Hell's Feast

Deacon didn't need to take his eyes from the scene to find the slugs he wanted. His fingers could feel the runes inscribed on the shells as he slammed them into the gun. He raised the weapon and fired.

The slug tore into the 'shifter's side, spinning him around. He dropped his victim and she hit the pavement, hard, and lay still.

Deacon was about to fire again when he saw the explosion of white flame from the 'shifter's wound and heard his target's ragged scream. The fire flew across the figure's body and he stumbled a few steps before hitting the ground, writhing. The flames burnt themselves out shortly after, but their work was done.

Deacon advanced, cautiously, an oily stench of burnt flesh in his nostrils. There was no reason to believe the 'shifter wasn't really dead, but no reason to take stupid chances, either. What he had thought had been black garb had been the creature's skin, sleek and smooth, designed to merge with the shadows. Vicious talons emerged from the shifter's fingers and rows of needle-like teeth filled his mouth.

Deacon prodded the body with his foot. Nothing.

He turned toward the woman then, still lying where she'd fallen. Her blouse had been torn open and there were deep scratches on her throat, but less blood than he would have expected. He took her wrist, the skin chilled by the night, and felt for a pulse. He didn't find one.

Deacon cursed. All of that, and he had been too late to keep her from dying.

He turned back in time to see her eyes snap open and her lips part in a smile. And suddenly he knew that he had been a few centuries too late.

Bloodshadows
Welcome to the World of *Fantasy Noir*

It's a mean old world out there.
The sorcerer upstairs conjures too loud;
the guy down the hall drinks
blood from a six-pack;
that stiff you left in the alley is
up and walking around.
If you're lucky, the Guild will pay
you for tonight's work;
if you're not, you're going home in a box.

A small box.

HELL'S
FEAST

by Greg Farshtey

HELL'S FEAST
A West End Games Book/April 1994

First Printing: April, 1994.
Printed in the United States of America.

0 9 8 7 6 5 4 3 2 1

ISBN: 0-87431-375-9

Cover Art by Ken Barr

Cover and Graphic Design by Stephen Crane

Map Art and Interior Illustrations by Thomas ONeill

Edited by Ed Stark

West End Games
RR 3 Box 2345
Honesdale, PA 18431

For Ciara;
For questions answered, though never asked;
And for all the mysteries still unsolved.

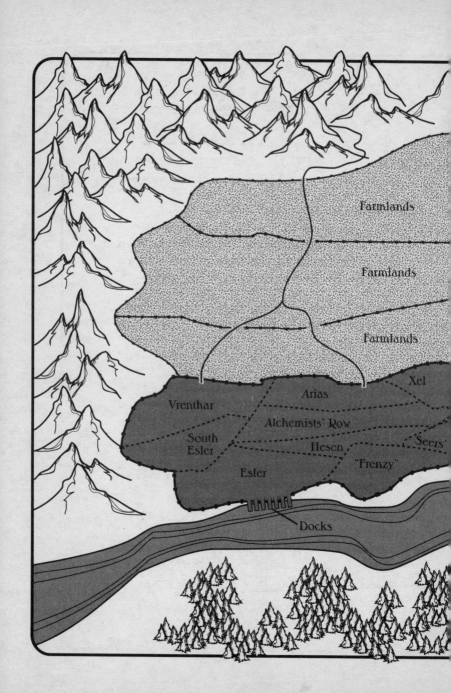

GALITIA
and Surroundings

Das Eldred

Canons

arters

RIVER SKORN

Prologue

Two men stood in a dimly lit room. Through a partially opened window, the sounds of the city street demanded attention — an infant crying, a woman laughing a little too loud, the off-key singing of a drunken man. The smell of smoke from a far away fire mingled with the scent of blood in the apartment.

The men did not speak for a very long time. They kept their attention focused on a third figure in the room, its owner, and the pool of dried blood at his feet. His body was transfixed to the wall with a crude spear, which had pierced his abdomen and emerged from his back, severing the spinal cord in its passage. The corpse's chin rested on his chest, giving him the aspect of one staring in wonder at the weapon that had killed him.

The taller of the two men turned away and began to wander the room, running an appreciative finger along the furniture. It was all meticulously handcrafted, oak and mahogany and polished so that it shone, even in the pale light of the lantern. The floor was covered with a brightly colored rug, imported at great expense from the city of Dela. The sight of the handsome carpet drew his eyes unwillingly back to the dark stain that had spread across it.

"He lived well," said the man. He was past middle age, with silver hair and pale blue eyes. He prided himself on his taste in furnishings, wines and precious stones.

"Too well," said his companion. "He drew attention to himself. This was bound to happen eventually, Merr."

"But not so soon. None of us expected that it would be so soon," Merr said, taking a step closer to the body.

The deceased had been a fine looking man, with jet black hair and a rugged complexion. He had taken pains to stay in good shape and his well-muscled form testified to his success. He was dressed in materials which, if not the best or most expensive available, were more than respectable.

Now, of course, they were covered in blood. He had vomited the stuff in the moments immediately following his impalement and his crisp white shirt now looked black.

His eyes were open. Merr wondered if, somehow, the last image he had seen might still be drawn from them. Then he reminded himself that there wouldn't be time for such luxuries.

"No signs of a struggle," Merr muttered finally.

His companion, Chase, nodded. "Probably didn't want to damage the furniture, the bastard." The short, plump man reached out and lifted the dead man's head slightly, revealing the burnt, blackened flesh of his face. "Akar's teeth, they made a mess of him."

"It's their way. How long has he been dead?"

There was a long pause. Both men were, in their own ways, strangers to death. Not that they had not killed or seen their share of corpses, but the final sleep was something that came for those far removed. This death made them … uncomfortable.

"Six hours, perhaps. Do we take the body with us?"

"No."

Merr turned away and looked out the window. Down below, night laborers were hurrying home, looking neither left nor right. The battered wooden buildings leaned in close, as if trying to protect their charges from the storm that was brewing overhead.

Merr closed his eyes and willed himself to see beyond surface appearances. No … no, there was no one watching the house. Strangely, he realized that he would have felt more comfortable if the foe had been there, waiting.

"It will be dawn soon," Chase said. "We had better be going."

Merr's eyes remained on the thinning crowds in the street. "We have to prepare. When we get back … you know who to contact."

Chase nodded, his eyes darting to the jagged bolt of lightning that flashed above the roof of the building across the street. For a moment, he wasn't certain if it had come from the sky or the structure.

"Tell her …" Merr paused, as rain began to lash the window.

"Yes?" Chase prompted.

"Tell her to do what she must. And that there will be no protection. She must see to herself."

"As do we all."

Chapter
One

Jack Deacon sat at the counter of an unfamiliar diner, nursing a cup of coffee grown cold. All around him, mill workers just come off shift were enjoying drinks before heading home for the night. Conversation revolved around the usual topics among such men: sports, women, tirades against the city for letting the glow-stones down the road burn out. It was nothing he hadn't heard before, but he listened anyway.

The waitress, a plain girl named Ella with dirty blonde hair and a sweet smile, came over and picked up his cup. She placed it on the upturned palm of her hand for a few moments, then set it back down, steam now rising once again from the surface of the brown liquid.

"Thanks," Deacon said, with just enough sincere gratitude to catch her attention.

"You're welcome, Mister," she replied. She ran a hand idly across the scarred wooden counter while trying to think of something else to say. Finally, she settled on, "I thought I knew everyone in this part of Galitia. Are you new here?"

Deacon shook his head. "Me? No, but I don't get down this way too often."

"Here on business?" she asked, all the while rearranging the condiment bottles so she would look busy for her employer's benefit.

 4

Deacon nodded and glanced at three men as they entered. Their faces weren't familiar, but the aroma they gave off shouted that they worked in the flesh mill down the road. He saw faces clench like fists as they passed.

"What do you do?" Ella asked, drawing his eyes back to her.

He smiled. "I sit around diners, waiting for something to happen. Once in a while, something does."

Ella didn't seem to know how to react to that at first, then decided to laugh. "It's nice to talk to someone with a sense of humor. Most of these guys are too tired even to say 'hello' when they walk in."

Deacon made sympathetic noises and pretended not to notice Ella looking him over. He was a handsome man, in a strange sort of way — tall and very thin, with a shock of reddish-blonde hair and blue eyes. He spoke with a slight accent, the consequence of being born and raised in the Eldred section of the city. The heavy overcoat he wore prevented the girl from telling how well he dressed, but he looked healthy enough. Ella decided he was worthy of further attention.

The street door opened and closed again, and Deacon could hear the sounds of the night workers moving by outside. In this area, the roads were for walking — few around here could afford an automobile, even one powered by steam rather than sorcery. And as they were not inclined to move aside for a vehicle, anyone who did try to drive through the neighborhood often found themselves late in arriving at their destination.

"I guess you hear a lot across this counter," Deacon said casually. In the background, the owner was arguing with a customer who claimed he'd been served the wrong drink. He eventually won his point and got a new glass, but Deacon wondered what might have been added to the beer in the meantime. Most likely, the loud customer would wake up tomorrow with stomach cramps and blood pouring out of his nose.

"If it happens around here, I hear about it," Ella agreed. "You looking for news?"

"Could be. What do you know about the brownstone around

5

the corner, the big one? Ever meet anybody who lived there?"

Ella shrugged. "Now and then. Why?"

"Anybody feuding over there? Any bad blood?"

"Not that I know of. Listen, if you're looking to start trouble —"

Deacon held up his hands, palms outward, to slow her down. "No trouble. I'm simply asking a question. I'm curious."

Ella's voice dropped a register to a conspiratorial whisper. "You a sentinel or something? Because if you are, well, I have a few things I could tell you. It's getting so a woman isn't safe around here after dark, even when the street lanterns *are* working."

Deacon cut her off. "I'm not a sentinel. Just a guy who makes a living asking questions."

Ella smiled, giving her green eyes an appealing sparkle. "I thought you sat around all day."

"That, too. But it's evening now, which means I have to start my second job."

"And that is?"

"*Standing* around and waiting for something to happen," he said, rising.

❦

Leaving the girl a liberal tip, Deacon shouldered his way past working men who reeked of grease and sulphur and naphtha to reach the men's room.

That proved to be a small, airless chamber with a glow-stone that provided barely enough light to see. The room smelled of urine and stale beer. Deacon was surprised not to see water pipes leading to the sink — apparently, the owner was well-off at one time and paid for water magic to be impressed into the tap.

Deacon twisted the rusty faucet and was rewarded with a stream of ice cold water. He splashed a little on his face, then leaned back against the tiled wall and tried to collect his thoughts.

The note that had brought him here nestled quietly in his hip pocket, along with the money that had accompanied it. He had found it slipped under his office door early in the day, the words written in a feminine hand:

Urgently require your services. Believe my life to be in danger. Watch the brownstone on Dover St., second floor, center, tonight and follow woman who comes out. Important she not know she's being trailed. Hope this is sufficient for your retainer. More later.

R

Ordinarily, he would have tossed such a note aside and pocketed the money. But he was between jobs right now, and there was something about the words — mannered and calm, yet obviously written in a hurry — that caught his interest. There was enough cash included to hold it, too, but not so much that it screamed set-up.

So he had pocketed his revolver and some spare slugs and made his way to the Canons section of the city, home to a good number of the mills and some of the better "disorderly houses," as the upper classes liked to call the brothels. He'd spent an hour or two wandering the neighborhood, trying to scout the target building without being too obvious about it. Street talk was about a multiple murder in the Seers' Quarter not far away and the need to crack down on the blood cults. None of this news was less than a week old so he had filed it away in the back of his mind and gone about his business.

He opened his eyes and took in his reflection in the cracked mirror above the sink. The young man who had left the sentinels to seek his fortune was long gone, replaced by a tired, middle-aged detective who hadn't been able to learn anything new about a case in twelve hours. With a ragged sigh, he realized there was nothing for it but go engage in a staring contest with an apartment building and hope it blinked first.

❧

It had begun to rain. Deacon stood in a doorway across the

7

Greg Farshtey

street from the object of his interest, a square of pale yellow light
on the second story of a shabby brownstone. He had been
watching for six hours now, and had seen nothing more than an
occasional shadow flit across its surface, then retreat.

He shifted slightly, trying to keep his muscles from stiffening
in the bitter cold. His vantage point did little to protect him from
the elements, but did provide sufficient shadows for conceal-
ment. The few people on the street this time of night knew better
than to take notice of a stranger, so he was left alone to question
his common sense.

The street itself was unspectacular. Two blocks down to the
west was a textile mill and a creditable weaponsmith. To the east
was the Seers' Quarter and the darker neighborhoods beyond it.
Diagonally across the road was an apothecary, who advertised a
sale on white cinnabar with garish signs. Next to that was a
newsstand, with headlines blaring about possible cult connec-
tions to everything from purse-snatchings to armed theft to
butchery at a phoney school for mages.

The brownstone had been built when the neighborhood was
better off, perhaps thirty, forty years ago, along with several
others. All the rest had been torn down — or had fallen down —
but this one still stood, battered but intact. It was home to laborers
who couldn't afford any better and a few grifters who could, but
preferred that no one know of their good fortune.

Deacon took his eyes off the building long enough to glance
down the street. Someone was coming, staggering along the
opposite side, looking for all the world as if his supper had been
served in a glass. The figure had almost reached the brownstone
when something shouted a warning to Deacon. The man's
movements were forced, the doggerel was just a little too loud, he
couldn't be sure what made it feel *wrong*. But his hand inched
toward the pistol in his overcoat pocket.

It was as if Deacon's movement had shattered a spell. The
figure froze, then straightened, his gaze falling on Deacon. For a
split second, the stranger's eyes were two pinpoints of red,
gleaming in the darkness. Then the man bowed his head and

walked briskly past the brownstone and down the road, until he was swallowed by the night.

"Nothing like doing your bit to get drunks off the streets," Deacon said, a grim smile on his lips. He let go of his gun, unsure if his palms were damp from the rain or from fear. Then he turned back to the building and it didn't matter anymore.

The light had gone out.

꽃

Deacon sank deeper into the shadows. There were two exits from the building: the main door, steel painted to look like wood, and a fire escape along the side. Both were visible from where he stood, so it was just a matter of patience.

He didn't have to wait long. The door swung wide for barely an instant, as if the building didn't want the darkness outside pouring in. Then the woman came out and, without a glance to either side, turned and began walking toward the Seers' Quarter.

She was there and gone so quickly Deacon barely caught a glance. She was tall, brunette, wearing a black leather coat that reached to her knees and a broad-brimmed hat. He gave her a good minute's head start before slipping from his refuge and following.

As they walked, linked by an invisible chain, he tried to decide whether she was to be the killer or the intended victim. There was no fear in her step, but there was purpose. Although Deacon felt painfully conspicuous on this otherwise empty roadway, his quarry never stopped, or turned, or quickened her pace. She simply kept moving, as the rain turned colder and the wind began to cut through Deacon's overcoat like a rusty knife.

Twenty minutes went by in this fashion, Deacon growing more and more curious about what had brought such a woman out on such a night. Even from a distance, he could tell the coat she wore was genuine, and thus wasn't cheap. And men didn't walk alone down these streets, let alone women.

But then, she isn't alone, is she? he thought. *Let's hope "R." is willing to cough up the money to treat the pneumonia I'm*

9

catching.

Now they were at the far edge of the Quarter and the foul smoke of the flesh mills was beginning to obscure the sight of her. All the common sounds of the city had faded, to be replaced by the moans of the seers and their clients, a not uncommon reaction to the face of the future. Too often, it looked too much like today.

The buildings were older here and the streets more narrow. Now and then, Deacon caught sight of people peering out of their windows, probably thinking he was stalking a sweet young thing. That would explain why they ducked back inside and closed their ragged curtains, anyway.

The attack, when it came, was so sudden it took a full second before Deacon could comprehend it. A figure dressed entirely in black leapt from an alleyway and caught the woman, slamming her into the side of a building. The attacker had one arm around her neck and the other tearing at her coat and blouse. She was fighting back, but her opponent had size, weight and surprise on his side.

Deacon drew his revolver and fired in one smooth motion. The bullet caught the other man in the shoulder, but the only reaction it provoked was a grunt, more of annoyance than pain. Deacon was too far away to see if his target was bleeding, but putting everything together, he suddenly doubted it.

"Goddamned 'shifter," he muttered, dumping the bullets from his revolver with one hand while the other reached into his left pocket for different ammo. The ... thing had the woman pressed against the wall and was going for her throat. She landed a solid knee to her assailant's groin, but to no effect.

Deacon didn't need to take his eyes from the scene to find the slugs he wanted. His fingers could feel the runes inscribed on the shells as he slammed them into the gun. He raised the weapon and fired.

The slug tore into the 'shifter's side, spinning him around. He dropped his victim and she hit the pavement, hard, and lay still.

Deacon was about to fire again when he saw the explosion of white flame from the 'shifter's wound and heard his target's ragged scream. The fire flew across the figure's body and he stumbled a few steps before hitting the ground, writhing. The flames burnt themselves out shortly after, but their work was done.

Deacon advanced, cautiously, an oily stench of burnt flesh in his nostrils. There was no reason to believe the 'shifter wasn't really dead, but no reason to take stupid chances, either. What he had thought had been black garb had been the creature's skin, sleek and smooth, designed to merge with the shadows. Vicious talons emerged from the shifter's fingers and rows of needle-like teeth filled his mouth.

Deacon prodded the body with his foot. Nothing.

He turned toward the woman then, still lying where she'd fallen. Her blouse had been torn open and there were deep scratches on her throat, but less blood than he would have expected. He took her wrist, the skin chilled by the night, and felt for a pulse. He didn't find one.

He found a piece of glass near the alley's mouth and held it over her lips, but there was no breath to fog it. He remained crouched beside her for a long moment, then rose to find something to cover her pale, beautiful face.

Deacon cursed. All of that, and he had been too late to keep her from dying.

He turned back in time to see her eyes snap open and her lips part in a smile. And suddenly he knew that he had been a few centuries too late.

Chapter
Two

You saved my life," the woman said, in a voice almost a whisper. She was standing off to the side, her coat wrapped tightly around her in an effort to conceal some of the alabaster flesh exposed by her shredded clothing. She had been watching Deacon for some moments in silence, as he dug into the ruined flesh of the 'shifter with a jackknife.

He didn't respond to her comment, so she tried again. "My name is Larissa. Larissa Martel. What's yours?"

This earned a glance from Deacon, but no more. He turned his attention back to his grisly work.

Larissa frowned and watched a while longer before saying, "Violating a corpse was still against the law, last I knew. Just what are you doing?"

Deacon's answer was to pull a bloodstained bullet out of the body and hold it aloft for her to see. He knew her eyesight would be keen enough to make out the ornate carvings on the shell.

"These things cost money," he said. "I can't afford to waste 'em."

"I'm surprised that a man of your … talents doesn't have enough to cover all his needs," Larissa said, more sharply than she had intended.

"Yeah, that's what my mother says, too," Deacon answered, rising. "Okay, he's all yours. I wouldn't wait around here too long, though. Even 'shifters have friends."

Larissa looked at the still-smouldering corpse with undisguised revulsion. "I have no use for the dead."

Deacon shrugged. "Neither do I, Miss Martel." He turned and began walking back toward the Seers' Quarter. "See you around."

He hadn't gone more than three steps when she cried out, "Wait!" He turned to see that she had moved toward him, her face suddenly illuminated by a flash of lightning. Her night-black hair was wet and framed her face as if it were a work of art, and that was not far wrong. Deacon couldn't remember when he had seen such a beautiful woman — but he also couldn't forget the sharpened canines her smile had revealed.

She reached out and laid a hand on his arm, more than a hint of warmth in her blue eyes. "I owe you a debt."

Deacon shook his head, reaching into his pocket for the money that had come with the anonymous note. "I've already been paid. This is yours, isn't it?" He stripped a few bills off the top and tucked them away. "This will take care of my time and expenses. You can have the rest. Give it back to 'R.,' if he even exists."

She looked at the money as if it were a foreign object and made no move to take it. "The deception was necessary. You would not have taken the job otherwise."

"Damn right I wouldn't," he snapped. "If I'd known what you were, I would have let the 'shifter have you."

Anger warred with what looked like disappointment on her face for a moment. Disappointment won. "Oh. I see," she said, quietly. "I had thought a man in your line of work might be a bit more … broad-minded."

She tied the belt of her coat tightly and then folded her arms across her chest. "Or do you think only the troubles of those who match your definition of a living being are worthy of your time?"

"Don't give me that!" he shot back. The rain had soaked through his coat and into his clothes, which did nothing to help his mood. "First I get a note slipped under my door that's right out of some Grade-B potboiler, then I get to chase you around on a night any sane person would be home with a bottle. And then you go

13

into this 'And what's your name' crap, as if you think I just happened along to save your ass! Why the hell should I trust you?"

"I'm not asking you to trust me. Not yet," Larissa answered. She brushed a wet lock of hair from her eyes. "All I ask is that you listen to what I have to say. Put aside … what I am and what you think about that for a moment, and just listen. Then, if you want to walk away, I won't stop you."

Larissa paused, her eyes meeting his. Then she said, "And if you need another reason to trust me, here it is: you know some of the truth about me. In my circle, that gives me the right — almost the duty — to kill you. And, as good as you are with that gun, you know I could do it.

"But I'm not going to."

Deacon looked hard at the face of the woman before him. There was no telling whether she was speaking the truth, or whether she just wanted to get him out of the open before she tore him apart. But something in her tone said this was about more than just her next meal.

Finally, he shrugged and said, "Can we get out of the rain? I don't listen well when I'm cold and wet."

She allowed herself a slight smile. "I have a place near here." Then she gestured toward the shapeshifter's corpse. "What about that?"

Deacon laughed, but there wasn't any humor in it. "In this neighborhood? There'll be nothing left by morning. Let's go."

❧

Larissa led Deacon to a crumbling brick building not far away. They were well outside of the Seers' Quarter now, in an area populated by those who had cast one spell too many and paid for it with everything from physical deformity to madness. The official name of the district had long been forgotten — everyone called it "Frenzy."

The building she made a home in had once been a simple apartment house for local workers. Now it was more like a

 14

fortress, with bars on the windows and heavy padlocks on the doors. There probably weren't many "normal" people who willingly lived in "Frenzy," Deacon thought, and those who did took steps to protect themselves.

I wonder what they'd think if they knew who … what was living with them, he said to himself. *Or maybe they don't care, as long as they're not on the menu.*

Larissa had vanished down a short flight of concrete steps that led to the basement. Deacon approached in time to see her standing before a heavy wooden door, looking with some annoyance at the padlock that kept it secure.

"Don't you have a key?" Deacon asked.

She turned, frowning. "I've never needed one before. I don't normally bring guests here." She paused, then added, "Not the kind who still need to use doors, anyway."

With a casual shrug, she tore the lock free and dropped it at her feet. The aged door opened with a shriek like that of a damned soul falling to Hell.

"That the only lock?" Deacon asked.

Larissa had already stepped inside, but now turned back to look at her somewhat reluctant guest, still standing at the top of the steps. "No one in this neighborhood can afford a mage, Mr. Deacon. That's part of what gives the place its charm. Are you always so cautious?"

Only when I'm about to go into a dark cellar with an Undead, he thought. But all he said was, "Little habit I've picked up in my travels. It's called survival."

She smiled. It would have been a beautiful expression if not for the two wickedly sharp teeth that marked her as a predator. "Then we have something in common, after all. Come in, Mr. Deacon, we have much to discuss."

❧

The room they entered was lit by lanterns — the real thing, not the sorcerous variety — but the light did little to dispel the chill of the place. The basement was cavernous, broken up only by the red brick pillars that supported the building above. The stone floor was covered with a thick white coat of paint that gave a bright, almost garish look to the place. Down the center of the floor ran a jagged crack, as if the foundation had tried to split apart at some point not long past. The room was sparsely "furnished" — mostly old chairs and and tables piled in corners, along with an ornate, antique modesty screen.

Deacon was most interested in what wasn't there. He was far from an expert on vampirism, but everything he had heard indicated that they needed a coffin, a crate, something filled with their native earth in which to sleep the day away. But there seemed to be nothing here that could serve that purpose.

Larissa had stepped behind the screen and was changing out of her ruined clothes. She noted Deacon's eyes sweeping the room and her own flashed in amusement. "Looking for the bed? You are a fast worker, aren't you?"

"Just trying to figure out if this is the bedroom ... or the dining room," he answered.

"Touché. I do rest here occasionally, at times when I can't afford to be selective. That crack in the floor is the 'box' you're looking for, by the way."

Deacon knelt down and examined the fracture. It looked too narrow for even an insect to pass through, but then there weren't many places a vampire couldn't go, he supposed.

"It's very convenient," Larissa said. "I can rest beneath the building, undisturbed, and no one will ever seal that crack. It's one of the advantages of living in 'Frenzy' — no one cares about appearances."

She stepped out from behind the modesty screen, clad in a tight, dark blue dress that showed off the figure of a woman seemingly in the bloom of youth. Deacon was struck once again with how beautiful she truly was and the fact that there was nothing overtly supernatural about her allure. The soft, dark hair, the light blue eyes, the perfect features, these she had been born — and died — with.

Deacon rose. "So ... you're a native of Galitia?" he said,

gesturing toward the crack and the soil that lay beneath it.

She laughed. "Don't believe everything you hear from the streetsingers, Mr. Deacon. Dirt is dirt."

The dress Larissa wore had a high neckline, but not high enough to cover the ugly scars the 'shifter had left on her. He could see she had already begun to heal, but it would still be at least a day before they faded completely.

"You run with a rough crowd," he said.

"Sometimes," she conceded. "I'd like to ask you why you're unwilling to work for me. Is it because I'm a vampire? Or because I lied to you?"

Deacon thought for a moment before answering, "Both."

"Well, I can't do anything about the first and I can only apologize for the second. If what I paid was not enough —"

"This isn't about money," Deacon said sharply. "You knew that thing was going to come after you, so you get me to follow along behind and blow it away. That way, you don't get blood on your hands. Or do you just like having a shadow, Miss Martel?"

Larissa's voice was stone cold. "I've had blood on my hands more times than you can imagine, Deacon. I'm perfectly capable of doing my own killing. I didn't hire you for that. I need a bodyguard, not an assassin."

"I'm not for sale as either. I've done a lot of things since I started in this business. I've peeked through keyholes; I've beaten people for no other reason than that they owed money they didn't have; I even broke a strike at one of the Nivashi talisman works. But I can't see protecting the life of someone who's already dead."

Larissa took a step closer to him. He caught a scent of her perfume, light and sweet. She ran a surprisingly warm hand down the side of his face. "I could pay you in other ways, you know," she said softly.

He stepped backward, not willing to risk being tempted by her. "I'm sorry, Miss Martel. I'm not interested in your kind of kiss. You'll have to find someone else."

Larissa's lips curled into a bitter smile. "I can see and hear things you cannot; I can fly with the night winds; and I would wager that my love of life is far fiercer than yours. Perhaps you should reconsider which of us is really dead?"

"I didn't come here to discuss philosophy," Deacon growled.

"Of course you did," she said hotly, the words flying like daggers. "You came here to prove to yourself that I'm some kind of animal who should be put down. Then you would have permission to walk away and go back to your miserable existence with a clear conscience.

"Well, I'm going to disappoint you, Mr. Deacon. I love and hate and fear as much as any living woman, if not more, and no one has the right to judge me."

She wheeled, her passion spent, and stalked to the far side of the cellar. She did not look at Deacon as she said, "Go, then. I was a fool to expect your help. Go to hell in your own way, Mr. Deacon, and leave me to go in mine."

Deacon watched her in silence. Her words had not had the effect she had intended — he felt no shame about his attitudes, or any particular compassion for her. But the things she had said had awakened his curiosity. What was she so afraid of?

Deacon leaned against the wall and tried to do exactly what she had suggested, put aside what she was and look at the situation objectively. Larissa was intelligent, beautiful and probably as strong as ten men. Anything that could frighten her badly enough to drive her to a mortal for help could mean trouble down the line for everybody. The money was good, too.

And if that 'shifter does have friends, I'd just as soon she be around when they show up.

"All right, Miss Martel. I'll take the job," he said, blaming the chill that ran though him on the cold rain that fell outside.

❧

The food at the Dw*elling Place* was barely edible, but the drinks were cheap and not watered down any more than usual. So Deacon hadn't objected too much when Larissa had chosen the dark, smoky bar for their next rendezvous. He sat nursing a gin while he waited, listening to the sounds of laborers who'd had too many and whores promising delights a veteran mage couldn't manage, even with pictures to work from.

The low murmur was interrupted by a sharp burst of static. The barman, a hulking, slow-witted type named Karl, had switched on the radio. It was an old set and most of the crystals had run out of power a long time before. The owner had fallen on hard times and didn't have the cash to buy new ones from the local stations, so it was only able to pick up one signal, and that poorly. Still, the announcer's voice caught Deacon's attention and held it.

"This is KLXR news on the hour. Sentinels are investigating the murders of three men and two women in the Esler section. Reports indicate the women were stabbed multiple times and mutilated after death. There is no word yet on the circumstances surrounding the other murders. Cult involvement is suspected.

"An explosion rocked the main offices of Nured Mills this morning, the third such incident in as many days. Witnesses reported seeing flames in a storeroom just prior to the blast, but whether they were sorcerous in nature is not known at this time. A spokesman for owner Zach Nured dismissed rumors that the bombing was tied to recent labor troubles.

"We'll be back with tomorrow's weather forecast, after this message ..."

Deacon stopped listening. Good, there had been no word on the dead 'shifter. Whoever had set him on Larissa's tail would figure he was dead, but there was no need for anyone else to know. The last thing he needed was sentinels elbowing their way in, at least until he knew what was going on.

Larissa had told him next to nothing, saying he "didn't need to know." He had balked—loudly—and wrung a promise from her that she would at least provide an outline of her troubles. She had also made a point of telling him that she wouldn't be spending the night in the brownstone, in case he was harboring any ideas about betraying her.

He'd laughed it off, knowing better than to take it personally.

Paranoia came with the pale complexion and the restricted diet. It was how her kind survived.

He looked up from his drink to see her walking out of the moonlight and into the bar. She was wearing a white dress, lighter than the weather called for. She seemed happy to see him and offered a smile as she sat down at the table.

"Good evening. Have you been waiting long?"

"Only a few minutes. What are you — ?"

Deacon stopped talking as Karl lumbered over. Larissa smiled at him, too, and ordered a Scotch and water before sending him on his way. Seeing the look of surprise on her companion's face, she explained, "Places like this expect you to order something. But I'm afraid I can't hold my liquor. Have you eaten?"

"Sure." He paused a moment before adding, "Have you?"

She didn't answer. But he had already noted how much … healthier her skin tone appeared, and her eyes were practically sparkling. It was a dramatic change from the ghostly, frightened woman of the previous night, and he wondered how long it had been between feedings for her.

She waited until Karl had brought her drink and retreated behind the bar before she spoke again. "We have a great deal to do tonight. Things are moving faster than I anticipated."

"What things? If I'm going to protect you, I have to have some idea who's after you."

She nodded and her voice was little more than a whisper. "You heard about the Esler murders?"

"Does that involve you somehow?" Deacon asked. Vampiric involvement with cults was ancient history, primarily because the average cultist generally didn't know enough to keep his mouth shut about his "great and powerful masters."

"It's a symptom, that's all. The disease is much worse. But there will be more of that sort of thing in the weeks to come."

"And you're trying to stop it?"

"No. I'm trying to survive it."

Chapter
Three

Larissa had a car waiting outside the bar, but was saying nothing about their destination. The vehicle was big and black, and looked new. At first glance, Deacon didn't see any steam emerging from the idling machine and revised his estimation of his new client. Cars run by elemental magic had been a fact of life in Galitia for decades, but they were still expensive to purchase and maintain.

He and Larissa climbed into the richly upholstered back seat and she ordered the driver to begin. Smoothly, almost soundlessly, the vehicle pulled away from the curb and began wending its way through the narrow streets.

Deacon eyed the chauffeur. The young man was no giant, but his broad shoulders suggested someone who would be formidable in a brawl. "How come he's not doubling as bodyguard?" he asked, gesturing toward the uniformed driver.

"Narses is an excellent servant, but I prefer to keep him out of harm's way." She pulled shut the soundproof panel that separated the front seats from the rear. "Some years ago, he was attacked by one of my cousins. It was a brutal, sloppy effort, and Narses' vocal chords were damaged. He's completely mute."

Deacon frowned. "Is he … like you?"

"Somewhere in between. He ages more slowly than most, but he does age. And he still requires food and drink, just as you do."

"I'm surprised he would work for you, considering —"

"I saved his life, Deacon," Larissa said, sharply. "We're not *all* ravenous monsters, you know. If we're going to work together, you had better learn that."

"Meaning what?"

She turned to him, something hard and cold in her eyes. "Meaning you can't make assumptions about how our enemies might behave, based on what they are. When people go beyond mere humanity, they don't get run through a mill and all come out the same."

"There are some things common to all hunters, Human or not."

She gave him a rueful smile. "I could introduce you to a number of people like me who wish they only had to be hunters."

Deacon glanced out the window. There were few sections of the city that were unfamiliar to him, but he could see they were riding through one of them. "Where in hell are we going?"

Larissa laughed, but there was no humor in the sound. "You're not far wrong." She pulled the glass panel aside and said to Narses, "Take us to East." The chauffeur turned and seemed to consider arguing the point, then thought better of it.

Deacon suddenly spotted a landmark, a warehouse he had seen far too much of a few years before. He'd been investigating an extortion scheme — a scribe at one of the news rags was blackmailing an ex-con arsonist into torching buildings. Everything was going along fine: the firebug had his fun, the scribe got to be first on the scene of the fires. Then along came a seer who had something better on the torch and got him to talk about who put him up to the jobs. Suddenly, the scribe is the one doing the paying, and he wasn't happy.

He had hired Deacon to clean the whole thing up. But the seer had friends — big friends — and he'd spent a week or so getting beaten bloody in that warehouse. The sight of that place brought back one important fact about the neighborhood: it doesn't matter how loud you yell if the people who can hear you are too scared to help.

For just a moment, he felt the pain of those blows again. Worse than the broken bones and the blood had been the feeling of being out of control, and he suddenly realized that was how he felt now. He had left the familiar behind when he had gone into that cellar with Larissa, and despite his dealings with sorcerers, he wondered if he was up to this.

He washed the doubts away with anger — at Larissa, for leading him around in the dark, and at himself, for not striking a match.

"I think I want some answers, lady," he said, turning back to the woman. She, too, had been staring pensively at the shabby buildings going by, but now she met his eyes and nodded.

"I had decided not to tell you anything," she began. "After you left last night, I began to think it was a mistake to involve you at all. Then I remembered that the choice isn't mine to make anymore. I have to take my allies where I can find them."

"You sound like we're going to war."

"It's already started," she replied. The car made a sharp right turn, deeper into the nest of empty warehouses. Even with the windows shut, the smell of decay seeped into the vehicle.

"I will tell you what I can," she continued. "I am looking for someone, Mr. Deacon — in fact, I'm looking for a number of people. I have information for them, information they may not want to hear. They may react … violently to the news, I don't know. That is why I need you."

"And this East is one of them?"

She shook her head. "No, he's another potential ally. A source of information, but a difficult one. He will try to bait you, Deacon. Don't give him the satisfaction of responding in kind."

The car slid to a stop in front of a wooden shack. Beyond it was a junkyard and, beyond that, the river, which stank worse than the piles of garbage that abutted it. As Deacon and Larissa emerged from the vehicle, a sickly looking cat screeched and sped through the partially open door of the shack.

"I will go first," Larissa said, advancing on the house, which seemed on the verge of collapse. Deacon could see a single naked bulb burning within, but the windows were covered with too much grime for anything more to be revealed.

Larissa paused before the door and knocked gently. There was no response from inside, save for the rotting door opening a few inches wider.

"East?" she called, taking a step into the shack. Deacon was right behind her, gun drawn, but she signalled him to stay back. He heard voices raised in argument for a few moments, hers and another's, which sounded like tree branches scraping against a window. Then Larissa waved for him to come in.

The interior of the shack made the outside look pleasant. Clothing was piled everywhere, much of it stained or torn. Books, magazines, and newspapers covered every inch of the floor and the walls were papered with headlines of various disasters, both natural and man-made, along with a fair share of deaths and disappearances. He didn't need to see the dates to know that many of them dated back decades.

But the most arresting item in the room was its owner, who rocked slowly in a cane-backed chair and watched the newcomers with the darting eyes of a serpent. He was ancient, with wisps of white hair and beard framing a face that was little more than a skull, thinly veiled in flesh. His clothes were simple and somehow gave the impression of not fitting correctly, although the evidence of the eyes did not support this. It seemed to be all the old man could do to manage a nod of greeting and absentmindedly stroke the scrawny cat that sat on his lap.

It was the eyes that intrigued Deacon, however. They held neither enthusiasm for life nor resignation to the inevitable — they were cold and dead, and despite himself, Deacon felt a trace of fear. He brushed it aside as if it were an annoying insect.

"East, this is Mr. Deacon, the gentleman I told you about," Larissa said.

The old man shifted in his chair — Deacon could swear he heard bones creaking — and offered a skeletal hand. Deacon shook it gently and wondered what made the man perspire so in the cold room.

"Welcome," East said softly, a malicious twinkle suddenly

coming to his eyes. "I get so few visitors these days. If I want to see someone … I always have to go to them."

Deacon found himself wishing he was back outside among the garbage. It felt very close in the little shack and the old man's gaze was making him uncomfortable. Thankfully, East shifted his attention to Larissa.

"Did you bring me someone?" the old man asked.

Larissa shook her head, an expression of distaste on her face. East almost rose from his chair, apparently angered by her answer, but Deacon could tell he was shamming.

"Then how do you expect me to help you?" East croaked petulantly. "You know I have to have someone! Everyone knows that! Now what am I to do?"

Larissa was not at all cowed by his outburst. Deacon thought that, were it not for the man's advanced age, he could have stood some slapping around. East subsided into muttering for a few moments, ignoring both his visitors, bony fingers scratching the cat between the ears. The animal shut its eyes and began to purr softly.

Deacon began to say something, but a look from Larissa stopped him. He realized her warning had been accurate: East liked games. The only way to handle someone like that was to refuse to play. So he joined Larissa in silence, waiting for the old man to grow tired of his muted tantrum.

Suddenly, East's expression brightened. "Ah, well, we must make do, then," he said, cheerfully. With an unbelievably swift movement, he snapped the cat's neck and tossed the limp animal aside. It flew into a stack of books, upsetting them, and they ended up serving as its monument.

East let out a long, satisfied sigh. "That's much better. Be a help, Mr. Deacon, and toss the poor thing outside. I think the rats would appreciate the irony of feasting on a feline, for a change, don't you?"

"Maybe I'll put you out while I'm at it," Deacon replied. "Or don't they eat their own?"

East's chuckle sounded like glass breaking. His eyes lit on

Deacon, dark amusement at play in them. "Oh, of course they do. Rats will eat anything, no matter how large or how small. They understand that, in the end, all that matters is staying alive. Aspirations to anything higher are simply the means we use to rationalize doing the things we must to survive day to day. Meaningless." East paused, then added, "They are admirable creatures, in that regard."

"I'd rather see them dead," Deacon said, letting some of his loathing for the old man creep into his tone.

East recognized the emotions he provoked in Deacon and gave him a death's head grin. "But they won't die, Mr. Deacon. No, they will outlive ... most of us. They have mastered the fundamental principle of survival in a hostile world: there is strength in numbers. That is why you're here, isn't it, sir? Or did the lovely Miss Martel simply want to ensure there would be someone to bury her one last time?"

"That's enough," Larissa said sharply. "I haven't the time for this, East. I came here for information."

East shifted his ancient form in the chair to look directly at the woman. "So you did. So many people have had questions for me lately. Chase came to me just a short time ago, full of wild fears and suppositions. I did what I could to calm him, of course." An expression of regret came to the old man's face. "Probably a mistake. The next day, someone tore his head off. And it was such a nice head, too."

"If this guy's on 'our side,' I think I'd rather we lost," Deacon said. He felt certain that, whatever East might be, he had a bullet that would do the job. It suddenly seemed that nothing would be as satisfying as seeing this vile old creature dead.

"I'm not interested in your opinions right now," Larissa said, impatiently. "East knows full well that he is in as much danger as anyone. Things have been quiet for a long time, but that is changing, isn't it, East? And when the bloodshed starts, you can be sure someone will see to it that you contribute your share."

For the first time since their arrival, East seemed genuinely concerned. *His kind always thinks they can sit on the sidelines and watch the fun,* Deacon thought. *They don't like it so much when somebody drags them into the game.*

"I'm a humble dealer in information. My death is of no use to anyone," the old man said, sounding as if he were trying to convince himself.

"Perhaps not. But they might find it amusing, just the same."

"There is that," East agreed. "We live in such a violent world, don't we? You heard about the Esler killings, I suppose? Shameful. Cults dumping bodies in an alley, for all to see. That is what rivers are for."

"Then those were cult killings?" Deacon asked, intrigued. If Larissa's business was tied up with cults, things could get nasty very fast. It might be wise to visit Belrand and see about weaponry.

"Did you set out to hire a guardian this dense?" East inquired of Larissa. "Oh, but of course you did — only that kind would be no threat to you. Put simply, Mr. Deacon, yes, they were cult killings. Cutpurses rarely take the time to carve a woman's heart out of her body and burn it. The pawns began moving on the chessboard weeks ago."

Deacon wanted to ask him what he meant by that, but Larissa spoke first. "You know why I'm here?"

East settled back in his chair, elbows resting on its wooden arms and fingers steepled. "You seek the *tral.* Galitia has more than its share. But there is no telling how many of them will welcome you. Not everyone enjoys their work as much as I, you know."

The room had begun to smell even worse. Deacon guessed that the cat had voided its bowels after death. He glanced around to find the nearest window he could crack open, then noticed something strange. The clothes thrown so haphazardly about were of varying sizes, ranging from those of a child to adult garb. And Deacon had been to enough murder scenes to recognize the stains on the garments.

He looked back at East with a knot forming in the pit of his stomach. Just what was this rotting old skeleton? How many *people* had he killed as casually as he had the cat? And how had he gotten away with it for so many years?

The old man was scrawling something on a slip of paper, his hand trembling so badly that the words were almost unintelligible. "This is the only one I know of, Larissa," he was saying. "There are more, but I will need time to find them out."

"How much time?" Larissa asked, taking the paper and tucking it away in her coat pocket.

"Some," East answered. "Within a few days, I should be able to get around more freely than I can now. Then I will find you. No, you need not tell me where you will be. I will find you, wherever you are."

"You had best be careful," Larissa warned as she started for the door. "The advantage is theirs now. They will kill to keep it."

"They are more likely to seek you out than I," East replied. "And if they should find you … I will see to it that your grave is well tended to." He paused, suddenly seeming to remember Deacon was there. He fixed his serpentine eyes on the man and added hastily, "Excuse me. *Both* your graves."

Larissa moved back into the night, Deacon a step behind her. He barely heard East's call. "Mr. Deacon — a moment, if you please?"

Deacon waved Larissa away. "Go on. I'll meet you at the car."

East was beckoning him forward, a smile of pure malice on his lips. "I merely wanted to give you some advice. I strongly suggest you reject Larissa's money — or whatever else it is she is giving you for your services — and stay as far away from her as you can. This is not a good time to be her friend."

"Or yours?" Deacon asked.

East's laugh became a cough. It was a moment before he could speak again. "I have no friends, Deacon. My lifestyle does not preclude them, necessarily, but they always seem to come and go so quickly. When I am weak and tired, as I am now, they grow bored and uncomfortable. When I am feeling more … energetic, they cannot keep up with my whims. Thus I have learned not to grow attached." He gestured toward the dead animal in the corner. "To anything."

"Is that all you had to say?" Deacon asked, turning to go.

"No, you fool. I am trying to give you some helpful counsel, the first I have given in some time and the last I care to. You think yourself a man of some strength, but you do not belong in the netherworld. Get out of it."

Deacon wasn't going to give East the satisfaction of knowing he had been thinking much the same himself, having seen Larissa's idea of an ally. "What's the netherworld?" he asked instead.

East tapped his chair arm with a long fingernail. "The world you don't see. The world where Larissa and I live, in the shadows of the one you move through every day. You are out of your depth, Deacon, a naked man walking through a nest of vipers. Keep moving deeper into this and it will be your death."

Deacon remembered the feeling he had experienced on the way over, the sensation of being out of control. It had returned now, doubled and redoubled in strength. As much as he hated to admit it, East was probably right — the smartest thing he could do would be to run, get away from Larissa, get out of Galitia, if he had to.

But something inside told him it was already too late for that ...

Without a word, he turned from the old man and walked out into the darkness.

Chapter
Four

The neighborhoods improve somewhat as you move from the east side of Galitia to the center of the city. Some of the squalor and vice is left behind and the buildings enjoy better maintenance. The sentinels pass through a little more often, rousting the homeless and the insane off the streets and sending them back toward the waterfront, from whence they came. Instead of relying solely on streetlamps, some of the sidewalks are dotted with large glow-stones that provide a dull illumination at night.

The city's heart is a magnet to the men and women of power. It's here that traders come to meet with their brethren from other towns, bankers consider investing in expeditions into the Wilderness, brokers cast runes and try to predict the direction of the gold market. The presence of so much money means the restaurants serve better fare (and there are far fewer reports of missing dogs from their neighbors); shopkeepers take the time to wash the soot from their display windows; and the whores stay indoors and take callers by appointment only.

The businessmen leave at dusk and the neighborhood is itself once more. The residents are thankful to have escaped the eastern section of the city and a few still harbor dreams of reaching the townhouses of the west side. Some of them are immigrants from other cities, who came to Galitia seeking fortunes and settled for a living wage. They are a bit more self-sufficient here — a man with a leaky faucet will study a "do-it-yourself" grimoire and try to fix it himself before giving in and calling an elemental mage.

It was to a rowhouse in this area of the city that Deacon directed Narses. They had dropped Larissa near the *Dwelling Place* shortly before dawn. Deacon had planned on getting home under his own power, but Larissa had suggested it might be better if Narses delivered him to his door.

"Your concern for my welfare is touching," Deacon had said, wryly.

"It's not strictly yours I'm worried about," Larissa had answered. "But you do make a tempting target."

Deacon decided not to try and decipher the meaning of the smile that came to her lips as she said that and accepted the ride. But he was still picturing her expression in his mind even as Narses slowed the car to a stop in front of his building.

Dawn was breaking, golden shafts of light lancing into the faces of the modest stone buildings. Deacon nodded a thank you to his silent driver and climbed out of the car, his heart filled with boundless affection for the concept of bed.

His room was on the second floor, able to be reached through the house itself or via the fire escape. Today, he opted for the more orthodox method of entry, climbing the hardwood steps and walking the twelve paces down the darkened corridor to his door.

It wasn't until he went to undo the lock that he noticed something was wrong, testimony to his fatigue. When he slipped his key into the hole, the door moved a fraction of an inch — it wasn't locked, wasn't even shut tight. All of which meant the spell he'd had focused into the lock no longer worked, or someone else had a better one.

In a perfect world, a beautiful blonde would have slipped into his room while he was out and be waiting, naked and willing, under the covers for his return. Deacon reminded himself that this was far from a perfect world as he drew his gun and kicked wide the door.

"Tell me true, Deacon — did you really think that low-power doorseal was going to keep anybody out?" a gruff voice said in welcome. "Gods and devils, man, I've got lockpicks down in the cells who could have cracked that old wheeze wide open when they were still in nappies!"

Deacon lowered his gun, reluctantly. Seated in the apartment's best armchair was Thom Banff, long-time sentinel, connoisseur of cheap ale, and one of the few men ever to down two gallons of Mesquer's while singing all twenty-seven verses of "The Shrublovers' Lament." His stocky form was nestled comfortably in the chair, a bottle of his unwilling host's ale in his beefy hand. He was in "uniform" — a rumpled suit with the gold badge of the sentinels proudly displayed on the lapel.

"Come on in. Make yourself at home," Deacon said, sarcastically, tossing his coat over the nearest piece of furniture. "Since when are you up before noon?"

"Since you started spending your nights with a 'vision in white, her hair woven darkness,'" Banff answered. "That's poetry, you know. Wrote it myself."

"Got a new stencil, huh?" Deacon said, opening up the coldbox and grabbing an ale. "All I want right now is some sleep, so unless this is important, I'd appreciate your getting lost."

"Oh, it is important," Banff said, turning in his seat to look right at Deacon. "It's very important, or so I'm told by the snot-nosed runt who sits at the captain's desk these days. Who's the looker you've been out with, Deacon?"

"None of your business."

"I could make it my business."

"Fine. I'll retire and you can have the office and all goodwill. I'll even introduce you to my creditors, as lethal a bunch as ever bled stones. Of course, they draw the line at breaking into a man's house and drinking his beer, but then they're not guardians of the law."

"Spare me the righteous wrath, you fleabitten son of a sorcerer," Banff growled, rising. "One of my men saw you at the *Dwelling Place* with a woman that could send anybody down to Alchemists' Row for some ground *gharb* horn. You were seen to leave with her. Who was she?"

"Get your own dates."

"This is sentinel business," Banff said, an unmistakable note of warning in his voice. "I'm not asking this for my health, you miserable excuse for a muckwader."

"And I'm not telling you, for mine," Deacon replied. He took a long swig from the ale bottle before adding, "After all, how long do you think I'll stay in business if it gets around that I tell everything to an overweight swamp ape that someone trained to wear clothes? I've got a reputation to protect."

Banff's face turned a deep red, the standard sign that good-natured kidding was over and things were turning serious. "I'll say this in small words, so that even you can understand it, Deacon: the last three cult-related murders we've had, your girlfriend's been spotted in the crowd around the bodies. She's a tough one to miss, I've been told. Now when you consider the fact that all three incidents took place in different parts of the city, it begins to seem a little strange."

"Maybe she likes watching your guys work," Deacon offered. "Maybe she goes for slobs in uniform."

"And maybe she comes back to see her handiwork," Banff said, loudly. Someone downstairs began banging a broomstick on their ceiling. Banff ignored it. "Something ugly is happening in this city, Jack. All the high priests and exalted wizards and great lords of the still waters are at each others' throats, and their followers are raising holy hell out there! I don't know if they're fighting over territory, theology or who gets the last piece of pie, but I've been up to my knees in blood for weeks now."

"The Esler killings," Deacon said, more to himself than to Banff.

"Yeah, and a whole mess of others," the sentinel said hotly. "It's like somebody's been stoking them up for this all along and just let them off the leash. Right now, they're only killing each other — but how long before some poor working stiff gets in the way of one of their knives? How long before some cultist decides that the next block is home to the enemy and lobs a fireball or two at it?"

"So round up the usual suspects, Thom. Why pick on me?" Deacon said, already guessing the answer.

"Because I think the looker is right in the middle of this thing, and that might put you right there with her. What are you working on, Jack?"

"You know I can't tell you that," Deacon said irritably. He turned away from Banff and went to the window, staring through the pane at the street below, which was starting to come to life. "As for the woman — she's someone I met in a tavern. Like you said, she's got something. I took her out, we had a few and went back to her place. She's as good as she looks. End of story."

Banff grunted and went to get his coat. "You should have been a streetsinger, Deacon. You tell a mighty fine tale."

Deacon emptied his bottle and tossed it in the can. The bottle slowly dissolved and was gone in a matter of seconds. He waited a few moments out of respect for the dead and then got himself another.

Banff returned to the living room, frustration evident in his features. "I'll be back. I'm waiting for a report on what killed the two women in Esler. Once I know what kind of blade I'm looking for, I may pay your girlfriend a visit."

He was halfway out the door when Deacon's voice stopped him. "Thom ... what do you think is happening? What's set them all off?"

Banff shook his head. "Damned if I know. I'm just the guy who cleans up after them. But if you want my advice, stay out of it. There's going to be a lot of blood flying around town and I'd rather none of it be yours."

Deacon frowned, a deep V forming between his eyes. "You're the second man who's given me that advice today."

"Then maybe you should start listening, Deacon," Banff said, walking away. "Maybe you should start listening."

❦

Deacon slept for four hours. His dreams were not pleasant ones.

❦

Late in the afternoon, he left his rooms and headed back toward the east side. He noted that, even here, there seemed to be a little extra snap to everyone's step. Word had traveled fast about what seemed to be a cult war, and most people were wary enough of those groups to prefer being off the streets if they were at odds.

Cults had been a part of Galitia — indeed, of most cities — for as long as anyone could remember. They ranged from the fanatically ascetic to the shamelessly hedonistic, and sects could be found at every point in between on the spectrum. Although their beliefs were often unorthodox, their memberships often included city elders, high-ranking sentinels, even priests of the more widely accepted religions.

Public opinion of cults varied. Those in the public eye tended to impose strict moral codes on their members, contributed heavily toward the Sentinel Benevolent Society, and as a general rule, did nothing to frighten anyone. At worst, the jealous way in which they guarded their secrets fostered some resentment or scorn in non-members.

But no one was foolish enough to believe these kind of groups to be typical of the secret sects. Demon cults had been a fact of life dating back to the Middle Ages, the last time there had been armed conflict between the groups. Occasionally, sentinels would raid a "temple" somewhere and haul in apparently respectable citizens who were in the process of dismembering animals or raping suspected virgins. In a few cases, the rituals proved to be just show — but more often than not, the blood cults were all too real and all too dangerous. They seemed to worship no single deity or demon, but any one of a host, with a fervor bordering on mania. When crossed, they showed no qualms about shedding the blood of their enemies, even if some of their members were killed in the process.

The only thing that had kept them from becoming major threats to peace in the last millennium was a lack of organization. It was rare for two cults to agree on anything, let alone work together. That, Deacon guessed, was what had the sentinels so worried: a cult war meant the sects had coalesced into two or more factions, with the potential to cause wholescale slaughter on a whim. Unless they were stopped — or at least persuaded to quiet down — there would be a bloodbath.

But stopping them meant learning why they were fighting in the first place. And there was always the chance that *they* didn't know …

Deacon looked up to see that his musing had brought him to the debris-strewn side street that housed Belrand's Curios. The pawn shop had a prime location and sufficient sorcerous protection to discourage would-be thieves. Even the bright green awning that proclaimed its name had somehow survived for more than five years. Though coated with grime, the window offered tantalizing glimpses of musical instruments, stained-glass chandeliers, wind-up toys and framed stamp collections. It was a waystation for goods whose owners needed a few extra coins to make it through the night, and so parted for a time with the things they treasured.

He opened the door, the soft jingle of bells announcing a visitor. The shop was empty, but the strong smell of a musky cologne said its proprietor had not been gone long. Deacon slipped behind the counter and opened the door that read "No Admittance."

His quarry had gone to ground in the back room, what most customers doubtless believed to be only a storage closet. In fact, it was the site of Belrand's more lucrative line of work, a sorcerous armory into which Deacon had poured money on more than one occasion. Belrand was fast, efficient, and only about two hundred percent more expensive than legitimate dealers.

Belrand was also asleep, as it turned out. The squat, baldheaded man was dead to the world, slumped over his work table with his tools still in hand. He had been in the midst of carving a flute, but Deacon did not recognize the designs carved into the sides.

The detective reached out and shook the craftsman awake, as gently as possible. Belrand still leapt a good two feet out of his chair and let out a shriek. His frantic movements didn't cease until the identity of his visitor registered in his brain.

"Hell's bells, Deacon, what are you doing, trying to scare ten years off my life?" Belrand snapped in his high-pitched voice. "I thought you were a sentinel, on my heart, I did!"

"Well, you were wrong by about six years, Rollie. Besides, what would sentinels want with you? You're just a simple arms dealer. Town's full of them."

Belrand drew himself up to his full height — four feet eleven and three-quarters — and gave Deacon a look of wounded pride. "I am an artist, that's what I am. Am I or am I not the best 'smith in Galitia? Why, I have weapons, charms, talismans in here that High Mages would give their grandmother's grimoires to get a look at!"

Deacon nodded, chuckling. "That they would. But you haven't answered my question: why would the sentinels be scouting you?"

Belrand's face took on a sour expression and voice dropped to a hoarse whisper. "It's these damnable killings. Until they know just what weapon was used, they are making life … difficult for all of us who design and build in a small way of business."

"So they think there was something special about the knife used?" Deacon asked. It wasn't unusual for cults to use arcane weaponry, but the reports he'd heard sounded like standard slice and dice. It wasn't as if the corpses were up and walking around, after all.

"Deke, they are not even sure it *was* a knife," Belrand answered, as if he were sharing one of the great secrets of the universe. "Or a hatchet. Or an axe. They can't match the wounds, friend Jack, and that is the truth."

No wonder Banff is so upset, Deacon thought. *I think I'm going to have some questions for Miss Martel tonight.*

"But enough of that," Belrand said, with a grin. "You came here for a reason, I expect? Perhaps to help fill an old man's coffers, eh? What is it to be today, more of those very special bullets?"

"That, and a few other things," Deacon said, pulling out one of the bills Larissa had given him. "How much will this buy?"

Belrand's eyes widened to the size of five-pieces. "Name it, friend Jack. 'Have I ever told you about my wife's sister? A fine woman, she is, and regrettably alone at present. If you would like —"

"Save it, Rollie. I've got troubles. I need a few boxes of the special ammo and something I can carry with me. Something portable."

"I have just the thing," Belrand said happily, tearing into a pile of guns, knives and other assorted melee weapons. After five minutes of cursing, tossing items around, and knocking his head on the corner of his worktable several times, he emerged with a small black rectangle of metal.

"This is my pride and joy," he said, presenting the item to Deacon. "And for you, only one thousand."

"What's it do?" Deacon said, reaching out to finger the item.

Belrand snatched it away from him. "Oh, you must be very careful with this one, my friend. Very careful indeed, yes. You see, you pass your finger over this notch here and —"

As he spoke the words, a wickedly sharp stiletto sprang from inside the object. The box reshaped itself before Deacon's eyes so as to become a hilt, with grooves for fingers. Belrand's eyes gleamed brighter than the blade.

"Cute," Deacon said. "But I need something a little stronger than a dagger on this job."

Belrand looked hurt. "Would I waste my genius on a simple knife? Watch."

With a shrill yell, he lifted the stiletto into the air and plunged it into the side of a tool box. The blade bit deep into the wood and stuck fast. Both Belrand and Deacon watched it for a moment, but nothing else happened.

"Sticks real well," Deacon muttered. "If I get attacked by furniture, I'll be sure to come to you."

Belrand spat a particularly vile curse and smacked the knife hilt with a hammer, driving the weapon further into its resting place. Suddenly, the blade emitted a blinding flash and there was a strong smell of wood smoke. When Deacon could see again, both knife and box were still intact.

"I don't think so, Rollie," he said. "The flash effect is nice and all, but —"

"Shut up and watch closely," Belrand said sharply. Then the little man bent over, brought his lips close to the tool box, and blew hard at it. The crate and its contents flew apart in a cloud of foul-smelling ash, the knife dropping to the floor.

"You see now?" the craftsman said, fanning away the cinders. "It's quick, it's neat and no bodies to dispose of when you're done. The spell focused into it is guaranteed untraceable."

"Guaranteed for how long?"

"For the lifetime of the owner," Belrand answered proudly. "I used to do it for the lifetime of the product, until someone pointed out that if the item doesn't work, the owner won't be around to collect on the warranty."

"I know. I'm the one who mentioned it," Deacon said. "All right, I'll take it. Put it on my tab."

"But what about the cash you showed me? The big bill?" Belrand sputtered.

"I asked you how much it would buy. I didn't say I was going to use it here," Deacon replied, smiling. "Besides, if I owe you money, it gives you a vested interest in my staying alive. Makes for better quality goods."

"Point taken," Belrand said unhappily. He busied himself bundling up Deacon's purchases, then said, "You really think you're going to need all this? Who are you going up against, anyway?"

Deacon started to answer, then remembered the predatory look he had seen in East's eyes when they had parted. "I don't need them for my enemies, Rollie. But I may be using them on some friends before all this is over."

Chapter
Five

An Undead with an aversion to sunlight will sleep anywhere from eight to 12 hours out of every 24, depending upon the season of the year. Although some cult literature on the subject refers to this period of inactivity as a "coma," it is actually only a very deep slumber. The central nervous system — the only part of an Undead that functions in a manner similar to that of a living being — does not shut down completely, but simply closes down a part of itself.

And in that state, so near and yet so far from the final sleep beneath the earth, the Undead dream …

For Larissa, safe in one of her many refuges, the dreams were always the same. She would see the smiling face of Roald, her lover, as he explained what he needed from her. She had known all along what he was, of course, and knew she risked damnation in the eyes of her church by associating with him. But it was somehow the danger that appealed to her, and perhaps she even harbored the foolish notion that her love could bring him back to true life. There was so much about that time that she could not remember, even in dreams.

Roald had made her a promise, she was certain of that. He told her that what he would do would be out of love; that he would only take enough to sustain him; that nothing very bad would happen to her. She hadn't wanted to show her fear, afraid of hurting him, and so she consented.

Had he lied? Or had he simply overestimated his own inner strength? Whichever, once he had begun to feed, he did not stop. By the time she realized what was happening, she was too far gone to push him away — not that she could have prevailed against his strength, anyway. All that was left to her was sweet darkness.

When she awoke, she was in a coffin. But she felt none of the terror a normal person might feel in such a situation — she knew what she had become, what *he* had done to her. He had not even bothered to remain nearby to ease her transition to the world of the Undead. He had fled, afraid of being found out and hunted down.

A desire for vengeance gave her purpose. It helped her retain some shred of sanity in those early days. And the dream grew dark …

It took her months, but she found Roald again. He had moved on to another city, living a life of parties, theatre and clubs and taking his victims from among the poor and homeless. The ones who wouldn't be missed, that was his fare now, for he had grown cautious in his second century.

Larissa began to follow him on his nocturnal hunts. As soon as he would close on a kill, she would snatch it away from him. He grew enraged, tried to slay her, but she was younger and faster. She merely laughed at him until he fled, and then she took up the chase again.

By the end of the first week, he was reduced to consuming the blood of rodents. His once-handsome form could be seen skulking through alleyways, upsetting trash cans in his search for sustenance. She considered leaving him be, letting him live with the humiliation. But all feelings of compassion were gone from her heart now, and it would be many years before they would return again. She shifted her form to that of a night creature and drove the rats away.

He was too weak to fight back, too weak even to run. Dawn was fast approaching — she would have to leave soon and be cheated out of seeing him die. And so she dragged him away to a cellar and kept him safe from the sunlight, the better to watch him die from blood starvation when the night came again.

The dream ended.

Larissa awoke in the here and now, still clinging to fragments of the dream. She knew it was important that she remember when she had died. Somehow, the ability to recall when she last felt the sun on her skin meant all her humanity had not yet fled. It had been eighty-five years and five months ... or was it six months ago? Damnation, why couldn't she *remember?*

She willed herself to mist and slipped through a crack in the door of her tomb, floating across the silent churchyard to reform in the abandoned rectory. She was nude, her body as trim and supple as it had been when she had lived, and far stronger in Undeath. She had learned long ago that the idea that one's clothes would miraculously still be clean after eight hours buried in earth was a myth.

She slipped into a black dress, one that highlighted her pale skin. She had made plans to meet Deacon in the crafts district at 10 pm, there to seek out the first of her targets. Narses had to be alerted and preparations had to be made if the night's work was to be a success.

But none of that mattered now. It could wait until she had fed.

❦

Sandel Hogue walked the brightly-lit path back that led from his workplace to his nicely appointed home. He was late — he hoped Indries would not be too worried, what with all these murders in the city. No, she knew him too well, knew he took only the safest routes wherever he went. At worst, she would be angry that dinner had grown cold.

Still, it had been worth it. For weeks, little Anya had begged for a new doll, one that cried real tears. He had saved his coins and scoured the city trying to find a toy shop that carried such a thing. And now it was his, wrapped securely in brown paper and tucked under his arm. He could picture the expression on his daughter's face — perhaps he would have a bit of fun first and tell her the package was just a cut of meat from the butcher's. Then he would tear it open before her eyes.

Lost in imagined squeals of childish delight, Sandel Hogue never heard Larissa approach.

Three nights later he would return to his family, the doll forgotten, and give them another sort of gift. A year from now, his head would be blown apart by bullets with religious symbols inscribed on them. Twelve years after that, Indries would die from exposure to sunlight in northern Dela. Anya would put her innocent appearance to good use and survive for a century before finally succumbing to blood starvation.

❦

By most standards, Galitia is a young city. It was founded a mere nine centuries ago by the remnants of an army, who constructed a ramshackle "fortress" on the site. This was during the last period in which the cults were actively killing each other, but at this time they were not striking from the shadows. Great armies took to the battlefield and met in bloody clashes that lasted for weeks at a time.

It was during this time of worldwide horror that the tales of creatures who were beyond Human were born. After the war's apparent end, people still held to the truth of these stories. After all, even the greatest scholars had an imperfect understanding of the sorcery that was a part of everyday life, so who was to say that such things didn't exist? The conventional wisdom became that the dark things had been drawn out by the carnage of the war, and would only return if wholescale bloodletting began again. How much of a role fear of these creatures of legend played in keeping future wars small ones can only be guessed at.

The men who came to where Galitia now stands were all who were left from an army that had numbered in the hundreds. Butchered by worshippers of a minor deity named Skorn, it was a miracle that any of that company had escaped. They traveled to the largely unexplored northern wilds and chose a spot near a broad river to make a stand. To keep the memory of the fate they had narrowly avoided, they named the river Skorn.

In time, merchants and traders came to Galitia and a town sprang up within the walls of the fort. Although the town fathers were never able to attract the Mage Academy they dearly wanted, the city became known for its craftsmen and metalworkers and made a convenient stop for those traders bold enough to sail the river.

Of course, much changed over the course of centuries. The city grew to the point where the ruins of the old fortress are now surrounded by row upon row of buildings. Skorn has become polluted by the waste products of alchemical plants (and other things which people don't care to talk about). Poverty, vice, crime and all the other plagues of modern urban living had arrived and taken root.

And the old feuds that a party of soldiers had fled from 900 years ago had also found Galitia ...

❧

Although he had been born and raised in the city, Jack Deacon had only a vague knowledge of its history and little interest in it. Before meeting Larissa, he had always said that people who had been dead a thousand years made lousy suspects and worse clients.

He had heard the stories about things like Larissa and East (whatever the hell he was) as a child. His parents used them to try and keep him from going out and playing in the streets after dark, with no success. As he grew older and more aware, he learned that not every murder was done with a gun or a knife, and not every murderer had reason to fear hanging. But like any other sentinel *cum* private investigator in a big city, he had only encountered traces of such things during his career. He had seen enough to know the need for being prepared on any case, the same way that a householder barred the door in a rainstorm, for it might turn into a gale.

Deacon's mother had wanted him to be a craftsman, even going so far as to apprentice him to a woodworker. It hadn't worked out — he had shown no talent for even the most basic spells someone in that line had to know and had hated being cooped up all day. His boss had finally kicked him out, calling him "magically uncoordinated."

That left trading (too sleazy, to his way of thinking) and a post in the sentinels. This was ideal, since all you had to know was "spot the suspect, warn the suspect, shoot the suspect," and sometimes the second part could be ignored. It didn't matter if you didn't know how to cast a really good fireball, as long as you had something that would drop the guy who did.

After six years chasing whores off street corners, breaking up bar fights, and running in minor mages who worked the shell game by making the pea disappear — and a case that left a bad taste in his soul — Deacon got tired of taking orders. There was more money to be made in private work, providing you were smart enough to keep one foot on either side of the law.

And I'm sure living the good life now, Deacon said to himself, as he walked down a dark street in the crafts district, listening to the telltale tread of a tail.

❦

Larissa had given him the address, but not the name, of their target. That Deacon had found out for himself through a little legwork and a few calls. Pau Gresh, age 34, no arrests, though the records showed he had been in his share of brawls. He ran a smithy, his specialty constructing engines for automobiles. Most of his money came through contracts with elemental mages, who needed someone to build the housing in which they would focus their magic.

The image the sentinel artist conjured up was of a well-built man with a sullen expression. Not as tall as Deacon might have expected, he still had a formidable look about him. The boys charged with walking his neighborhood warned Deacon that Gresh had a short temper. The closest he had ever come to being brought in was when he had cracked the skull of a creditor with one blow some months past. Everyone else on the street had sworn it was a case of self-defense, although that description probably applied more to their willingness to back Gresh's story.

All in all, he sounded like the type who best understood the weighted end of a club. Deacon was beginning to understand why Larissa had felt the need for a bodyguard.

He rounded a corner and she was there, as if she had been born from the alley's shadows in that moment. For an instant, he didn't recognize her and caught himself trying to decide on a pick-up line. There was something about her, something that was a far cry from the woman he had met on two previous occasions. The sparkle was still present in her eyes, though it didn't dance as it had before, but the aura of vitality about her was almost overwhelming. Deacon had a sudden desire to take her in his arms and say to hell with the rest of the world. He had known many women in his life, but never one who seemed so *alive* —

It was that thought that shattered his fantasy. Suddenly, he was back in the here and now and Larissa truly was like no other woman he had known.

She gave him a questioning look. He knew what she was asking. "I had a shadow. I shook him," he said matter-of-factly.

"You're certain you weren't followed?"

"Yeah. I'm also sure you were."

"How — ?"

"Just trust me," he said, giving her a less than gentle push toward the alley. "This is what I was hired for, remember? Let's go."

The two of them walked briskly down the alleyway, Larissa not needing to be told to keep her eyes forward. Their passage among the piles of garbage disturbed a pair of cats at their nightly feast and the animals dashed away as if devils were in hot pursuit.

The alley opened on to a broad avenue lined with woodworkers' shops and smithys. There were lights on the upper floors of a few buildings, but no one out on the street. The craftsmen were all in bed for the night, or else washing away the day's troubles with an ale, Deacon guessed.

He steered Larissa into a sharp right turn and signalled her to say nothing. "Keep going," he whispered. She hesitated, about to question, then thought better of it and moved off.

Deacon flattened himself against the brick wall and waited, the muscles in his stomach knotted with tension. He was rewarded by the appearance of a young man clad in the simple clothes and leather apron of a butcher's apprentice. Deacon caught sight of the cleaver in the new arrival's hand and sprang.

His attack caught his target by surprise. Deacon caught the young man's right wrist in a firm grip and began to twist, but could not get him to drop the knife. The apprentice kicked backwards and snapped Deacon's left knee, the pain almost making him let go.

"All right, we'll do it the hard way," Deacon said through gritted teeth. He seized the back of the young man's neck in his free hand and propelled his foe face-first into the brick wall. He heard the satisfying crunch of bone and cartilage and the sound of the knife striking pavement.

He yanked backwards to get a look at his catch. The young man couldn't have been older than twenty, with a face that would have been handsome if it hadn't been streaked with blood. Surprisingly, the collision with the wall had been enough to knock him out — his eyes were closed and his body limp. Deacon let him fall and turned to call Larissa.

A second later, it was Deacon who was on the ground. A blow like a sledgehammer had struck the small of his back and brought him to his knees, pain rocketing through his body. He heard the sound of the boy rising behind him.

"Get up." The voice was cold like a night wind, the words those of someone who relished delivering pain.

Deacon groaned and began rubbing his right wrist, as if he had sprained it in the fall. An instant later, he felt the knife slide from his sleeve into his hand. He passed his thumb over the hilt the way Belrand had showed him and the blade appeared, but he made certain to switch off its sorcerous energy. He wanted this one alive.

The boy came closer and seized Deacon's overcoat, lifting him to his feet. Deacon whirled and plunged the knife into his opponent's left arm, just above the elbow, and the boy screamed and released him. Deacon took two steps forward and turned, knife at the ready.

The wounded arm hung uselessly at the boy's side, but he seemed not to care. His nose was smashed and bloody, but somehow there was still a smile on his ruined lips. And his eyes gleamed red …

❦

Larissa heard the scream, but didn't turn back. She reminded herself that this was what she was paying Deacon for, and if he died in her service, well … she decided she would not tell East. She did not want to listen to the old man gloat.

❦

Deacon and the boy were circling each other. Twice, the detective feinted to the left and then went right, trying to score on his foe's wounded arm. But the boy was too fast and Deacon narrowly evaded a kick that would have put him on the ground again had it connected.

Tactics ran through his head at blinding speed. All he needed was one good strike with the knife, its magic now reactivated, and the boy would be ashes. But his movements were sluggish from the blow to the back and his legs felt like they were made of lead.

Still, it was only a matter of time, he thought. No matter what was keeping the boy on his feet, he bled like a Human. Eventually, that would take its toll … Deacon hoped.

Suddenly, the boy lashed out with a fist. Deacon barely caught the blow on his left arm, which went numb. He staggered back a few steps, his back now against the wall of a building. The boy swung again, but this time he telegraphed the blow and Deacon had time to duck. There was a sickening crack of bones as hand struck stone.

Deacon lunged with the knife, but the boy was already falling back. He made a second stab at the wounded arm and this time managed a gash across the wrist. The cost of doing the damage was almost fatal, as he slipped on a pool of blood and almost went headlong toward his foe.

The boy was looking from his pulverized right hand to the blood flowing from his left with seeming detachment. Deacon made another thrust and the boy swept it aside, still smiling.

"Is this what you want?" he said, gesturing toward his dead arm. He reached across his body, grabbed hold of it, and with one sudden motion, tore the arm out at the shoulder. A geyser of blood erupted from the gaping wound as he casually dropped the limb at Deacon's feet.

"I can lose a dozen of these bodies. How about you, Deacon?" the boy said. Then the red glow faded from his eyes and he collapsed to the ground, like a puppet whose strings had been cut.

Deacon staggered back to the alleyway and began to retch.

Chapter Six

When Deacon caught up to Larissa, he had regained some of his composure: the color had returned to his cheeks, his heart rate was back in a normal range, and there was nothing left in his stomach to cough up. It wasn't until he saw the look on Larissa's face that he noticed his clothes were covered in blood.

"Your enemies, or mine?" she asked quietly.

"Is there a difference anymore?" he replied, wiping the sweat from his brow.

"Did you kill him?"

"I had a hand in it. He did most of it himself."

As they walked the last few blocks to the metalwarper's shop, Deacon related the details of the fight. Larissa nodded occasionally, but said nothing until he had finished.

"I wish I could say I was surprised by this news, but I'm not," she said, eyes fixed on their destination. "What you fought was a minor demon called a relkazar. I'm not certain if they have a physical form of their own, but they've turned possession into an art form. They make excellent scouts, but they have no real stomach for confrontation."

"Tell that to my aching back tomorrow," Deacon said hotly. "Better yet, tell that to the kid in the alley back there with his arm ripped off."

Larissa stopped and turned to him, a mixture of grief and anger

 50

on her face. "Many more innocents are going to die before this is over, Deacon. You can't afford to begin bleeding for them all."

"The day I stop feeling those deaths, I'm no better than you," Deacon said, walking away from her. "Maybe the only value Humans have for you is for what's pumping in their veins. Maybe you've had to convince yourself that we're no more than that in order to survive. But don't expect me to shrug off murder."

"Spare me your self-righteous posturing, Deacon," Larissa snapped. "'Every man's death diminishes me,' isn't that the line? If you believe that, then Humanity has been diminished past the point of no return for centuries. Your kind has been judging whether people like me have the right to live for generations. Your hands aren't clean."

"Not everybody recognizes your right to exist at the cost of others' lives," Deacon answered angrily. "Prey has the right to judge the predator."

"Oh? Should we then have the beasts of the fields and the fish in the stream meet to decide the fate of Humanity?"

"That's not the same thing, and you know it," Deacon growled.

"Isn't it?" Larissa answered quietly, then noticed where the argument had carried them. "We can continue this later. We've arrived."

Gresh's smithy was a barn-like structure with two great wooden doors that slid aside to allow entrance. It was not as old a building as it first appeared, but Gresh had allowed it to get covered in grime. A fresh, new smithy did little to attract customers, who demanded an atmosphere of soot, ash and sweat.

Deacon tried the doors and found them locked, but could see the fire of a forge and the telltale glow of metalwarping magic through the crack.

"Looks like he's home," he reported, then turned back and rapped on the door. When no answer came, he rapped a second time.

An angry bellow came from inside. "We're closed! Come back tomorrow!"

Deacon looked at Larissa. She nodded. "I've had an accident!"

Deacon yelled. "Broke an axle! It's just down the road!"

"Come back tomorrow! I'm busy!"

Deacon frowned and began kicking one of the doors, rattling it on its frame. After a few moments, he heard a chain lock being undone and the door opened with a crash.

Pau Gresh was a short, stocky man with a fringe of black hair around his head and a thick moustache. He had broad features and his nose had been broken at least twice, inexpertly set both times. His body was all muscle and he reeked of sweat.

"I said we're closed!" he snarled at Deacon. "Beat it or they're gonna have to carry you away!"

Deacon had seen this type before. You got nowhere with them if they weren't taught some respect. "Little guys always talk tough, don't they?" the detective said, looking Gresh over with thinly disguised contempt. "What's the matter, pal, they won't let you on the adult rides at the fair?"

Gresh was surprisingly fast for his build. The fist he swung at Deacon had only slightly less stopping power than an anvil, but the detective sidestepped and watched the blow splinter the door. Deacon took advantage of the opening this gave him to land a jab to Gresh's kidneys, then another to his throat. The smith charged and caught Deacon around the waist, driving him into a building across the street.

Deacon cursed and brought a knee up into Gresh's stomach, forcing the smith to break his grip. With a little more room to maneuver now, he smashed Gresh's jaw first with a right, then a left. The bull-like man was rocked by the blows, but didn't fall.

"Are you done?" Gresh said, driving his fist into Deacon's chin and lifting the detective off his feet. Deacon hit the ground and rolled barely in time to avoid a wicked kick aimed at his groin. Hearing Gresh approaching, Deacon grabbed an old piece of pipe and swung.

Gresh's laugh was harsh. A bright light flared from his outstretched palm and the pipe turned red, then white. Deacon dropped it with a yell of pain.

"Never try a pipe on a metalwarper," Gresh said, smiling.

"Now get on your feet and let's finish this."

Deacon looked up at him and spat blood. "Come and get me."

Gresh took a few steps backward and charged toward his fallen foe, leaping at the last moment. Deacon swung his legs up in the air and caught Gresh in the gut, using the smith's own momentum to send him flying overhead and into the wall. The smith crumpled to the ground as Deacon got to his feet. He cast a rueful glance at his burnt hand.

"Was all that necessary?" Larissa asked. "We're only here to talk."

"He'll be a much better listener now," Deacon answered, dragging Gresh with difficulty toward the smithy.

❦

A pail of cold water in the face was sufficient to wake the smith up. Aside from a few nasty bruises and a massive headache, he seemed unharmed. He was on his feet and halfway toward Deacon when Larissa interposed herself.

"That's enough," she said firmly. The smith pulled up short and looked her over, all but licking his chops.

"Whatever you say, lady," Gresh said. "Are you with him, or are you as smart as you look?"

"Sit down. We have things to discuss," Larissa said, her tone one of command. Deacon stood behind and to her left, gun in hand. Gresh's eyes went from her face to the pistol and then back to her.

"It's like that, huh? If you're looking to rob me, I haven't got enough to buy a bottle," he said, defiantly. "Spellslingers are quick to hire, slow to pay."

"We're not here to take anything," Larissa said, gesturing toward a chair. Gresh took it, never taking his eyes off the gun barrel pointed at him. "We're here to give you back something you've lost."

Larissa's voice was soft now as she stepped closer to the smith. "Remember? There was a time, long ago, when no one could stand in your way, Gresh. You lived for the sounds of battle and the smell of blood."

"What are you, crazy?" Gresh said, harshly. "I've never been in a war, lady, you've got the wrong guy. Now take what you want and get out of here. Shoot me down, if that's what you're going to do."

Larissa reached out and placed her hands on his wrists, drawing close enough that her lips almost touched his. Deacon thought he saw a light playing on Gresh's face, but he couldn't discern the source.

"Listen to me," Larissa said. "It's buried deep inside you. The truth was locked away centuries ago. It's time to set it free."

"What truth? I don't know what you're talking about!" Gresh said, trying to pull away from her. Deacon could hear the doubt growing in his voice.

"Set it free," Larissa repeated. "It's time now, Gresh. All of this has been a sham, an illusion. Let go of it."

"Let go …" Gresh muttered. "Are you sure?"

"Yes. You're needed now. We're all needed. Let go, Gresh. It's time for the lies to end."

Shortly after Jack Deacon had learned to walk, he ventured under the stoop of his building and stumbled on a bloodfly nest. The matriarch was away at the time, else he might never have survived to master running. But the brood was there, locked away in fleshy cocoons, waiting for the moment they would emerge.

That time came before an infant's awestruck eyes. The cocoons began to shiver, then their substance was torn apart by the newly-metamorphosized insectoids within. A fine mist of blood filled the dank space beneath the stairs. The child screamed and bolted, a fortunate circumstance since bloodflies come into this world hungry.

Deacon's memory of that incident was lost to time, but the fear he had felt then was of a primal nature that never truly vanished from the soul. He felt it again now, as he heard a sound like cloth ripping and saw Gresh begin to change.

The stocky man was on his feet, in too much pain even to scream. The flesh along his arms had split apart and jagged edges of bone were fighting their way free. Then the same thing began to happen to his legs, blood and tissue flying as his skeleton expanded, shredding his skin.

Deacon shook himself free of the shock that had paralyzed him and started toward the convulsing man. Larissa put out a hand to stop him.

"There's nothing you can do for him," she said, her expression unreadable. For the first time, Deacon noticed what looked like a gem buried beneath the skin of her throat, and aglow. "There can be no birth without pain."

With a roar of terror and agony, Gresh reeled backward as his face began to swell and his eyes filled with blood. With an explosion of flesh, his skull broke free of its prison and began to mutate. When it was done, it resembled a warrior's helmet from a woodcut, with a broadly curved bone at its crest that ended in sharp horns.

Suddenly, Deacon realized that the thing that was Gresh had grown larger as well, now closing on three meters high. He was now no more than a skeleton, but unlike any Deacon had ever seen, with wickedly sharp daggers of bone emerging at odd angles from its limbs. And there was something inside, seemingly protected by the skeletal structure, a reddish, vaguely humanoid mass that glistened sickeningly in the light cast by the forge.

At the feet of the Gresh thing lay the skin of the smith in a pool of blood. With a casual gesture, he kicked the remnants of his old life aside. He no longer had any eyes or mouth as such, but Deacon somehow knew he could see and speak.

And the thing was looking at him.

When Gresh spoke, it was in a voice that sounded like gravel being ground down to dust. He gestured a skeletal hand toward Deacon's gun. "Go ahead and shoot. Maybe you'll get lucky and you won't hit bone. I'm beyond pain now, anyway."

Deacon's aim didn't waver. "Good for you. I get the same way after ten or twelve ales. I'm betting that if I put a slug between your ribs, you'll feel it."

The mass of tissue moved slightly, but the skeleton remained in place. Gresh turned his attention to Larissa. "He's a tough guy, isn't he? Maybe I should show him what these can do," he said, swinging one arm at the wall. The boards splintered before the blow, and the bone daggers tore great gashes in the wood that had survived. "Just like I remember."

Larissa turned to Deacon. "Put your weapon down. This is Gresh's true form. He won't hurt you."

"Much," Gresh added.

Deacon took a step backward and kept the gun levelled on both Larissa and Gresh. "I'm packing the same slugs I used on the 'shifter. It's time to play question and answer, sister. I want to know what this is all about."

"There isn't time!" Larissa said, strain obvious in her voice. The gem had ceased to glow, but she looked as if the experience had drained her strength. "We have to get out of here before they arrive. It's only a matter of time —"

"Until what?" Deacon demanded, color rising in his neck. "Damn it, I can't go any further in this until I know what game we're playing! I don't know who's after you, I'm not even sure you do! I have to be sure you know what you're doing, that we're not just blundering around in the dark hoping not to get killed today!"

Gresh took a step forward. "I'm here now. You don't need him."

"Don't be a fool!" Larissa snapped at the skeletal creature, before turning back to Deacon. "There isn't time for a full explanation now. What I said before is true: we are in the middle of a war, Deacon. The other side is marshalling their forces, and we must do the same. That's my task — mine and others', in other cities."

"Whose side are you on? And who's the enemy?"

Larissa shook her head. "It would take too long to explain. We must get out of here!"

Deacon knew he should press for the whole story now, before things went any farther. But he could tell Larissa was not acting

— *something* was coming, and she didn't want to be around when it got here.

"All right," he said, still holding the weapon steady. "We'll go. Bones walks in front of me. When we're safely away, I get the story, start to finish, or I'm through."

"Last part sounds good," Gresh said. There was a predatory smile in his voice, if not on what now passed for his face.

Deacon was about to explain just who he would take with him if he went when his eyes caught something near the battered door. At first, he thought it was a trick of light and shadow. Then Larissa saw it, too, and he knew his first impression had been right — the darkness *was* moving.

There was no sound or smell to mark its passage. It was not thick enough to be oil, and though it floated on the air and seeped through the cracks in the walls, it was not smoke. It was the substance of night, black and cold, and it moved around and through every obstacle in its path to the three.

Gresh roared and backed away from the ebon tendrils as they came closer. Deacon fired toward the doorway, but the slug passed through the attacker without doing any harm.

"You can't stop it that way!" Larissa shouted, pushing both Deacon and Gresh toward the far wall. The substance was coming from three sides now. In one spot, it paused before an anvil, enveloped it, and crushed the massive iron object to dust before moving on.

"What the hell is that?" Deacon said, shoving furniture out of the way in order to gain them more space to retreat. The cloud of liquid was flowing like a river through the holes Gresh's new and improved arm had made in the wall.

"It's a darkfield," Larissa replied. "I never dreamed they would use that!"

Gresh swung a spiked fist at the oncoming darkness, only to have the target catch one of the bone spurs in its grip and snap it off. Gresh snarled and fell back.

"It's a conjurers' rite," Larissa continued, as she tore a rack of shelves free from the wall and hurled it at the cloud. "It will destroy everything in its path, friend or foe, until the spell's energy runs out."

"When's that?" Deacon asked, feverishly working at the timbers of the wall with a crowbar.

"There's no way to tell," she replied, even as her body grew insubstantial. Now no more than mist herself, she began to drift toward the ceiling, darkfield tentacles trailing after her. "We're not armed to fight this. Gresh! Open the way!"

The creature of bone hesitated, reluctant to run from a fight. Then the mass of tissue shrugged and drove a spiked fist through the rear wall. Grabbing hold of one of the boards, he tore a hole large enough for a man to run through.

"Go! Move!" Larissa shouted, already diving for the opening with the darkfield only inches behind her. Deacon shot through the hole and scrambled to the top of a pile of stone before turning around. Gresh was clambering up behind him, rock sliding down behind as the creature struggled to gain purchase.

Deacon hesitated for a split second before reaching down and helping Gresh to the top of the pile. The creature nodded in his direction and said, "You thought about it first, didn't you? Now you're catching on."

The darkfield had completely enveloped the barn and the structure was beginning to fragment in its grip. A few tendrils had begun to reach for the stones at the bottom of the slope.

"Keep moving," Gresh ordered. "It is."

Deacon slid down the rockpile and caught the scent of the river. The docks weren't far from here. The alley before him was narrow but uncluttered and he made for it, with Gresh pounding along behind. Ahead of him, he could see Larissa reforming.

She beckoned them to follow and began to run. Behind him, Deacon could hear the sound of stone being pulverized as the darkfield consumed the pile of rock, glass and wood. He could imagine it was already seeping into the warehouses he was passing, moving inexorably forward.

He bombed out of the alleyway, Gresh at his heels, and found himself on a dock that extended several meters out to the river.

Larissa stood at the end.

Deacon wheeled around. The cloud had moved faster than he had anticipated, already engulfing a one-story warehouse and reducing it to splinters. More of it had floated down other alleyways, cutting off escape to the right or left. The only route open to them was the river itself.

"Looks like we swim," Deacon said, out of breath.

"It's too fast," Larissa said. "You and Gresh could never outpace it in the water, and I'm too weak to fly from it."

"You brought me back for this?" Gresh snarled.

The darkfield had reached the beginning of the dock and was rolling toward them. Deacon took another shot at it — this time, it almost seemed as if the cloud recoiled. Its substance was beginning to lessen as well, no longer the solid black wall it had been.

Deacon dropped to one knee and fired three more times. Now he could see the slugs erupting in the cloud, sending fiery streaks through its substance. It faded some more, going from cloud to mist. One wisp brushed across Deacon's face sending an icy chill through him. Then the darkfield spread wider and wider and finally dispersed, what little was left drifting away with the night wind.

"It's gone," Larissa reported, her voice weary. "The spell's duration has expired."

"What's to stop them from sending another one after us?" Deacon asked, rising slowly.

"It's not an easy spell to cast. The sorcerer will need rest before he can conjure another such thing. We must use that time to get away from here."

Gresh and Deacon followed her as she led them along the docks, no one speaking until they were well away from the scene of devastation. Nothing pursued them — at least, as far as they could tell.

"Maybe they think we're dead," Deacon offered.

"No. They would know if the darkfield had slain us. They would have felt it. But much good has come out of this, Deacon."

"How do you figure that?" the detective asked, trying to ignore the massive creature that lumbered along beside him.

"We have Gresh. And we know now that the enemy wants us dead far more than I would have believed possible. Perhaps they are not as secure in their strength as I had been led to believe."

"I'd hate to see what you think of as bad news, lady," Deacon muttered as they moved farther into the darkness.

Chapter
Seven

The safehouse Larissa led her two companions to was a far cry from her other haven. Where the other had been a shabby basement, this was a richly appointed penthouse atop one of the better-known inns in the city. Huge windows looked out over the slumbering Galitia, the lights of glow-stones making the town seem almost festive. From this high up, things looked clean and beautiful, a conjurer's illusion that could last forever, as long as one never came down.

"This is more like it," Gresh muttered. Deacon tried not to let his surprise show on his face as the smith withdrew the bone daggers back into his skeletal frame, apparently by strength of will alone. That done, the creature stalked off in search of the kitchen and food.

Narses had been waiting for them when they arrived. The driver did not so much as glance twice in Gresh's direction. *Maybe he's seen worse,* Deacon thought.

"Make yourself comfortable," Larissa said. "We'll spend the day here and try to contact East tomorrow night." She sat down on the golden couch that dominated the center of the room and gestured for Deacon to take a chair. Instead, he walked to the windows and looked out over his city.

He had a lot to think about. In the morning, someone would report Gresh's disappearance and the destruction of the smithy, not to mention two or three warehouses. If anyone had spotted him or Larissa in the area, there would be no putting Banff off this time. The sentinels would want in and they would walk over him to get there, if necessary.

Maybe I should let them, Deacon said to himself. *Larissa has Gresh for a watchdog. Let him deal with darkness that follows you and people bursting out of their skins. East was right, I don't belong here.*

As soon as the thought crossed his mind, however, he saw a flash of the butcher's apprentice lying dead in an alley. Then he remembered the warehouse smashed into kindling, and wondered if there might have been squatters inside, taking shelter from the night air. This war of Larissa's wasn't going to disappear if he walked away, and so far no one else involved seemed to care very much if innocents were killed.

"Are you afraid, Deacon?" Larissa asked. She had come over to stand next to him without his even being aware. Now he looked at her profile, fine and beautiful, and found himself thinking how far she must have come from the living woman she had once been.

"Sure, I am," he answered. "Shooting at 'shifters is one thing. Hell, I did that when I was wearing a uniform. But standing around while you bring back a nightmare like Gresh …"

"Do you want to quit?" she asked quietly.

He turned to face her. For a moment, they were a man and a woman standing in the moonlight and Deacon felt an urge to talk her out of all this. If they went far enough away, maybe East and Gresh and their like wouldn't be able to find them. Maybe …

All he said was, "I want to know what I'm a part of. I've never been one for kneeling down and praying to gods I can't see or hear, but I'd like to know how close I am to damned for all time."

"Why? Why must you insist on knowing?" she demanded, moving away from him. "Can't you just do what I ask of you without question?"

"No, Larissa, I can't. I don't mind living ignorant, but I won't die that way."

Larissa said nothing, just looked at him for a very long time.

He could see her weighing options, then realizing she had none if she wanted to retain his services. When she finally spoke, her voice was clear and cold. "There are forces at work beyond your experience, Deacon. This is a war about power, and more, about fear of what would happen if the other side were to win."

"Most wars are," Deacon commented.

"The opponents have been known by many names. I suppose the clearest, if least accurate, labels for them would be 'Chaos' and 'Order.' Their struggle dates back to the beginning of existence and it's been fought on many worlds, on many planes, in time as well as space. The last time they warred here was nine hundred years ago — the soldiers who built this city were fleeing from that conflict."

"Who's winning?" Deacon asked, already guessing the answer.

"There's never been a victor. Oh, skirmishes go to one side or the other at times, but the forces are too evenly matched for one to ever vanquish the other completely. The battle shifts from one theatre to another, seemingly at random, and some of us spend our lives waiting to be called to service again."

"Doesn't sound like much of a life," he said, walking back to the living area and taking a chair. "So you wait for someone to tell you the war's come back here, then you go around and wake up the troops. Have I got it right?"

"Essentially," she answered, nodding. "This is the first time the *tral* have needed to be awakened on this planet — as I said, the fight has been elsewhere for most of the last millennium."

"Why here? What, did someone pick our name out of a hat? Some diviner's rod point toward our planet and the generals decide we were overdue for a slaughter?"

"No, there was a reason why the conflict began again here, and why it began with the cults. Yes, of course they're a part of this — they worship the servants of Chaos and Order and act as scouts, spies and conjurers' fodder. And they were the first to realize that something new — a third faction — had been added to the mixture. Something no one expected, but which could mean final victory for my side … or the enemy."

Deacon regarded her carefully, not yet sure just how much of all this he believed. Abstract concepts going to war seemed a strange excuse for cult members knifing each other in alleyways. But he would play along and see where it all led. "So what's this new factor? Or is that a military secret?"

"Hey! What are you talking to him for?"

It was Gresh, teeth and jawbone stained with blood, spikes abruptly returning to his hands and arms. His words were addressed to Larissa, who did not look at all intimidated by him.

"That's none of your concern, Gresh," she said flatly. "I felt he deserved to know."

"Oh, you did, huh?" the creature said, moving toward Deacon. "How do you know he's not working for the other side? Maybe that's how they knew you were coming to see me. Why don't you take off for a while and let me explain a few things to him?"

Deacon looked up at him, doing his best to seem unimpressed. "If you're not careful, Gresh, somebody's dog is going to bury you in their backyard one of these days."

"You won't need no dumb animal to bury you, friend," Gresh snarled in response. "I'll do it myself."

"Gresh has a point, Deacon," Larissa conceded. "I may have said too much. The more you know, the more of a target you become."

"And a bullseye would clash with my suit, is that what you're saying?" Deacon said angrily, rising. "Fine. You and your new friend here can toss bat wings into a steaming cauldron, or whatever it is you types do in your spare time. I'm going out. When you need me, try and find me."

Without waiting for a reply, Deacon slammed out of the penthouse and headed for the street. He didn't have any particular destination in mind — but a lover's quarrel with a bottle sounded like the best idea he had had in a long time.

❧

Larissa stood staring out at the night for some minutes, in

 64

silence. Gresh knew enough not to join her at the window, where he might be seen, but saw no reason to refrain from voicing his opinion.

"Let him go," he said in between swigs of ale. "We don't need him. He's not one of us."

"Until a few hours ago, neither were you," Larissa replied. "How long ago was your true nature buried, Gresh? Do you even remember?"

Gresh paused in thought before shaking his head. "I remember tearing my way through a mob of demons with wings. After that ..."

"You were wounded in that battle, or so I've been told," Larissa said, watching her new ally for any sign of memory returning. "The healers were working on you when the war shifted somewhere else. The decision was made to preserve you, in case the fight returned here."

"So they made me Human," Gresh spat, as if the very word disgusted him.

"To all outward appearances, yes," she agreed. "For almost a millennium, you've been living, dying and being reborn. You've enjoyed countless Human lifetimes, without being aware of what had gone before or what was to come. And if I hadn't found you, you might have spent another thousand years that way."

"So what do you want? You want me to say 'thank you?' You didn't bring me back out of the goodness of your heart, you did what you were told. I know what your kind thinks of mine, lady, and I'm giving you fair warning: when the fighting starts, don't get in my way."

Larissa's eyes flashed fire. She was on Gresh with impossible swiftness, lifting him into the air with one hand and baring her fangs. "Are you threatening me, Gresh? Is that what you're doing?"

Gresh growled a vile curse. With a dark laugh, she hurled him the length of the room and watched him slam into the wall. A fissure opened where he had struck. He slumped to the floor and was a few moments regaining his senses.

"I am in charge here," Larissa said, ice in her voice. "You will

65

fight when and where I tell you to. You will run as quickly and as far as I tell you to. Or maybe you would prefer an introduction to East? He's been looking run-down lately."

Gresh withdrew the spikes that had sprouted all over his skeletal armor. "You're stronger than I expected," he muttered. That was all the apology Larissa could hope for.

"I'm stronger than a lot of people expect," she replied coolly. "Get up. Do you remember how to conceal?"

Gresh nodded and began to concentrate on the Human form he had worn for the past thirty years. In a few moments, his new body — blood-red tissue encased in a massive skeleton — was gone, replaced by that of Gresh, the smith. It was only an illusion, and would not last long, but Larissa hoped it would be long enough for what she needed done.

"Follow Deacon. See where he goes, who he meets with. Make sure he hasn't been tagged."

"What are you so worried about him for? Afraid you might miss a meal?"

Larissa ignored his jibe. "I brought him into this, Gresh, and I can see he doesn't understand. He thinks he'll be able to go back to his old life when the job is done. He may not know the danger he's in."

Gresh started for the door, then stopped and turned. "Is that the only reason?"

Larissa cast her eyes down to the floor. "No. I'm wondering how the other side knew where we were tonight. I need to know —"

Gresh gave her a vicious smile. "If he's gone over, I'll save a little of his blood for you."

❧

Deacon regretted his choice of bars almost as soon as he walked in. It was a sentinel place — the room was crawling with uniforms and off-duty patrollers, and it made him feel like he'd taken a step into the past. Still, the booze was better than average, and he hadn't crossed any sentinels lately. He took a seat at the bar, ordered an ale, and tried to figure out just when he had lost

66

control of this case.

He finally decided he had never had any to lose. From the minute he'd looked into Larissa's eyes in that alleyway, his common sense had taken a walk. What was he thinking? That somehow he could make her something other than what she was — a dead looker who drank blood to stay up and walking. When she had no further use for him, he would be just another potential snack.

It wasn't as if he was new to dealing with Unnaturals. In his time, he had encountered a few 'shifters, two or three vampires, and something he thought sure had been a lich. There were relatively few of the things in Galitia, and those that were around kept a low profile, for obvious reasons. But despite sentinel efforts to keep it covered up, everyone with any street sense knew that, now and again, there were deaths that couldn't be explained away.

Unnaturals had been a fact of life for centuries, just like glow stones, insane prices for a simple conjuration, and women who wouldn't be satisfied with anything less than a fur wrap from Dela. Most people feared and hated them, but few had ever actually met one (or would know, if they had). The chances of being attacked by a *fexast* or a *varr* were probably less than that of getting struck by lightning — twice.

At least, that's the way it always had been. There were stories that, during the war, non-Humans were everywhere, whole armies of them. That certainly jibed with Larissa's story — though he still had a hard time accepting that all these things were coming out the shadows to fight a war they couldn't win.

Of course, it was possible that Larissa had been "educated" by one of the blood cults — maybe the whole yarn came out of a high priest's fevered imagination. Judging from the talk around the bar, cult violence was still escalating. For a moment, Deacon thought back to his youth, when the existence of cults made for a great argument with an unwilling girl ("You know, I hear there were a few girls kidnapped across town last week. They say the cults are planning more sacrifices. Guess it's safer nowadays not to be a virgin").

He was startled out of his happy memory by a beefy hand landing on his shoulder. This was followed by Banff's gravelly voice saying to the bartender, "Anything but what my friend here is having. He's got less taste in wine than he does in women."

The sentinel took the chair beside Deacon. He looked worn down and about ten years older. For an instant, Deacon wondered if his old boss had taken a drink from the wrong fountain.

"Where's your lady friend, Deacon?" Banff asked. "She letting you go out to drink all by yourself these days? Or did she just have other business?"

Deacon looked up from his ale. "No, the human sacrifice ran overtime," he answered. "She pulled skull-washing duty."

Neither man laughed at the joke. The bartender handed Banff a mug full of dark golden liquid. From the sweet scent, Deacon knew it was no ale — probably something the innkeeper whipped up in the back with one of those "do-it-yourself" grimoires.

"Gods and devils, Deacon, you are a wonder," Banff said, shaking his head. His manner was light, but his brown eyes held no mirth in them. "Here I sit down to tell you a story about a sacrifice, and you guess that it has to do with your Miss Larissa Martel. It's no wonder you've made it to the middle of your profession."

"Peddle it to a newscribe with parchment to fill, I'm not interested." Deacon started to rise, but Banff's hand on his arm restrained him.

"I think you'd best be sitting down for this one," the sentinel said, in a tone not far from his command voice. For the first time, Deacon noticed that the man's normally florid face was pale. "And if you're thinking of walking away, well, I'm not the most popular man on the force, but I'd guess a lot more people in here like me than you."

Deacon sat down.

"We've got bodies stacked like so much cordwood in the morgue, Deacon. Dr. Bligh wanted to hire some help for the cutting and cataloging, but I reminded him that the last time he did that, three or four necromancers slipped in as ringers. Next thing we knew, there were murder victims wandering the halls and frightening the wits out of the cleaning people."

"More cult killings?" Deacon asked, signalling for another glass.

"People who belong to cults. People who got in the way of cults. People who got in between cults. A few whose closest connection to this business is that they know how to spell 'cult.'"

"Any more details on the weapons used?"

"Oh, I've got piles of evidence, Deacon. I can tell you what the murderers used, where they stood, where they went when they were done and what the sons of swine had for breakfast that morning. What I still don't know is why."

"And you still think Larissa's involved?" Deacon asked.

"Now that's where things grow interesting," Banff said, one elbow resting on the smooth oak bar. "I did some checking on the lady. Found everything in order — where she was born, where she apprenticed, facts, figures, numbers, dates, even her mother's midwife's middle name. Nice and neat and tied with a ribbon."

Deacon sighed. "Let me guess — you hate 'nice and neat and tied with a ribbon.'"

"Like I hate my ex-wife's pet *haftun*," Banff agreed. "Like I hate bookstores that serve pastries and tea. Like I hate half-witted independents who think they have a higher responsibility to a client's cash than to the safety of their city."

"If you're so convinced she's behind all this, why don't you bring her in?" Deacon said angrily. "Flog her, tie her to the rack, use the thumbscrews, make her listen to some dried-up old crone explain how sorcery works for three hours. And when you're through, she can lay a curse that will make you wish you only had plague."

"We tried to find her," Banff said, trying to keep his temper in check and his voice reasonably low. "But she's not to be found. Neighbors at her listed residence haven't caught sight of her for weeks; her employer is beside himself; and the only time she seems to make an appearance these days is when there's been

Greg Farshtey

another killing. In fact, my men have seen her on opposite sides of the city within a few minutes of each other."

Deacon saw where this was going and didn't like it at all.

"Which leads me to my next question, Jack," Banff continued. "Just what manner of beastie have you been sparking with these past few nights?"

A hundred possible answers flashed through Deacon's mind in a split second, any one of which would keep the sentinels off Larissa's trail, at least temporarily, but would be certain to land him in a cell. The debate over whether to simply tell the truth he postponed indefinitely.

The sound of window glass shattering saved him the trouble of choosing the right lie. Someone had tossed a rock into the bar … no, not just a rock, Deacon realized. It was giving off a bright, white light and was about to —

"Get down!" Deacon shouted, tackling Banff and driving him away from the "conjurers' stone" as it exploded into flames. Panic set in immediately as sentinels, guardians of law and most especially order, fought among themselves to reach the exits. Deacon somehow managed to avoid getting trampled and rose, helping Banff to his feet. Acrid black smoke had already filled the room. Off in a corner, Deacon could see the bartender struggling to remember his elemental water magic (not that it would do any good against sorcerer's pitch).

"Get out of here!" Deacon shouted at Banff. "I'll get the bartender out!"

Either Banff had chosen to be reasonable or already had a lung full of smoke, because his only response was to turn and make for the door. Once outside, though, he began to bellow at his fellow officers to act like sentinels instead of dungbeetles in a thunderstorm.

The heat was growing intense and the smoke was making it impossible to see more than a few inches ahead. Deacon banged into more than a few tables and chairs on his way to the far corner of the room where the bartender still stood, making ineffectual motions with his hands.

"Save it for a drought," Deacon barked, lifting a chair and hurling it through the nearest window. The blast of night air made the fire leap higher. The sight seemed to rouse the bartender, who promptly scrambled through the new exit, followed hard by Deacon.

Outside, the fire brigade had arrived and were putting their mages to work calming the flames. A few of the bar's patrons were still milling about, but most had wandered off. Banff was nowhere to be seen. As for the bartender, his face wore the look of a man who was watching most of his life vanish.

Deacon saw a knot of people further down the street, little better than a mob, who had a man pinned against a building. One or two off-duty sentinels were watching the action with interest. Deacon started off that way when a small voice stopped him.

"Mr. Deacon, don't go down there," the voice said. "Come with me instead."

Deacon turned. In the mouth of a darkened alley stood a four year old boy, face and hands streaked with soot. He was wearing a simple outfit of dark grey and one shoe was untied. His hair was copper-colored and curly and he had the cherubic face of an angel. But there was something about the eyes that seemed uncomfortably familiar ...

And then Deacon remembered where he'd seen them before.

The little boy smiled sweetly. "Come along, Mr. Deacon. You wanted to play in the netherworld, you have to follow the rules." He turned and toddled into the alley, Deacon following close behind.

When they were well away from the street, the little boy sat down on the pavement. "How did you like my little di ..." The child's mouth seemed to have trouble getting around the word for a moment. "Diversion?" he finally managed.

"Who are you?" Deacon asked, not wanting to believe his own instincts.

"You know very well who I am," the little boy said, as if scolding the detective. "As for why I am what I am, let's just say I'm young at heart."

"What are you doing here?" Deacon said, trying to sound less disturbed than he truly was.

"Looking for you, naturally," the child said, tracing shapes in the dust of the alleyway. "When I found you, that unpleasant little man was asking you all sorts of questions. I decided to save you the embarrassment of what would almost certainly have been a very poor lie. But I suppose I got a little carried away. Still, at least no one was killed."

"Looking for me? Why?"

The little boy reached into his pants pocket and pulled out a crumpled, dirty piece of paper. "To give you this. Take it and run along. No, no, don't read it now, the sentinels will be along any minute."

Deacon shoved the paper into his coat. "What about you?"

"I'll be fine," the little boy answered. "I want to sit and watch the flames a while longer. Maybe I'll be a firemage when I grow up, hmmmm?"

Deacon backed away a few steps, watching the child tossing a pebble in the air and catching it in one pudgy, dimpled fist. Then he turned and headed for the street, forcing himself not to run.

❦

Sentinel Stenten Gill was voicing his doubts about the circumstances of Banff's birth when he turned into the alleyway and saw the little boy. No older than his sister's little girl, the child was sitting on the pavement and crying pitifully.

Gill put on his best "the sentinel is your friend" face and knelt beside the little boy. "Shhh. It's all right," he said, reaching out to wipe fat tears from the child's cheek. "What's the matter?"

"I can't find my Daddy!" the boy cried. "He told me to wait here while he went to have a drink, and then there was a crash and a fire, and now I don't know where he is!"

Then the child was wracked with sobs again. Gill patted the child on the head and waited for him to cry it out. Then he smiled and said, "Well, you know, I'll bet I can help you find your Daddy. I'm a sentinel, you know, and helping people is what we do best. Why don't you tell me your name?"

For the first time, the little boy's eyes stopped spurting salty tears and he actually managed a sweet smile. He reached a tiny hand toward Gill.

"My name is East," he said happily.

The boy's fingers brushed ever so gently against the side of Gill's face. The sentinel had the unique experience of feeling his blood vessels explode, one after another, the sweet terror of knowing Death was approaching, the bitter realization that he had made the one mistake each living thing is allowed. Then he fell dead to the pavement.

"And you've already been a great help," East said, skipping past the corpse and on to the street.

Chapter
Eight

Deacon walked for eight blocks before pausing to look at the message the child — East, somehow, he was frighteningly certain — had given him. It was no more than a name and address: "Cardiff Black, 1816 Rendout Road." The name wasn't familiar, but the street was in the crafts district, not all that far from Gresh's splintered smithy.

Thirty seconds after he had left the scene of the fire, he had sensed a shadow. By stopping to stare in shop windows and the like, he had been able to confirm that Gresh, back in Human form, was making a clumsy effort to tail him. The awkward way the man moved fueled a suspicion in Deacon's mind, one he needed only another block or two to confirm: the Human body was just a mask. Gresh's footfalls were still those of the … thing he had become.

Deacon frowned. He hadn't decided yet whether to deliver East's message to Larissa or Banff, and the last thing he needed was her pet monster coming along to bloody the waters.

The detective slowed. His pursuer didn't. Deacon waited until Gresh was just the right distance behind, then ducked into a doorway in a quiet sidestreet. The former smith lumbered by a moment later, and Deacon stepped out, gun drawn. He was careful not to get too close to the illusory Human form, wanting to stay out of the creature's far greater reach.

"Nice day for a walk, isn't it?" Deacon said quietly. "I won't ask you to keep your real hands where I can see them, since I can't see them. I'll just point out that I remembered the good bullets today, and leave it at that."

"How'd you pick me up?" Gresh growled.

"When I heard a herd of *sabvas* coming up behind me, I knew it had to be you," Deacon answered. The Human Gresh's lips were moving, but his voice was coming from considerably higher. "Whoever taught you that spell robbed you blind, Gresh. You couldn't fool a dead man."

"Nice choice of words," Gresh chuckled, turning and taking two quick steps toward Deacon.

"I warned you," the detective muttered, firing at his target's leg. The bullet flew a few feet and exploded with a bright flash that illuminated the creature's true form. Bright golden bands of energy coiled themselves around Gresh's legs and constricted, bringing him crashing to the ground.

"Those won't last long, but they're effective," Deacon commented. "And you don't want to see what they'd do if I aimed higher up. So we'll start with why you're following me."

Gresh writhed on the ground, unable to free himself from the bonds of sorcerous energy. His only answer was a curse.

"One of these days, I'm going to wash your mouth out with lye," Deacon said, a hard smile on his face. "Right now, I don't have time. If you'd like, I can fire a few more times and leave you trussed up on the sentinels' doorstep. They might not be sure what to do with you, but I'm sure they could take a guess. A drop in the river, maybe — you'd make a hell of an anchor."

"All right, already," Gresh grumbled. "Larissa wanted you followed. She wanted to make sure you hadn't gone over to the other side."

"How could I? I don't even know which side I'm on now."

"Listen, Deacon, let's make a deal," Gresh said, twisting himself around to look up at his captor. "With your brains and my brawn, we could be running Galitia by the end of the week."

Deacon shook his head. "Sorry, Gresh. My landlord doesn't

allow pets, and besides, it would cost too much to feed you. And what about this war of yours?"

Gresh shrugged. "I like a fight. It's what I'm best at. But last time I went down, it was nine centuries before I was myself again. I'll go along until I find a better deal, then the big boys can find themselves another neck-breaker."

"Sounds reasonable," Deacon agreed, wondering how many more of Larissa's "allies" were lukewarm to the idea of resuming the war. "I've got places to go, Gresh, and I don't need a shadow. When those bands wear off, make like a witch wind and blow."

"This isn't over, Deacon, not by a long spell," Gresh said menacingly. "And what the hell am I supposed to tell the wolf bitch?"

"If you mean Larissa, I'll handle her," Deacon said, turning away. "I'll tell her somebody tried to use you to flavor their soup. She'll understand."

Deacon walked off, Gresh hurling obscenities at his back. The detective felt better than he had in days. As the sun rose over the city, he headed for his apartment and a few hours' sleep.

And now he knew what to do about East's message.

❧

Cardiff Black tugged on the reins and bade his horse turn into one of the narrow, cobblestoned streets that led to his shop. The wagon in which the tall, thin man rode bounced as it rode over ruts in the avenue, jostling its cargo.

Black smiled as sweetly as he could manage and nodded at the passersby. He had never been a man who made friends easily — perhaps because he had never cared sufficiently to pursue anyone else's company — but he recognized the importance of maintaining good relations with his neighbors. It wouldn't do to have any nasty whispers circulating about him. No, that wouldn't do at all.

Oh, there were some who wondered about him, he was sure. More than once, one of his customers had asked why a man who made (apparently) a decent living repairing automobiles should persist in driving a horse and wagon through Galitia. Surely, they would say, you must have some desire to drive one of the cars you spend your days fixing.

"No, no," he would say, shaking his head and laughing. "Where I go, I have no need of a car." *And neither does anyone else,* he would add silently.

Still, there was no need to worry so, particularly not tonight. It had been an exceptionally good evening. He had found just what he was looking for not once, but twice, and acquired them without a hitch. For tonight, they would be safe in the back of the wagon. The delivery — and the payment — would wait for tomorrow eve.

He took a deep breath and enjoyed the scent of fresh flowers. He could dimly remember, as a youth, loving the smell of roses. How fortunate he had been to find a second career that allowed him to be around flowers so often. *And to be paid so well for the privilege*, he thought happily.

Black turned his mind to more practical matters. His pale grey mare would need to be fed once back home, as would Tobias. This last was particularly important — last month, the little brute had gotten into one of his deliveries and cost him at least a few coins, when all was said and done.

Wending his way down the darkened alleyways that led to his home/place of business, he passed a young streetsinger making a mournful tune. Something about a bloody business to the north, having to do with cults. Black wrinkled his nose at the lyrics — he hated that sort of violent behavior, hated it with a passion. More than once he had wondered about the intelligence — or lack of it — among men who felt compelled to carve up their fellows. If death was what one wanted to achieve, there must surely be quicker, cleaner ways than that to achieve it.

The streetsinger — Ellen, that was her name — smiled charmingly at him. He reined the wagon to a stop and tipped his cap. "Good evening, dear. And how are you?"

"Chilled to the bone, I'm afraid, Mr. Black," the girl answered, wrapping her jacket tightly around herself. "I worry what the night air will do to my voice."

"Ah, your sweet tones would drive away any demon who tried to silence you," Black answered, all charm and good humor. He reached into his jacket pocket and produced a handful of coins. "Here now, girl. Buy yourself some hot coffee, or an ale, if you like. Hardier folk than you have caught their death on a night like this."

The girl accepted the coins eagerly and tucked them away in her coat. "I wish there were more men like you," she said warmly.

Black's smile grew wider. "But if there were, you would have less cause to appreciate me. And I, less time in the light of your smile. Good evening to you now."

Ellen watched her benefactor drive off, enjoying the sweet smell of flowers that seemed to follow him everywhere.

Black was surprised to find a man waiting for him outside of his garage. A formidable looking fellow, the mechanic noted, and from the look on his face, one here on business. Black made an obsequious gesture as he slipped down from his wagon, sliding his oaken cane out from under the seat with the most casual of gestures.

"Good evening, sir," he said. "May I be of some service?"

"Maybe," Deacon answered.

"You have a vehicle that needs repair, perhaps?" Black asked politely. "It is quite late, but if you'll show me where it is —"

"Nothing like that. But I do have business to discuss with you — providing you're Cardiff Black."

"That I am," Black affirmed. His face retained its benevolent expression, but there was wariness in his eyes now. "You have the advantage of me, I'm afraid."

"Can we talk inside?" Deacon asked, aware that he might have had a shadow he hadn't spotted. He half expected Black to refuse, but the man simply nodded.

"If you like. Allow me to stable my horse and we can sit down and talk like gentlemen."

Deacon waited impatiently while Black saw to the feeding of

his animal. The rear of the wagon was filled with lilacs and other flowers, tossed haphazardly on top of a burlap tarp. More flowers stuck out from beneath the cover, but there was no telling what else might be under there.

"Moonlighting as a florist?" Deacon asked, gesturing toward the cut plants.

Black chuckled. "In a small way of business, sir. I have always loved growing things — and the paradox that men kill them for use as grave decoration. That way, every death takes some beauty from the world, even if the deceased had none of his own."

The man — probably not more than middle-aged, now that Deacon had a closer look at him — went back to feeding his horse, who he referred to as "Brother." His clothes were rumpled and worn, the knees of his trousers particularly, and these were stained with what looked like earth.

When Black was done, he led Deacon into a small, poorly furnished sitting room. The fireplace was filled with cold ashes and the lone glow stone was dim. Black gestured his guest toward the least worn of the chairs.

"I have little to offer a guest," the mechanic said with a shrug and a smile. "But then, as someone once said, distance is the only thing a rich man will allow a poor one to call his own, provided he keeps it."

Deacon wasted no time. He reached into his jacket pocket for his wallet. "I'm here to do you a favor, Mr. Black," he announced. "Maybe the biggest favor anyone's ever done for you."

Black's smile never wavered, but the suspicion in his eyes had hardened and begun to creep into his voice. "And just what might that be?"

Deacon opened the wallet and took out a few bills, offering them to his host. "There's a few hundred here. Take it and get out of the city. Go anywhere, just leave, and do it tonight."

Black looked at the money as if it carried some dread disease. "Leave Galitia? Surely you realize what you're asking, sir? Why, it would be worth my life to dare the Wilderness, and that's a fact. I've heard many a tale of the dark things that wait to claim a man beyond the walls, and I'll not risk their wrath."

"There are some pretty dark things inside the walls, too, pal," Deacon said.

"But my home, my business — what would become of me? And why ever should I wish to leave? I'm quite happy here. Oh, my surroundings may be modest, but I have Brother and Tobias and want for little else. Where would I go?"

"I've got friends on the docks. There's a trader sloop leaving for Dela in a few hours. Pack your things and be on it. I know how this sounds, Mr. Black, but I have reason to believe your life is in danger if you stay."

Black shook his head in disbelief. "From whom, man? I haven't an enemy in the living, breathing world! I repair autos in the day and gather blossoms at night. Who would want to threaten me?"

Deacon stood up and glanced out the cracked window. "I haven't the time to explain. You'll have to take my word for it, you'll be much better off somewhere else."

Black's voice grew low and its tone one of dismay. "Are you a sentinel, then?"

Deacon turned, surprised to see, not fear, but something almost akin to menace in his host's features. *Maybe he's got a sweet deal going here and doesn't want to transplant it,* the detective thought.

"No, I'm not. Just somebody concerned for your welfare." Deacon put the money down on the scarred, wooden table. "Take it. Use it to skip town. There are people a whole lot worse than any sentinel who are going to try and make you stay."

Black rose and began to gently guide Deacon out of the room. "I'll take your money, if it will ease your mind, friend. But I think you are worrying over nothing. I've never harmed a living soul and I'm of no importance to anyone. That's the great advantage to being a poor man — you're overlooked by all, including those who would do you harm."

The two men stepped into the stable, which connected Black's home to his garage and the street. Deacon felt Black stiffen and then saw what had provoked the reaction: a large, smoky blue cat was rooting through the flowers in the wagon.

"Tobias! Get away from there!" Black roared, charging forward with his cane held high. The cat turned to look at its master, hackles rising.

Deacon reached the wagon just as Black did and wished he hadn't. Tobias had torn part of the covering away and commenced to chew on Black's cargo: a Human body, still marked with the soil in which it had been buried. The shape beside it, still concealed by the tarp, could only be another corpse.

Black snarled and brought his cane down toward Deacon, but the detective wheeled and caught the stick with his right hand. Gone was the modest, unassuming businessman — in his place was a man filled with murderous rage who forced Deacon back into the wagon.

It was taking all of Deacon's strength to keep the cane from landing on his skull. Black grabbed the detective's throat with his free hand and began to squeeze, Deacon trying desperately to wrench it free. But bent back over the wagon and with no leverage, he was getting nowhere. His muscles were starting to turn to water before Black's onslaught, and in a few seconds, the grave robber was going to have three bodies to sell.

Suddenly, Deacon heard a screech and saw a dark shape leap on to Black's shoulder. It was the cat, angry at having his dinner disturbed, clawing at his master's face. Black let go of Deacon's throat long enough to swat the beast away, and the detective took advantage of the break to swing a hard left. The blow connected with Black's mouth, staggering him enough that Deacon was able to reach his feet.

He never got the chance to press his newfound advantage. Black spat blood and smiled as a strong smell of ozone filled Deacon's nostrils. He let go of the cane and tried to dodge, but the lightning bolt that flashed from the end of the stick slammed into his chest and hurled him to the floor, in the embrace of sweet oblivion.

Chapter
Nine

The idea that the area between life and death is marked by a glowing path with a bright light at its end is, of course, no more than a streetsinger's tale told to comfort those who fear the inevitable. In truth, no place where men — or their souls — have trod can be neat and orderly. The region beyond what Humans consider living is littered with the detritus of existences left behind, and populated by the newly dead and those too disturbed to move on.

Deacon wasn't sure which analogy fit the place best, a packed wharf waiting for a ship to arrive or a tank of hungry *arkan* fish. The room in which he found himself was crammed with the bodies — or rather, spirits — of thousands of people. Most bore wounds of one kind or another, all of them mortal, and the floor was sticky with dried blood. The vast majority were in shock and babbling incoherently. The minds of those abruptly slain, perhaps only seconds before, mingled with those of the insane, who had haunted this region for centuries.

None of which inspired Deacon to want to stay. He turned to the woman standing next to him, who was smiling sweetly despite the fact that her body had been torn open and both hands were occupied with keeping her organs internal.

"Where are we, Cassandra?" It was only after he spoke her name that he wondered how he had come to know it.

 82

"I don't know," she answered. "The last thing I remember was the knife, and even that, not very clearly. I suppose I'll forget it in time. What brought you in?"

Deacon glanced down at the burns on his chest. "A florist with an attitude," he answered. "Are we just supposed to stand around here? Isn't there a line we should be on or something?"

A man standing nearby, blood still oozing from a bullet hole in his temple, began to laugh for no discernible reason. It was a high-pitched, grating sound, and it seemed to inspire some of the others to laugh as well. The cacophony rose to deafening heights before stopping abruptly, when everyone noticed that the man who had begun the hilarity was gone.

"A suicide," Cassandra muttered. "He's gone to torment."

"Where?"

"They'll clean him up and send him back. The best punishment for someone who wants to die is to make him live again. You'd be surprised how many people you meet on the street are reincarnated suicides."

"So we stand here until someone gets around to disposing of us?" Deacon asked, beginning to feel claustrophobic in the close quarters.

Cassandra didn't answer right away, being busy tucking a pesky intestine back in. Then she said, "You can sit if you'd like, Deacon, if you don't mind being bled on."

"This isn't quite what I expected," Deacon commented, looking around at the otherworldly charnel house he had happened upon. The only things missing were flies — *dead insects must go somewhere else,* he mused.

"It never empties out long enough for them to clean it," Cassandra replied. She planted an elbow in the side of a heart attack victim with wandering hands and he moved off in search of less aware prey. "It's been particularly bad lately, what with the cults. That's what happened to me."

Deacon didn't ask her what had happened, but she started telling him anyway. There was not much else to talk about here. "My boyfriend told me he had influential friends who could land me a job as a tavern singer in Dela, or Cham, or maybe even Selastos. He took me to meet them. Turned out all they wanted was a woman to take turns with, while he stood there, grinning like an animal."

A small tear ran down her cheek and mingled with the blood still trickling from her mouth. "When they were done, they … sacrificed me. Oh, they made a big show about showing obeisance to some entity or other, but it was really that they were afraid I'd talk."

"What was your boyfriend's name?" Deacon asked.

"Simms. Morgan Simms. He's a bank manager in Galitia."

Deacon was about to ask her something else when she began to fade. There was no time for a goodbye. He hoped she was going someplace better than this, or at least, less crowded.

"Deacon!"

He ignored the shout. He was tired of people shouting at him. He tried to strike up a conversation with the man next to him, but the fellow had had his jaw broken and his words were unintelligible. A trio of babbling lunatics were in a corner tormenting a alchemist who'd been blinded — and killed — while trying to mix one element too many. Deacon shouldered his way through the crowd, with great difficulty, and frightened them off.

"When I felt the life leaving me, I thought, 'Well, at least I'll be able to see again,'" the alchemist said, bitterly. "But, no. The secret every philosopher has sought since the beginning of time, and I can't see any of it."

"You're better off," Deacon said, trying not to look at the blackened pits where the man's eyes had once been. "This place is a nightmare."

"Death isn't neat," the alchemist muttered. "But somehow I always thought I'd die in bed."

"So did I," Deacon agreed, though not meaning it in quite the same way. "Cassandra said something about forgetting. Is that what happens?"

"I suppose. After all, it wouldn't do to have souls settling old quarrels all over the place. One of the things that makes people fear death is the thought of seeing all those relatives they were well rid of again. As it turns out, your Aunt Dottie won't know you from any other dead man."

"But I still remember everything," Deacon said, more to himself than to the alchemist. "Does that mean I'm not supposed to be here?"

"No. It means you're a stubborn bastard," the blind man answered. "Let go. What did life get you but death? Find yourself a corner and make yourself comfortable, like everyone else does."

"Deacon!"

There it was again. Fainter, this time. Good. Maybe it would go away completely. He had enough problems without having to deal with someone else who wanted something from him.

The crowd nearby parted for just a second, long enough for Deacon to make out a doorway. *Anyplace is better than this,* he reasoned, making for it. He barely avoided stumbling over a lamplighter who'd been run over in the street, and evidently had decided to go through the afterlife on his face.

The door was painted white and had no sign on it. The knob was cool to the touch, which comforted Deacon somewhat — since, according to legend, there was at least *one* place worse than this.

He opened the door and slipped inside. The room was warm and pitch dark. He reached out and found the wall, using the feel of its rough surface to guide him. The opposite wall was within arm's reach as well, leading him to believe he was in a hallway.

The wall to his right vanished and one appeared in front of him. The corridor had curved and he went with it, now drawn forward by a spotlight in a room beyond. There was no visible source of the light, it simply was.

As he drew nearer, he saw that it shone on the figure of a nude young woman, who lay on the floor in a fetal position. Deacon said a few words of greeting, but she didn't answer.

"Deacon!"

He moved forward and crouched beside her, brushing dark

locks away from her face. He recognized the features instantly — it was Larissa, eyes wide open, but unseeing. Her flesh was healthy and pink, but cold to the touch.

Deacon ran a hand across her cheek, his mind filled with questions. Had someone slain her? East, maybe, or Gresh? And if this truly was her, as it appeared to be, why was she like this? How come she wasn't up and walking around like everyone else?

"What did you think, she couldn't die like the rest of us?"

The voice came from off to the right. A man walked out of the darkness and stood beside Deacon. In the harsh light, the wounds on his throat were apparent.

"Who the hell are you? What is this place?" Deacon asked, rising.

The man snapped his fingers and a second spotlight appeared, this one focused on a chair a few feet away. Without a word, he walked away and sat down, his eyes on Larissa.

"I asked a question," Deacon said, angrily.

"You asked two," the man corrected. "My name is Sandel Hogue. I was her last victim. Nice to meet you."

"What happened to her?" Deacon said, gesturing toward the beautiful woman at his feet.

"She's been like that for years," Hogue answered. "Some part of her had to die when she became a vampire, after all. That part came here, but it can't go anywhere till the rest of her joins it. Kind of a rule."

Both men turned their attention back to the silent woman. "Looks pretty pitiful, doesn't she?" Hogue asked.

"What are you, a guard?"

"Who'd want to steal her?" Hogue answered. "No, just another rule. Last victim gets to spend a few days in here before going back. Then I forget all about it. Someone out here has a sadistic sense of humor, if you ask me."

"Deacon!"

"Are you going to end up … like that?" Deacon asked.

"I guess," Hogue answered, without evident emotion. "I guess there are a lot of these rooms. I wonder where my body is now?

I wonder if someone had it buried. Do you know where yours is?"

"Eaten by a cat, most likely," Deacon said. He bent down and touched a finger to Larissa's lips. Was this her humanity, then, her compassion, set aside until it was needed again? Had she ever noticed it was gone?

"Why don't you get going?" Deacon said. "Go on, beat it. I'll watch her for a while. Maybe they're serving drinks outside."

"What if someone comes looking for me?" Hogue asked, nervously. "I don't know what will happen if I'm not where I'm supposed to be."

"Neither do I," Deacon answered, spitting the words like daggers. "Why don't we find out together?"

Hogue thought better of arguing with the shade in front of him and simply vanished. Deacon made a note of the trick, determined to learn it while he was here.

Alone now with the still form of Larissa, he felt a profound sense of loss. He had never know her while she was alive, but somehow he found himself missing the Human woman. When she finally died, would this fragment of her past get dragged along to whatever hell her soul would be bound for?

"Deacon!"

The voice wasn't much than a whisper now, but it was recognizable. Or maybe he had known it was Larissa calling from the beginning, and didn't want to acknowledge it.

"Damn it, what do you want of me?" he growled at the ether. "Why should I go back, just so you can kill me? Why should I risk spending eternity like this?"

"It's not eternity," someone said from behind. The voice was young and old at the same time, but the speaker was unmistakable.

"East!" Deacon shouted, charging into the darkness. There was nothing there but another wall. He turned to see his quarry standing near Larissa, going from child to youth to old man and back again at a rapid pace.

"You seem surprised to see me here," East chuckled. "You shouldn't be. Some of my best friends are dead ... with a little

87

help from me, of course."

"And you?" Deacon asked, riveted by the horrific sight of East aging, decaying and being reborn.

"I have a visitors' pass," he answered. "Now, as I was saying, this miserable state is not for eternity. Eventually, Larissa will meet her final death, the one she won't saunter away from. Sooner, rather than later, if you choose to remain here."

"An old man with a lightning bolt took me out," Deacon shot back. "I'm out of my league here. How am I supposed to protect her?"

"It was evident to me from the start that your usefulness is limited," East answered, smugly. "But you operate with few of the prejudices that shackle Miss Martel."

"Meaning?"

"Meaning that she is too blind to see that she has a great deal more to worry about than the servants of Chaotic deities. There are forces at work here that are far too subtle for her to comprehend, and there are events she is as yet unaware of. In the end, the true threat may come from behind her, not before her."

"You're talking in riddles again," Deacon muttered.

"Well, this is the place for it. Your choice is a simple one: go back and act on the knowledge I've given you — oh, yes, you'll remember all of this, that's part of the fun. Or wait here and moon over this Human vegetable until her Undead counterpart comes to join you. Maybe they'll even give you two adjoining pillars of fire. Won't that be nice?"

"Deacon!"

East smiled. "Well, Deacon, are you going to answer her or not?"

❦

The first thing he was aware of was the searing pain in his chest. Someone was applying salve to his burns and it hurt like hell. His throat was parched and sore but he managed a grunt just before his eyes opened.

Larissa was standing over him, looking haggard. She didn't

seem happy to see him back among the living.

"You fool!" she shouted. "You could have been killed!"

"Then I would have fit right in with the rest of you," Deacon rasped. Looking past her, he could see Gresh and Black in conversation, Narses off to one side. The grave robber didn't seem any different — had East's note been a sham? Was he only what he appeared to be, and not one of Larissa's troops?

He glanced around. He was still in the stable, lying on a bed of straw, thankfully not in the wagon. The smell of burnt flesh was in his nostrils.

"How long have I been out?"

"A full day," she answered, going back to cleaning his wounds. "The sun set only a little while ago."

Deacon gestured toward Black. "I was trying to —"

"I know what you were trying to do," she said sharply. "You were trying to warn him off so I couldn't revive him. Fortunately, I have other sources of information besides East. It took me a little longer, but I found him."

Deacon noticed that her collar was open. Yes, his eyes had been telling the truth back in the smithy. The glow he had seen playing over Gresh's face before his transformation had come from her, from the gem embedded beneath the skin of her throat. Its radiance had yet to fade completely.

With an effort, the detective sat up. Black looked at him and smiled, offering an exaggerated tip of a battered hat. Was it imagination, or were the man's teeth a trifle sharper, his color a little off?

"So what is he?" Deacon asked.

"You would call him a ghoul," Larissa answered, putting away her herbs and taking a roll of bandages from a small bag. "They don't look very much different from Humans. Makes it easier for them to pass."

"And the corpses in the wagon?"

"A profitable sideline," Black answered, coming nearer. "One I can only assume I was drawn to through some unconscious knowledge of my true nature. You see, Mr. Deacon, the city's flesh mills cannot always get all the bodies they need through legitimate channels. So if one company gets an extraodinarily large book-binding order or some such, they call on me, and I obtain a healthy specimen for their work. Illegal, regrettably; immoral, perhaps; but a mutually agreeable business arrangement."

Glancing at Deacon's wounds, he added, "My apologies, sir, for my behavior. But I thought surely you must be a sentinel, your offer of money just a blind to win my confidence. And once you saw Tobias at my wares, well, I couldn't let you leave with that information, now, could I?"

"No, of course not," Deacon said, sitting up and reaching for his shirt. Putting it on was painful, but he made a point of not grimacing. Why give Black the satisfaction?

"Your wounds are serious," Larissa said, some of the anger gone from her voice. "You should rest here a while."

"I go to sleep around here, I might never wake up," Deacon growled. "What time did you say it was, sister?"

"A little after dark. Seven o'clock, I think. Why?"

Deacon pulled on his coat, relieved — and surprised — to find his gun still in the pocket. He checked to make sure it was loaded. "I've got someplace to go."

"What are you, crazy?" That was Gresh, all half-ton of bones of him. "You just finished proving we can't trust you. I say we tear him into little pieces right now. Black looks like he could use a meal."

"Try it, boneyard," Deacon snapped. "I've taken down guys who'd use your ribs for toothpicks."

Gresh started forward, but Larissa held up a restraining hand. "There's been enough violence here. We're lucky no one heard your scuffle, Cardiff, or we would have had to leave you to your fate." She looked at Deacon as she added, "We're all expendable, you know."

"And I'm on top of the list, right, kid?" the detective said, a bitter smile on his lips. "I got in the way of the recruitment drive of this private little war you have going on. You know, the one where maniacs in business suits carve up girls 'cause they think they have permission, they think anything goes. Oh, this cult war is beautiful — stiffs turning up in alleys every day, when they're not dragged off by your friends here. And everybody decides that the old rules don't apply anymore, it's panic time."

Deacon drew closer, his expression that of a wolf closing in on prey. "And through it all, there you are, my little angel of death, making sure all the corpses are well and truly dead. Or do you just get off on seeing all the blood, like a kid in a candy store? Is that why you're in the crowd everytime the sentinels find a body?"

Larissa's body was rigid with barely controlled rage. "Whatever you may think, my mission is vital to a war that's older than any Human law. I'll do whatever I have to to succeed … and survive. I told Gresh before, I tell you now: I'm in charge here."

Deacon's smile grew broader and his voice was laced with contempt. "Well, good for you. But you're not in charge of me. Not anymore. I'm quitting."

"We can't let him go," Gresh barked. "He knows too much!"

"It would seem a poor course of action," Black agreed. "And in his current state, he would be easily dealt with."

Deacon regarded them without fear. "Come ahead, then. Make your play. Maybe you're right, when I'm six feet under, all your troubles are over. Or maybe I had a mage friend of mine focus the whole story into a scribe capsule and left it with a friend, to be opened in the event of my death, disappearance … or digestion. Could be that friend's a sentinel, too — wouldn't that throw a *dask* jaw into your precious operation?"

"You're bluffing," Gresh snarled, long, sharp spikes emerging all over his frame.

"Call me," Deacon countered. "I hear they're putting together a special unit to deal with the cults, and anything they might summon up. Maybe they'd like to practice on you."

"Hold still, Gresh," Larissa said, her own anger cooled a bit. "We have no way of knowing whether he's telling the truth or not. But if he wanted to betray us to the sentinels, he could have done so by now. What are your terms, Deacon?"

The detective shook his head. "No terms. No conditions. No deals. I walk out of here, free and clear, and that's the last I want to see of the lot of you. I got a hint of where you're going, and where I'll end up if I hang on with you, and I want no part of it."

Larissa started to answer, then paused, truly looking at Deacon for the first time since his revival. "What did you see when you were gone?" she asked softly.

"You knew once," he answered, turning to go. "Believe me, you don't want to know now."

His back to her, Gresh and Black, he walked out of the stable. No one tried to stop him.

❧

A detective in any big city, Galitia included, makes a lot more enemies than friends. But the people he does stay on good terms with are invariably those who can be of some use in the future. On this particular evening, the conjured image of an ex-bank bandit gave him information he needed to know.

Deacon arrived at the Alchemical Bank's Hermes Ave. branch just as the manager was closing it up for the night. He was a youngish type, handsome in an arrogant sort of way, better dressed than his income should have allowed. He gave Deacon a glance, saw he wasn't a wild-eyed eclectic mage with his brains leaking out his ears, and went back to securing the locks and seals.

Deacon stopped five steps away from him. "Your name Simms?"

The man turned, startled. "Yes. Yes, it is. If you have business to discuss, it will have to wait until morning."

"No business," Deacon said, drawing his gun. "Just pleasure."

Before the bank manager could cry out, he fired once, making a nice, neat hole between the man's eyes and a big, nasty one in the back of his head. The body hit the ground like a stone.

"Cassandra says 'Hi,'" Deacon muttered as he walked away.

Chapter
Ten

Over the next few days, Deacon went back to his regular routine: out of bed by noon, breakfast from an ale mug, sort through the scribe capsules, scanning the letters and tossing the bills. Then roughly an hour of kidding himself that a client was going to walk through the door, followed by a nap at his desk. That brought him to dinner time and the local tavern, where he spent the evening telling lies to the regulars or panting them to a whore.

He took comfort in the familiar, be she blonde or brunette. One night, he found himself with a pale vision with dark hair, whose name he never learned. They thrashed hungrily about on the mattress before getting down to business in earnest, but he found himself distracted by a persistence of memory. He kept seeing Larissa as she had been in the afterlife, catatonic and helpless. The girl tried to recapture his attention by giving his neck a small bite. He shoved her back on to the mattress and stormed out.

For the first week after he'd quit, Deacon had two shadows. The first, and most obvious, was Gresh, cloaked in Human form but still hopeless as a tail. The detective took great pleasure in leading the ex-smith around, making sudden attempts to lose him as if headed for some significant appointment. Then Deacon would circle back around and start following Gresh, as the creature struggled to pick up his trail.

The second shadow went unnoticed. He'd begun by following Gresh, until realizing that was not an effective means of keeping track of Deacon. Then he switched to the detective, keeping watch on him from both near and far. Long after Gresh gave up in frustration, this unseen presence kept to his task.

He was watching when the detective and his night's amusement were awakened from a fitful sleep by pounding on the door. With a string of curses, Deacon pulled on a robe, undid the doorseals, and flung it wide. Strategy centered on punching out whoever was knocking at such an obscene hour and going back to bed.

Thom Banff stood in the doorway, beefy arms folded across his chest. He didn't wait to be invited before stepping inside.

"You know what time it is?" Deacon asked, because it was expected.

"That I do," Banff replied. He was poking around the apartment, sticking his head in the various rooms. A shriek of protest indicated he had found the bedroom and its shapely contents. Said contents immediately began explaining that she hadn't received a coin from Deacon and this was strictly for pleasure, and who the hell did Banff think he was bursting into a private bedroom in the middle of the night?

Deacon asked the same question, less politely. Banff gave him a weary glance. "I was looking for your Miss Martel. I have some questions to ask her."

"You're some detective, Banff," Deacon replied, pulling the bedroom door shut to allow his guest time to get dressed. She would put the bill on his tab — better that than getting dragged downtown by a sentinel with a slab on his shoulder. "I've been off the Martel case for over a week. I don't know where she is."

"That's too bad. It would have made things a little easier all around," Banff said, his brow furrowed. "All right, Deacon. Get the girl on her way and throw some clothes on. We're going for a ride."

"Where to?"

"You may not know where she is, but one of hers knew where

 94

you are. Only he never quite made it here. Someone — or maybe something, considering the company you've been keeping — stopped him. Knowing how you feel about losing potential business, I thought you'd want to know. Maybe you can give us an identification, since Miss Martel remains among the missing."

"Not in the crowd for this one, huh?"

"If she had been, lad, I'd have her in a cell so deep she'd feel the flames of Hell licking at her feet," Banff answered. They were the last words spoken until he and Deacon reached the scene.

❦

It wasn't a pretty sight. Sentinels were trying to keep the crowds back while sorcerers with an affinity for fire doused the last few sparks. Banff flashed his badge and the knot of morbidly curious citizenry parted to allow him and Deacon through, stepping carefully to avoid puddles left by the night's showers.

"At least it stopped raining," Banff muttered. "Bloodmages raise holy hell when all the red stuff's washed away before they get here."

The automobile wrapped around a lamp post was unmistakably Larissa's, its front end now crushed and mangled. Escaping elemental energies always posed a danger of explosion, but the relatively relaxed postures of the sentinels hinted this had been dealt with.

The body lay half out of the driver's seat, eyes open, blood staining his dark suit. One arm was outstretched, fist clamped tightly shut. Even from a distance, Deacon could tell that the wounds on his throat weren't the result of the accident. Someone had slashed his jugular vein, the new and fatal injury mingling with old scar tissue.

"His name was Narses," Deacon said quietly.

"So you do know him," Banff said, no surprise in his voice. "Figured you might. He'd been seen in the company of Larissa Martel on more than one occasion. What was their relationship?"

"He was her driver. She had saved his life once … or so she said. How do you know he was coming to see me?"

"We're not sure, Deacon, not really. Somebody picked him clean — wallet, everything. Only thing they left behind was your address on a slip of paper tucked in his breast pocket and whatever it is he has in his hand. He was traveling west when the accident happened, so it's possible. How well did you know him?"

"We never spoke," Deacon said, moving over to look at the corpse more closely. "Knife do this?"

"Most likely. We won't know for certain until tomorrow. We figure the attacker was hiding in the back, jumped out and cut him."

"Then vanished out of a moving car? Or did he walk away from this accident? Was there any blood besides Narses' around, Thom?"

Banff frowned. "You know the routine. Bloodmage will do a thorough check of the area. And we both know there are things abroad in this city that can vanish when they want to, or walk away unharmed from things like this."

Deacon didn't answer. He was examining the car, hoping for one of those classic dying clues — a word written in blood, a snatch of newscribe parchment, anything. But that sort of thing only happened in stories, the same ones that had fooled him into thinking detecting was a glamorous profession. They never mentioned dark, cold nights and bodies covered in blood.

"How long ago?" he asked.

"Not more than half an hour. We asked around — everybody heard the crash, nobody saw anything." There was an uncomfortable pause before Banff added, "Just for the record, Deacon, where were you?"

The detective didn't take offense. "You know where I was, and what I was doing, Thom. The girl will confirm that."

"I believe you. Gods and devils know, this isn't your style. But don't place too much faith in the tramp — somebody slips her a little more loose change, she'll swear she never saw you before."

"Just cause they won't go near you is no reason to slander their profession," Deacon replied.

Banff's retort was cut off by the approach of one of his men, his hands cupped around a sphere of sorcerous energy. "We finally peeled his fingers loose, Sarge," the officer reported. "He was holding on to this like his life depended on it."

Deacon moved over to take a look. Ever since the Sarcen scandals of a few years back, all evidence taken from a crime scene had to be encased in an arcane sphere to prevent tampering. Long-range alteration spells had turned more than a few murder weapons, drug caches and the like into piles of dung in sentinel storerooms.

Within the clear capsule of energy hung suspended three coins, adding up to roughly a week's pay for a millworker. They looked new and clean, and that alone made them stand out from their surroundings.

"Guy was holding them so tight, they left marks in his palm," the sentinel said, chuckling. "Maybe he refused to give somebody their fare back, eh?"

Banff snorted. "Bring that in, Canel, and keep the cute cracks to yourself. And get somebody to keep those crowds back."

Deacon looked around. In fact, most of the crowds had already dispersed, now that they were certain the dead man wasn't going to do anything entertaining. A brief spate of killings by an impatient necromancer had made murder a spectator sport for a while, since the bodies had a habit of getting up and walking around after death.

Not everyone had lost interest in this scene, though. A redhead with an ample figure and a "come hither and get yours" smile stood in a doorway, watching the sentinels at play. She was wearing a thin dress that might have been white once, but now was more of a gray, spotted in places from rain drops. She noticed Deacon's attentions and assumed a position that might have been provocative a few hundred customers ago.

"Do you need me for anything else, Thom?" Deacon asked, not taking his eyes off the woman.

Banff turned and followed the detective's gaze. "Kaphet's trousers, Deacon, one day you're going to follow the scent right into trouble. Try sleeping diagonally once in a while, boy, it will do wonders for your temper."

"Right. Then I can be cool and calm like you," Deacon replied, already walking away. "See you, Thom."

❦

The woman didn't make a move as Deacon climbed the steps to where she waited, leaning against the side of the doorway. Her expression was one of lust painted over boredom.

"You don't look like a uniform," she said, in a voice made husky by too many nights inhaling cheap incense.

"You don't look much like a dress," he answered, looking her up and down. "More like one of those silky things they make in Vazar, the kind that come in plain wrappers."

She laughed. Deacon decided that a person could get used to that sound without too much trouble. "So what are you? One of those morts that gets off on the sight of blood? Or do you just like to watch them cart the body away and pretend you did it?"

"No, I get aroused by all the usual things. How about you?"

She shrugged. "Been so long, I can't remember. Anyway, this breaks up the evening, until I find something better. Are you something better?"

"Maybe," Deacon answered. "Why don't we go inside and talk about it?"

She gave him a look that turned hard. "How do I know you're not a sentinel? You were with them, acting pretty friendly."

"Now I'm with you, acting friendlier. But I don't do your job, either."

She reached up and traced the line of his jaw with her finger. "I like you. What's your name?"

"Jack. Are you going to invite me in, or are we going to keep making sparkling conversation on your stoop?"

"I'm thinking about it, Jack," she said playfully. "My name's Tara. I'm 28, no visible scars, been on the game for six years, no diseases that I know about. And if you have a badge underneath that coat, I'll scratch your eyes out."

"That would be a damn shame," he replied. "Then I couldn't

look at you."

Her laugh was loud and sharp now, filled with scorn. "Don't you have the alchemist's tongue? I stopped being anything to look at a few thousand tumbles ago. But that little bit of gold has bought you a ticket inside."

She turned and opened the door of her building, beckoning him to follow her inside. The air was stale and damp and smelled of dust and urine. She led him up a battered stairway and stopped at a door at the end of a long hall. At one time, golden letters had marked this as apartment 12, but the "2" had long since fallen off. The impression of the number was inscribed on the grime coating the door.

Tara favored him with a smile while she unlocked her place of business. She underestimated herself, Deacon realized — true, the years hadn't treated her kindly, but her blue eyes still held some sparkle. When her smile wasn't forced, it showed flashes of the sweet girl she'd been before poverty, or booze, or the wrong man at the wrong time had led her to this life.

Her apartment was small; bedroom, kitchen/living area, bathroom and one closet. The atmosphere was heavy with cheap perfume. The bed was unmade.

"Don't worry, the sheets are clean," she said, dimming the only illuminated glowstone in the place. "I make enough to get the good ones. They scour themselves in between times."

Tara slipped out of her dress in one easy motion and let it fall to her floor. Her large breasts were still firm and she was well-rounded in the right places. She climbed on to the bed and held out a hand to him.

"Come on over," she whispered seductively. "Maybe you can teach me a few things."

"I'd rather learn from you, Tara. Can we talk for a little while?"

She shrugged, all the while pulling a sheet up to her waist. "Don't tell me you're bashful?" she teased. "Trust me, once we get started, everything will be fine. And if you need some help ... well, I've got everything you might need. Ground unicorn horn, powdered henbane, good stuff."

Deacon took off his coat and draped it over a chair. He was wearing his revolver in a shoulder holster, and Tara's eyes went wide at the sight of it.

"Hey, what are you doing with that?" she asked, bringing the sheet up to her neck. "You're not one of those guys who likes to hurt, are you? I don't like that."

"No, Tara, I won't hurt you," Deacon said softly, sitting down on the edge of the bed. "I just want to ask you a few questions."

A look of betrayal stole on to her face. "You are one of them! A sentinel! Damn, I knew it!" she said angrily. "All right, what will it take to make you leave me alone? If you want a pay-off, my money's all with a Gris named Linx."

"Would you shut up?" he snapped, louder than he had intended. She stopped talking, looking frightened again. "I'm not a sentinel, and I'm not here to beat you up or run you in. I'm a private detective. My name's Deacon. The guy who was killed out there tonight might have been coming to see me. I'm trying to find out who stopped him."

"I don't know anything about that," she said sullenly. "And if I did, why should I tell you? You'll walk out of here fine, but I have to live in this neighborhood! Suppose whoever killed your friend comes back for me?"

"Don't worry. I'd guess he's long gone by now. This isn't some wandering necro at work. This was planned, and he got who he was after."

"What's in this for me, Jack?" she demanded. She wasn't pretty when she was angry.

Deacon pulled out his wallet and tossed a few bills on the sheets. She reached out to grab them and he caught her wrist. "Not till I get some answers."

She wrenched her arm free. "I was only checking to see if it was real. You might as well take it back, cause I didn't see anything. I heard the crash like everybody else and came out to see what happened."

Deacon picked up the money and glared at her. "First time I ever met a prostitute who was a bad liar."

"What the hell is that supposed to mean?" she spat, a little too loudly. Her eyes held equal parts fear and anger.

"What it means is that you work the stoop, kid. Everyone else in that crowd poured out after the car had crashed, but you were outside when it happened."

"How do you know where I was?"

Deacon reached down and picked her dress up off the floor. His words flew like bullets. "This was damp from the rain when I met you, Tara. But it had stopped raining at least an hour before I showed up, and a good thirty, thirty-five minutes before the crash. You were outside all that time, waiting for a customer to go by, and you saw the whole thing."

She shrugged. The gesture made her breasts move in a distracting fashion. Deacon did his best to ignore them.

"What if I did?" she said, looking away from him. "In my business, you see lots of things. You don't last long by opening your mouth to every *lyke* that comes by."

Deacon frowned and tossed the money back on the bed, then peeled off one more bill and added it to the pile. "What did you see, Tara?"

She did some mental addition and giggled. That would be enough to get her a ride in a wagon out of town, maybe even a car! A new start, that was all she needed, she reasoned. And if all this guy wanted what she had seen and heard, why not?

"Okay, Mr. Detective," she began, leaning back against the pillows. "I was standing outside, like you said, waiting for somebody to go by. Suddenly, I see this big, black car turn the corner and start down the street, so I straighten myself up and get ready. He's driving really slow, like he's looking for an address, or maybe a woman.

"Next thing I know, there's a shout. The car skids, goes out of control, and smacks into the lamp post. End of car, end of guy, end of story."

"Did you see anybody leave the wreck?"

"No, Jack. I had my eyes shut for just a second when he hit, and when I opened them, everything was like you saw it. But if anybody had been back there, they had to be a devil to walk away from that."

"There was somebody back there. He didn't cut his own throat," Deacon said darkly. He pushed the money a little closer to her. "Take it. You've earned it."

"No, I haven't. Not yet," she said softly, her hand on his. "I've got my pride, Jack. I don't like being paid for a job I haven't done."

She pulled him down to her and kissed him like she meant it. Deacon wasn't about to insult a professional pursuing her craft.

❧

The sky was brightening when he stepped out of the building and on to the street. The thought of going home again was unappealing, so he headed for his office.

His brain was full of questions. If Narses had been coming to the apartment, why was he coming alone? Had Larissa sent him, or did she not even know he had left? And why was he holding on to that money for dear life?

Not that it matters, he reminded himself. *I'm off this case.*

And that was what was bothering him, he realized. He was off the case, and somebody didn't want him back in. Somebody who was willing to kill to keep him out, and next time might not stop with the messenger.

Chapter Eleven

After a few hours of staring out his office window, too many smokes and too few ales, Deacon came to a decision. The sun was high in the sky by now, which gave him plenty of time to do what he had to. If it worked, the real action wouldn't start until after dark.

He went down to the street and hailed a driver. The car was small and noisy — cheap elemental spells, Deacon guessed — but the driver didn't waste a lot of time in conversation. He didn't even make any rude comments when he heard the first of Deacon's destinations.

For the rest of the afternoon, they cruised the city from one end to the other. Deacon visited the alley where he had killed the 'shifter; the bar where he and Larissa had rendezvoused; the ruins of Gresh's smithy; Black's stables; and all the other places that had figured in the case so far. At each stop, the detective got out and nosed around finding, as he expected, no signs of Larissa or her recruits. Even East had gone missing, for which Deacon was more relieved than he cared to admit.

He was heading back to the office after visiting the now abandoned penthouse when he spotted Banff. The driver obligingly pulled over and Deacon tossed him the fare before climbing out.

"Have a nice ride around the city, Deacon?" Banff said. "I've been trying to find you all day. Where the hell have you been?"

"Like you said, seeing the sights. And being seen," Deacon answered, falling into step with the sentinel. He wasn't sure where they were headed, although with Banff for company, a tavern was a reasonable guess.

"What's that?"

"Nothing, Thom. What did you want to see me about?"

"The first few reports on last night are starting to trickle in. I haven't had an easy one in three years, Deacon, and it looks like I won't be starting now," Banff grumbled. "To start with, the bloodmage says all the red stuff flowed out of the corpse we've got. No blood in the back seat or within three blocks of the accident. Whoever he was, he walked away clean."

"And?"

"And Bligh is done with the body. It might interest you to know that your friend Narses wasn't a mute."

Banff smiled at the look of surprise on the detective's face. "That's right, sometimes we sentinels are a step ahead of you independents. Oh, he's got plenty of scar tissue, but nothing that affects the vocal chords."

"Maybe it was shock that silenced him," Deacon said.

"Could be. But it wasn't physical, that's what the doctor said, anyway. Seems he drank, too — nothing chronic, probably, but more than he should have."

"He didn't seem like the type."

"Neither do we," Banff muttered as they passed through the doors of the bar.

"I'm glad you're off this one," the sentinel said when they both had ales in front of them.

"How do you read it?"

"From what you told me, the guy by himself isn't important," Banff paused to take a long drink. "He wasn't robbed, that we know of. That leaves a warning — to you, or to your lady friend. Seen her, by the way?"

Deacon smiled. Banff had never learned to do a subtle interrogation. "No. Spent the day looking for her, too. She didn't even leave footprints in the dust."

"Why were you trying to find her? You're better off staying away from that poison, Deacon."

"'Cause I don't like being pushed. I walked away from this case because I wanted to, and I'll walk back in for the same reason. And if somebody wants to send me a message, I'm making myself available to hear it."

Banff's face went red with anger. "Gods and devils, Deacon, you're making yourself a target! Damn you, I ought to run you in right now!"

"On what charge?"

"I'll make one up, if I have to! I'll toss you in a cell and forget you're there till this whole thing settles down."

Deacon stood up, tossing change on the table. "I'm not going to sit around waiting for someone to lob a fireball at me. And I won't run and hide. Let them think I'm back in and maybe they'll come out in the open."

"And suppose they're too much for you, you pile of *ghef* dung? What then?"

Deacon turned at the door. "If they kill me, Banff, you'll be the first one I'll haunt."

❧

The sun had set by the time Deacon made it back to his office. The corridor leading to his door seemed longer tonight and the sounds of the building settling were like thunder in his ears. With relief, he noted that the doorseals were still intact, as was the iron lock. But he drew his gun along with the key anyway.

He opened the door and stepped inside, reaching to turn up the glow stone. Suddenly, there was a blinding light, and then darkness again. He had shut his eyes barely in time to keep from being blinded, but colored spots still danced before him.

"Sit down, Mr. Deacon," a cold, quiet voice ordered. Deacon could barely make out a figure sitting in the chair behind his desk. "My name is Whisper. You are most fortunate that I have not been waiting long, sir. Otherwise I would have burnt out your eyes just now."

Deacon fought to clear his vision, without much success. He found a chair — the one normally used by clients — only because he knew from memory where it was. The gun was still in his hand. If his visitor kept talking, he would aim at the voice.

"I have business to discuss with you. It won't take long. When we are done, I will leave here and you will be both wealthier and wiser."

"Sounds good to me," Deacon answered. "But we're closed. Come back in the morning."

Whisper laughed. It sounded like ice cracking. "I have been told you are a stubborn man. You do not seem to know how to take a warning, even when it is to your benefit to do so. It might interest you to know that I have been following you for some time. I have come to know your strengths and weaknesses, perhaps better than you yourself do. I can assure you that I am acting in your best interests."

"Well, that makes two of us, then."

Deacon's eyesight was slowly coming back. His visitor was tall and rail-thin, clad in a three-piece, black suit and a tie whose pattern couldn't be made out. The man's hands were bony and his fingers were long, like a pianist or a safecracker. Deacon guessed the man was neither.

"My employers have asked me to speak with you," Whisper continued. "Before we begin, I would appreciate it if you would put the pistol away. It's distracting."

"Sorry, pal. I feel naked without it."

Whisper shrugged and reached into his jacket, pulling a revolver. Without a word, he put the gun to his temple and pulled the trigger.

The noise was deafening and the muzzle flash threatened to start the spots dancing in front of Deacon's eyes again. Still not speaking, Whisper put the gun back into his pocket and turned his attention back to Deacon.

"Keep the gun if you wish, then. But I prefer you harbor no illusions about it. Now — you are acquainted with a woman named Larissa Martel?"

"I know lots of people," Deacon replied, yawning. "I'm a friendly guy. Ask anybody."

"You were hired by her to do a job. She paid you a great deal of money?"

"That's the way the business sometimes works, yeah. You a tax collector?"

Whisper tried again. "Are you still in her employ?"

Deacon moved restlessly in the chair. "Look, pal, let's get past question and answer. If you have an offer to make, out with it. You're boring me."

Whisper's eyes flared red for a brief moment, then subsided. Deacon had a flash of the butcher's apprentice with one arm torn off. "Very well, Mr. Deacon. My employers are willing to offer you twice what Miss Martel is paying."

"To do what?"

"To do nothing. Go on with your life as if Miss Martel had never existed. Stay out of matters that don't concern you."

Whisper reached into his jacket again and pulled out a handful of bills. Put together, they added up to a formidable amount of zeros.

"You should have thought of this before you killed Martel's driver," Deacon said. "It would have saved you a lot of trouble. Why did you kill him, anyway? What was he on his way to tell me?"

There was a long pause before Whisper answered, "That is none of your affair. Will you take the money or not?"

Deacon shrugged. "Hell, sure, I'll take the money. But what's to stop me from … misbehaving once I've got it?"

There was a bright flash as the money burst into flame. The light illuminated Whisper's face, long with strong features and jet-black hair. He watched the bills burn for a few moments before releasing them to drift to the desk as ash. Then he smiled and held out his right hand to Deacon, palm upward.

"I presume we have a deal, then," he said. "But before we shake upon it …"

Before Deacon's eyes, the flesh of Whisper's palm began to bubble and heave, as if something were fighting to get out. With sickening swiftness, it began to stretch, twist and mold itself, moving as if there were maggots beneath it. When it was done, the figure of a man stood upon Whisper's palm, no more than a few inches tall. It stood at silent attention, and Deacon noted with revulsion that its face had no features.

With a lightning swift movement, Whisper closed his fist on the figure. There was no sound to mark its "death," but red-black blood oozed from between Whisper's fingers and began to pool on the desk. Deacon's mouth went dry.

Whisper opened his hand again. It bore no sign of the creature that had risen from it only moments before.

"It is just that easy, Mr. Deacon. Remember that."

Deacon didn't bother to reply. He didn't have to, for Whisper had vanished. All that was left behind was a sheaf of bills, now made whole again, resting in a pool of drying blood on the desk blotter.

Deacon would stare at that spot for a very long time.

Chapter Twelve

"My advice? You're asking my advice? Well, then, friend Jack, my advice is to pack your satchel and disappear from Galitia for a while. Six months, a year — see some other cities. You could even do some business for me while you're gone."

Belrand mopped the sweat off his bald pate and pushed aside a pile of bullets he had been reloading with powder and an assortment of noxious chemicals. Deacon had chosen an inconvenient time to visit — this was a rush order — but when he heard the story of Whisper's visit, he decided to be big about it.

"Even if everything he did was illusion — the fire, the homunculus from his hand — you are still dealing with a sorcerer of no little ability. And if it wasn't illusion ... I'd strongly suggest staying under the bed for the rest of your natural life."

"What's my second choice?" Deacon asked, all the while playing with a flute he had found on the floor. With a cry of alarm, Belrand snatched the instrument away from him.

"What are you trying to do, blow up the shop? Even the low notes on that can fell a tree, let alone what the high notes can do. And your second choice is to go about your business with your head down and hope this unpleasant fellow has more important things to worry about than a cut-rate detective."

"Do you have anything I can use?"

"Against that one? It would take a few days, Deacon, and even then, I can't promise anything. Maybe I can whip up a charm of protection or something," Belrand answered, sounding not at all certain it would matter if he did. "Come back end of the week. And this one will cost you, friend Jack."

Deacon nodded his agreement and left the shop. He was no more than two steps on to the pavement when he heard the screech of tires. He turned in time to see a big, black car bearing down on him, with intent to kill.

There was no time for thought, only movement. Deacon dove for the sidewalk, but the car clipped his leg as it roared past, sending him flying into a set of metal trash cans. He hit the ground and lay still amidst the garbage. The car sped away, its driver apparently satisfied.

Deacon regained consciousness a few minutes later. The first face he saw was Belrand's, looking anxiously down at him.

"Are you all right, my friend? Should I call a healer?"

Deacon shook his head and sat up. His right leg ached and the world took a while to stop spinning, but other than that — and the horrible smell of the trash — he was okay. Physically, anyway.

"I am afraid your suit is ruined," Belrand said.

"If I had hit the wall instead of those cans, something else would have been ruined," Deacon muttered. Belrand helped him to his feet and brushed some of the loose refuse from his coat.

"Come back into the shop. We can contact the sentinels from there."

"No thanks, Rollie. I got a look at the driver. I know where to find him."

"Where?"

"City morgue. He died the night before last."

Despite the size of the city, the Galitia morgue was a relatively crude affair. Located in the basement of the main sentinel station, it was stone and slabs and icy cold. It stank of cleaning solution, herbal mixtures, and death, not necessarily in that order.

Dr. Oswald Bligh had originally wanted to be a surgeon, but

a pathological fear of making a mistake and killing a patient hampered his work. He had switched to the coroner's art early on, finding happiness in a job where cutting the wrong thing didn't matter. Nothing ever happened in the "heat of the moment" down here.

And Bligh was the best of a bad lot. Most coroners were budding sorcerers who wanted bodies to practice on. Once they had the parts they needed for this week's incantation, they vanished. The city would have to hire someone new then, and in the meantime, the bodies piled up.

Right now, Bligh was wishing he had taken his mother's advice and gone to work in a slaughterhouse. This was the third badly mutilated corpse that had been dropped on his doorstep in the past week — each time, there seemed to be less for him to examine.

Deacon had stopped only long enough to change clothes before heading to see the coroner. Banff had been waiting for him at the station, and now both men were doing their best to hide their discomfort.

"What are you saying? You are saying a man I certified as dead is not dead? You are drunk, or insane?" Bligh sputtered.

"Take it easy," Banff said gruffly. "We just want to take a look at the body. That's not too much to ask."

Bligh turned, muttering something in a language Deacon didn't recognize. They followed his slope-shouldered form to the back of the morgue, where one wall played host to an assortment of drawers and their grisly contents. Once a month, a sentinel mage came down and reinforced the spells that kept the bodies cold.

The coroner was still talking to himself as he ran a finger down the rows, looking for the right name. Finally, he chanced upon the one labelled "Narses" and yanked it open.

This time, Deacon recognized the words Bligh was saying. He had heard dock workers spout them in the midst of a brawl.

The body on the slab wasn't Narses.

"So what happened?" Banff asked, starting to pace the room.

"Did he just get up and walk away?"

"He was never here," Deacon answered, forcing himself to take a closer look at the body. "The wounds are all the same as the ones we saw on Narses that night. This is the guy who was in that car."

"You mean a conjuring trick?"

"And a damn good one. Somebody cast a rite on this guy, making him look like Narses, right down to the scar tissue. But the spell only worked on the outside — it couldn't duplicate the damage to Narses' vocal chords. That's why Tara heard a shout just before the accident."

"Who the hell is Tara?" Banff demanded.

"Never mind. I had a feeling something was wrong then, and when you told me the body Bligh examined wasn't mute, I knew it. But that business with my night visitor last evening overshadowed it — until the real Narses tried to decorate my face with tire tracks."

Bligh had finally caught on. "And this spell's duration, it has worn out? That is why we are seeing him as he truly is now?"

"Right. Somebody paid him to pose as Narses for a day. That was the money he was clutching in his hand. Maybe they were using him as bait, trying to see if anybody was close enough to them to bite — and somebody was."

"Makes sense," Banff concluded. "Doc, did you ever identify the weapon used?"

Bligh frowned. "Ah, yes, sir, I did. This man, he was not killed with a knife blade. No, it was the same as the last dozen bodies brought to me."

"If not a knife, then what?"

"Claws, Sergeant," Bligh said quietly. "Very sharp claws."

❧

"They had to know this would come out sooner or later," Banff said later. He had invited Deacon upstairs to his office while he filled out the mountain of paperwork the changed body mandated.

"Why? The guys who slap him in the ground wouldn't know what he looked like in the first place. They fooled whoever killed him, and they fooled me — as far as their enemies were concerned, Narses was dead."

"So why did he come out of hiding and try to run you down?"

"That's what I'm going to find out, Thom. And I think I know where to start."

❦

Deacon spent the next few hours visiting every tavern and flophouse he could find, starting from the riverfront and working his way west. Banff had gotten a sentinel mage to create a "living sketch" of Narses, based on Deacon's description. Now the detective carried it with him and showed it to everyone he ran into.

No one had seen the mute. Deacon hadn't expected that they would have. But if he had guessed right, news that he was looking for the man would drift back to someone who could answer his questions.

He didn't have long to wait. A black auto — driven by someone other than Narses — slowed to match his walking pace as he headed from the twentieth bar toward the twenty-first. The rear passenger door flew open and a voice inside said, "You've been very naughty, Mr. Deacon."

The detective turned to look into the face of East, now a young man of twenty-five. With only a moment's hesitation, Deacon slid into the seat beside him and pulled the door shut.

❦

The detective gave his host a long look as the car began to move. East was wearing the body of a coldly handsome youth of medium build, and dressed in a suit that probably cost more than Deacon's office rent for the year. The face of the old man to come could be seen in the young, and as before, the eyes were a dead — in more ways than one — giveaway.

Deacon wanted to ask about Larissa. He wanted to ask about

Narses. But the first question that came to his lips as he stared at East was, "What the hell *are* you?"

"I'm a survivor," East said, glancing out the window. "Some men sow, others reap — I exist. I have an innate talent for staying alive, and next to that, all other abilities pale."

"That doesn't answer my question."

East smiled thinly. "Tell me, Deacon: if you die today, and someone reanimates you tomorrow, do your former friends have the right to destroy you? After all, at this hour you are free to walk the planet — does the accident of death and a few hours in the ground erase that privilege?"

"I was raised to believe the dead should stay that way," Deacon replied.

"Were you?" East said, chuckling. "It seems to me that I recall chatting with you in a very different setting, not so long ago. For all your talk, you wasted little time in returning to life."

"Is there a point to this, East, or are we just playing word games?"

"Oh, there's a very substantial point of procedure at stake here, my boy. You believed Narses to be dead, then found he was not so; you now feel an obligation to return him to his former state. Now why do you Humans feel this holy duty to keep the dead buried?

"And while we're on the subject, if an entity of some sort possesses a corpse a-mouldering in the grave, why do you object? Would you prefer it possess the living? After all, no one has any further use for the body, except those in Black's line of work."

The car had picked up speed. Deacon recognized the area they were moving through as the downtown area, the borders of the theatre district.

"You've been making quite a nuisance of yourself, Mr. Deacon," East continued, in the tone of a parent delivering a deserved scolding. "You tried to warn Black away from his destiny. And why? Because you wished to save him from a 'fate worse than undeath.' But the only difference between him now and what he was then is that now the corpses he unearths are put to far better use. Rather than see them turned into lampshades and bookbinding, he has returned them to the food chain, where they belong."

"I thought he could do better than go back to fighting a war that can't be won," Deacon said quietly.

"It can be won, sir ... that is the problem," East responded, the note of challenge leaving his voice. "And if you are to survive the battles to come, both you and Larissa will have to cast off your damnable Human compassion. It will only get in the way, you know. One of the advantages to having never been Human is escaping that curse."

"We seem to be back at my first question: what are you, East?"

East folded his arms and leaned back in his seat, amused. "Very well, Deacon. I do not know if there is a name for it — I have never bothered to come up with one. Put simply, I have been favored with virtual immortality, of a sort. I live out my lifespan from month to month, aging from child to adult to ancient in harmony with the phases of the moon. The price of this in one I am most willing to pay: the lives of others. One a day."

"Human lives?" Deacon asked coldly.

"By choice, not design," East answered, as if proud of the fact. "I could simply snuff an insect each morning and fulfill my contract — but I much prefer the challenge of eliminating thinking creatures. It strikes a far better balance."

"You lousy —"

"Save your indignation for your own kind!" East snapped. "The netherworld doesn't operate by your rules. Parts of it don't operate by *any*, and it is those aspects that are so feared by Larissa ... and myself. They are the 'enemy' she speaks of. But as I told you before, they are not the only — or even the most dangerous — foe she faces."

"Let me get this straight: all of this bloodshed is because some other ... things won't play by your rules?"

"Not *our* rules, Mr. Deacon. *Any* rules. Think of it: everyone knows such things as we exist, but few ever encounter us. If the Chaotics triumph, we will all be far more visible. They have less to fear, for it is harder to slay a creature who does not operate in a predictable fashion. But they would bring attention — and destruction — upon Larissa and those like her. Already events are getting away from us. Your involvement is proof of that."

"I'm off this case," Deacon said, though not as convincingly as he had intended. "The only reason I'm pursuing this is that Narses tried to run me down."

"Narses is a fool!" East snarled.

"Why's he after me, East? And where is he?"

"As you have no doubt discovered, Deacon, we sent a sorcerously-created double out in his place two nights ago. We wished to see how close the enemy had come to tagging our operatives. And, if they believed Narses to be dead, he would be able to act with greater freedom.

"It worked perfectly. Then word came back that you were on the scene. Narses panicked — if the charade was exposed, he would be in mortal — or immortal, as the case may be — danger. He tried to handle the problem on his own, and botched the job."

"So you're here to finish the job," Deacon concluded.

East looked at him, surprised. "If I wanted you dead, Deacon, I would have left you watching over Larissa's still form. You're far more amusing alive, I assure you. But your continued involvement is proving troublesome — and presuming you are a man who hates to leave things unfinished, I am going to help you solve your current case."

The car slid to a stop in an alleyway. Deacon looked out the window and saw lights playing on the rear of an old building across the street.

"How?" he asked. "And who's over there?"

East sighed happily. "Those men — or one of them, anyway — killed the poor, drunken sot who posed as Narses. And we are going to bring them down, Deacon. Together."

Then the young/old man began to laugh. But Deacon didn't feel much like joining in.

Chapter
Thirteen

By the time the two had slipped out of the car and made their way closer to the target building, East had amended his statement. Oh, he still intended to help Deacon solve Narses' "murder," and more than a few others, besides. But he wasn't going to do anything that would allow the believers in Chaos to trace the incident back to him.

"Then why don't you go back to your car and get the hell out of here?" Deacon whispered harshly. They were standing in an alleyway, only a few doors from where respectable looking men in business suits were filing silently into what appeared to be an abandoned theatre. The windows were boarded up, but the barricades had been torn off the side door, and this provided their means of egress.

"I want to watch you at work," East replied, unruffled by Deacon's anger. "I do very little myself. Like the spider, I prefer to remain in the center of the web and wait for my prey to come to me. I rarely go out and actively hunt anything down. I'm looking forward to the experience."

"Wonderful," Deacon muttered. "Maybe they'll sell postcards. I'm beginning to think we should just call in the sentinels."

"And have them find what? An empty theatre? Are you so foolish as to think that these fellows don't have someone inside that august body to warn them against raids?"

"All right, already," Deacon cut him off, then drew his gun. "If these guys are cultists, they're bound to have a sentry posted at that door, if only to keep an eye out for rivals. We'll have to take him out.

"Alleys run all through here. Give me sixty seconds, then take a walk down there and distract him. I'll handle the rest."

East nodded. "How strange. The last man I heard speak so confidently of an impending confrontation was the fool we disguised as Narses. You might wish to learn by his example, Deacon. Sixty, fifty-nine, fifty-eight …"

Deacon took off down the alley, turned left, then right, then left again. As he expected, it wasn't hard to find an indirect route that would bring him behind the theatre. He recognized it now, the Calyricon, once home to top-of-the-line plays. When it fell on hard times, the owners started booking shows that featured more "flesh and flash." It had been closed for six years.

It was almost pitch black. It wasn't until the sentry used a heatstone to light a cigarette that Deacon spotted him. He was young, built like he should be pulling a plow somewhere. Unlike the men who had gone inside, he wasn't wearing a tailored suit. Probably wasn't a full member of the cult, just local muscle they had hired to watch their backs.

Deacon had been counting down the seconds. When he reached zero, he heard East's footfalls. The sentry doused his smoke, but the detective had a fix on him. He started forward even as East said, "Pardon me, I seem to have lost my way."

If Deacon had been unsure where to land his blow, the guard erased it by barking, "Keep going, friend, or you'll lose more than that!" Guided by his foghorn voice, Deacon brought the butt of the revolver crashing down on his head. The guard hit the ground, still breathing but of no use to anyone for several hours to come.

Almost anyone. East hovered over the body for a long moment before joining Deacon at the door. "So full of life," he said, voice tinged with regret. "But there is wisdom in restraint."

Deacon produced a glowstone from his coat. The iron latch on the door had been broken, but that was meaningless. It was much more likely there was a doorseal of a different kind in place.

The detective looked around the floor of the alley until he found a jagged piece of glass. Cautioning East to stand back, he tossed the shard at the doorknob. As soon as glass touched metal, there was a bright spark and the smell of ozone. When the two men opened their eyes, the glass was gone.

Deacon repeated the process two more times until he was certain what was invested in the door. "Cheap, but effective," he commented. "Put the spell in the metal — doorknob, hinges — and leave the wood alone. That's enough to discourage casual burglars, especially when there isn't much of value inside."

Moving closer, he wedged his fingers in between the door and the frame and pulled. East joined him a few seconds later, and between the two of them, they were able to yank it open.

They found themselves looking at a darkened stairway leading up. From deep in the building, they could hear voices raised in chant, but no words were intelligible. A faint aroma of melting wax drifted out to them.

"Sounds like the party's already started," Deacon said. "Let's go."

Together, they climbed the stairs which led to stage level. Deacon motioned for East to keep going up a second flight to the balcony.

From their new vantage point, they could see most of the theatre. Roughly a dozen men were assembled on the dimly lit stage, having exchanged their suits for crimson robes. Only one, standing toward the rear, had his hood raised. The rest, despite the arcane words pouring from their mouths, still resembled shopkeepers and warehouse foremen playing dress-up.

The stage boasted only one piece of scenery, an altar that appeared to be stone but was most likely painted wood. It seemed vaguely familiar to Deacon — then he realized that he had seen it used in a cheap skin play here almost a decade ago.

"Are you sure these are the guys?" he whispered to East. "This looks like Talent Night at the local coven."

"The one in the hood. He's the one you want," East assured

him. "The trappings may be shabby, but they are said to worship one of the more powerful Chaotics. If he chooses to manifest himself through them, we could enjoy a very short evening at the theatre."

Deacon glanced back at the stage as the hooded cultist moved toward the altar. Judging from the way the others moved aside for him, he was evidently the high priest. Strangely, he said nothing, simply raised his arms toward the heavens in supplication.

That was when Deacon saw the claws. Long and sharp, extending from each finger like a stiletto. Just like what Bligh claimed had killed the corpses streaming into his morgue.

Deacon checked his weapon. Not certain what he would encounter on his hunt for Narses, he had opted for a mixed load. If it came down to it, he might have a few surprises for the cult members.

He and East peered over the rail of the balcony as the ceremony began. The cultists formed a semi-circle behind the altar, while the hooded priest stood beside it. After much chanting and dropping of the name "Erom," the priest dropped his arms. Two of the cultists immediately disappeared into the wings.

"Sacrifice?"

"Of course," East answered. "Probably some whore who thought she was attending a costume party. Don't interfere, Deacon. Better to wait until they have had their fun and indulged in some post-bloodletting wine."

The remainder of the cultists were chanting again. "Hear us, Erom, heed the words of your faithful servants. We pray thee appear in all glory, and spill the blood of our enemies. For yours is the power, great Erom. Accept this sacrifice in your name ..."

It went on like that for several minutes, straight out of a bad shadowplay. Deacon didn't know whether to be frightened out of his wits or stand up and start throwing rotten vegetables at the stage. East's expression was grim, though; the blood shed on the boards tonight would not be any sham.

Deacon was about to say that he had no intention of sitting around while maniacs in robes cut someone open, but his reply was cut off by the sight of the two cultists returning. Between them, they half-led, half-dragged a lithe, raven-haired woman in a loose white gown toward the altar. She was struggling, but not with much success. When she stumbled halfway across the stage, one of the men slapped her hard across the face.

Even from the balcony, Deacon knew who it was.

"Larissa!" he whispered, shocked. "East, that's —"

But East was gone.

Deacon cursed under his breath. but couldn't waste time looking for his "partner." Larissa had evidently been drugged, otherwise there was no way the cultists would have been able to manhandle her the way they were. A few tore at her dress as she went past, but a gesture by the high priest brought such behavior to a stop.

The two cultists lifted Larissa into the air and deposited her on the altar, then went back to their places among the others. The chant rose higher and the priest moved into position, raising his right hand and then bringing it slashing down at Larissa's pale white throat.

Deacon squeezed the trigger. The slug was one of Belrand's favorites: as it flew, spikes emerged from the sides and the bullet began to revolve, faster and faster. It was hell on accuracy, but the damage done was incredible.

As the cult leader found out. The slug drilled into his shoulder and ripped through muscle and bone until his right arm was hanging by little more than a few strands of cartilage. He screamed and hit the floor.

The other cultists had spotted the muzzle flash and surged forward, off the stage and in among the seats. Deacon spotted a few break off from the pack and head for the staircase to the balcony.

Deacon decided the mob needed a lesson in intimidation. He spun the chamber until his finger found the bullet he wanted, the one with the jagged rune on its shell. He aimed at the leader of the mob and fired, the lightning caged in the bullet incinerating him where he stood. That was enough to persuade the rest of the cult

121

to go for cover. A few pulled revolvers and opened up on the balcony, poking holes in the cheap plaster and chipping wood off the rail. The noise had started to revive Larissa, but she was evidently still too weak to make a break for it on her own.

The sound of men pounding up the stairs alerted Deacon to his way out. There were no more than two of them — perfect for his needs. He shot across the balcony and flattened himself against the wall beside the entrance. As the first cultist came through, Deacon tripped him up, sending him flying against the far rail. Then the detective whirled and fired into the dark stairway, sending his other foe up in a burst of bright red flame.

Deacon turned to find cultist number one up on his knees, trying to shake off the stars he was seeing. A bullet punched a hole in the railing and just missed his head. Deacon dove on top of the man and wrapped an arm around his throat. He stuck the barrel of the gun against the cultists' temple.

"Nice and easy," Deacon whispered harshly. "And let's hope you owe money to somebody down there, or they might just blow your brains out to get to me."

Deacon hauled the man to his feet and thrust him toward the front of the balcony. The cultists stopped firing.

"Put the guns down. Now!" Deacon shouted. Reluctantly, the cultists complied, never taking their eyes off him or his hostage. "My friend, here, and I are going to take a little walk down there. Behave yourselves, and maybe you won't have to clean him off the walls."

The cultist started struggling when they reached the pile of ash that a few minutes before had been a man. Deacon tightened his grip, saying, "They only have to *think* you're still alive for this to work, pal."

The trip down the two flights of stairs took an eternity. Deacon could feel the man sweating through his robe. He was gambling that these men were playing at being a blood cult, all but their high priest, anyway; if they weren't, neither he nor Larissa would be walking out of here in one piece.

How the hell did she end up here? Deacon asked himself. *And*

*why didn't East tell me? He had to have known. Did he lead me
here so I would save her?*

They reached the last landing. The stage was clear except for
the altar bearing Larissa. The high priest had crawled off, leaving
a trail of pale blood behind him. The cultists were still standing
amongst the rows of seats, a captive audience for a different kind
of entertainment.

Deacon brought his prisoner into the wings. "We're going to
make a trade," he shouted toward the men. "Your friend for the
girl."

"No!" one of the cultists bellowed in reply. "We need her for
the sacrifice!"

Deacon smiled and took the gun from his hostage's temple,
levelling it at the speaker. "I think we've had enough death for
one night. But if you want a sacrifice, I'll be happy to oblige."

No reply came from the cultists. The one in Deacon's grip had
begun to cry.

"I want one of you up here," the detective continued. "Get the
girl on her feet and bring her over to me."

After a few moments, one of the cultists got the nerve up to step
on to the stage. His eyes on Deacon, he went over to the altar and
helped Larissa off of it. She seemed more steady than she had
been when brought in and there was recognition in her eyes at the
sight of Deacon.

The cultist started to guide her toward the wings, but she shook
him off, walking slowly toward where the detective waited.
When she was within two paces, Deacon shoved his hostage
forward and grabbed her arm, pulling her to him.

The freeing of their member seemed to give the other cultists
courage. They charged for the stage, guns drawn, as Deacon
pushed Larissa toward the door to the alley. He shot down one of
the mob, but there were too many, moving too fast. He needed
something to buy them time.

His left hand went into his coat pocket and pulled out the knife
Belrand had sold him. With a flick of the wrist, he sent it flying
through the air, burying itself in the floor of the stage just in front

of one of the cultists.

With a wicked grin, the robed man stooped down and yanked the dagger free. He had only a split second to regret his action, as the enchantment in the blade caused the floorboards to crumble to dust beneath his feet. A half dozen of the cultists plunged to the stone floor of the basement below, while those still in the aisles found themselves cut off from the fleeing Deacon and Larissa.

She was waiting in the alley. "We've got a few minutes, at most," Deacon said quickly. "Once they get through the front entrance, they'll be all over us. Can you run?"

"I'll be all right," Larissa answered, still trying to shake off the daze she had been in. "Let's go."

A glance toward the street revealed that East's car was gone. *We may have to discuss just what "virtual" immortality really means, East,* Deacon said to himself.

The sound of wood splintering signalled that the cultists had made it through the front door. Deacon took Larissa's hand and the two took off down the alleyway, hoping to lose their pursuers in the maze.

The next few minutes were a kaleidoscope of darkness, sound, sweat and pain. There was no way of knowing where they were, or even if they had doubled back on themselves and were heading back toward the theatre. The shouts of the cultists were enough to let them know they were still the hunted.

Deacon glanced behind him at Larissa. Too weak to transform, she was doing her best to keep up. But she wouldn't last long, he could see that. And when she fell, he would have to decide whether to make a stand with her, or keep running.

Suddenly, the cries of their pursuers stopped dead. Somehow, the silence that followed was worse. Deacon paused in a futile effort to get his bearings and catch his breath.

"Why are we stopping?" Larissa asked. "We have to keep going."

"It doesn't sound like they're back there anymore," he answered. "Maybe they gave up."

"No," she said, in what sounded like a cry of pain. "Can't you feel it? We're still being followed. But now it's something else …"

Deacon scanned the rooftops. His eyes had adjusted to the darkness now, but there was nothing to see.

"What? What do you think is out there?"

"The shadows," she replied, moving through the alley like a caged animal. "The shadows are watching us, Deacon. We have to keep moving."

"All right," he agreed, wondering briefly if the experience with the cult had broken her. "Any ideas?"

"This way," she said, taking the lead. He kept as close behind as he could, straining to filter out the sound of his own breathing and hear any telltale sounds of pursuit. But there was nothing to be heard.

Larissa's stride began to falter. At one point, she stumbled, reaching out to an alley wall to catch herself.

"We've got to find someplace to hide," Deacon said, putting an arm around her shoulders to support her. "If we make it to daybreak, we'll be all right."

"That's a long time from now," she answered wearily. "But you're right. We won't escape them this way."

Salvation proved to be an abandoned tenement, a stone and mortar affair that stood four stories high. Deacon tore loose one of the boards that barred entrance through the back and climbed inside, then helped Larissa through. It was damp and empty, the floors covered in who knew how many years' worth of accumulated dust. But right then it felt to Deacon like a mighty fortress against an unseen enemy.

"The basement?" Larissa suggested.

"No. Ground floor. If they tumble on to us, there's no way out of the cellar." He paused, then added, "For me, anyway."

"Then I'll stay here with you."

"Concerned for my health again, sister?" Deacon asked, grinning sardonically.

"If you're here alone and are discovered, you might not have time to shout a warning," she replied.

Deacon took a good look at her. She was paler than usual,

listless, weak and the detective had an uncomfortable feeling he knew why.

"So how did a nice girl like you end up with a crowd like that?" he asked, sitting down on the floor beside one of the windows. He could see the empty street outside through a slit in one of the boards.

"Even a vampire can be taken, if you know the right ways to do it," she said, sounding embarrassed at the thought of her capture. "They might have trailed Narses back after his attempt to kill you. That's the most likely explanation. If you hadn't found me —"

"I didn't just happen along," he interjected. "East brought me there."

"East …?" Larissa repeated. She paused in thought for a moment, then shook her head angrily. "Damn it, I can't focus! If East knew there were Chaotics there, why didn't he say something before this? Am I the only one who knows this isn't some game we're playing?"

"No, you're not," Deacon answered grimly. The barely contained rage in her voice had confirmed his suspicions. "How long has it been, Larissa?"

She gave him a look of pure hatred, but when she spoke, her fury had subsided. Her tone was one of resignation. "Almost two days. That's how long they'd held me. Their priest finally said the sacrifice would have to be now, if the cult didn't want to offer a rotting corpse to its gods."

"Will you make it?"

She gave him a knowing smile. "You're afraid, aren't you, Mr. Deacon? Afraid you'll fall asleep and awaken to find me drinking from your veins." The smile faded as swiftly as it had appeared. "And maybe you should be. I've seen … others on the third day. It's painful and hellish. It's easy to lose control under those circumstances. All in all, a very bad way to die."

"There aren't too many good ways, lady," he answered.

Neither spoke for a long time. Deacon saw her flinch and grab her side — *just like any other addict,* he thought. *Withdrawal is setting in.*

"There are probably rats in the basement," he offered uncomfortably.

It took her a moment to comprehend what he meant. Then she shook her head. "No, I'm afraid not. It has to be Human blood, Deacon. I can't digest anything but that. My own personal curse."

She looked at him from across the room and for a moment there was tenderness in her eyes. "It seems a strange thing to thank someone for, but I appreciate your making the suggestion. Don't worry. Chaotics have notoriously short attention spans; they'll probably be gone in a few hours. Then we can leave and I can ..." Her voice trailed off.

"Do what you have to do," Deacon finished for her.

❦

Deacon tried to concentrate on the street for the next hour, rather than watch a beautiful woman die by inches. He knew there was something he could do to ease her pain, but it was an option he refused to consider. *She chose the life she leads,* he told himself. *This is part of it.*

Still, he turned when he heard her stirring. She rose unsteadily and glanced out one of the windows. There were still a couple of hours before dawn. She was far from her best, but she knew things would get no better from here. If she was going to try and slip away, it would have to be now.

Before Deacon's eyes, Larissa transformed from flesh to mist, albeit slowly. The cloud hung in the air for a few moments as she struggled to maintain her concentration. Then it vanished through a gap in the windowsill and out through the night.

A minute passed. Two. Deacon waited in the uncomfortable silence, suddenly aware that he was holding his breath.

Then there was a flash from outside, as if winter lightning had struck close by. The next moment, Larissa's body came flying through wood and glass as if she were a toy tossed away by a bored child. She struck the wall with a sickening thud and slid to the floor, bruised and bleeding ichor.

Deacon was at her side immediately, cradling her head in his hands. Parts of her gown had been burned away and the flesh beneath seared. As consciousness returned, a moan of pain slipped from her lips. Her eyes fluttered open and then went wide with what could only be fear.

"What is it? What happened?" Deacon demanded.

"Pure energy," she said, in a voice as quiet as the grave. "There's an arcane barrier all around the building. I tried to get through but ... it's too strong. It forced me back into Human form, and — "

"Spell it out, Larissa," Deacon cut in. "What's this mean?"

Larissa shut her eyes, as if for the final time.

"It means we're trapped, Deacon. It means it's all over."

Chapter
Fourteen

When the sun's rays began to steal their way between the rundown buildings that surrounded their prison, Deacon carried Larissa to the basement and left her to rest. She hadn't spoken again after her grim prophecy, simply staring up at the cracked ceiling. He had never thought of an Undead as being able to experience hope, but the loss of it had affected her as it would a Human.

Back upstairs, he glanced through the ruined window. There was no sign of any shield or barrier outside, but something had stopped her escape. He pulled up a rotted floorboard and broke it in two, tossing one half out the window. Nothing acted to impede the stick's progress, but what fell to the ground on the far side of the alley was nothing more than ashes.

Over the next few hours, Deacon tried various experiments, all the while remembering what it was he hated about sorcery. Apparently, sound could not carry through the spell that surrounded the building, and either it warped the sight of passersby or Galitia's citizens were even more indifferent to others than Deacon suspected.

Frustrated, he began to pace. The amount of power required to maintain a spell like this was tremendous, that much he knew. Was it possible that something in the building was feeding the rite? But that would mean someone had known they would go to ground here, maybe even had encouraged them to do so. It seemed farfetched, but worth checking out.

The rest of the afternoon was spent inspecting the tenement from top to bottom, searching for some sort of talisman that could be acting as a focus for the barrier spell. Deacon searched through every closet and in every corner, even punching holes in the ceiling and looking in the crawlspaces.

When it was all over, he had discovered rats and insects, both living and dead, mold, dung and lots of dust. But nothing that looked out of place — save for himself and the woman in the cellar.

Thought of Larissa reminded him that dusk had arrived. She would be waking soon. And as much as a part of him didn't want to be there to greet her, he knew he had to be.

He returned to the first floor to find her already risen. She looked like hell — dark circles surrounded her eyes and her features mirrored the pain that racked her frame. It was the third day without blood and her system was beginning to devour itself.

She did not so much lower herself to the ground as sink to it. She never lifted her eyes from the floor as he approached. When he bent down and touched her shoulder, she started violently and bared her fangs.

For a second, Deacon thought she was going to attack. But she fought a war with herself and won, forcing her muscles to relax and the hungry gleam from her eyes.

"You … should be more careful," she muttered, her voice hoarse.

"How are you feeling?" he asked, then mentally kicked himself for such a stupid question.

She smiled weakly. "Like someone who should have died a long time ago, Deacon. Don't let anyone fool you with the myth of 'glamorous vampiric immortality.' Our lives are spent wondering where next we'll feed … and after we've fed, we begin wondering where the next repast will come from. After a while, you find there's little time for anything that does not lead to precious blood."

"Sounds like the *vahis* addicts. Always looking for more money for their fumes."

"No! It's nothing like that!" she snapped angrily. "The blood is nothing, Deacon. It's *living* we grow addicted to! There is no cure for this condition save death, don't you understand? I never asked to become like this, but I have never been strong enough to choose nonexistence. It's ironic that the most powerful and longest-lived vampires may be those with the weakest characters."

Larissa doubled over as pain shot through her. Without blood, the nervous system of the vampire rebels, punishing its host until it get what it needs. When the seizure had passed, she looked at Deacon again, tears now running down her face.

He reached out and brushed them away, all the while thinking of the beautiful, innocent young woman whose body lay in a darkened room somewhere beyond this life. Did that part of her know what was going on here?

"You should save your energy," he said, gently. "You'll need it when we get out of here."

"Don't patronize me, Deacon. I've come to know you too well — if there were a way out, you would have found it by now. I didn't choose you at random, you know."

"Here I thought I'd just had a bad day," Deacon said. He took off his coat, wadded it up, and placed it on the floor. "You can rest your head on this."

Larissa nodded and stretched herself out on the floor. "I wouldn't have brought you into this if I'd had a choice, Deacon. But my people couldn't protect me — too many of them had been tagged by the enemy. They knew the other side was too close. I would have to be on my own."

A shudder of pain ran the length of her body. He laid a hand on her forehead, expecting it to be ice cold. Instead, her flesh was burning hot to the touch.

"You didn't make a great choice in bodyguards, kid. I'm no good against stuff like this," he said, gesturing toward the window and the invisible barrier that lay beyond.

131

Greg Farshtey

"But that's why I wanted you, Deacon," she said, struggling to sit up again. "Think of sorcerous ability as a source of light. The better you are at magic, the more light you give off, and the easier it is for you to be seen. Now that the battle has been joined here again, anyone truly adept at sorcery will be recruited by one of the factions. And if they can't recruit him, they might just kill him to keep him away from the enemy."

"So where do I figure into this? I don't know enough magic to light a match. I'm no good at it, never have been."

"Exactly," she agreed. Her skin was beginning to glow the way a brain fever patient's did just before the end. He tried to get her to lay back down, but she shrugged him off with surprising violence.

"Your lack of magical skill makes you almost invisible to those of us who can sense the expenditure of sorcerous energies. That's why I had Gresh following you, and they had their people doing the same. If someone isn't physically watching you, we don't know where you are. You can't be tagged — that's what made you so valuable to me."

It made sense. Deacon had never realized failing miserably as a mage would be such an asset. "What do you mean, 'tagged?' They have some way of finding you?"

"Magic is an energy source that's manipulated by a person's will. That means that if six people cast the same spell, there will be subtle differences in the way the energy is expended. The more powerful the rite, the more obvious the differences. And there are those among us who can sense those patterns and trace down spellcasters using them."

She rose to her feet and began to pace the room, running, Deacon expected, on whatever passed for adrenaline in her kind. "That was why we had to fake Narses' death. With him 'gone,' they would stop looking for his pattern. He could move more freely."

"And you didn't care that some poor slob was going to die in his place?" Deacon said hotly.

Larissa shook her head. "No. No, I didn't. I've told you, this

 132

is a war. There may not be armies meeting in open fields with banners flying, like nine centuries ago, but it's a war nonetheless. And innocents die in wars."

"Then maybe the war isn't worth winning."

She shrugged and began to say something, but a wave of pain cut her off. It was a moment before the words came out. "Those choices were made a long time ago. There's more at stake here than one city or one planet. I don't expect you to understand."

"Try me."

Larissa leaned against the cold stone of the wall. Her wan appearance and tattered dress made her look like a streetsinger who had fallen on bad times. But the story she had to tell was far more serious than anything that had been spun from a singer's imagination.

"Order and Chaos have been fighting since the first living being recognized them as concepts. As I've told you, neither side has ever won a complete victory, and so life for most people consists of elements of both. But if we stop fighting — if we let the Chaotics win — millions would be wading in blood, just waiting to be cut down in turn. We have to keep them from victory."

Deacon frowned. "If I know anything about war, right about now someone on their side is saying the same things about you and yours. Order without Chaos might not be so great, either."

"It's preferable to the alternative," she said, in a tone that did not invite argument. "And this debate is pointless. We all do what we are destined to do. The nature of the struggle can't be changed anymore than … I can go back to being Human."

She walked to the broken window and stared sadly out at the night. After a moment, he went to join her, and they stood in silence for some time. He could see her shivering from the night wind, which somehow was able to pass through the sorcery that imprisoned them. He put an arm around her shoulders.

"Sometimes I miss the sunlight," she said softly. "When I was a child, I was afraid of the dark. So much seemed to change when the sun went down — the familiar wasn't, anymore. But I've been living only by night for so many years now … you learn to adjust."

"Do you?" he asked. She turned to look into his eyes.

"No, Deacon, you don't. Not really. You never get used to the fact that you will never truly love a man; never bear children; never grow old and die peacefully beside another. And the only thing that keeps you sane is that you're too busy trying to stay alive to think about it."

He wasn't thinking now, as he put his arms around her and kissed those lips that had tasted so much blood. She clung to him like a drowning woman would a rope, as if his touch could make her Human again.

Then, abruptly, she pushed him away. "No. You mustn't, Deacon. I'm not like you anymore. I only know one way to … all I could hear was your heart beating. All I could think of was the rich, warm blood in your veins."

She walked away and stood with her back to him. "This is wrong. I should never have involved you."

"But I am involved," Deacon said.

"No, Jack. It isn't you they want." She turned to face him. "They knew I was weak from blood starvation. Another day or two, at most, and I would be dead. And if I claimed you, well, they would find another way. But they haven't the power to maintain this spell for too long. Trust in me; if I'm gone, they will let you go."

"What are you saying?" he demanded, though he knew full well the answer.

"I'm going to die, Deacon, slowly and painfully. I'm afraid of death, that's why I still am what I am. And that is why I want to ask a favor of you.

"I want you to kill me."

It wasn't what he'd expected to hear. Once again, she had taken him by surprise and he didn't know what to answer.

"I won't fight you," she continued. "You can use a piece of wood from the window. I would prefer it through the heart, but it doesn't matter, as long as the task is done."

"I don't want to do this," he said quietly, staring at the beautiful woman — yes, she was still a woman, even though long dead, he admitted to himself.

"You would have my gratitude," Larissa said, not meeting his eyes. "The alternative is much more painful. I would prefer to avoid that."

Deacon walked over to her and lifted her head. "There is … there is another option, and we both know it, Larissa."

"I won't ask that of you," she said firmly. "Please, do what I ask. It hurts so badly. I don't know how much longer I can —"

"I'm not being noble, Larissa. Hell, I don't know how. I hate what you are and I don't want to become anything like it. But if you can take what you need without killing me …"

"I can't promise you that, don't you understand? A long time ago, a man told me he would only drink enough to survive. When he was done, I had lost a part of myself I would never be able to reclaim. I've been three days without blood, Deacon — if I pierce your throat, the chances are great that I will murder you."

Deacon nodded. "I know that. But I don't think you will."

"I don't want your blood on my hands."

"And I won't have yours on mine, Larissa. It's my choice to make."

"Deacon —"

He silenced her with a kiss, warm and tender. "You hired me to keep you alive," he whispered. "Let me do my job."

They kissed again, as he undid the laces of her gown and let it fall at her feet. She began to moan softly as he ran his hands along her body, and he could feel her nails digging into his back. Her mouth found his again, kissing him hungrily even as he lowered her to the floor.

She broke away only long enough to look deeply into his eyes and ask, "Are you certain?"

"I've never been less certain of anything, Larissa," he answered. "But it's the only thing I can do."

For the next hour, they explored each other's bodies. He knew she couldn't take pleasure in the same ways as a Human woman, but she still responded to his touch. For her part, Larissa kept a tight rein on herself, surrendering only her passion to feel and experience. For the sake of her own conscience, she needed this to be about more than her bloody appetites.

Finally, she could restrain herself no longer. She kissed his throat and clasped him tightly to her, then plunged her fangs into his jugular vein. The warm, salty taste of blood was sweeter than any nectar to her, and she drank deep.

At first, he felt only the pain, like white-hot needles jabbed into his throat. Then he became lightheaded as the blood flowed freely from the wound. He could feel her tongue brushing against his neck as she drank the lifegiving fluid.

He understood now what she had meant. Dizzy and weakened, he would not be able to push her away if she went beyond what she needed to survive. All he could do was trust in her.

Larissa had lost track of time and how much blood she had consumed. But a voice inside her warned that it was time to stop, that she was dangerously close to ending his life. A part of her rejected the voice, revelling in the renewed strength the blood was giving her.

And then she remembered whose body was pressed against hers, whose hands had caressed her. Somehow, she found the strength to push herself away from him while his humanity was still safe.

She wiped her mouth on her white gown, then used it to dab at the wounds she had made. The blood was already coagulating; he would be weak for a while, but would survive. Smiling, she bent low and kissed him on the lips.

His eyes opened. Immediately, he felt the pain of the wounds. When he tried to sit up, the world began to spin.

"Rest easy," Larissa said, running a hand along his face. "It will take some time for you to get your strength back."

"Did you —?" he began.

"Yes, Jack. You are still among the living."

"I guess I must be. I can't believe I could feel this lousy and be dead," Deacon answered, struggling to get his vision clear.

Her expression turned serious. "There's no way I can thank you, Deacon. I know all too well what you risked for me."

Deacon reached out and took her hand. Her flesh was cool again, a sign that her strength had returned. He pulled her down on top of him, saying, "We'll think of something, Larissa."

❧

They would spend another day in the tenement, but by the following night, the barrier had evaporated. Her dress ruined, Larissa donned Deacon's trenchcoat for their trip into the night.

"Hopefully, our pursuers will be a while restoring their energies," she said as they made for a main avenue and the relative safety of the evening crowds.

Deacon hailed a cab. "Somehow, I don't think Whisper's going to be very happy with me, though. I'm going to have to stop at Belrand's tomorrow and see if he's put anything together for me."

After they were on their way to his office, Larissa turned to him and asked, "Who are you talking about? Who is this Whisper?"

Sticking to the high points, Deacon told her about his visitor of a few nights' past, the one who had warned him off the case. Larissa's expression grew more and more grim as he sketched the details.

"You should have told me about this before," she said finally. "This changes a great many things."

"Like what?"

"There's no time to explain. Devils take me, why didn't I see it before?" she exclaimed. Leaning forward, she ordered the driver to pull over. "May I borrow your coat for a while? I'll have someone return it."

"Where are you going?" he demanded, trying to bar her exit. But her strength far exceeded his at the best of times, and this was not that.

"Deacon, you helped me find something tonight I thought was long gone from the life I lead. I owe you a great deal for what you did and for the trust you showed in me. But what I have to do now

137

has to be done alone."

"And that's it?" he said angrily. "'Thanks for everything, see you around'?"

She laid a hand on top of his. "I will see you as soon as I can. I may be worrying over nothing." She kissed him gently on the lips. "I love you, Deacon."

Then she was gone.

Deacon sat in silence for a long time before the driver's voice broke in. "Where do you want to go, pal? The kind of spells I've got in this baby don't grow on trees, you know."

"Yeah, I know," Deacon said, rubbing the wound on his throat, which had begun to ache again. "The hell with the office. Take me home."

❦

Deacon's thoughts were tangled all the way back to his apartment. Why should he care where Larissa was going, what she was going to do? His part in all this was over, wasn't it?

What is it? Ego? he wondered as he fumbled with the doorseals. *I gave her a tumble ... well, sort of ... and she cuts and runs on me. So what? There are plenty of other women. Some of them even breathe.*

He pushed the door open and stepped inside. His welcome was an iron pipe crashing down on the back of his skull, an explosion of light and color, and an instant's worth of incredible pain.

Then nothing but darkness.

Chapter
Fifteen

Thom Banff pounded his meaty fist against the door and waited for an answer that wasn't coming. The elderswrath in his pocket, the one with Jack Deacon's name scrawled on top, felt like a lead weight. He was trying hard not to think about what he had to do tonight. He was concentrating instead on the stiff drink he would have when it was over.

Behind him stood two Hugors — Human/Ogre breeds — in ill-fitting sentinel uniforms. They were both showing off their bad teeth in what were supposed to be smiles and chuckling at nothing. If Deacon tried to run, they had orders to each take one leg and make a wish.

Banff really hated working with Hugors. They all traveled in pairs, staying with their identical twin for life. Some figured their relationship might be symbiotic — one drawing energy from the other — because when you got them apart, their jaws turned to glass. But in the same room, they could lay out a *queskworm* in heat.

This particular pair were a little more Ogre than Human, evidenced by the greenish cast to their skin, the incredibly foul breath, and the coarse, black hair that covered their bodies. They were both well over two meters tall and masses of muscle. And they made Banff damn nervous.

He tried knocking one more time. Another pair of "Hugos," as they were called, were posted in the alley behind the building, just in case Deacon tried to *skesh*. But there had been no sounds at all from inside, let alone that of a window opening.

"All right. Break it down," Banff said wearily.

One of the Hugos snorted with satisfaction and splintered the wooden door with one punch. Surprisingly, there was no flare of eldritch energies in response — Deacon had locked the door from the inside, but not activated the doorseals?

The apartment was a mess. Furniture turned over, empty ale bottles all over the floor, and Deacon stretched out on the rug. Banff directed the Hugos to check out the other rooms while he looked at Deacon.

The detective was unconscious. His clothes and breath stank of strong ale. There was a lump on the back of his head the size of a conjurer's stone. Banff rolled him over and shook him awake.

The Hugos came back, shrugging their massive shoulders. Banff wasn't surprised — the two of them together had the awareness of the average slab of rock. They helped him get Deacon into a chair.

The detective looked at Banff through bleary eyes and rubbed the bruise on his head. "Hi, Thom," he said. "How'd you know I needed a fourth for bridge?" His eyes strayed to the two Hugos. "And a second. And a third."

"What happened, Jack?" Banff took out his scribepad. Every word Deacon spoke from now on would appear on the paper, complete with punctuation and notes on his body language.

"Had yourself a party?" Banff asked.

Deacon winced as his fingers massaged the lump. "If I did, nobody invited me. I walked in and somebody socked me. I've been out cold since then."

Banff nodded, but didn't look convinced. "What time was this?"

"Early. Nine, ten o'clock. What time is it now?"

"A little after four." Banff left Deacon with the Hugos and walked into the bedroom. There were more ale bottles scattered about, but his attention was drawn to something else. One of

Deacon's shirts had been wadded up and tossed into a corner. Spread out on the bed, there were obvious stains on it — not blood, but not far off, Banff guessed.

The sentinel threw open the closet. A few suits, some shirts and trousers, but one thing was missing. Banff picked up the shirt he'd found and went back into the living room.

Deacon had found a flask and was taking a drink from it. "How many did you have before you came home?" Banff asked.

The detective shook his head. "None."

"But you made up for lost time."

"I don't know where all these bottles came from," Deacon answered irritably. "Maybe my cleaning lady's a boozer." He noticed the white shirt in Banff's hands. "What's going on here, Thom? I wake up to find you and the Terror Twins wandering around my place, and now you're collecting my laundry."

"Where were you a little after midnight?" Banff asked sharply. *Damn you, Deacon,* he grumbled to himself. *Give me an answer I can work with.*

"Dreamland," Deacon replied. "Tell the muscle to quit shedding on my rug."

"Did you leave your coat there, too? I don't see it in your closet."

"I didn't wear my galoshes out either, Mom," Deacon snapped. "If you've got something to say, Thom, say it. Otherwise, get out and let me die in peace."

Banff's face colored. "Okay, smart guy. Two of my men found a woman in an alley about an hour ago. She was beaten and carved up, worse than I've ever seen. Even stranger, she was stark naked except for a trenchcoat.

"At first, they figured she was just some whore whose client got out of hand. Then one of the boys recognized what was left of her face. That's when they called me." Banff could tell from the expression on Deacon's face that he had guessed the punchline.

"It was your ex-client, Larissa Martel, Jack. She's dead."

Banff watched Deacon's features carefully. He saw shock and, more surprisingly, grief. It looked genuine, too.

"When did you last see her, Jack? And, gods and devils, for your own sake, don't lie to me."

Deacon took a long drink before he answered. "Tonight. We shared a cab." He threw the glass against the wall, smashing it into bits. It didn't make him feel any better.

"Easy," Banff said. "I know about the cab. The driver gave us a good description. He said a lot of other things, too."

One of the Hugos laughed. It was more of a grunt, really. Banff decided that the only thing he disliked more than smug sentinels was smug sentinels who could snap trees in half on a whim.

"Any idea where she went after she left you?" Banff asked.

"No. She said she had business to take care of."

"Yeah. I don't doubt it," Banff replied. "It looks more like her 'business' took care of her. Why was she wearing your coat? I thought you were through with her."

"It's a small city," Deacon answered. "We ran into each other at the theatre."

"Right," Banff said. He pulled the elderswrath from his pocket and showed it to Deacon. "I've got a warrant for your arrest, Jack. You've got a right to face a judge and an inquisitor and plead like hell for mercy. Do you understand that right?"

Deacon managed to rise. The two Hugos moved in and pinned his arms behind him. He struggled, but Hugor grips are legend.

"Get these beast boys off of me, Thom, or so help me —"

"Take it easy!" Banff said, beginning to pace angrily around the room. "Put yourself in my shoes. I've got a witness that has you arguing with her not long before she died. She was wearing your coat. And I'd lay more than one gold piece that a bloodmage will find traces of her brand of ichor on that shirt of yours."

"I was sapped two seconds after I walked in!" Deacon shouted. "The only thing I've killed tonight is time in the dark. Even you ought to be able to see this is a frame!"

"We'll finish this downtown," was all Banff said.

The two Hugos began to shove Deacon toward the door. As he passed, Banff held out a hand to stop the procession and said, "You know me, Jack. Whether you did it or you didn't, I'll do the best I can for you. Don't know that I'd blame you, knowing what she was."

Banff paused, his eyes fixing on the wound on Deacon's throat. He looked back at his friend, then, seeing him in a very different way now.

Neither man said a word all the way down to the station.

❦

The interrogation room was stark and bare, save for a long table and two chairs. There were runes inscribed in the walls that could provide a subtle push toward truth-telling, if the questioner felt the need to use them. The temperature was a little below normal, just enough to be uncomfortable.

Deacon sat at the opposite end of the table from Banff. The two Hugos had been posted outside the door. Since Deacon wasn't a spellcaster, the manacles on his hands were unenhanced iron.

The questioning had gone on for three hours already. Deacon had decided early on that there was no point in hiding anything from Banff, except for those things that fell under detective-client privilege. And so he related the events of the night before — Larissa's rescue from the cult, the siege of the tenement — over and over until it was beginning to seem like a litany.

"Then what happened?" Banff asked for what must have been the hundredth time.

"I unlocked my apartment. I walked in. Somebody sapped me. I never saw him," Deacon repeated mechanically.

"And then he left, locking the doors and windows from the inside?"

"With the crowd I've been running with, he could have turned to smoke and slipped through the crack under the door, for all I know. But apparently he decided to have a few drinks before he left."

Banff slapped the table. "Okay, Jack, now let me give it to you the way the inquisitor will give it to the judge. You and Miss Martel had an argument. Maybe she welshed on a payment. Maybe she bit you once and you wanted more, but she wasn't

143

having any. You dropped her off and went home. But once you were there, you had a few too many and decided to go out and teach her a lesson.

"You tracked her down. Maybe you knew where she was going to begin with." Banff paused, obviously uncomfortable with what he was going to say next. "You argued again. You tried to rape her, and when it was all over, you got scared. You carved her up, hoping no one would recognize her face and make the connection to you. Then you went back to your apartment."

"And hit myself on the head?" Deacon asked, incredulously.

"The inquisitor will say you had a few more bottles of ale, slipped, and hit your head. The important thing is you've got no alibi for the time of death. Undead or not, judges frown on you independents. He'll clap you in Cairngate just to set an example to the rest of your lot."

"If I killed her in a drunken rage, where's the knife?"

"In an alley somewhere, or a trash can, or maybe you paid somebody to make it disappear," Banff said. "The way I see it, the best chance you've got is self-defense. If you can prove she attacked you — or even someone else, for that matter — you were within your legal rights to destroy her. We'll have a healer examine your wound and —"

"Don't bother," Deacon said. "It was voluntary. There wasn't any violence involved." He vaguely recalled meeting one of Larissa's victims in the vision he had had after "death." But, little by little, that experience had begun to grow hazy and he could not recall the name.

"Do you think that's what it was?" the detective asked. "Somebody found out she was a vampire and put her away?"

Banff shook his head. "No. I wish it were that simple. If you ask me, all those mutilations were a cover for something. The inquisitor says sexual assault, but I'm not convinced. Although in 'Frenzy,' it's not impossible. Besides, she was carved before her spine was snapped — that means somebody strong enough to hold a vampire when she doesn't want to be held."

"That lets me out," Deacon replied dryly. "That takes brute

strength or sorcery. I'm not known for either."

"And that may be what saves you, if I can get a judge who'll listen. Meantime, we'll have to hold you. The bail's pretty high — anybody I can call for it?"

Deacon thought for a moment, but no longer. He didn't know that many people with money, so the choice wasn't a hard one. He threw out Belrand's name.

Banff rose and rapped on the door. The two Hugos came in, accompanied by a Human sentinel. Banff told the Hugos to round up Belrand and bring him down, then gave Deacon into the care of the Human.

"Take him to solitary," Banff ordered. "I don't want him in with the cult boys, understand?"

The sentinel nodded. "Understood, sir." He took Deacon's arm at the elbow and followed behind him as they left the interrogation room and headed for the cells.

Neither Deacon nor Banff noticed the crimson gleam in the sentinel's eyes as he did his duty.

❧

Well, Jack, now what?

Deacon lay on the hard bed in his narrow cell. He could hear the shouts of sentinels and inmates from all over the cell block. Banff had rounded up scores of cultists from all over the city, intending to hold them for the night and see what developed. If nothing else, the fights breaking out in the cells gave him an idea of which cults were fighting with which others this week.

If Banff was wrong about the good sense of the local judges, three stone walls and bars on the door were going to be something Deacon might have to get used to. Provided, of course, they didn't just torture him to death.

Now that's a cheerful thought. Where's Belrand with that bail money?

He wasn't going to have a lot of time on the street to find out who had killed Larissa. He closed his eyes and began to review what he knew.

Larissa was working as a sort of recruiter for people — in the loosest sense of the term — who claimed to worship Order. They'd been fighting a gang war with others, who believed in Chaos, for thousands of years. Now Galitia and the rest of the planet were going to be the site of the next battle, and she was sent out to gather the troops.

But something was wrong. The enemy was too well informed and moving too quickly. Her superiors panicked and told Larissa she was on her own, so she went out and hired Deacon to watch her back.

Nice and clean, so far. Then things got hazy. Apparently, the war had shifted back here because some third force — a wild card, from the sound of it — was looking to play spoiler. That meant there was no real way to tell from which direction any attack was coming. Larissa revived Gresh with a jewel embedded in her throat, but somebody was on to them. Black was next, after he killed Deacon.

Fortunately, I got better, the detective said to himself.

And all the while, in the background, there was East. Supposedly a silver mine of information, he didn't seem to be on any of the three sides, only his own. No matter what he did or said, he left you feeling like you'd been played.

The only face to face contact with the enemy had been a butcher's apprentice who looked to be possessed. The same sort had been prowling around Larissa's building the night she and Deacon met, when she'd been attacked by the 'shifter. The face of the foe changed, but the will behind it seemed to stay the same.

What Larissa had been up to after bringing back Black, Deacon didn't know. From what she'd said, his quitting the case threw a scare into her. She dispatched a bum disguised as Narses to smoke out the enemy, and sure enough, he did, getting killed in the process. When Deacon looked into it, the real Narses got scared and tried to run him down. Then he went into hiding. He'd made someone else nervous too: that was when Whisper paid a visit and warned him off.

Suddenly, there was East again, leading Deacon to where a

blood cult was about to sacrifice Larissa. Her story of how she ended up in their hands was fuzzy, but her weakness was real enough. The power thrown against the building they were holed up in seemed beyond what so small a cult could manage.

That made the cult one starting point. The second was Whisper, because it was mention of him that sent Larissa out on her own and right into her killer's blade.

He tried to drive away the image of her corpse as Banff had described it. Then one of the missing pieces of her murder suddenly came into view, and he struggled to visualize her body. The mutilations had been wild, brutal and the killer had cut seemingly at random, or so the sentinel had said. There was only one spot where the knifework had been precise and careful:

Her throat.

Deacon sat bolt upright on the bed. He saw in his mind's eye the golden glow playing across Gresh's face as Larissa had exhumed his buried nature, turning him back into the creature he truly was.

And suddenly, he knew what her killer had been after …

Chapter
Sixteen

Deacon dreamt of Larissa.

They were back in the tenement, she in her tattered dress, but this time all was different. They were there because they wished to be, and as she flew into his arms, he knew he would be content to stay there for the rest of his life.

Her kiss was soft and sweet and there was none of the desperate hunger he remembered. When he looked into her eyes, they were alive with love.

And then she smiled.

Deacon felt as if chains had been struck off his limbs. The signs of the Undead were gone from her. She was a living, breathing woman again.

"I'm free," she whispered. "Now we can be together, Jack. We can get away from Galitia, go someplace where they can't find us. There must be someplace where they can't find us."

She reached out to him and he went to take her hands. But his had turned misty and insubstantial and passed through her substance. Her expression hardened.

"Stop playing games," she said, anger and frustration mingling in her voice. "There isn't time. Damn it, Deacon, do you want me or not?"

This time, when he tried to embrace her, she pulled away. But the shocked look on her face said she hadn't intended to, and the shape that materialized behind her stood as mute explanation for the event. His features were hazy at first, then coalesced into the face of Banff. The sentinel was dragging Larissa away. Deacon tried to pursue, but his legs wouldn't respond.

Then Black was at his side. "She's not for you, Deacon. She's one of the dead now. She belongs to all of us."

"She asked for it," Gresh growled from behind him. "Always acting so high and mighty."

Banff and Larissa were barely discernible in the distance now. She was struggling in vain. Black and Gresh were laughing.

Then another figure appeared. Without knowing how, Deacon was certain it was Whisper. The sorcerer took three long strides toward Larissa. The next few moments moved with agonizing slowness, yet still too fast for Deacon to cry out a warning. He saw Whisper raise his hand and bring it across her throat, tearing at the soft flesh. He saw the blood fly in silhouette. Then Banff dropped her limp body to the floor.

Whisper turned. In his bloody hand, he held a gemstone. It began to pulsate and glow, rapidly growing larger until the sorcerer had to release it. Soon, it was as big as a man, then it dwarfed them all, its light blinding. Deacon found himself wondering how the building was able to contain the massive jewel.

The next instant, there was a high-pitched shriek and a bolt of energy flew from the gem to strike Gresh. The fiery blast seared through bone and tissue, reducing him to a pile of ash. Black tried to backpedal, but the jewel fired again and destroyed him as well.

Deacon waited for the end.

The jewel paused, as if it were having difficulty mustering the energy needed to burn the detective. Deacon heard a low rumble and saw a vibration pass through the gemstone. Cracks began appearing on its multiple faces. Finally, with an explosion of sound, it shook itself apart and crumbled to the ground.

Larissa stepped out of the smoke and dust, whole once again. She walked up to Deacon, tears in her eyes.

"I'm so very sorry," she said softly. "I would have liked …"

Then she faded from view.

Deacon awoke, feeling like his heart had been torn out.

❧

Banff showed up a little while later. He didn't look happy.

"Belrand won't be posting bail," he reported. "Somebody beat him almost to death last night. His place was turned upside down. Nobody in the neighborhood had the guts to summon us."

Deacon sat up on his bunk. "Will he make it?"

"Hard to tell. Only thing certain is he won't be talking for a while. Anybody know about your connection with him?"

"Other than you? Well, I was coming out of his shop when Narses tried to run me down. You know as well as I do you can't keep a secret in this burg."

"Then maybe the safest place for you is right here, Jack," Banff said. "At least until we know who's after you."

"Or who isn't," Deacon replied. "But I can't do anything to clear myself from in here, Thom."

"I'm doing what I can. The healer will be by to take a look at your wound later on. Maybe we'll get lucky — if she was sloppy about it, the edges might be ragged. We could blow that up and make it look like the results of an attack."

But Deacon wasn't listening. His mind was on the dream. "Thom, was anything found on her body? Or in it?"

"What do you mean?"

"A jewel," Deacon explained, walking over to the barred door. "She had a jewel embedded in her throat. I saw it once. You said somebody had cut her neck, and I was thinking that might have been what they were after."

Banff frowned. "There was nothing in the report about it. I'll talk to the boys that found the body. Hell, I'll run a dowser over them, if I have to. Sometimes they like to pocket trinkets. You know how it is."

"I'd appreciate it. If the jewel was taken from the body, that might explain Belrand's joint getting tumbled."

Banff nodded. "Right. Somebody figures you killed her and

took the gem, so they start turning over places you might have hidden it. One more reason for you to stay where you've got some protection."

"I've always been able to protect myself," Deacon answered, starting to pace. "As long as I'm stuck here, it might be a little harder for somebody to get at me, but they know right where to look."

Banff shrugged. "Without somebody to make bail, it don't make much difference. The inquisitor will be by in an hour or so. I'll send somebody to get you."

The sentinel moved on down the hallway, pausing only long enough to direct a guard to break up another fight in the cells. Deacon peered through the bars and saw them dragging a bloodied worshipper of Caina off to the healer's room.

If it's this bad here, what are the streets like? he asked himself. *Every death is more bottled thunder on the pile, just waiting to be set off. If things don't settle soon, we may not have a city to worry about much longer.*

❦

As Banff had promised, a sentinel showed up a little while later. "Time to take you upstairs," he said.

Deacon nodded and gave the guy a smile. He saw it was the same one who had escorted him to the cell, and it never hurt to get on the good side of a guard. "No blindfold? No last meal?"

The sentinel grinned. "Not this time," he said unlocking the cell door. When Deacon stepped out, he directed him to the left, explaining, "Banff doesn't want you going past the cells. Afraid one of the other inmates might get an idea about selling your location when they get out. So we're going the back way."

Deacon did as he was bid, but felt more than a little wary. The guys in the other cells had seen him get brought down early that morning — why hide his presence from them now?

The corridor made a sharp right turn. The cells down this way were empty, most of them in some need of repair. The sentinel had Deacon pause before a metal door whose legend read,

"Authorized Personnel Only," then began undoing the doorseals.

"The last one always sticks," he said, struggling to work a counterspell. "Budget cutbacks, you know. We ended up getting some really cheap spells for this place. You'd think they'd come up with the money for sentinel work, wouldn't you?"

"They're spending it all on fancy clothes from Dela and Gimm," Deacon said.

The sentinel laughed. "Guess so. My name's Mallory, by the way." With an audible hiss, the last doorseal dissolved and the door opened. Beyond it was a dark tunnel, the walls lined with narrow pipes. Deacon could hear water dripping from somewhere within.

"Where are we going?" he asked.

"This is an old maintenance tunnel," Mallory said. "Lets the watermages get right up close to the plumbing. The other end comes out at the far side of the building, not far from interrogation. Don't worry, Mr. Deacon. There's nothing living inside there."

"That's not what I'm worried about," Deacon muttered, stepping inside. An instant later, Mallory shut the door behind them and the tunnel was plunged into darkness.

"Just a second," Mallory said, producing a small glowstone from his pocket. Its dim illumination revealed damp walls, but left most of what lay ahead a mystery.

"I've got to tell you, Mr. Deacon, I admire what you did," the sentinel continued. "I know it couldn't have been easy. Some of the boys told me she was a real looker. But the way I see it, the world would be better off without all them bloodsuckers."

"I didn't kill her."

"Right. Of course not," Mallory said hastily. "Wouldn't want you to think I was trying to get a confession out of you or anything. Me, I hope you walk, know what I mean? Sure, I know that we're all supposed to feel sorry for them and applaud the ones that stand on bloodlines for bags of the stuff instead of sucking it out of the citizenry. But it's my tax money that's paying for all that blood! Let 'em starve, that's what I say."

Deacon kept walking. By his reckoning, they were maybe a third of the way through the tunnel. His ears were open for any sound that didn't belong, any sign that this was a trap. So far, he hadn't seen any side tunnels where ambushers could hide, but that didn't mean there weren't any.

"Why should we do anything for them? The Writs say living off the flesh and blood of another is sin. Any right-thinking person knows none of us will be safe as long as we let that sort live in the cities right along with us. You see that, don't you?"

Deacon nodded. "The way things are, I'd agree none of us are safe."

"Is that why you killed her, Deacon? Or did you just get bored with her charms?"

Mallory's voice had grown cold. Deacon heard a rustle of cloth, as if the sentinel were taking something out of a pocket. He whirled in time to see Mallory striking at him, and got his forearm up in time to block the blow.

Deacon got lucky. Mallory had pulled a blackjack, and had that struck the detective's arm, it would have shattered bone. As it was, he struck the sentinel's wrist and followed it up with a punch to the solar plexus that brought an explosion of air from Mallory's lungs.

The sentinel responded with a left to Deacon's kidneys and then swung again with the sap, barely missing. Deacon charged and grabbed Mallory around the waist, slamming him into the wall.

"You did so well against my last tool that I thought I would get one in better shape," Mallory said. But one look at the red glow in his opponent's eyes told Deacon it was not the young sentinel speaking, but something that was using his body.

And using it well. Mallory's hands clapped themselves over Deacon's ears and the detective's world became a dull roar and a jolt of pain. He let go of the sentinel, staggering, waiting for his opponent to move in for the kill.

Mallory didn't disappoint. Holding the blackjack above his head, he came at Deacon. The detective shot up like a spring that had uncoiled and slammed a fist into Mallory's jaw. The blow didn't do much more than rock him, but he dropped glowstone and sap.

With a grunt of rage, Mallory reached out and tore a water pipe free from the wall, sending a mini-geyser into the air. He swung for Deacon's head, but the detective ducked under the attack and scooped up the blackjack. Mallory was winding up to try again when Deacon smashed the sap across his face, shattering bone and teeth.

Mallory dropped, blood pouring from his mouth and mingling with the rapidly forming puddles of water on the floor. He was shaken, but still conscious. Deacon kicked the piece of pipe away from him and then took a step back.

"If you can talk through a mouth full of broken teeth, now's the time," the detective said, trying to get his breath. "This is the second time you've tried to waste me. I want to know why."

The Mallory thing sat up, coughing and spitting out pieces of dental work. "It's been a long time since I've tasted Human blood," he muttered absently. "Never liked it. And blood-drinkers always come to such bad ends."

"Answer the question," Deacon said coldly. "This thing can do a lot worse than knock some teeth out. And I'm having a bad week."

"I wasn't after you the first time," the relkazar answered in Mallory's voice. "I was after the bloodsucker. You got in the way."

"And now?"

"Now she's dead and a certain … item has gone missing. When you were picked up, my employer thought —"

"Whisper thought I killed her. That is who you're working for, isn't it? Tell him he can join the club. And if I killed her, naturally I know where the 'item' is, right?"

"Something like that."

"How'd you figure to get any answers by beating my brains in?" Deacon asked hotly.

Mallory shrugged. "I love my work."

"Well, you can go back and tell Whisper I didn't kill her, got it? And if he sends another red-eyed freak after me, I'll —"

"But you do have the gem?" Mallory said, struggling to his feet. It was more of a statement than a question.

Deacon did some fast thinking. If they thought he knew where the jewel was, he had some value to them alive. Otherwise ...

"No, I haven't got it," Deacon answered. "But I might know where I can get it. I want you guys off my back once and for all. Maybe we can make a deal."

For a guy — even one demonically possessed — who'd had his teeth broken only a few moments before, Mallory moved fast. His hand was in his vest pocket and out again with a small but nasty revolver faster than Deacon could move to stop him.

"This is my kind of deal," Mallory chuckled. "I get what I want or you get dead."

Deacon dropped the blackjack and put his hands in the air. But his manner remained calm. "You might as well put the gun away, pal. First off, you're bleeding all over it. Second, if you shoot me, I can't tell you where the jewel is. Whisper wouldn't like that very much."

"Different game, different rules than you're used to," Mallory replied. "If I kill you, Whisper knows maybe twenty guys who can bring you back. You won't be much at parties, but you'll be walking around. And you'll be just enough of a conversationalist for our purposes."

Damn it. Should've expected something like that, Deacon cursed. "So what's the plan? You walk me out of here at the business end of a gun through a building full of sentinels? Don't be a fool. You won't make it two steps toward the front door before they gun you down."

"I know another way out. Move. Whisper's waiting."

Mallory moved so that his back was to one wall to let Deacon pass. Both men were soaked from the spray in the narrow tunnel. The detective considered three or four ways he could try to get the gun away from his captor, but all of them ended with a shot going off and Mallory laughing over his corpse. He did as he was told and heard the relkazar fall into step behind him.

The tunnel went through its share of twists and turns. Deacon tried to make conversation a few times, but Mallory didn't answer. The only words he spoke came when the detective stumbled over a raised step on the tunnel floor.

"Hold it. This is our way out."

Mallory let the light of the glowstone play on the floor. The step had a sealed hatch in its center.

"Open it up," Mallory ordered.

Deacon bent over and took the handle with both hands. The hatch came open with surprising ease, to reveal another tunnel and a rusted iron ladder leading down. The smell of Human waste coming from below was overpowering.

"That ladder leads to the sewers. Even if the rest of the inmates knew it was here, there aren't many who could stand the trip," Mallory said. "Hope you've got a strong stomach, Deacon."

The detective glanced down the dark hole. All the stories he had heard as a child about the Dark Things that lived beyond the cities coming in by way of the sewers ran through his head. He looked up to see Mallory gesturing with the gun.

"Answer his questions and maybe Whisper will give you a new suit of clothes. The ones you're wearing are going to stink."

"Will he give me a new nose, too?" Deacon asked, reluctantly starting down the ladder.

Mallory began to laugh. It was an abrasive sound and Deacon was about to tell him to knock it off when someone else took care of it. The laugh became a liquid scream and a new stench joined the ones from the sewer.

Deacon saw the gun hit the tunnel floor first. Then his eyes traveled to Mallory's face, which was melting and running like candle wax. The flesh was sliding off his skull, his hands, his whole body and forming a pool at the sentinel's feet. Soon, there were no features left, just a gray skull still locked in a scream. Then bones and clothing collapsed into the puddle of melted skin and muscle.

And now the man who had been standing behind Mallory

became visible. East, now distinguished and late middle-aged, took the gun ever so gently from amidst the liquid flesh and wiped it clean with a monogrammed handkerchief. The smells of sewage and roasted Human seemed not to bother him at all.

"We do run into each other in the strangest places," was all he said.

Deacon pulled himself out of the hole, taking care not to step in what was left of Mallory. "I'll take the gun."

"What?" East asked, surprised. Then, as if only just realizing that he held the revolver, handed it over. "Oh, of course. I wouldn't know what to do with it, anyway."

"I won't bother asking what you're doing here. You'd only start dancing around the question again."

"And I dance rather well, don't I? Actually, I came to pay you a visit and found you in the company of one of the more odious Chaotics. That was a nice bit with the blackjack, Deacon, but I hope you've learned a lesson about banking on your enemies keeping you alive because they might need you. It's a maxim of the netherworld that most people are far more cooperative after they've been dead a while."

East balled up his handkerchief and dropped it on the floor. He then took another out of his coat and mopped his brow. "You had best be on your way. It's no longer safe for you here, if it ever was. Next time, they won't send an entity to do a demon's job. Not to mention what the sentinels will do when they find 'one of their own' melted to slag."

"I could always give them you," Deacon said, now aiming the pistol in East's direction.

East snorted in derision. "Gun or no gun, you don't have me to give. Whatever you may think of my lifestyle, I am your only ally right now. Those who matter in Galitia think you have the gem of restoration or know where it is, and they won't stop until it's theirs."

"Meaning they'll beat a path to my door," Deacon said grimly. "And what about you? Don't you think I killed her?"

East shook his head. "I know you didn't. Larissa was the one who introduced you to all this, and even with the performance I put on for you the other night, it was her allure that brought you back into it. Killing her would have been the smart thing to do. And I don't credit you with that much sense, Deacon.

"Go down into the sewers and get away from here. Find someplace to hide. Don't worry, it's no deeper than the darkness you've still to walk through. Stay away from your home and your office. They'll be watching. And if you want to live the rest of your life as something other than a hunted animal, find that gem."

"And her killer with it," Deacon said, more to himself than to East. He slipped the revolver in his pocket and started down the ladder into the depths.

"My last bit of advice to you," East called."Treat this like any other murder: start with her friends."

Then the hatch closed above him and Deacon was alone in the pit.

Chapter
Seventeen

There's an old saying among those who make their living on their backs, or "on the game," as they prefer to refer to it: "Never sleep with anyone who has more troubles than you do."

So when Tara Hemsath opened her door to find Jack Deacon, soaked and stinking of raw sewage, her first instinct was to slam it in his face. Bad enough she had squandered the money he had given her on a few really good bottles, but now he was back, bringing Akar knew what kind of a mess with him. She was still half-convinced that he was some new sort of sentinel, and *that* kind of trouble she didn't need.

She had just about decided to tell him to get lost when she made the mistake of looking into his eyes. Unlike most of the men she met, there was no pleading there, no self-pity, no desperation. Instead, there was an understanding that she had no reason to let him in and would probably be better off if she didn't.

Tara's friends had always told her she was her own worst enemy. She stayed true to form and brought Deacon inside, already thinking about how she would get the smell out of the carpet.

"Had a bad day?" she asked, looking him over. "Or are you selling perfume door-to-door now? You better find a new line, Jack."

"I went for a swim," he answered, leaning against the wall and shutting his eyes. If he wasn't completely exhausted, he was at least in the neighborhood. "It's a long story."

Tara took a step back and crossed her arms over her ample chest. "Uh-huh. It usually is. As much as I'd like to hear the whole, sad song, it's going to have to wait until we can breathe again. Get those clothes off and take a bath. I'll take them out and burn them."

"I don't think anything of yours will fit me," Deacon answered, waking up just enough to renew his appreciation of her figure.

"I don't know," she chuckled. "I have some garters and stockings that would go great with your eyes. But I've got some money scattered around, too, Jack; I'll buy you something to wear."

"I'll pay you back."

"Damn right you will," she said, pulling on her coat. "You're going to pay for the fumigation spell I'm going to have to get cast on this place, too. When I get back, you can tell me your story. Make it good, Jack."

"It's still missing an ending," he said, heading for the bathroom.

"Those are the best kind."

❦

Tara returned an hour later with a plain brown suit and an assurance from the pawnbroker that there was nothing living in it. She insisted that he come out of the bathroom and get it until he growled at her to stop playing games and give him the gods-be-damned suit.

She did as she was told and pouted for a few minutes before finally sneaking up and throwing the bathroom door open. He was standing there, fully dressed, slipping a gun into his pocket. The smile faded from her face.

"Something's gone real wrong, hasn't it?" she said softly. "This isn't some two-bit sorcerer with a mad on for you, right? This is the stuff."

"As real as it gets," Deacon said. "Thanks for the clothes, Tara. But I did some thinking while you were gone. I can't stay here. I don't think I was followed, but I can't be sure."

"If you were, you could smell them from here," she replied. "If you're in it that deep, Jack, then I've already risked my neck by helping you. You're not walking out of here without giving with the whole story. Sit down and start talking. I'll go conjure some coffee."

Deacon made it short and simple, leaving out what had gone on between he and Larissa. What emerged was a not so pretty picture which, like Deacon, had turned out to be suitable for framing.

"And that's all they have on you?" Tara asked, incredulous. "You knew this piece, had a few words, and she winds up dead? Any one of a thousand Gris could have done that."

"Somebody think it's enough, or maybe they just want me off the streets. I don't know."

"So what are you going to do?"

"Everybody thinks I have this jewel. Unless I want to spend the rest of whatever proving them wrong, I'd better find it. But since my roadmap through all this died a few nights ago, my best bet is to stir things up. If I play smart, maybe I'll make somebody nervous."

"And maybe they'll make you dead!" Tara said angrily. "What if you're being too slick for your own good? What if they don't want the jewel back, Jack? What if they want it to go away, and you with it?"

"I'll cross that Undead when I come to it," Deacon said, rising. He felt better since the bath, but hadn't caught any sleep and it showed. Tara reached out and laid a restraining hand on his arm.

"Don't leave," she said. "Wherever you need to go, it can wait until dark."

Deacon thought about protesting, but fatigue made a more persuasive argument. He took off his jacket and turned around. "I seem to be spending a lot of time thanking you."

"That's okay. I'm used to it," she answered, smiling. She took his hand and led him to the bed. "I'd stay, but then you wouldn't get any rest. I'll be back by sunset."

Deacon's ego wanted to talk into her coming to bed with him. He could never be too tired for that, could he?

Yes, I can, he said to himself, collapsing on the mattress and falling sound asleep.

❦

Deacon awoke to the sensation of soft fingers kneading the muscles in his back. He rolled over to see Tara clad in a tight, silken dress sitting on the bed beside him.

"Wake up," she whispered. "Sorry I'm late back. The inn was busy today."

"What time is it?" he mumbled.

"After eight," she answered, sliding the straps of the dress off her snowy white shoulders. She bent over and gave him a long, gentle kiss. When it was over, she smiled and said, "It's nice having someone to come home to."

Deacon suddenly felt a powerful attraction to Tara, as if her words had opened the door to some part of his heart closed long ago. He pulled her down on top of him and kissed her again, letting his lips wander down her throat and across her shoulders. She made a small sound of pleasure and pulled away, then began kissing his neck.

And suddenly she was on her feet, backing away from the bed, eyes wide with fear. Deacon sat up, confused. "What's the matter?"

"Your neck! You've been bitten by an Undead!" she cried. "Gods, and I almost let you —"

Deacon got off the bed and went toward her. She grabbed his jacket and took the revolver from the pocket, shakily pointing it at him. "You stay away from me! I knew a girl who got involved with one of you. I saw what happened to her. When she wouldn't go on the bloodline, they cut her heart out!"

"Tara, I'm not a vampire. The wound wasn't fatal. You don't have anything to be afraid of," Deacon assured her. "Put the gun down."

"How do I know you're telling the truth?"

"Because if I was a vampire, I would have taken the gun away from you by now," he answered. "And that pistol's only packing lead, kid. It wouldn't stop any Undead I ever heard of."

Tara looked at the gun, then back at him. Tears had begun to spill from her eyes, running down her face and neck before disappearing into the sweet divide between her breasts. She dropped the weapon and began to sob.

"I'm sorry," Tara said. "You don't know what this life is like. I'm so scared all the time. And Linx warned me that Undead like whores because nobody cares what happens to us."

Deacon picked up the gun and put it on an end table, then took the frightened woman in his arms. "It's all right. We're all afraid. There's a lot out there to be scared of, Tara."

He gently lifted her head and wiped a fat tear away with his finger. "But you don't have to be frightened of me, kid. I don't want your blood." He kissed her willing mouth passionately while one hand found a soft breast to caress.

"Everything else, but not your blood," he said, leading her back to the bed.

❦

"When all this is over …" Tara began, when their lovemaking was through.

"What?"

"Will you take me away from here? From Galitia, I mean?"

He turned to look at her. The hard shell she wore as part of her trade was gone. Its loss made her that much more beautiful. "Most people don't like to leave the city. You're always hearing stories —"

"I don't care about that," she replied, turning over to face him. "When you find this jewel, will you have enough money for us to go somewhere?"

"Honey, right now my only client is myself, and I pay lousy," he answered. Her face clouded.

"Oh," was all she said.

"But who knows? Galitia may not be too healthy for me when this is done. There are a couple of ship masters who owe me favors. Maybe we could take our chances someplace else. But are you sure you're not afraid to go outside the walls?"

She nestled close to him and lay her head on his chest. "Dying doesn't scare me as much as living here, Jack. Understand that, and you'll understand me."

"I don't think I'll ever understand either of us, kid," was his reply.

❦

Deacon left Tara's a little after midnight. While she had slept, he had begun planning. What East said about focusing on Larissa's friends made sense, but there was one other lead he wanted to run down first. Belrand had been beaten and his place ransacked not long after Larissa's death. If his assailants had been looking for the jewel, there might be a clue left behind that would lead Deacon to them. The only game he could think to play was to set any factions against each other and hope they knocked each other off. But he couldn't do that till he knew who all the players were.

It took a good deal longer to reach the shop than Deacon had expected, largely because he had to keep to the back alleys and sidestreets all the way. It was possible that Banff would keep the escape quiet to keep the detective from becoming a moving target, but not likely. Too many other people would have to keep their mouths shut for that to work, and if it got out that he had covered for Deacon, Banff would be washed up.

No, it was a lot better bet that every sentinel in the city had seen a conjured image of Deacon and had their eyes wide open. A few knew him and might just as soon let him go rather than shoot him down. He opted to spare them the tough decision and keep out of sight.

The scene at Belrand's was pretty much what he had antici- pated. Normally, the scene of a crime is protected by spells that keep out anyone who isn't carrying the proper talisman. This lets the bloodmages and others do their work without disturbance by newscribes or morbid bystanders.

In the case of Belrand's place, though, the spells had been removed early. What this meant was that the sentinels assigned to the case had been especially efficient and had already looted the shop of anything they thought might be valuable. The rest they left for the locals to pick through.

Deacon slipped in through the back way, the route Belrand's attackers had taken. The door frame was scorched, most likely by the rite that blew away the seals that protected it. The intruders hadn't bothered with picking the standard lock — they had simply smashed the door to kindling and walked right in. The detective stepped over the splinters of wood and did the same.

Both rooms of the store, front and back, looked as if a whirlwind spell had hit them. It was impossible to tell what damage was done by the assailants and what by the sentinels. In the rear of the shop, all of the worktables had been overturned and split apart. The flute Belrand had been working on lay snapped in two in a corner, surrounded by the shattered remains of a hundred other weapons, amulets, charms and the like.

The side of the shop the public saw was in similar condition. It was here that his attackers had cornered Belrand — blood spattered on the walls was testimony to the violence of the assault.

Deacon looked around and frowned. Nothing done to him would hurt Belrand so much as seeing his precious shop like this.

Forcing himself to put the image of a broken man surrounded by broken works out of his mind, Deacon started searching. There wasn't much left that was intact and of any use, but he did find three boxes of bullets buried in the back of a cupboard behind some alchemical powders. A quick examination revealed that they were enchanted, and something more besides: they had all been used. A few still bore bloodstains. They had been dug out of their victims and resold to Belrand, probably at a substantial loss to the seller. Now the only question was whether or not Belrand had ever gotten around to replenishing the enchantments in them.

Deacon pocketed the ammunition and went back to work. It

was simple enough to reconstruct the scene. After beating Belrand almost to death, the intruders went into the back room and tore it apart in increasing frustration. Unless there was a mob of them, at least one had strength beyond Human. Oak tables that had been bolted to the floor were torn loose and thrown around like leaves in a windstorm.

He walked back to the ruined door and knelt down. There were plenty of tracks going in and out, but most of them were made by sentinels. None of the fragments of wood had caught so much as a string off of anyone's clothing. Beyond the bullets, this trip was looking like a dead end.

He was about to give up on the whole thing when his eye caught something in a corner. He had seen it before, but passed over it as another blood spot, albeit in a strange place. But now that he saw it more closely, he could see that though it was crimson, it was no bloodstain.

He reached out and touched it. It was soft and moved in the slight breeze created by his gesture. He snatched it up and and brought the fragile thing closer.

It was a rose petal.

At first, Deacon didn't make the connection. Belrand was allergic to all sorts of growing things — even children, he contended — and hated flowers with a passion.

But there was somebody with very different feelings. Somebody who loved flowers and had worked with them before Larissa had found him.

Black.

It made all too much sense. Narses would have told them about the connection between Belrand and himself, if they hadn't known already. When Larissa turned up dead and her "killer" was temporarily out of reach in jail, Black must have figured that he had left the gem with someone he trusted. So he and Gresh came to Belrand's and tried to beat the information out of him.

Deacon felt a dark, cold rage well up inside him. All of this pain and destruction, all for nothing.

He took out his revolver and emptied the lead slugs, replacing them with the ones he had found in Belrand's cabinet. He test-fired one into the floor, watching with grim satisfaction as the acid spell it contained ate a hole through the boards and into the foundation of the building.

"Start with her friends," East had said.

I'll start with them, all right, Deacon thought, slamming a bullet into the cylinder. *And I'll finish with them, too.*

Chapter
Eighteen

A dirty snow had begun to fall by the time Deacon made it to
Starkwood cemetery. A chill wind had come in from the east,
bringing with it the first taste of winter and driving all but the most
desperate bums off the streets. Even sentinel patrols had been
unusually light — *this is the kind of night you get your pay-off
from the whores,* Deacon remembered. *Sure beats booze for
keeping warm.*

If the weather was enough to chill the body, the look of
Starkwood took care of chilling the soul. Originally designed to
compete with some of the ritzier private burial grounds, it had
ended up as the dump for the poor, the unnamed, the criminals,
and a few things that refused to stay in the ground. The owners
stayed afloat by saving space, and the cemetery's reputation for
mass graves had led to a joke: if you don't like crowds, don't drop
dead near Starkwood.

One of the other coin-cutters was the lack of any kind of
security. Most kirkyards employed ex-sentinels as watchmen, or
at least invested in "flash and bang" spells. Stepping in the wrong
spot meant a sudden burst of light and more explosions than a
clumsy alchemist could provide, usually enough to startle all but
the most determined body snatchers.

But Starkwood's security was a laugh. The lock on the rusted,
wrought-iron gate wouldn't keep out an infant with a hairpin and

the stone wall could be scaled by a crippled newsie with bum lungs. If its contents were less than prime, it was still an easy mark, and everyone knew it.

That was what had brought Deacon here in the middle of the night. With Larissa out of the picture, it was a good guess that Gresh and Black were cut off from her bosses and running out of money. The quickest way to get some was for Black to go back to what he did best, especially if Gresh could be conned into doing the digging. The streetsingers weren't humming about any big hauls, so Black was probably just getting his spade out now.

Sure, Starkwood might be a long shot. Deacon had hit with enough of those to decide it was worth taking.

After glancing around to make sure there was no one on the street — fortunately, cemeteries make for quiet neighborhoods — Deacon pulled himself up over the wall. He landed softly in the overgrown grass of the graveyard. Although the snow wasn't sticking to the ground, it had turned the turf soft and Deacon could feel the mud clinging to his shoes as he walked.

Monuments and headstones in various stages of decay were scattered around the cemetery. There was no reason for anyone to care for the markers — after all, nobody had given a damn about the people they "honored." Deacon picked his way among the stones until he found a good-sized hunk of stone in the shape of an avenging angel. It seemed appropriate, so he took up position behind it, gun drawn, and waited.

Hours melted into each other as the snow tapered off and finally stopped. Every once in a while, Deacon stretched to keep his muscles from stiffening. Something about the situation — the dark, the cold, the all-pervasive silence — reminded Deacon of another night, one long ago, when he had still worn a uniform.

❧

He and Banff had been on the docks waiting for a trader to come in. Smugglers were a rare breed — the profits to be gained from the business were usually outweighed by the risks of travel. But now and then someone would chance upon a load of silks or alchemical powders and decide to pick up some quick silver by dumping it out of town. In this case, the crew of the *Leilah* had found themselves a few dozen crates of cinnabar and were planning to palm them off on the Galitian market.

Just where their boss had gotten the tip that the boat would be coming in — and almost a week ahead of schedule — Deacon had never bothered to ask. All that he knew was that he and Banff were growing roots waiting for the vessel to show up.

Deacon had taken out a flask and handed it to Banff, who took a long swig. "Think they changed their plans?"

"This bunch?" Banff replied. "More likely, they got lost in the dark. They'll be here. Remember the drill — wait for them to tie up the ship, then do your warning. If they move, drop 'em."

"What about the cargo?"

"That's not our job. We let Property handle that. And one of these days, their fingers are going to get a little too sticky and we're going to get to run them in, too."

Their conversation was interrupted by the sound of water lapping against the side of a boat. It was running without active glowstones. Most likely, there was a lightmage on board to help the pilot steer without tipping off the ship's position. It slowed as it approached the dock and Banff gestured for Deacon to get down behind some crates.

The crew was good. They steered it in without a scratch and moved quickly and quietly to secure the line. Banff peered around the crate and saw the last knot put in place, then signalled Deacon.

"Sentinels! Stay where you are!" Deacon shouted, rising to his feet. Banff followed suit, both their guns aimed squarely at the ship's master.

Deacon had spent a lot of bottles over the next few years trying to forget the images of that night. The crewmen put their hands in the air. One stepped from the boat on to the dock. The master made a sudden movement. Banff shouted something.

Then something exploded from out of the hold. Deacon never got a clear view of it — maybe it moved too fast or maybe it was just too horrible to bear looking at. Razor-sharp claws tore through the ship's master, shredding him into dozens of bloody pieces. Deacon and Banff both fired as the crew scattered, but their bullets didn't even annoy the thing. Two of the smugglers found some courage and went at it with firestaffs, but it carved them neatly in half before they were near enough to use their weapons.

The thing had freed itself from the hold now and was moving toward the dock. Deacon had slapped some sorcerous slugs into his revolver and was taking aim when Banff charged. He had a knife in his hand and Deacon shouted after him, thinking he was going to take the thing on with no more than a blade. Worse, he was blocking Deacon from getting a clear shot.

Suddenly, Banff dove, but not for the ship. Instead, he slashed at the line holding the boat to the dock, cutting it clean through. The tide carried the vessel downriver, the creature still aboard.

Deacon stepped out from behind the crates. His partner was still standing and watching the ship and its hideous stowaway drift into the darkness. "Now what?"

"Now, nothing," Banff had replied. "Either it will go back where it came from or it will make landfall someplace else. It's not our problem anymore."

Deacon holstered his weapon. "What was it?"

Banff turned on him, a look in his eyes Deacon had never seen before. "I don't know. I don't want to know. If you're smart, neither will you. This never happened."

Later, Deacon would learn that ship masters and others whose business forced them to travel from city to city occasionally found themselves making better time than they'd thought possible. There seemed no rhyme or reason for it — but creatures like the one in the *Leilah's* hold seemed to come with these "short-cuts." It was something travelers knew about, but didn't speak about in public. What money was to be made in ferrying people from city to city would dry up if it was generally known what sort of things waited outside the walls.

Deacon would spend the next few days in one bar after another, trying to forget the thing he had seen or that he had stood there while Banff had set it free to kill again. Sure, they wouldn't have been able to stop it — but he had been enough of an innocent in those days to think it was their job to die trying.

When he had sobered up enough to make the decision, he'd turned in his shield and gun. For the first few weeks afterwards, he had been shadowed by some of his old friends, just to make sure he didn't have a few too many and start babbling things that would be unhealthy for the city's coffers.

❦

Now, years later, he was walking down the same road. He could have let Larissa and her "people" be someone else's problem — Banff's, even. But he couldn't let it go — and once he had held Larissa in his arms, he couldn't let her go, either.

The image in his mind of Larissa faded, to be replaced by the face of Tara. Was it possible he had fallen for her, so soon after losing Larissa? Or was the fire he felt for her nothing more than a way of ignoring Larissa's death and what it meant?

He was saved from trying to find an answer to that one. A faint sound came from the cemetery gate, that of an iron lock torn free. Deacon crouched down behind the angel monument as the barrier swung wide. A few seconds later, he heard Black speaking in soothing tones to his horse while Gresh unlimbered shovels and spades from the back of the wagon.

"You sure you're not just looking for a meal?" Gresh muttered, slinging the tools over a skeletal shoulder.

"I've told you, my friend, I am a poor man. I managed to save only a few coins, hardly enough to keep both of us. But with you as a partner, we can make enough from the flesh mills and others with … unusual tastes to keep us comfortable for some little while."

"Yeah, well, I don't like it. If they could skrag the wolf-bitch, they can do us. And here we are, right out in the open!"

"Hardly that," Black answered, calmly. "No one walks this lonely way, Gresh. Those few restless forms who wander among the graves of an evening have more on what's left of their minds than us, I assure you. Now that seems a likely spot — freshly turned earth and only a rock for a marker. Start digging."

"What about you?" Gresh snarled.

"Someone has to keep watch, Gresh. I feel certain we were not followed. But you would not want to end up like our fair Larissa, now would you?"

Gresh's only answer was the sound of spade striking soft earth. Deacon forced himself to stay still and wait. He was close enough to them to hear Gresh breathing, but they were still two to his one. That hole the boneyard was digging would be his edge.

He waited while Gresh turned over the earth, until the first corpse had been found. He could tell the two would-be resurrectionists had gotten lucky by the overpowering smell that drifted across the graveyard. "Gently, now, gently," Black implored as his ally bent to scoop up the body. It was not as recent a death as Black had hoped, and the rotting corpse fell apart in Gresh's hands.

"Rotten!"

"You could hardly expect preservation spells at work among such damned souls," Black scolded. "We'll take what pieces are still whole for sale. It won't mean as much silver as an intact body, but better than nothing, just the same."

Deacon tensed. Gresh bent down into the hole and emerged with a forearm, the hand attached only by a thin strand of muscle. Shrugging, Gresh tore the hand free and tossed it away. Black took the proffered piece and turned to place it in the wagon.

That was when Deacon sprang from cover, reaching the open grave in one quick stride and levelling the gun at Gresh's skull. "You boys should get a hobby," he said.

Gresh stood stock-still. Deacon knew there was a good chance the boneyard could grab the gun and tear him to pieces, but there was a better chance he'd squeeze a shot off first. He was glad to see Gresh apparently shared that view.

Black turned slowly, smiling, and casually edging his hand toward the wagon seat where his cane lay. "We merely desired a change of air, Mr. Deacon."

"Move that hand again and I'll give you a change *from* air," Deacon shot back. "Move away from the wagon and get in the grave. You'll feel right at home."

Deacon took a step backward as Black approached, but the ghoul did as he was told, sliding into the pit to stand beside Gresh. It had begun to snow again.

"Give me a reason not to make that pit your new home," Deacon said coldly.

"What do you want with us?" Gresh grumbled. "We haven't done nothin' to you. You're the one killed our boss."

"Looking for a new hole in that thick head of yours?" Deacon asked. "'Cause I'm dying to give you one."

"Yeah, you're real tough with that gun in your hand. Let's see you —"

"Be quiet," Black commanded. Gresh fell silent, more out of surprise than anything else. "If you're going to kill us, Deacon, I commend your choice of location. But do get on with it."

"There's not much I'd like better. But I want some answers first, Black: why'd you hit Belrand's place?"

The ghoul shrugged. "There's little point in lying to you, I see. Very well, we thought the gem might be there, Larissa's gem. I thought perhaps some interested party would want to buy it once it was found."

"You were wasting your time. Belrand doesn't have it."

"Because you do?"

"Maybe I know where it is," Deacon answered. "But it's too hot for me to handle. I don't know who to deal it to."

"Perhaps we could enter into an … arrangement, then," Black said, greed and something else, something Deacon couldn't identify, dancing in his eyes. "We could act as your agents in this matter."

"You're going to deal with this sunnuva —"

Deacon fired. The bullet struck Gresh in the shoulder, actually chipping the bone. He bellowed in pain and rage.

"Somebody's got to teach you some manners. Yeah, Black, I might be interested in making a trade. But first I want whoever killed Larissa."

Black looked nonplussed. "Surely, you did? Else, how did you get the gem?"

"Let's say I have my sources. I need a name, someplace to start."

"There was someone Larissa had mentioned a time or two. I believe it was Gadsden … yes, Erl Gadsden. He lived in Canons, and she spoke of him as if he were her superior. Perhaps he could be of more help to you. How soon can you produce the gem?"

"It may take a while. Your lead may go nowhere. But there is another possibility."

Deacon looked at Gresh, still nursing his wound, then back at Black. There was a partnership that could stand splitting. "The sentinels don't care about the gem, but they do care about the murder. If we can give them someone, anyone, they'll back off. Then you can sell the gem in peace and we split the profit."

Black evidently liked the sound of that plan. "You have someone in mind, I take it?"

Deacon nodded, a predator's smile on his lips. "We give them Gresh. He's perfect for the role, and grotesque enough that the newscribes will have copy for months. And then we only have to divide the gold two ways instead of three."

Even in pain, Gresh was aware enough to know he didn't like the direction this conversation was taking. He glanced at Black, saw his partner was giving the matter some serious thought, and charged at him.

"You lousy —"

Deacon took a shot and missed — on purpose. Black might normally have been able to elude Gresh's blows, but in the narrow confines of a grave, it wasn't so easy. Deacon waited until Gresh had drawn some blood from the ghoul before winging him with a second shot.

"Maybe this wasn't such a great idea," Deacon said. "Gresh isn't going to walk in there. Dead, he's of no use. I know Banff — he's going to want a live suspect he can grill over a slow flame. No, we'll just have to be patient while I check out this Gadsden."

Black shrugged, all the while glaring at Gresh. The skeleton was staring back and Deacon felt he had done a good night's work. Black wouldn't forget the pain of his wounds, and Gresh wouldn't forget that his partner was all set to hand him over to the sentinels. It would be a while before either one slept easy around the other — *if they do sleep,* Deacon added.

"All right, you two, get going. And next time you get hungry, Black, remember that this joint isn't take-out."

Black's expression was unreadable. Gresh, missing two fragments of bone lost to Deacon's ensorcelled bullets, hauled himself painfully out of the grave. The only thing left to do would be to trail them home, so he could find them when he wanted them.

A sudden explosion changed Deacon's plans. One of the grave markers nearby went off like a bomb, sending chunks of stone through the air like cannon shot. One piece clipped Deacon in the knee and he hit the ground, somehow managing to hold on to his gun.

Black and Gresh made for the gate, but the two monuments nearest there chose that moment to explode, driving them back into the graveyard. It reminded Deacon of nothing so much as the raid on a cut-rate alchemist who had buried *thunder* potions all over his front lawn. Headstones were going off three, four, five at a time, and standing up amid all that flying stone would have meant resembling a sieve in about two seconds.

Deacon pulled himself along on his belly and rolled into the open grave, landing on top of a weeks-old corpse that had been flattened by the weight of Gresh and Black standing on top of it. The stench was straight out of a nightmare and he was a long while deciding whether he really needed cover this badly. In the end, he barely got his head below the lip of the hole before that grave's stone exploded, sending debris everywhere.

Deacon poked his head back up and saw Gresh fighting his way through wave after wave of rock. As long as it struck off his bones, he was all right. It was only when it found its way through his ribcage and slammed into his tissue that he staggered. But he seemed determined to get where he was going — unfortunately, he was heading further into the graveyard and farther away from any exit.

Three more stones went up, loud enough to shatter eardrums if there had been anyone close enough (not that someone next to them would have to worry about hearing, or any other sense, after that).

So Black had been wrong, Deacon thought. The two of them were followed and killing them in a cemetery meant eliminating the middle man. The graveyard looked more like a battlefield.

Gresh was gone from sight now, lost in the darkness and the rain of stone. But where was Black?

There! The ghoul was charging toward Deacon's hole, head low, trying desperately to dodge the flying chunks of monument. He was halfway through his leap toward the grave when a piece of concrete shrapnel tore him in half, sending a shower of blood and gore to the barren ground before the two portions of his body followed suit.

He didn't even have time for any last words. Deacon figured that was what Black was griping about now, standing in the spectral waiting room trying to keep his body joined at the hips.

A few minutes later, the explosions stopped. Only a few of the headstones were still intact. The ground was littered with the shattered remains of markers and Black. For most of the people buried in Starkwood, that was probably a better monument to their lives than what they'd had before.

Deacon stayed in his hole for as long as he could stand it. He'd thought that the long-distance vandals might have wandered in to check on their work, but evidently they had better things to do. He decided that he did, too, and pulled himself out.

First on the list was checking Black's corpse. The geyser of blood had subsided and what was left of the ghoul's torso looked like a stiff breeze could blow it away. Deacon did his best not to think about what he was doing and started going through the dead man's — *a damned stretch of that word,* he reminded himself — coat pockets.

Three of them were empty. The fourth contained a narrow metal box. Deacon ran his fingers over it and the blade obligingly popped out. It was the same kind of knife he had bought from Belrand. As he pocketed it, he found himself wondering if it might be the same *knife* he'd bought, the one that gave the blood cult such a nasty surprise.

He'd set aside some time later to give that some thought. For now, he was better off gone — even in a neighborhood like this, someone might have heard the sounds of a small war going on and sent for the sentinels.

Deacon started for the wall, then decided his heart had taken enough of a pounding for one night. He headed for the front gate, thinking that at least Belrand's account had been squared. But the body count on this case was going way up.

And if he wasn't real careful about his next move, they'd be adding one more to the tally.

Chapter Nineteen

Deacon was halfway back to Tara's when a voice from an alley stopped him.

"Soldier."

His hand was on his revolver, but the figure that emerged from the shadows wasn't carrying anything. He was shorter than Deacon, and maybe in his early thirties. His hair was white and shoulder-length and his eyes were shaded by the bill of the leather cap he wore. The man's hands were buried in the pockets of his dirty trenchcoat.

"Talking to me?" Deacon offered.

"That's right, soldier," the man said, smiling. "Thought ya might like some free advice."

"It's usually worth what you pay for it. What's the subject?"

"That." The smoky-voiced man flipped something at Deacon. The detective caught it in mid-air and saw it was a playing card. Suicide king — twin images of royalty with a sword through his head.

"What do I have to do to get the other fifty-one?" Deacon said, unimpressed.

"You don't understand. That's whatcha call 'symbolic,' soldier."

"What's with this 'soldier' stuff? I'm not in any army."

The man chuckled and wiped his nose on his sleeve. "Sure ya

are. We all are. 'Course, some people are still pickin' sides."

"This card supposed to help me decide?"

The man brightened. "That's good, soldier, that's real good. Yeah, see, the two big boys — Chaos, Order — they're past it. They're done. Neither side can win the scrap and neither side can quit fighting. I ask you, does that sound like a bunch of guys who should be deciding for you and me?"

"You going to run up a white flag, friend?"

The man laughed again and picked up a brick. He tossed it in the air a few times, then shied it toward Deacon. The detective had no trouble catching it, but couldn't hold it. Suddenly, the stone weighed a ton. He let it drop and saw it crack the concrete sidewalk.

"Only way to stop the two sides is to beat 'em both down. This is straight dope, pal: this war's gonna be won by its deserters. That's us."

Deserters? Was this the 'third faction' Larissa had said had been added to the mix? Was this why the war was shifting back here? Deacon wondered.

"I don't think you'd want me," he said finally. "Flat feet."

"You're a funny man," the "deserter" said, but he wasn't laughing. "We're more interested in something you've got."

"Stumble on a jewel and you get real popular," Deacon mumbled in reply. "What are you offering?"

"Name your price," was the reply.

"What do you want it for? Or shouldn't a good salesman ask that?"

The man looked confused for a moment, then said hurriedly, "Want it? We don't want it. We want you to take it out of play. Drop it in the river. Bury it. Whatever it takes."

Well, this is a new one. "Let me get this straight: you're offering me a pile of money *not* to give you something?"

"Us, or anybody else," the man corrected.

"And what do I tell all the folks who want it enough to kill for it?"

The man shrugged. "That's your problem, shamus. Not ours.

 180

We got a deal or not?"

Deacon frowned. "I'll think it over."

"Think fast. Word on the street is that murder charge is the least of your worries. Seems some of the junior Chaotics aren't too happy with how you treated the guy they sent to bust you out of jail."

"'Bust me up,' is more like it," Deacon replied. "How is it you know so much?"

Another shrug. "We spy on them. They spy on us. This war's still cold, but it's heating up fast. The Order camp's been taking its lumps for a while now. The vamp's death is just the latest, pal. They've lost a lot of their top people in Galitia."

Whatever this "third force" might be, it was damn talkative, Deacon decided. "Ever hear of a guy named Gadsden?"

The card-player screwed his face up as he thought. His answer was a definite, "Maybe."

"Know where I can find him?"

"Check the Twelfth St. bloodline. He has friends there."

"Thanks, pal. How do I get in touch with you?"

"We'll find you," the man said, already backing into the alley.

"Well, no one else has had a problem doing that so far," Deacon said dryly. "Anything else I should know?"

The man paused but didn't emerge from the shadows. "Yeah. Two things. We haven't had nothing to do with anything that's happened to you. We're your pals, get me? And whether you take our gold or not, get ridda that jewel. It's nothing but trouble. Order wants it back to bring their troops around; Chaos wants it, too, maybe for ransom, maybe just to keep the other guys from having it. You're in the middle."

"It's my favorite place to be, friend," Deacon said, moving on down the street.

❧

Deacon was looking forward to a shower and a few hours' sleep back at Tara's. She had some friends who were "crash and grab" experts and was going to send them over to his place. With any luck, some of his clothes would still be there. Anything of value would be in the hands of the sentinels assigned to watch the place by now.

When he reached the second floor of Tara's building, one of breed alchemy's bigger mistakes was waiting for him. A long time ago, some potion-popper had gotten the cute idea of combining Hugor and Human blood, along with some other odds and ends lying around the lab, and seeing what happened. He ended up with a squat, muscular breed that nobody wanted to claim as their own. Legend said that their creator dubbed the first ones "grisly," and it had been shortened to "Gris" since then.

This particular Gris was named Linx and worked as Tara's "manager" — a nice name for pimp. Deacon hadn't met the sweaty, green-eyed slob before, but Tara had spoken of him often enough. Linx was about three hundred pounds, all of it muscle, which was pretty amazing when one considered most Gris subsisted on garbage. This particular specimen had greasy hanks of black hair hanging down around his eyes and a nasty scar on his cheek. The jagged red line stood out harshly from his pale yellow skin.

Deacon stopped with a few feet to go before reaching the Gris. Linx looked him over and snorted, "You're trespassing. Take a walk."

"I just took one," Deacon answered. "Try again."

Linx straightened up and wiped some hair away from his right eye so he could get a better look at the guy he was about to pound. "I'm being nice here. You've been keeping my girl out of her place. She screws somebody at an inn, maybe I don't know where she is all the time. Maybe I don't know how much money she's getting. Maybe somebody's even trying to get her off the game. All that's not good for business. So beat it while all your moving parts still work."

Linx didn't so much talk as wheeze his threats. Gris acted tough because they were — Hugors were bigger and stronger, but lacked the knowledge of dirty fighting that Gris seemed to have from birth.

For his part, Deacon had been beaten, jailed, bitten by a vampire, gone swimming in a sewer and dropped dead, all in the past few weeks. He wasn't in the mood for a Gris with an attitude. And the thought of this thing with its paws on Tara …

"Tell you what I'll do," he began. "You get out of my way and stay the hell away from Tara, and maybe I won't turn you into the sentinels. Maybe I'll even let you keep the use of both arms. Hell, if you're real nice, I'll only break half your ribs. What do you say?"

Linx lunged, snarling, "Get outta my face!" Deacon side-stepped the blow as best he could in the narrow hallway, caught the Gris by his hair and slammed his head into the wall three or four times.

"What face?" he asked as the Gris hit the floor.

Linx spewed a string of curses and pulled a knife from his tunic, catching Deacon in the thigh. The detective grunted in pain and landed a kick in the Gris' ribcage. It felt good, so he kept kicking until Linx let go of the knife.

The Gris made it to his knees and charged again, this time slamming into Deacon and carrying him the length of the hall-way. Seizing his advantage, he landed a hail of blows on the detective's face, all the while having his best laugh in months.

When one of Deacon's eyes had swollen shut, Linx took a few seconds between punches to admire his work. This was a mistake — Deacon managed to get an arm up to block the next blow, then hit the Gris with a combination to the stomach and the mouth. Linx gave ground little by little, but Deacon had a feeling his fists would give out before the Gris' jaw would.

Linx came to the same conclusion and started hitting back, sending Deacon back toward the landing. Apparently reeling, the detective dropped his guard, while blood started flowing from a half dozen cuts on his face.

Linx wound up for one last punch, but his target had moved to the side at the last instant and the blow sailed over his left shoulder. Deacon came up with an uppercut and rocked Linx, then brought a knee up into what passed for a Gris' groin.

Linx doubled over and howled, though not much sound came out of his mouth. Deacon stepped to the side, grabbed him by hair and tunic, and allowed the wall, the floor and the staircase the honor of ruining what was left of the Gris' face.

When Tara came home a few hours later, the sentinels had already scraped Linx off the lobby floor. Nobody had looked too hard to find who had beaten the Gris — it would probably just have turned up another Gris, and who wanted to deal with that?

Tara unlocked her door and spotted Deacon sitting on the bed. She turned up the glowstone and gasped at the sight of his battered face.

"What happened?" she asked, shocked.

Deacon smiled, then winced when his bruises protested the expression. "You're under new management," he said.

❧

They spent the next few hours gently celebrating her resignation from Linx's service. The festivities were interrupted by Tara's friends, who had managed to get their hands on some of Deacon's older suits and a gun the detective's precise directions had led them to. Deacon was particularly pleased to see that. Carrying the false Mallory's revolver brought back too many memories of the man melting before his eyes.

The boys had even been lucky enough to find some cash he had stashed around the apartment, although they announced they were planning to keep most of it as a "finder's fee." Deacon's newfound gun convinced them otherwise. He tossed them more than a few bills as payment for their work and they left as they had come, through the window.

There was no point in heading over to Twelfth until dark, so Deacon and Tara found ways to amuse themselves until the sun went down.

❧

When vampires and their kind first became a problem in Galitia, the policy was a simple one: hunt them down and kill them. A special division of the sentinels was created to do the job — it was lousy duty, not much better than being a ratcatcher. Find the vamp, stake the vamp, and listen to the watermage bitch about getting all those bloodstains out of your uniform.

Somewhere along the line, things changed. Elders of the city decided that too much money and too many resources were being poured into "pest control," and a more liberal movement arose, asserting that vampires could be "productive members of society," as they had been in life. The trick, they claimed, was to make the Undead's predations unnecessary by giving them the blood they needed.

In the end, the city started bloodlines. Every few nights, vampires — or those who thought they were vampires — could line up and get their ration of stale blood left over from surgeries, drained at flesh mills, and from some even less appealing sources. It was good for little more than keeping body, if not soul, together, and no one really believed it satisfied the bloodsuckers. But every night, a small, haggard line would form at sites around the city while wary Galitian civil servants handed out containers of the red stuff.

Current law said that only vampires who could be proven to be a danger to the public could be hunted down without penalty. One of the ways of showing you didn't intend to bite your neighbors was to register for a bloodline. How many of those who appeared on the lines went after live prey an hour later was anybody's guess (and city officials preferred not to talk about that possibility, for obvious reasons).

The Twelfth Street bloodline was one of the more active, located, as it was, on the east side. The vampires that gathered here were a far cry from the glamorous pictures of their kind painted by the streetsingers. They were dirty, poor, sometimes insane; none of them lived in huge mansions or had thought to stash any money away during their centuries of life. More than a few had had brushes with blood starvation, and bore the scars of that experience along with those accrued in turf battles.

As Deacon rounded the corner, he saw perhaps a dozen

Undead in what could only loosely be called a line stretching from a storefront out into the street. Inside the store there would be coldmage-treated cases to keep the blood semi-fresh until it could be given into pale, dead hands.

Most of the beggars were too far gone to pay much attention to Deacon as he approached. Three at the rear of the line, though, were bored with waiting and looking for some amusement.

"Check out the warmflesh," the largest of the three said, using a derisive Undead slang term for those still living. His companions dutifully chuckled.

"What do you want here, warmflesh?" the second vampire said, a tall, gangly type with scars running up and down his arms. Sometimes, in the depths of starvation, vampires had been known to cut themselves and try to drink their own blood. Hunger made them forget they didn't have the red stuff circulating in their veins anymore.

The third Undead was short and stocky, younger than his friends and clad in foul-smelling rags stained with earth. He didn't say anything, just stepped forward to block Deacon's path.

Deacon looked the three of them over, then said, "I know where you can get better stuff than this."

"So do I," the short Undead said menacingly, looking pointedly at the detective's throat.

"Save it. My blood's nine-tenths alcohol. I don't think it would sit well on your stomach. I've got a friend who works a flesh mill. He can get you stuff right out of the stiffs."

"Dead blood isn't any good," the tall vampire said, turning away and running a hand down his scarred arm.

"Live blood gets your spine snapped," Deacon answered. "Interested or not?"

The first vampire folded his arms across his chest and spat on the ground. "How much?"

"A few answers."

"What if we don't like the questions?"

"Then keep your mouths shut. That's what the city wants you to do, anyway, right? They'll probably have a few bags of week-old stuff by the time you reach the front of the line."

The tall Undead stopped scratching himself and turned to look at his companions. The other two considered their options for a minute before nodding.

"So what's the question?" Short and Stocky asked.

"A guy named Gadsden. Ever hear of him?"

"What's to keep us from lying to you?"

Deacon gave the Undead a tight smile. "Your good sense."

Short and Stocky snorted. "Warmflesh, we had any sense, we'd be in the ground. Yeah, I've heard of Gadsden. Worked his way up from the bloodlines, got himself a nice apartment. Don't know where he made his money."

"Where'd he live?"

"Dover."

Deacon relaxed a little, now feeling fairly certain the vamps were telling the truth. This case had started for him on Dover, watching a building and waiting for trouble to walk out.

"Valari. Nured Mills. Tell 'er Jack sent you."

Deacon turned and headed back where it all began, part of him wondering if Larissa would walk out the door of the brownstone when he got there, a bigger part hoping she would.

Chapter Twenty

A little nosing around on Dover revealed that Gadsden did live in the building Larissa had departed from weeks ago, leading Deacon into a mess he still wasn't sure he'd be able to get out of. It was still early evening when he stood before it, wondering why somebody with money enough to impress the three corpses on the bloodline settled for this old brownstone instead of something further west.

On the way over, he had heard somebody's crystal set warning about a "dangerous escapee, wanted for two murders," who strangely enough matched his description.

Two murders? he wondered. *Either they found Mallory—and they figure I had a really effective fireball spell on me — or somebody stumbled on Simms in front of the bank. Hell, maybe I've started killing people I don't know about. Can't put anything past a menace to society like me.*

Deacon was actually grateful that he had no idea what Gadsden looked like. It meant there was no point in another night of watching and waiting. Instead, he could use the direct approach.

He was planning on pulling the old "wave your hand in front of all the doorwards and hope someone opens up" trick, but the bright red sign reading, "Apt. For Let" in the front window made that unnecessary. He climbed the front steps and knocked on the door.

It was opened by a dumpy blonde who had seen better decades, wearing a nightdress and a thick blue robe bound so tightly at the waist it was a wonder any blood was reaching her brain. She looked at Deacon with a sour expression reserved for those who had interrupted her favorite conjurevid.

"Whadda you want?"

"I saw the sign. Thought I might look at the apartment."

"At this hour? Come back tomorrow!" The landlady moved to shut the door. Deacon's foot moved faster, keeping it open.

"I work all the time. Evening's when I'm free. I just want to take a quick look at the place."

The woman's expression shifted from distaste to greed, with a healthy dose of wariness mixed in. "What do you do?"

"I deal in lead," Deacon replied, figuring the best lie was always the truth.

The landlady smiled. "Oh! An alchemist! Well, come on in. The apartment's on the second floor."

As she waddled down the hallway and up the stairs, Deacon made appropriate noises about loving old buildings and such. Then he cast a line, saying, "What really interested me about this place is that I have a friend who lives here."

"Really? Who?" the woman asked over her shoulder, now almost unbearably pleasant since she'd discovered she was escorting a professional man.

"His name's Gadsden."

The landlady stopped halfway up the stairs and, with difficulty, turned to face him. "You're a friend of his?"

"That's right."

"When'd you see him last?" she asked, with that same look Banff always got during interrogations.

Deacon played it safe. "It's been a while."

That seemed to settle her mind. "Well, when you see him again, tell that bum he owes me a month's rent. And if he thinks he's getting his deposit back from me after the condition he left that place in, he can think again!"

"He skipped out?" Deacon said, in mock surprise.

"Damn right," she answered bitterly as they reached the second floor landing. "Over a month ago, without so much as a 'So long, sister,' he takes off in the middle of the night. All I know is, he must have been in some kind of trouble. Left his clothes, all his furniture, everything."

"He didn't seem like the type," Deacon offered.

"You never can tell. Anyway, it's his apartment I'm showing. You still interested?"

Deacon nodded and followed her down the corridor until they came to number 15. She slipped a key in the lock, twisted it, then whispered something to the jamb. The door opened with a slight squeak.

The apartment was spacious, made moreso by the absence of any furniture. The view of the apartments and warehouses across the street was unspectacular now, but would be better in the morning. The building faced east, after all, and the sun would shine brightly through the series of windows. The floor was covered in a lush rug, dazzling in its beauty.

"Three rooms and a bath. The kitchen's through that door, although from the looks of it, he never used it much. The rug belonged to him, but I'm keeping it in lieu of rent."

Deacon made a show of wandering around the living room and poking his head into the kitchen and bathroom. It wasn't until he made his second pass that he noticed the stain on the rug. The look of dried blood was something he knew all too well. There had been obvious efforts to scrub it clean, but it would take a really skilled watermage to get it out, and they cost.

The landlady started babbling before Deacon even had a chance to ask about the stain. "I found that here when I finally broke in. There was some blood on a pile of clothes I found in the corner, too. I figured he probably cut his hand or something, maybe used his shirt to bandage the wound till he found something better."

"Or till he was out of blood," Deacon said, squatting down to get a better look at the mark. "Did you ever think that maybe he was taken out of here? Maybe you should have called the sentinels when he turned up missing."

"And how would that look, all those big brutes tramping up and down my front steps? I run a respectable place here," she snapped, her fat face flushing. "I've got a reputation to keep up."

Deacon stood and shut the door. Hidden behind it had been a spot of new plaster on the wall, roughly the diameter of a man's fist.

"What's that?"

"Your pal left a great, big hole in that wall when he left. Naturally, I had to get it filled in before I could try to rent the place."

"Naturally," Deacon agreed. "Where's his stuff?"

She was getting suspicious again. Deacon decided he didn't care. "What is this? Do you want to rent this place or not?"

Deacon frowned. "We can do this the easy way or the hard way. If I walk out of here and tell the first sentinel I meet that my friend has turned up missing, he's going to be hacked off at me for interrupting his ale. When I tell him that his landlady didn't bother to report blood on his carpet and a hole in his wall, he's going to be even angrier at you. He'll find something to charge you with, if it takes all night. So where's Gadsden's stuff?"

The landlady looked good and scared. *And if she had a clue about what really happened here, she'd look a lot worse,* Deacon thought. "I put all his junk in the basement. Figured maybe I could sell some of it. You're not going to call the sentinels, are you? I've got a reputation to keep up!"

Deacon shrugged. "I'd rather not. I've got better things to do than watch some badge make reports. Gadsden had some of my stuff, so I'm going to go down to the basement and get it. Right?"

The woman nodded vigorously. "Sure. Right. Go right ahead. Take it all, if you want to."

❦

The basement was dark, musty and crammed from ceiling to floor with the accumulated junk of years. After a brief search, Deacon managed to find the panel that turned on a dim, overhead glowstone. If anything, it made the place look worse.

The vast majority of what was rotting in the cellar had belonged to Gadsden, or so the landlady had said. Just looking at the dresser was enough to tell Deacon the man had expensive tastes — a glance at the fine fabrics in the drawers confirmed it.

Whole place would make a hell of an antique shop, Deacon thought. *Surprised the old broad didn't think of it herself. Must have been the blood that put her off.*

It took a solid quarter hour of searching to turn up a balled-up pile of clothes in a dark corner. Shirt and trousers were heavily stained with blood, and there was a ragged hole in the shirt to boot, front and back. Deacon felt pretty certain that, matched with the hole in the wall of Gadsden's apartment, they'd make triplets.

The old lady's going to be waiting a long time for that back rent …

There was still one piece missing, and it was a long shot that it would still be around. Deacon fought his way to the back of the basement and the woodpile — insurance in case the building's heat spells wore off. It was all the way on the bottom, but it was there: a good-sized, do-it-yourself stake, maybe three feet long, roughly the same diameter as the three telltale holes. It was wickedly sharp, but the wood wasn't as hard as one would expect in a vampire-killer. Looked more like someone had carved it from a fence post on short notice …

There was one more interesting aspect of it. There was no blood on the point or anywhere on the portion that would have been in the victim's body. All of it was concentrated on the end that would have been sticking out from his chest.

Meaning there was no blood in the body … except maybe in his stomach. And it didn't stay down long. Must have been a bad year.

Deacon sat down on a dusty armchair that half the curio dealers in the city would have killed for and started setting the scene. There might not have been positive proof that would convince Banff of the victim's identity, but he was willing to go out on a gallows and bet Gadsden was dead. It was also a safe guess that neither he nor the landlady would have let someone in the door who was carrying a damn spear, so the killer or killers had to have some way to conceal it. And it wasn't the sort of thing easily hid under your coat. *Are you planning to stake a vampire, or are you just happy to see me?*

With all the furniture and bric-a-brac moved downstairs, there was no way to be sure whether there had been a struggle or not. The landlady hadn't mentioned any noise. So Gadsden lets his killer in the apartment. Maybe they argue, maybe they don't. Things get nasty and Gadsden gets pinned to the wall like a bloodfly in somebody's collection. The whole thing upsets his stomach and he pukes blood all over his expensive clothes and nice rug. Then the killer beats it.

And the body …

Deacon got a mental image of the sun rising through those big, east-facing windows. The ones whose shades would have been open because it was the middle of the night. The sun would have struck the body flush, providing the killer remembered to shut the door behind himself. Enough of that and all you have left is a very old pile of dust in a nice suit.

That left who and why.

Larissa? She'd definitely been to his apartment, but after he was gone. She was capable of it, though. But Black had said she talked of Gadsden as if she'd worked for him. It might have been his death that forced her to look for outside help. And better to set up a rendezvous at a location the enemy already knew about than give away one of her hideouts.

But did the enemy know about it? Would Gadsden have opened his door for a Chaotic? Maybe — if he didn't know what the guy was, or if he was working both sides of the war and expecting a pay-off.

And then there were East's words: "In the end, the true threat may come from behind her, not before her."

Were Gadsden — and maybe Larissa, too — killed by one of their own?

Deacon shook his head. That last possibility put a whole new slant on things. But short of bringing in a temporal mage — and where would you find one at this time of night — there was no way to get even shadows of what had happened in Gadsden's apartment. He had learned all he could here.

He climbed the steps, tipped his hat to the landlady, and went out the front door. He had just hit the sidewalk when the big, black car pulled up to the curb. The back door flew open and a guy who might have been an oak tree last week got out.

"People want to see you," the bruiser announced.

"Good looks are a curse," Deacon agreed. "Tell 'em they'll have to talk to my manager."

"I wasn't askin'," the big man snarled. Deacon looked him over and realized he had seen walls that looked less solid. He'd seen walls with more personality than this guy, too.

The thug reached out and grabbed Deacon's shoulder in a hand so big that the detective's whole head could have fit inside, with room for a ham sandwich besides. "Get in the car."

Deacon shrugged as best he could under the circumstances. "Well, who am I to keep my public waiting?"

He slid into the back seat. When he saw the man-monster was getting in the front, he thought maybe his luck might be turning.

That feeling lasted until the stocky, balding driver turned around and flashed a smile.

Gresh.

Chapter
Twenty-One

The car, with Deacon an unwilling passenger, drove deep into the west side, well past where any industry could be found. They were in the domain of the big rich now, with houses whose light bills alone would be enough to pay for glowstones for most of Galitia.

Gresh turned right, steering on to a broad, semi-circular driveway. The house wasn't all that impressive — it wasn't as big as some cities Deacon had heard of, and the roof barely brushed the clouds.

"Moving up in the world, huh, Gresh?" Deacon ventured.

"Watch your step, Deacon, or you'll be moving out of it," Gresh answered, bringing the car to an abrupt stop in front of the mansion.

"I tried that once. It didn't do anything for me."

The walking monolith pushed his door open and lumbered out, then yanked Deacon's door wide. "We're here. Do what you're told and you'll go home in one piece. Give us any trouble and they'll be sweeping you up."

Deacon, his two escorts at his side, climbed the marble staircase that led to the massive mahogany doors. The inlaid carvings on them were real gold, not the alchemical stuff. Before Deacon could get a good look at what they depicted, the doors were opened by a woman clad in a tight black dress. She would have been beautiful by anyone's standards, but it was her silver skin and hair that really made her unusual. It wasn't until Deacon passed her by that he realized she was actually *made* of silver.

Before he could digest that little piece of information, he was being hustled through a marble foyer toward a set of double doors that even the wannabe giant could get through without bumping his head. When the trio reached the rich, wooden barriers to the unknown, Gresh and "Tiny" took a step back.

"You go on alone from here on," Gresh chuckled.

"I'll be sure to write from the other side," Deacon answered, smiling. "You boys take care of yourselves, now."

"Tiny" almost shoved him through the doors. "Get going before I get mad!"

Deacon laughed and reached for the golden knob to open the door. It saved him the trouble and turned itself.

The detective steeled himself and took a step inside. The room was huge and dominated by a massive conference table with beautifully carved chairs surrounding it.

A lone gas lamp was lit near the center of the room, providing a dull illumination. While everyone else muddled along with glowstones, the big rich favored gas that was piped right into their houses. Stones required separate spells for light, heat, etc. but gas did it all for one price, and you didn't need wizards traipsing all over your house, winter and summer.

A figure sat at the head of the table opposite Deacon. A finely tailored suit and hands that had never done hard labor, fingers steepled, were all that was visible, the rest obscured by shadow. A voice bearing a trace of a northern accent said, "So good of you to come, Mr. Deacon. Won't you sit down?"

Deacon casually pulled a chair out from under the table and sat. "I never refuse a polite invitation. Especially when it's delivered by guys big enough to rate as farm animals. Next time, keep your pets on a leash."

"But would you have come if I called?"

"Maybe. Depends on who you are and what you're selling."

"I didn't imagine you to be so well trained. Still, I am hoping there will be no need for a second meeting between us. I arranged this one because I felt that, sooner or later, we would have to meet. And I preferred it to be sooner."

Deacon stifled a yawn. "Good for you. Well, I'm here — are you going to stick your head out of the darkness or are we going to play 'shadows and light' all night?"

The man's voice turned stern. "We need to talk."

"Do we? Or do you talk and I listen? That seems to be the routine these days."

"You have made it known that you are investigating the murder of Larissa Martel. Who are you working for?"

Deacon shifted in his chair, trying to get comfortable. "Nobody. Miss Martel was a client. I make it a point to look into the killings of my clients, especially when they haven't finished paying me yet. It's a little extra service I provide."

The figure didn't sound convinced. "And now you are investigating the disappearance of Erl Gadsden? Why?"

"I forget," Deacon answered, doing his best to sound bored. "Kidnappings upset me, especially when I'm the one snatched. Make me forget things."

The figure leaned forward, allowing the gas lamp's glow to spill over his features. He was a little past middle-age, with pale blue eyes and silver hair brushed back tight against his skull. He had the look of a *baquest* player casting on his home stone.

"I would prefer straight answers to my questions," he said coldly.

"Great. Start asking me a few straight questions. Better yet, let me: who the hell are you? What's your stake in this? And what's the connection between Larissa's killing and Gadsden's murder — don't look so shocked, pal. It's my guess you've known all along what happened to Gadsden. He was one of your boys, wasn't he?"

The man's face hardened and he reached into his coat pocket, producing a sheaf of bills, which he tossed on to the table in front of Deacon. "There's a substantial amount of money there. You may count it, if you wish. Take it and drop this case."

Deacon picked up the bundle and tossed it from hand to hand, as if testing its heft. Satisfied, he threw it back at his host. "You know, that's the second time somebody tried to buy me off this case. Never have so many offered me so much to do so little. I'm a funny guy — people want me to stay away from something, I like to dig deeper and find out what has them so scared."

"You won't take my advice, then?" the man said, sounding vaguely disappointed.

"Sorry, no. I've got a murder charge hanging over my head. Unless I find the guy who did do it, I'm a candidate for a cell and maybe a blood boiling. All the gold in the world won't help me then."

"We can make the murder charge go away. I have friends among the sentinels, Mr. Deacon."

Deacon chuckled. "Yeah, I'll bet you do. Which brings us back to question one: who are you?"

The man sighed, as if conceding defeat on one point, at least. "My name is Merr. No. I didn't expect it would mean anything to you. In fact, I would be disturbed if it did."

Deacon decided to press his perceived advantage. "Fine, now we know who we are. Short of walking in front of a railrunner car, what else can I do for you?"

Merr glanced at the packet of money, but left it where it was. "I want the jewel. Larissa's jewel. If you're as smart as you pretend, you will sell it to me."

"That'd be a real tempting offer — if I had it."

"You told one of our agents that you did."

"I told Black what he wanted to hear. He seemed willing to deal. I thought I'd string him along, see how far he'd go before he tumbled. He was all set to throw Gresh to the pit vipers for a few gold pieces. Nice little army you've got there. By the way, how'd you find the boneyard, anyway?"

"We have our sources of information, Mr. Deacon. One of them found Gresh after the … incident in Starkwood and brought him to me." Merr said, matter-of-factly. "Can you lay your hands on the jewel?"

"Could be. As soon as I lay my hands on whoever killed Larissa. Or do you think I did that, and just don't care as long as you get your ice back?" Deacon stood up suddenly, kicking the chair and sending it crashing against the wall. "What are you wasting my time for? You knew before I walked in here I didn't have the jewel! All of this is just supposed to throw a scare into me, keep me out of your hair while you try to figure a way out of the mess you're in! Well, I'm not going away, Merr — I'm in this thing up to my neck, and if I go down, I'm taking the whole stinking lot of you with me!"

"Sit down, Mr. Deacon," Merr said quietly, barely containing his anger. When the detective didn't move, he rose to his feet, slammed a fist down on the table, and shouted, "I said, sit down!"

Deacon took one of the remaining chairs and sat. Merr followed suit, taking a moment to wipe the perspiration from his brow with a handkerchief that appeared in his hand from nowhere. "For a man in so much trouble, you seem very sure of yourself. If I'm so intent on having you out of this, why don't I just have you killed?"

"Because you didn't get all this —" Deacon said, gesturing at the rich furnishings that surrounded him "— by being stupid. We both want the same thing — Larissa's murderer — though maybe for different reasons.

"Your first guess was that I had the jewel. That's all wrong — if I'd had it, you would have known five minutes after I palmed it. Your second guess was that I knew where to get it. Well, that's half right — at least, I'm getting a few ideas."

Merr nodded with approval. "Very good, Mr. Deacon. Yes, I would have sensed it if the jewel were in your possession. It's the fact that I can't sense it — anywhere — that has me so concerned."

"What makes this thing so valuable, anyway?"

Merr smiled, a gamesman who saw himself being backed into an obvious trap. "A trade, then, since it is evident that cooperation might be to both our advantages. I will give you some background, and you will share your theories. Agreed?"

"Sure," Deacon answered. "You go first."

Merr leaned back in his chair, waving a hand at the gas lamp as it did so. Its luminosity increased, filling the room with light. "Have you ever heard the term 'erismata,' Mr. Deacon?"

"Sounds like it has dust on it."

"Yes. The language it sprang from died long before you were born. An erismata is the resumption of a conflict. The embodiments of Chaos and Order, their various priests, servants, and hangers-on have been warring since before recorded time, the erismata occurring over and over again on countless worlds, on countless planes of existence. Now it falls to this world, Marl, to act as battlefield.

"The rules of the game are fairly simple: awareness that the battle must begin again comes to the more powerful servants first, and from them, travels down the chain to the lesser powered, and finally to the cults. Both sides set about recruiting new followers and reviving those who survived the last war. That was Larissa's task here in Galitia. Using the jewel implanted in her throat, she was to restore truelife to our warriors here."

"And with it missing?" Deacon asked.

"We are at a … disadvantage. While we could bring in another with a jewel from someplace else, it would take time and it would leave that other city vulnerable. If we do not find the jewel soon, we will have to concede Galitia to the Chaotics — and whatever else might wish to claim it."

"The third group?"

Merr's face took on an expression of profound disgust. "Miserable pests! Wielding their pitiful magicks of the dirt and rock and threatening a balance that has existed for millennia!"

"Sorry I asked," Deacon said. "Let me ask you this: suppose Larissa knew somebody was closing in? Could she have removed the jewel herself and hidden it somewhere?"

Merr shook his head. "No. Once the jewel is in place, it can only be removed upon the bearer's death. It's my understanding that you prevented a shapeshifter from taking it a few weeks past."

"That's right, and I guess that makes this my turn. Okay, here's what I have: Black said Larissa talked about Gadsden like he was her boss, and I'm guessing he was. And you were his boss. The war was all set to start up again, but things were going sour for you Order fanatics. Too many of your people were getting offed. That meant Gadsden had to put Larissa to work, maybe sooner than expected.

"Only trouble was, Gadsden had made himself too visible. I saw his clothes — pretty sharp stuff for someone who ought to be trying to stay inconspicuous. Anyway, one night somebody shows up at his door, maybe somebody he knows. He lets 'im in, maybe they talk, then the new arrival rams a piece of fence right through Mr. Gadsden, sticking him to the wall. How'm I doing so far?"

Merr said simply, "Go on."

"The killer beats it and leaves you with a problem. My guess is only Gadsden knew the names of his contacts and you needed the list for Larissa to do any good. So somebody — maybe even you, since you were running out of pawns — goes to his apartment as soon as you get the word he's dead. You take whatever might identify him or connect him to you, in case the sentinels get involved before dawn. You don't bother with the body — Gadsden's a vampire, one of yours, which means he has to follow the rules. And rule number one is the sun will leave him a pile of ash on the floor. Nice and tidy.

"Larissa's ready to go, but she's got no protection. She figures the enemy would expect her to hire spellslingers, so she crosses them up and hires a guy who can't manage a card trick. But the other side is all over us from the start, and she's barely gotten started before she's dead. For good, this time. The jewel disappears, somebody hangs the frame on me so I won't be able to look for it, and things get a whole hell of a lot worse for you.

"That brings us to now. Black talks out of turn and gives me Gadsden's name, and when you find Gresh, he tells you all about it. As good as you are, you're worried you might have missed something at his place, something that would lead me — and

201

anybody's who's on my tail — right here. So you put the snatch on me and try to make me go away before I paint a target on you."

Merr began to drum his fingers on the table, more troubled than he wished to let on by Deacon's recitation of events. "And who do you suspect is behind all this?"

Deacon rubbed his jaw, feeling the beginnings of a beard. "Good question. The obvious choice is your enemies, the Chaotics. I'd guess the 'shifter was one of theirs. and there are more where he came from. That gives them means and motive and Larissa gave them the opportunity. But the demon that came after me in jail thought I had the jewel — if he was one of theirs, and they did it, why not just leave me in there to rot?"

"Maybe they had second thoughts," Merr suggested. "Maybe they realized you might know something that would damage their cause."

"Possible," Deacon agreed. "There are other questions, too. Gadsden was a big boy, and I doubt he would have let in a blood enemy or gotten caught flatfooted with a spear like that. No, he had to trust the person he let in — which means he was working the other side of the street or it was one of yours."

Merr's eyes widened a bit at that. "No. I refuse to believe that. Gadsden may have needed gold — perhaps he did sell us out. You would have to ask the Chaotics."

Deacon shrugged. "I'll look 'em up in the book. One more thing: why did Larissa take off when I mentioned Whisper? Who is he?"

This time, Merr's efforts to hide his surprise failed miserably. But he regained control of himself in an instant and said only, "I don't know. Perhaps someone she had encountered before we contacted her. Regardless, I believe Gadsden's treachery is the key to all this — find who he was in contact with and we will find Larissa's killer. And the jewel."

Merr rose and handed the money back to Deacon. "I wish to retain your services. Our people, for obvious reasons, cannot deal with the Chaotics at the moment. But you are still, in many ways, a free agent in this matter. I have no doubt you can find them and learn what we need to know."

Deacon took the money, did a swift count, and tucked it away in his coat pocket. "Where do you suggest I start looking?"

"There's a church on Coriander, a cathedral of Syl. My people report it has contacts with the other side. Seek out a shapeshifter named Redge."

"How do I contact you — assuming I walk out of there?"

Merr walked to the door and stood with his hand on the knob. "You don't. By tomorrow morning, I'll be gone from this house. A precaution, you understand. No, I will contact you. And there's one other precaution I feel we must take …"

So saying, he opened the door to admit Gresh and "Tiny," both of whom carried blackjacks. When Deacon looked back at Merr, the rich man was pointing a gun at him. "You can't very well leave here looking hale and hearty, Mr. Deacon. The Chaotics would suspect at once that we were allies and your life would be over."

Deacon rose and went for the window, but "Tiny" caught him and lifted him like he were a child's doll, then threw his newfound toy against the wall.

The detective found himself surrounded by a dark cloud that was rapidly closing in. He went for his gun but somebody stamped on his hand. Then Gresh's spiked fist was all he saw.

❦

When Deacon looked bloody enough for his purposes, Merr ordered him dragged back to the car and dumped near where he had been picked up. The detective was in no condition to object as "Tiny" threw his battered body over one shoulder and carried him out of the room.

Gresh moved to follow but a word from Merr stopped him short. "Keep following him, but stay well away. He will go to the Chaotics now and confirm what I already suspect. Once he's done that — kill him."

The twisted, bloody tissue inside the massive skeletal frame nodded happily.

Chapter
Twenty-Two

Deacon clawed his way back to consciousness and found himself in an alleyway, maybe an hour or so before dawn. There wasn't anything that didn't hurt — if there had been, he would have kept it to himself, though. The way his luck was running, the gods would send somebody down to hurt that, too.

He wasn't going to be able to get a cab in his condition. No driver was going to pick up the losing end of a brawl — the winners were usually the ones with the cash. But the railrunner ran down this way along iron tracks spiked to the street. They'd take money from anybody and didn't ask any questions. No one knew if that was because 'runner drivers were discreet, or just didn't give a damn about the answers.

Deacon didn't have to wait long. A car, one of the newer ones, made its silent glide down the avenue and slid to a stop in front of him. At this time of day, the wide car, lined on both sides with seats, was largely empty. Only a few drunks sleeping it off were there to share the ride.

The railrunners installed in the last five, ten years were ideal for catching shuteye. Elemental propulsion meant they were, for all intents and purposes, noiseless. The bad news was that they crept up so quietly that people enjoying a walk on the tracks more often than not never heard what hit them. Somebody started calling them the "silent death," and the name had stuck.

The older railrunners, of course, were anything but silent. Pulled by animals — horses, oxen, sometimes even domesticated rerbeasts — they clanked and clattered along, the stink of freshly-dropped manure suffocating the passengers and ensuring that these models would remain in use only in the poorer neighborhoods.

He took the railrunner as far as Tara's block and made his way to the apartment they were now sharing. Unfortunately, she was in, only lightly asleep, and wasn't happy when she saw the blood and the bruises.

"Is this what I'm going to wake up to the rest of my life?" she asked as she gathered bottled herbs out of a cabinet. "You coming in at all hours, beaten half to death?"

Deacon understood how she felt. Being a detective's lover wasn't much different than living with a sentinel or a firemage. There was always the possibility they wouldn't be coming back. It came with the job.

He tried to explain that to her as she dabbed at his cuts with a damp cloth. She wasn't buying. "I want to get out of here, Jack. Let's just forget this crummy town and go. If we get far enough away, maybe the sentinels will stop looking for you."

"We can't run, kid," he answered, wincing at the sting of a northern herb supposed to fight infection. "In its own way, this city's as much a prison as the kind with bars on the windows. We built the walls and sealed the locks a long time ago, praying that the devils outside would leave us be. Now we can sleep at night — but finding another town takes money, guts, and somebody to watch your back. And there's no telling if anyplace else would be any better."

"It has to be," Tara insisted. "I've heard stories ever since I was a kid about Dela and Gimm and how the people live there. They don't have to worry about 'shifters and gods know what else. They don't have to be afraid."

Deacon caught her hands in his and looked hard at her. "Listen to me, Tara. What's happening here in Galitia is just the start of something big. Pretty soon, could be no place is going to be safe.

Maybe Galitia's going to hell anyway, but there might be something I can do to slow down the trip. As long as there's that possibility, I have to stay and finish this."

Tara turned away, but there were no tears. She had known what his answer would be, but didn't welcome hearing it. "All you're going to do is get yourself killed," she said bitterly.

"Wouldn't be the first time."

She turned and kissed him softly on the lips, then broke away, saying, "I don't want to lose this, Jack. But I know it's not enough to stop you."

"I can't let it be, kid. Understand?"

She nodded and walked away, staring out the window at the street. Neither said anything for a few moments. Then she turned to him and the lover had been replaced by the woman who had worked the streets for most of her life. "And now?"

"I've got a hold of something. It's not much, but for the first time on this case, I think I know where I'm heading," Deacon said. He reached into his pocket and took out the knife that he had found on Black. The blade obligingly appeared at his request, sharp enough to split a harpy's hair. "People have been pushing me in and out of this thing since it started. I'm getting real tired of being pushed."

"What are you going to do?"

"That's easy," he said, the knife blade gleaming in the light. "I'm going to start pushing back."

❧

Services at the cathedral of Syl ran through dusk, so Deacon grabbed some sleep during the day and slapped together a hot meal before leaving in the early evening. News about the manhunt for him had ebbed, replaced by stories of fresher atrocities. The destruction at Starkwood was the subject of outrage by some scribes, indifference by most. Somebody called the "vandalism" a sign of a "crisis of faith" in Galitia.

"That's not what this is about," Deacon corrected the crystal set. "It's about too many people who damn well believe."

As a child, he'd had a little more exposure to religion than the other boys in his neighborhood. Though his father had been largely indifferent to the various sects that competed for souls in the churches, temples, shrines and corner booths, his mother had been a devoted follower of one of the thousands of gods credited with the creation of the universe. His father had always said that with that many alchemists mixing the elixir, it was no wonder the world had turned out the way it had.

At any rate, Sena Deacon had made sure her children learned the virtues inherent in asking for help from a church ceiling and blaming yourself when it didn't materialize. Jack had lost interest in organized religion right after he turned 19. His younger sister, Kaya, then 16, had been tapped to be a priestess of Tev and slated for missionary work. It later turned out that most of the missionary work done through that particular church involved the position of the same name. Deacon had barely avoided a prison sentence for beating the cleric bloody; Kaya, too ashamed to face her family, had left Galitia on a trader and not been heard from again.

Fifteen years later, the only things Deacon remembered from his religious training was that for every god, there's a devil, and that all too often the righteous lose because they don't have enough sense to duck when the shooting starts.

With that in mind, he checked his revolver as he climbed the steps to the cathedral of Syl. Carrying a weapon into a church was probably sacrilege — but if Merr had been telling the truth and Chaotics were working out of here, the place was already unholy.

In the grand list of deities, Syl was a footnote, a god who had just never made it. Maybe it was because too many of his scriptures dealt more with what his followers should do for his priests than what he would do for his followers. For a while, the faithful had tried swiping elements from more popular religions and incorporating them into their own, even loading the choir with tempting young virgins. But fierce competition meant this was the last shrine to Syl still standing in Galitia — most of the rest had been torn down or taken over by acolytes of hotter faiths.

The building was good and old, built during one of the boom times for religion locally — usually during or just after plagues — when a well-fattened flock existed to be sheared. Its spires brushed the sky and its ornate face was covered with images of holy men dying for their beliefs so that their descendants could get the reverence they deserved. Naturally, there were also a fair number of demons and devils carved into the walls to illustrate the fate of those who didn't think Syl's good favor was worth a few coins once a week.

The double doors were made of wood, but the hue and texture were strange. Deacon wondered if it might have been imported from somewhere outside the city. The priests would fetch a good price when they went to sell this place, he decided.

Even with services done for the day, one of the doors was ajar. It was traditional: churches and shrines stayed open all hours, always hoping for some late business. Most people don't really start regretting their sins until well after midnight, and they had to be snagged while they were still desperate for redemption. By morning, they would have convinced themselves that they hadn't really done anything that bad after all.

Deacon pushed the door open and stepped inside. Inside, the walls were of the same grey stone as without, but faded tapestries worked to cover cracks. Candles mounted in iron holders lined both sides of the nave, casting indifferent light on the empty house of worship.

But it was the pews that caught the detective's eyes. They were hewn from an unusual stone, one of pure white but laced with veins of some reddish mineral. Just for a moment, it seemed as if the benches were wounded and bleeding.

At the end of the nave stood a simple, unadorned pedestal where the priests — called Speakers — recited their sermons. Hovering above that was a painting of Syl, a haggard old man who looked disappointed in the turnout.

Although he felt like the sound of his footfalls must have been like thunderclaps in the stillness of the place, no one had come out to see why he was there. He was about to call out when he noticed a glowstone embedded in the wall near the doors that gave off a crimson light. A dim memory suggested that visitors were supposed to pass a hand before the stone to let the clerics know they had arrived.

It worked. A little old man clad in red robes came scurrying out from a room Deacon guessed was the sacristy. He was probably close to 70 and struggled with a pair of wire-rimmed spectacles that refused to stay in place as he almost ran down the aisle. Once he reached Deacon's side, he smoothed his snow-white hair and took a moment to catch his breath.

"What ... can I do ... for you, my son?" he asked, between deep breaths.

"I'm looking to talk," Deacon answered. "I have questions that need answering."

The old man smiled. "Then you have come to the right place, indeed, you have. My name is Speaker Gan and I invite you into this house of Syl. May his blessing be upon you."

Deacon acknowledged this with a nod and followed Gan down the aisle. "You seem troubled, my son," the Speaker said. "How may I help?"

"I've lost something that was important to me. A friend of mine was killed not long ago."

"Most regrettable. But sometimes ... sometimes when we we lose something, we find something as well. Have you, perhaps, found something, my son?"

They had reached the front of the church now, but Gan took a left and headed toward the sacristy.

"You might say that," Deacon answered. "But the trouble is in the keeping."

"If what you've found isn't yours, perhaps it would lighten your spirit to part with it," Gan said, his tone that of a benevolent grandfather. "But we can talk of such things later. For now, I would ask that you enter the chambers with me and purge your soul of its sins."

The chambers were two small booths joined by a thin wall with a screen mounted in the middle. Doors entered both sides, one for the Speaker and one for the supplicant. The latter related all the slips he had made lately and the cleric told him how much forgiveness was going to cost him. This was a common feature in most houses of worship, sometimes as a sincere form of spiritual relief and sometimes just a way to relieve suckers of cash. A few shrines had even been accused of entrapping their faithful into committing some really heinous sins so they could jack up the price of redemption.

Deacon hadn't been through a rite like this since childhood, but he had no illusions about why the Speaker was inviting him to participate. Walls listen well, even in churches. So he opened the door and ducked his head to fit inside the small booth, while the Speaker did the same.

When both were settled, the Speaker pulled aside a sliding panel to reveal a fragile screen. He sat with his back to the wall so that Deacon could not get a good look at him, another part of the tradition. It was designed more to preserve the anonymity of the confessor than the cleric, but it served both parties well.

"Now, my son, cleanse your soul of its sins. It will do you good," the Speaker assured him.

"It would take more time than I've got. I'm looking for somebody named Redge. Is he here?"

"Perhaps," the Speaker answered warily. "Many pass through our doors and some decide to stay a while. Why do you wish to see Brother Redge?"

"A friend of his named Whisper has been trying to find me. I thought I'd make it easy. Maybe we could do a deal."

"Whisper? And why does this Whisper want to find you? Have you sinned against him, my son?"

Deacon was running out of patience with this game. "Just tell Redge I'm here. Tell him I'm ready to talk in exchange for some of the action."

The Speaker clucked in disapproval. "These things take time, my son. You must guard against a reckless spirit, for it can cause a man to do many unwise things. Even murder."

The cleric's voice turned harsh and accusing. "And you have

murdered, haven't you, my son? A vampiress; a sentinel; even a banker; oh, yes, Syl knows all! And now you come to this holy place seeking to make deals with devils!"

The Speaker let out a moan of pain, almost lost beneath the sound of shredding cloth. When he spoke again, it was in a voice only barely his, deep, powerful and dripping malice. "You've been a very bad boy!"

Suddenly, a clawed hand smashed its way through the screen, reaching for Deacon. The arm behind it was sheer muscle, the skin gray and taut with shreds of the Speaker's garment still clinging to it.

Deacon narrowly avoided the lunge, drew his weapon and fired three times through the thin wall that separated the chambers. The response was a hideous screech and the thing, body awash in arcane energy, smashed its way into Deacon's booth.

The detective hadn't waited for it, though. Instead, he had kicked the chamber door open and found cover behind a stone pew. He put another shot into the thing as it emerged, then backed away again and took aim.

What had been the elderly Speaker was now a winged monstrosity, resembling nothing so much as a gargoyle off a cathedral's face. It was well over two meters tall, with wings that spread out to four meters. Its body was rock-hard and its hands and feet sported hooked claws. The head was hairless and topped with razor-sharp horns. The Speaker's new face had an overlarge mouth with pointed, crooked teeth, twin slits in the skull to act as nostrils and eyes the color of blood.

From behind a pew on the far side of the church, Deacon tried to figure his next move. Running for the street was out — with its wings, the outdoors would be that thing's element. The burns that crisscrossed its scaled chest proved it could be hurt. The trick was in finding out how much it could take before it fell down.

The detective, down on one knee, levelled his weapon at the thing, whose movements were ponderously slow. Its wings stretched to their full length and then curled in upon themselves as it took stock of the situation.

211

"Back off or the next one goes between the eyes," Deacon said. "I've taken your kind down twice so far. A third time won't bother me."

The thing smiled, an expression more frightening than its scowl. "Good, Deacon. You recognize us. You remember. The relkazar never forget an enemy, either. How do you like our natural state?"

"I can see why you go for Human bodies. It'd be kind of hard getting laid looking like that."

The relkazar shrugged. Its wings unfolded again, moving as if they had a life of their own. "This form has its advantages." It bent down and tore a pew free from the floor, hefting the massive stonework like it was a sack of feathers. Then, almost as an afterthought, it tossed the bench the length of the room and chuckled as it smashed into pieces against the wall.

"You've got no future as a mover," Deacon said, rising to his feet but keeping the relkazar covered. "Let alone as a priest. And why the big act, in the first place?"

The relkazar took a few steps forward, then stopped. "Knew you'd show up sooner or later."

"So now what?" Deacon asked. "We waltz around for a few rounds. One of us gets pretty dead. What do we prove?"

"Why does it have to prove anything? You're a fleshling; I'm a relkazar. Tearing the heads off things like you is what I do."

"Even when this head holds info you might profit from?" Deacon asked. "Like where your enemies are and what they're planning?"

Deep thought for a relkazar was like chin-ups for a fat man. Eventually, the demon decided it couldn't decide without some help. "What do you get in return?"

"The answers to a few questions. And I walk out of here the way I came in."

The relkazar didn't get a chance to respond. A booming voice from the sacristy answered for him. "Enough talk! Bring him here!"

"Is this your first meeting with a Chaotic, Mr. Deacon? Or do you greet all your hosts with undisguised revulsion?"

The questioner was Redge himself. He was a shapeshifter, all right — his picture would have been next to the word in the scribe's guide, if anybody could have kept his dinner down long enough to cast an image of him.

Redge was nature gone berserk, a shapeshifter with no apparent control over his transformations. He sat like a slug on a divan in the remodeled sacristy, nude, the changes running up and down his soft body in waves. When Deacon had walked in, his left arm had been furred and clawed, his torso changing from stone to flesh and back again, and his face midway through a shift from humanoid serpent to man. Deacon guessed that, fully human, he would have been unimpressive — a chubby, balding man who spoke with an arrogance that screamed for a fat lip. Given that, the detective thought, he was probably lucky that he was never fully Human.

"I've had a few run-ins with your friends," Deacon answered. "Now I'll ask one: do you always look like that, or is tonight something special?"

A soft chuckle came from the mouth of a horned ram. Twelve insectoid legs appeared and disappeared. "You have no doubt heard of men who wear their loyalties on their sleeves? I wear mine upon my whole body. It is all the happy result of an ancestor who tried to do too much with too little sorcery — or perhaps it was the other way around. You see, sometimes I remember it one way, sometimes another. Have a seat, please."

Deacon glanced back at the relkazar still standing in the doorway, looking as if it was tensed to spring. Then he turned to Redge, saying, "Isn't it time to let him out for the night? I've got business to discuss."

Redge waited until his right arm had completed its transformation to a leathery bat's wing before using it to order the relkazar out. Deacon kicked the door shut behind the winged creature and took a seat on a hard wooden bench. Redge's face had gone from ram to boar in the matter of a few seconds. His body was doing a good impression of a man-serpent, but only for now.

The shapeshifter made a few attempts to talk, but his newly-formed tusks got in the way. He waited impatiently until they receded and his face took on more birdlike aspects. "That's better. You say you want information. What do you have to trade?"

"How about the home address of Order's brains in Galitia?"

The boar came back long enough to snort in derision. Gossamer wings sprouted from Redge's back while his body fused into a fleshy lump. Then his face was human again, but horribly distorted. "You insult me, Deacon. Do you think me so foolish that I would believe Merr would share with you anything potentially dangerous to him? You know what I want!"

Deacon nodded, trying to keep from being distracted by the grotesque kaleidoscope of changes going on before him. He couldn't help but wonder if the constant shifting was painful. "You want the jewel. What I don't know is why."

"So that Merr will not have it, of course," Redge answered, now almost completely wolflike. "If nothing else, it will unsettle him. And I live to unsettle others."

"No kidding. Suppose I can get you the jewel, in exchange for some information now?"

The insectoid face that looked at Deacon somehow managed an expression of skepticism. "And why should you want to help me? I thought you fleshlings always preferred Order to Chaos. Don't your mothers put you to bed with stories where things like me get vanquished by those who follow the rules?"

"I'm not interested in politics," Deacon replied gruffly. "And I've got no reason to love Merr and his crowd. Play straight with me and I'll give you the rock. Take it or leave it."

Redge stretched and yawned. By the time he was done, his hands were claws and his skin was smooth and sleek like the 'shifter that had gone after Larissa. He had no facial features, but managed to speak anyway. "Very well, Mr. Deacon. I believe I will … take it. Ask your questions quickly before I change my mind. Or something else."

"A guy named Gadsden was murdered. He was —"

"I know who he was," Redge interrupted. "He was a posturing, preening little freak more interested in sexual conquest than survival, as it turned out."

"Meaning?"

A man-fish shrugged. "I don't know what it means. You're the detective."

"But he was killed by your people?"

"Oh, no! When sated, Gadsden was a fount of information. We much preferred him … well, as alive as he was able to manage, under the circumstances."

"Then Merr's people did it?"

Redge was Human for almost an entire split second before taking on a form something like his relkazar. "If Merr had known what a poor job his servant was doing, yes, he was quite capable of killing him. But Merr didn't know — in fact, there are a great many things Merr doesn't know."

"I checked Gadsden's place out. I think he knew whoever killed him."

"Or not," Redge corrected. "Suppose his killer was a sorcerer — one skilled enough to produce some truly wondrous effects?" So saying, Redge held out a Human hand that suddenly sprouted claws, clenched it into a fist and squeezed until blood flowed between his fingers.

And Deacon had seen that before. "Whisper!"

"Quite possibly," Redge agreed, looking with distaste as his legs took on the semblance of a segmented worm. "Perhaps he had procured for Gadsden in the past. Maybe he used his magics to convince the fool he had brought him another woman to satisfy his peculiar … appetites."

"But Whisper's one of yours."

"Whatever gave you that idea?" Redge hissed, running an elongated tongue over a new set of fangs. "Whisper is out of town talent, but he's Order. Always has been."

"Merr said he didn't know him."

"Merr lied. He does that. We all do. Get used to it."

Deacon frowned. "Let me get this straight. Whisper finds out that Gadsden is selling out and kills him."

Redge spread a set of ebon wings and bellowed, "Wrong, wrong, wrong! Whisper's reasons were his own. He could care less about this little disagreement going on here." Then the shapeshifter's leonine face brightened. "I like you, Deacon. You are one of the few men who has ever been able to spend more than a few minutes in my presence without running screaming into the night. I respect that, so I will share with you a little secret. Not all the Order deaths so far can be laid at our door, or that of the new players in this game."

"They're killing their own?"

"It's far easier than killing us, and it will end this war — at least on this world — just as quickly."

It made a lousy kind of sense. So did a lot of the things East had said, viewed this way. When he spoke, it was more to himself than Redge. "Whisper's working on his own. Or with others. Ones who want their side to lose. That's why Gadsden was killed. And Larissa, for the jewel —"

"Without it, they've lost Galitia," Redge said, sounding thoroughly satisfied by the prospect. Deacon didn't recognize what the 'shifter had become, but hoped he never encountered the real thing. "Now I've held up my end of the bargain. I assume you'll hold up yours?"

"One way or the other," Deacon said, rising. "Thanks for your help."

"It was purely self-serving, I assure you," Redge said, once again lacking arms and legs and having to make do with fragile-looking tentacles. "For obvious reasons, I won't show you out."

Relieved, Deacon left the sacristy. The relkazar was nowhere to be seen in the church proper. *Probably off stealing from the collection plate,* the detective said to himself.

He'd had a feeling before he came to the church that he was close to the end of this case. Now he was sure of it. Whisper was looking out for himself, trying for some reason to shaft his own side in the war. He killed Gadsden to slow Order down and make sure Larissa wouldn't have any protection, figuring Redge's people would take care of her. When she hired a detective, Whisper tried to scare him off.

But when Deacon mentioned Whisper's name to Larissa, she knew something was wrong. She left, maybe to confront him, maybe to inform Merr, and got killed for her efforts.

It all makes sense. It all fits perfectly. Whisper killed her to keep from being exposed and to get his hands on the jewel, Deacon said to himself as he walked down the steps of the church to the street. *So why do I still feel like I'm missing something?*

He turned the corner and started walking, trying to convince himself that he'd found the answer.

Across the street, a figure stood in a shadowed doorway. His eyes narrowed as Deacon approached. Then, forcing his hand to stop trembling, he raised a gun and pulled the trigger.

Chapter
Twenty-Three

From his vantage point in an alleyway near the church of Syl, Gresh's first thought was that the sentinels had finally tracked Deacon down. When he heard the shot and saw the detective hit the ground, he expected to see a squad descend on the body and haul it off. But nobody emerged from the shadows and Gresh decided maybe that was an example he should follow.

After all, Merr had only told him to follow Deacon and kill him after he left the church. Nothing had been said about what to do if somebody else was gunning for the detective. And as long as the shamus was dead, what difference did it make who killed him?

Gresh turned away from the scene, feeling good inside. In the morning, news of Deacon's death would be on the crystal sets. Maybe he could even claim credit for it with Merr — say he used a gun to make it look like any one of a hundred killings. Sure, that would work fine.

Meanwhile, his Human guise would get him into an inn. He was in the mood for a celebration ...

Deacon didn't know how his would-be murderer had managed to miss. *Either he's a lousy shot or I'm luckier than I have a right to be.*

 218

The detective had hit the pavement the instant the bullet had struck the wall of the building beside him. He had caught the muzzle flash out of the corner of his eye and knew right about where the shot had come from, but out here in the open was no site for a gun battle. Better to let whoever think he was dead and try to lure the triggerman in.

Of course, this strategy wasn't without its risks. The gunman might decide to pump a few more rounds into the "corpse" just to make sure it stayed dead. Deacon lay still, holding his breath, feeling his heart pound in his chest and sweat collecting on his brow. His eyes were open and fixed on the source of the shot, but nothing stirred.

He half-expected Gresh to appear. He had picked the boneyard up three seconds after leaving Tara's place, but made no effort to try and lose him. Frustrated, he might just double back and pay Tara a visit.

But guns weren't Gresh's style. So who —?

The question was answered quietly. That was the only way Narses could answer, after all.

The mute stepped into the light of a glowstone, gun hanging limply in his hand. He took a few steps toward Deacon, then stopped. The sounds of a far-away argument drifted along on the stale breeze. Narses glanced both ways and then began to run.

Deacon sprang to his feet and went after him. *This is the second time that son of a bitch has tried to kill me. It's going to be the last.*

Narses heard the heavy footfalls behind him almost immediately and flew around a corner, heading for one of the more upscale shopping districts. Most of the stores had been forced to close after dark, since few of their patrons wanted to be out on the streets with the cult war going on. It felt as if the whole city was sitting back and silently watching two men, one pursuer, the other pursued.

Narses had a good lead, almost a full block, and he was in good shape. But he didn't know the city as well as Deacon, hesitating just a second too long before deciding which way to turn. That let the detective gain precious steps.

A couple of times, Deacon had considered taking a shot and trying to hit Narses in the leg. But if he missed wide, he might lose his target completely, and if he missed high, the shot would kill the fleeing man and he'd get no answers. Neither prospect seemed appealing, so he kept running.

That brought up another problem. Narses was heading east and if he made it as far as the warehouse district, he'd lose himself in the warren of alleys and narrow streets. He was following the railrunner paths now, but they would end when he reached the warehouses, the roads not being wide enough for the cars to pass through. At that point, the 'runners went underground and curved toward the more populated areas to the north.

Deacon saw Narses turn left around a corner and started to follow, then checked himself. Some sixth sense warned him that it was a trap and he slowed himself down as he reached the spot. Cautiously, he stuck his head around and was greeted with a bullet that chipped off some of the brick just overhead. He fired off two rounds and Narses fled again, this time staying to the left of the paths.

Deacon cursed. If Narses went much farther, he would be past the railrunner tunnel going underground and among the warehouses. His only hope of catching his quarry lay in driving him under the streets.

The detective waited until Narses was only a meter or so from the tunnel entrance. Then he squeezed off a shot that ricocheted off the wall near his prey, sending stone fragments and dust flying through the air. Narses, startled, veered right and ran along the paths again, following them down the incline and underground.

Deacon reached the tunnel entrance and listened. The nearest station was a long run away, which meant Narses had nowhere to go. But the subpaths were dark — railrunners had their own lights, after all, and the ones pulled by teams boasted beasts with good night vision. Perfect spot for an ambush.

He reached into his pocket, grabbed a few bullets — standard lead — and reloaded his weapon. Then he started down the tunnel, listening for any sound that might betray Narses' location.

But there was none. He waited for his eyes to adjust to the darkness and edged along, feeling for the tunnel wall with his left hand. It was cold and damp and the tunnels stank of sweat and animal waste. *And it would be a hell of a place to die,* Deacon thought.

He walked for what seemed like an hour, but was really only a few minutes. A little voice in his head was wondering whether Narses had a way out of the tunnels Deacon hadn't been aware of. Maybe he had made it back to the street and was coming up behind even now. Maybe the hunter was getting hunted in turn.

Deacon told the little voice to shut up.

It was time to face facts. Narses was standing stock still, waiting for Deacon to get close enough to plug. In the dark, he could walk right into the barrel of the gun and not know it. But if Narses fired — and missed — he'd betray his position. Of course, it would take talent to miss under these circumstances.

Let's hope you're talented, pal, Deacon thought. Then he stopped and shouted, "Narses! Give it up! Drop the gun and you can walk out of here!"

He pausing, listening for one of two sounds: the gun hitting the ground or a rustle of cloth as the trigger was pulled. Neither came.

"Come on, kid! It's only a matter of time before I find you! I'm a hell of a lot better shot than you, Narses — don't make me prove it."

Nothing. Deacon felt a knot forming in his stomach. The gun felt like it weighed a ton. Narses was probably laughing to himself, just waiting for the right moment to shoot.

Time to quit playing around. "Narses!" he shouted into the coal-black tunnel. "What's this about? Larissa? Don't throw your life away on that slut! She thought of you as a pet! She told me so! Once she got bored with you, she was going to leave you where she found you and let the rest of her kind finish you off!"

That did it. Deacon had a quarter-second's warning, just the faintest sound of movement. He dove to the ground as the sound of a gun firing filled the tunnel and the muzzle flash lit it up like somebody had rolled a massive glowstone down the paths.

Deacon had been ready for the sudden light and was up and moving. Narses was no more than a few meters away and the detective slammed into him before he could react.

The mute tried to bring the gun down on Deacon's head, but the detective caught his wrist and slammed it back against the wall. Narses grabbed Deacon's gun hand and held fast, keeping the barrel of the weapon pointed at the ground.

Now it was a contest of strength, pure and simple. And maybe something more — Deacon was fighting for his life, Narses was fighting to take one. But this close to Larissa's former servant, Deacon saw something in his opponent's eyes. There was intelligence there, and pain, but they weren't the eyes of a killer. They were the eyes of a scared kid.

Unfortunately, Narses was a scared kid who knew how to use leverage. Deacon hadn't had any success freeing his arm from the mute's grip, and now he was losing the struggle to keep Narses' gun hand pinned to the wall. If he freed it, the last thing Deacon would see would be a bright flash.

Then it came, but it wasn't what he was expecting. Instead, this light spilled down the tunnel from the direction they had come, illuminating both men. It was golden and warm, but its presence chilled Deacon to the bone. He knew it could only be one thing: a railrunner was coming down the paths, straight for them.

Narses saw it too and began to push Deacon into the path of the silent vehicle. It was elemental powered, which meant the driver probably was paying no attention on this long straightaway. Not that he would be able to stop the thing in time anyway, not at the speed the car was traveling.

Now Deacon could smell the eldritch energies pouring off the car. He spared the railrunner a glance, judging how close it was, then went with the force of Narses' shove. He flew backwards over the paths an instant before the 'runner shot by, flattening himself against the tunnel wall, the edge of the car brushing against his coat.

Then it was gone.

And so was Narses.

 222

For only a moment, Deacon wondered if Narses might have made a leap for the passing 'runner and been carried away. After all, there had been some aftereffects of the vampire attack he'd suffered — maybe he had powers Deacon wasn't aware of.

The detective dismissed that idea almost as soon as he'd thought of it. *If Narses could do things like that, he wouldn't have bothered with a gun.*

Darkness had returned to the tunnel, so the possibility existed that he might have slipped away and be laying in wait again. Deacon was about to pick a direction and start walking when something caught his eye on the tunnel wall opposite him.

It looked as if a crack had formed in the stone, running from the ceiling to the floor. What made it unusual was that it could be seen — there was light shining through from the other side. By accident or design, Narses had left a beacon of sorts leading to his escape route.

Deacon crossed the paths and began running his fingers down the crack. There was barely enough of a gap for him to get a grip, and then it took most of his strength to move it even a little. He wondered if there was a trigger somewhere that Narses had known about, since he had managed to open and almost close it in the time it took the railrunner to pass.

When he had the hidden door open sufficiently for him to slip through, he stuck his head in and looked around. Narses was nowhere to be seen, but the chamber beyond the wall hid nothing of itself. It was brightly lit with glowstones and it didn't take a genius to see it had once been an underground station. At some point, budget cuts must have forced it to close and the place had been walled up to prevent anyone from using it to access the paths.

Someone was using it for something else now. A finely crafted stone altar sat in the middle of the platform, stained here and there with blood. Deacon didn't recognize the idol enshrined in the ticket booth, but the expression on its face said it was just waiting for a better temple to wreak havoc and destruction.

He wasn't surprised at the signs that a cult had been here or, for that matter, that Narses knew about it. Abandoned stations, empty warehouses, anyplace an altar could be slapped up and chanting wouldn't disturb the neighbors was ideal for a cult. All they wanted was privacy, except for those times when the public was invited in to serve as Human sacrifices.

There was only one exit from the platform, a staircase leading up. If this place was built like other stations — and there was no reason to think it wasn't — the stairway would lead to a maze of tunnels that would end at a second set of stairs leading to the street. These would be sealed off with an iron gate and whatever wards the city had been able to scrape up the gold for. Odds were most of those had been shot by the cultists, since it wasn't likely they were using the path entrance. People walking in and out of a tunnel all the time would look damn suspicious, even to jaded Galitians.

Deacon took the stairs two at a time, paused at the landing and glanced around the corner. Seeing no sign of Narses, he took off down the hall.

At each corner, he repeated the procedure — no sense running into a bullet. The station proved to be a labyrinth, but at least the hallways were lit, if dimly. He tried not to think about the possibility that the cultists who used the place were only out to dinner and would be coming back soon.

Around the second to last turn before the street exit, he caught sight of his quarry. He managed a burst of speed that brought him within striking distance just as Narses slipped around the final corner. Deacon readied his weapon — unless Narses had a key to the stairs gate, he was cornered.

Deacon pivoted around the corner, gun held in front of him. Narses was halfway up the steps, facing him, the locked gate still intact. The mute had his semi-automatic pointed at Deacon, but hand and weapon were trembling.

The detective caught his breath and then smiled. "End of the line, kid. You gave me a good run. Now drop the gun and let's get out of here."

Narses took another step up the stairway, weapon still trained, if unsteadily, on Deacon.

"Listen to me, Narses," Deacon tried again. "The way your hand is shaking, that baby is liable to go off. I don't want that, and I'm not sure you do either, though you've been doing your damndest to convince me otherwise. Want to tell me — somehow — what this is all about?"

Narses made no move for a moment, and then his brow furrowed ever so slightly. Suddenly, Deacon felt as if his brain was exploding with colors, sensations, information. He was looking at Narses and looking at himself at the same time, the two images flipping back and forth at dizzying speed. A scream forced its way out of him.

Then the pain eased. Deacon sensed that Narses was in his mind, apologizing for pushing too hard on initial contact. He had not used this ability in a long time. With Larissa, there had been no need.

"Why … why did you try to kill me?" Deacon asked.

There was another black jolt of pain that vanished almost as soon as it came. Then Narses answered, *You killed Larissa. Why did you kill her?*

"I didn't kill her, kid. You've got the wrong guy. I know how you feel, but I'm not the one you want."

Then who? Narses demanded.

"I think Whisper did it. She knew something about him, something he didn't want spread —"

Whisper? No, Deacon, that lie will not work. She sensed Whisper's presence. He would not have been able to take her by surprise in that alleyway. And only through surprise could she have been defeated.

Deacon dug out the doubts he'd had after he left Redge and dusted them off. "When did she sense Whisper?"

Not long before she hired you. She wasn't certain of his name, only his power. She believed Merr had brought him in to replace one of the fallen.

Deacon grimaced. The walls he thought he had been beginning

225

to tear down were reassembling themselves again. Merr hadn't brought Whisper into town, that seemed certain, unless the conspiracy to throw the war extended a lot higher than seemed likely. Now that he thought of it, for a guy who should have been lying low, given his task here, Whisper had made quite a show of himself. *First, he shows up at Gadsden's door, then at mine.*

There are thoughts that hover on the fringes of your consciousness at times, ones so horrible that you fight to keep them from crossing your mind. Deacon put up such a fight and lost.

Somebody sent Whisper to me — somebody who knew I would mention him to Larissa sooner or later. She'd know where to find him and, being one of her own, odds were she'd go after him herself. A perfect way to get her alone and unprotected, Deacon thought darkly. *They set her up and they used me to do it!*

"Whisper was a godsbedamned diversion!" Deacon exploded. "Bait to trap Larissa and a handy fall guy if Merr caught on. Narses, who knew Larissa could sense his presence?"

Narses lowered his gun. He had felt Deacon's thoughts, and more, now knew what the detective had felt for Larissa — perhaps better than Deacon knew it himself. *I knew — Gresh, Black, East — I assume her superiors knew as well, though I'm not sure.*

Deacon turned the names over in his head. Black was dead, killed in the cemetery. Gresh? Too stupid, unless he was putting on the greatest act of all time.

East? A definite possibility, and worth shooting on general principles even if he wasn't guilty.

"We've got to get moving, kid," Deacon said. "The guy who really killed Larissa and stole her jewel is out there doing gods know what while we're standing around here. I need your help."

Even after I tried to kill you?

"I'll get over it. We have to find East, but first there's somebody I need to get in touch with. Do you have a key for that gate?"

Narses raised the gun, ready to slip it into his pocket. *Yes, I —*

The air was suddenly split wide open by three explosions. The first two bullets tore through Narses' throat. The third took off the top of his head. His brains hit the wall a second before his body hit the ground. The smell of blood mingled with the stench of cordite in the stairwell.

The detective looked up to see a shadowed figure standing on the other side of the gate. The gun he held was aimed right at Deacon's heart.

Chapter
Twenty-Four

Deacon lifted his hands in the air, gun dangling from one finger. Narses' blood pooled at his feet. The figure looking down upon them both didn't move at first. Then he pointed the gun a few degrees to the left and fired, blowing the lock off the iron gate.

"Jack? You all right?" the gunman said as he shoved the gate aside. It was Banff's voice and Banff's stocky form coming down the steps now, doing his best to avoid stepping on the man he had just killed.

"Thom?" Deacon asked, surprised. "What the hell are you doing here?"

"And no 'thank you' I'm getting?" Banff said, holstering his weapon and glancing at the ruined corpse on the floor. "Gods and devils, if it wasn't for me, it might be you lying dead." Banff squatted down and shined a glowstone on Narses' face. "Isn't that —?"

"Yeah," Deacon said grimly. "The real one, this time. You didn't have to kill him, Thom. He was putting the gun away."

Banff rose, indignant. "And how was I to know that?"

"In the old days, you'd have warned him first."

"Well, these aren't the old days," the sentinel said, with more than a trace of bitterness. "This station is a known cult sanctuary. With those guys, you shoot first and use a medium to ask your questions."

Deacon slipped his pistol into his coat pocket. He understood

Banff's attitude, but couldn't help being furious. Narses' only real crimes were a desire to stay alive and a love for Larissa that made him put his neck on the line — pretty much the same record as Deacon's. And he might have helped clear this mess up, left alive.

"Come on. Let's get out of here," Banff said, starting up the stairs. "I'll call in the cold wagon for him."

"Aren't you forgetting something?" Deacon asked, lagging behind. "I'm wanted for a couple of murders, last I heard. Suppose one of your boys gets ambitious?"

Banff stopped and turned. His expression was unreadable. "I'm here alone. We're stretched pretty thin right now. And I never saw you."

Deacon followed him up to the street, more troubled than before, and the two men headed back toward the tunnel entrance. *Since when do they send guys out alone to haul in cultists? Manpower shortage or not, no sentinel'd ever go along with that.*

"So what brought you out here?" he asked. Banff was walking slowly, like he was in no particular hurry to get where he was going.

"We got a report of shooting in the tunnels. Somebody had to check it out. Now, since I'm the one with the badge, why don't you tell me what *you* were doing there?"

Deacon gave him an edited version, leaving out Merr and Redge. "I went to run down a lead and somebody takes a shot at me. I chased him down the tunnels and it turns out to be Narses. We got to talking."

"What about?"

"This and that. A guy named Whisper, mostly. It looks like he killed Larissa's boss, and somebody wanted me to think he killed Larissa, too. But I'm not buying. Whisper might have been the bait that got her into that alley, but somebody else held the knife."

Banff shook his head angrily. "Damn you, Deacon, why didn't you drop this case and let it stay dropped back when you had a chance? How long do you think your luck's going to last? Suppose I hadn't shown up when I did?"

"I might have learned something useful!" Deacon snapped. "I told you already, he was through with the fireworks."

"Sure, right. First he tries to run you down, then he tries to fill you with lead. He's a real pal. Maybe he killed her, did you ever think of that, and all this was just sorcerer's smoke?"

"He didn't kill her," Deacon said, his voice cold. "He loved her too much."

"And she was spending all her time with you. Maybe he got jealous. It happens."

Deacon wheeled on Banff, frustrated and angry. "He didn't kill her! She was murdered for a jewel and one thing more — some of her people have turned traitor. She might have blown their whole deal."

Banff nodded, obviously interested. "So they solved two problems at once. Plus they put you out of the way. How'd you escape, anyway?"

Again, Deacon cut a few parts out of the story, mainly those having to do with Tara. "'Mallory' let me think he was working for Whisper, but only because I brought the name up. Whisper didn't want me sprung — he knew I didn't have the jewel because he and his buddies did."

"And where is it now? Why hasn't it surfaced?"

"With them. Maybe it's too hot to move. And nobody likes dealing with traitors, Thom."

"You got names and descriptions for these guys?"

Deacon rattled off a brief description of Whisper, Gresh and, as best he could, East. He made a point that he wasn't positive which of the latter two were in on it, but had his money on East. Banff took no notes, just stood there frowning.

"I'll get elderswraths for the lot of 'em. East, for 'Mallory's' murder; Gresh, on assault; Whisper for suspicion. Why don't you let us handle it from here, Jack? Go underground until it's all over."

"I started it. I want to be in on the finish."

"Then consider it an order, 'in the interests of public safety.' Suppose some innocent taxpayer gets in the way of a bullet meant

 230

for you?"

"Next time, I'll let it hit me. Will that make you happy? Hell, Thom, you guys haven't been able to catch *me* yet — seems to me you'd welcome any help you can get."

"Well, I don't need your help, you two-bit shamus!" Banff growled. Deacon wondered at the tone of almost desperation in his old friend's voice. "Do what I'm telling you or, so help me, I'll clap the irons on you and toss you back in a cell for your own good! Are you looking to get killed? Get back to that girl, Tara, and stay with her, at least until we pick Gresh up! Who knows what will happen if he gets a hold of her!"

Deacon gave the old sentinel a long look and then said quietly, "Maybe you're right, Thom. Maybe this thing is bigger than I dreamed. Maybe I'd be better off not knowing the truth."

With that, the detective dropped back a step, pulled his gun and jammed it in the small of Banff's back. "I ought to kill you right now," Deacon said.

Even without seeing his face, the sentinel knew the man with his finger on the trigger was dead serious. Banff began to sweat. "Have you lost your mind? Cut the joking, Jack!"

Deacon's voice was stone cold. "I'm not kidding. I'm going to blow a hole right through that fat gut of yours."

"Gods and devils, you *have* gone crazy! This is Thom, remember? Your old friend! Do you know what you'd get for threatening a sentinel?"

"I'm already wanted for murder, Thom. They can only hang me once. And if they're going to do it anyway, I ought to get to kill somebody, right? Now get your hands in the air."

Banff did as he was told, trying not to show how scared he really was. He felt Deacon's hand reach into his overcoat pocket and take out his gun. "Fine. Do it," Banff said. "But before you end *both* our lives, mind telling me what this is about?"

Deacon steered Banff into an alley and shoved him away. "Turn around!" he commanded. "I want to see your face."

Banff turned. He expected to see a wild look in Deacon's eyes, but the detective was, if anything, unnaturally calm. Only the tone of his voice, betrayed the rage inside him.

"You played it real well, Thom," Deacon said. "You just happened along in time to keep Narses from talking too much. Damn right it's not the old days — back then, you couldn't be bought."

"Damn your eyes, Deacon!" Banff sputtered. "Speak plain!"

"Yeah, you almost had me convinced. Even mentioning Tara didn't give you away — I'd dropped her name to you in the morgue the first time Narses 'died,' and you could have guessed I was hiding with her. But, Thom — how did you know Gresh had found her place?"

Banff didn't answer. His mouth had gone dry.

"I didn't know Gresh had tracked me there until I left the apartment tonight. He's gotten better at tailing, but your boys haven't. I'd have heard their size 18 boots a block away. The only way you could have known was if Gresh — or his boss — told you."

Banff shifted uncomfortably, but didn't answer.

"What was the score, Thom? I was supposed to go to the Chaotics, find out they hadn't killed Larissa, and then what? Merr — you know him, don't you? — probably has a way to sense what I'm feeling — as soon as I stepped out of that church, he had confirmed what he'd known all along, that some of his own had turned. There was no more need for me getting in the way. Am I getting warm?

"It was Gresh's job to see I went quietly to my grave. When he saw me go down in the street, he probably thought his job was done. But when Merr found out Gresh had dropped the tail, he panicked. He needed to find me again, and he needed someone who could track a *vronast* through a sulfur bog. Preferably somebody I'd trust if I doubled back and ran into him. Who better than you?

"Turned out their fears were justified. I'd caught up to my would-be killer and we were doing the worst thing possible, in Merr's eyes: sharing information. Merr didn't want me — or anybody else — knowing just how much trouble his side was in here, did he? Maybe it wouldn't look good to *his* bosses if they found out their own people were undermining the cause. That's why he lied to me about knowing Whisper.

"And here was Narses — poor, stupid, lovesick Narses — spilling his guts about the whole thing. The Chaotics had put me on to Whisper, but Narses showed me the thing was bigger than one sorcerer with an attitude. One of Larissa's own little group had killed her."

Deacon took a few steps forward and shoved the gun barrel under Banff's ample chin. "Did they know Narses was gunning for me? What were your orders, Thom: kill the poor slob and me, too, if I'd found out too much? When did you sell out? When did you become no better than a hired gun?"

"You don't understand," Banff said, a note of pleading in his voice. "Every day was another few dozen killings. It was out of control. Merr's people approached me — told me they could bring the cults back in line — I had to listen. Damn it, I've got a responsibility to the people of this city!"

"And all you had to do was shoot Narses down in cold blood! What else did they offer you — gold? Higher office? Maybe even an Elder's seat?"

"No," Banff said, in barely more than a whisper. "They said they'd clear you. Merr said he'd find the one who killed Larissa and hand him over to me."

"He lied to you," Deacon said, disgusted. "Whichever one it is would know too much about Merr's operations in Galitia to turn over to the sentinels. At best, you'd get another corpse to add to your collection."

Banff's eyes darted down to the gun and then back to Deacon. "So what are you going to do, Jack? Kill me or let me walk out of here? It's your decision."

Deacon's face contorted with fury for a moment and Banff waited for the bullet that would tear through his brain and bring some peace. Then the detective pulled the gun away and took a few steps back. "No. Then I'd be no better than you, no better than Merr. You did all this for nothing, Thom. Narses had already talked. Merr will use his death to blackmail you into looking the other way from now on. You've let another monster go free because the alternative looked to be too hard, just like that day on the docks. And letting you live with that is a hell of a lot worse than killing you."

Deacon reached into his pocket and took out Banff's weapon. After emptying it of bullets, he tossed it back to his former friend. Then he gestured with his own gun toward the mouth of the alley. "Get out of my sight. Turn in your badge while it still stands for something. And give Merr a message for me: I'm going to find the one who killed Larissa. If he or any of his rotten crew get in my way, I'll drop them for keeps. Got that?"

Banff slipped past him and back to the street. He turned then and said, "Jack, I meant what I said before. Get Tara the hell out of her place. They know about her and they'll use her to stop you without thinking twice. You're right, Merr's more afraid of his superiors learning the truth about Larissa's death than he is about getting the jewel back or holding on to Galitia."

"Does he know who killed her?"

"I don't think he's certain yet," Banff replied. "But before I left, he said he had a line on Whisper. I'll … I'll try to find out."

Before Deacon could say anything more, Banff had disappeared into what seemed a deeper darkness than either man had ever known before.

❧

Deacon took Banff's advice and took a railrunner back to Tara's. The place was being watched from the front by a young guy in a ratty cloth coat. He seemed to be alone. He was making a pretense of reading a newspaper and doing a lousy job of it. But he'd picked a good vantage point — from where he stood, he could see the main entrance and the fire escape on the side of the building.

There would be time to deal with him later, Deacon decided, walking past the kid as if he hadn't noticed him. The important thing now was to check on Tara and get her packed and out.

The first thing he saw when he hit the second-story landing was that her door was ajar. This was followed by the sound of her voice, raised in what sounded like polite conversation with someone. He walked in to find her in one of the apartment's two chairs. The other was turned away from the door, so Deacon couldn't see who occupied it, only a man's hand holding a teacup.

Tara smiled brightly when she saw Deacon. "Jack!" She rose and came over to him, giving him a quick kiss on the lips. Her next words were said happily, but the expression on her face was a plea for help. "You've got a visitor. Why didn't you tell me you had such a charming grandfather?"

A silver-haired old gentleman peeked around the armchair and winked at Deacon. "Good evening, dear boy. Your lady friend has been entertaining me with the most amazing stories."

As gently as he could, Deacon pushed Tara to the side. He wanted a clear shot at East.

❦

"You haven't written. You haven't called. What's an old man to think?"

Deacon sat across from East. Periodically, he would glance out the window and observe the kid outside, still "reading" the same page of the same newspaper. He had sent Tara upstairs to one of her friends and, over her objections, told her to stay there until he called. The deciding factor for her was not the risk of Deacon's disapproval but the thought of spending more time in East's company.

Deacon more than understood how she felt. The bearer of "virtual immortality" wasn't quite as ancient as he had been when the detective had first met him, but he was getting close. He'd already been reduced to walking with a cane.

"Cut the crap, East. I've spoken to Narses."

"Really? That must have been a remarkably one-sided conversation. And what did our mute friend have to say?"

Deacon leaned back in the armchair. "He said you killed Larissa. You and Whisper."

He expected East to deny the charge, or else, almost playfully, confess. He didn't expect the burst of rich laughter that filled the room. "I killed her? Then, pray tell, Jack, why am I still alive? Why haven't you drawn your prodigious phallic symbol and ended my existence? Afraid to stain your rug?"

"I want to know why," Deacon said, though his hand did rest on his gun butt.

East leaned forward, both hands atop his cane. "Well, I can't tell you why, Jack, because I didn't kill her. Why, she was like a daughter to me — though given her chronological age, 'sister' might be more appropriate. I worshipped the ground she slept in."

"Why don't I believe that?" Deacon asked mockingly.

"Because you're a cynic, Deacon. And because you have a damnable prejudice against things you don't understand. Just because I kill midway between 300 and 400 Human beings a year, you think me incapable of the more tender emotions. Well, I cared a great deal for Larissa, innocent that she was.

"And if you don't believe that, believe this: my continued existence was tied into her success. Her death has made my position … uncomfortable. With her gone and her group scattered, I have been left to fend for myself."

"Give it a rest, East. You say you didn't kill her. Prove it: where were you the night she was murdered?"

East snorted in derision. "I expected better of you, Deacon, than such tired clichés! Where, then, are the naked light bulb and the thumbscrews?"

Deacon drew his pistol and aimed it between East's already dead eyes. "Will this do?"

"For now," East conceded. "That night, I was with an entrancing young woman named Charlotte. We danced, we drank and we repaired to her apartment for a more intimate conversation. I was in the bloom of youth at the time, or damned close to it. We pleasured each other for a time, and as she climaxed, I laid a hand on her brow and caused each of her body's cells to explode in succession, from her head to her feet.

"Then I bathed.

"I can show you the corpse, if you wish, or what's left of it," East added hurriedly. "I'm sure one of your necrophile friends could date the death back to the night Larissa was killed."

"That's one hell of an alibi," Deacon muttered. "But how does it prove you didn't kill Larissa, too?"

East shook his head. "I only murder one a day. I prefer to stay regular."

"Assuming you're telling the truth, that leaves Gresh," Deacon said, sounding unconvinced by East's story.

"Yes. That leaves Gresh. *If* he is the only other extant suspect."

"And Gresh is an idiot."

"Yes. Gresh is an idiot. Which brings you back to me. And I can give you three good reasons not to shoot that gun: one, there's no guarantee a lead bullet would kill me, and what I would then do to you would be infinitely worse; two, I can tell you the nature of the clumsy fellow watching this apartment; and three … I know where Whisper is."

Deacon shook his head. "No deal."

East threw his hands up in the air in frustration. "Blast you, Deacon, think about it! If I had killed Larissa, would I have come here and trusted to your dubious mercy? I'd sooner walk the Wilderness than bargain with you, but bargain I must."

Deacon gave it some thought. East was cunning and potentially treacherous, but he seemed to value self-preservation above all else. If he'd slain Larissa, he could have gone into hiding for a century or so and not had to worry about taking the fall. Instead, he came here …

"Give me the 'why' first," Deacon said finally. "I need a good laugh."

East rose and shambled over to the liquor cabinet. Hands that would be palsied in a few days poured a drink. "When first we met, Deacon, you heard Larissa warn that eventually the war would reach my own doorstep. And so it has. Too many of those I have come into contact with of late are dead or missing: Larissa, Black, Gresh — yes, he's vanished, too — and Narses. Don't look so surprised. News travels quickly in the netherworld."

He took a long sip from his glass. "I'm not a young man anymore, Deacon — at least, not for the next week or so. Whisper and his allies are a bit too formidable for me to challenge at present."

"Why come to me? I'm the one you had counted out from the beginning, remember?"

East favored Deacon with a smile. "Perhaps I've changed my opinion. You have survived a good deal longer than I've expected. In so doing, you've given nightmares to beings more accustomed to causing them. I like that."

East took his seat again and reached into his pocket for a few crisp, new bills. They had enough zeros on them to command attention. "A retainer. I believe that's customary."

"You're hiring me?" Deacon asked in disbelief. "For what?"

East pressed the money into the detective's hand. "Our unseen foe chose his weapon well. I've heard of this Whisper. He's skilled, he's intelligent and he doesn't like to lose. When you find him — and you will — I want him dead."

For the first time since they'd met, Deacon saw a real emotion in East's eyes.

And it was fear.

Chapter
Twenty-Five

The sun had risen by the time East left. He looked uncomfortable in the daylight, squinting his eyes against the sun's glare as he hobbled away. It wasn't that he was unaccustomed to the day — it was the sunlight's habit of bringing out every line in his face that bothered him. Pure vanity.

The kid watching Tara's apartment took no notice of East. The old man wasn't one of the two he'd been told to watch for and follow if they left, and so he was irrelevant. The dark-haired young man turned another page of the newspaper (not a line of which he'd read in the past six hours) and waited for something to happen.

All of this Deacon saw from the window two stories above the street. East had provided a few tips on dealing with the pair of eyes that had replaced Gresh, and a suggestion that Deacon refrain from killing him if at all possible.

"He's one of Merr's. A favored one, if you know what I mean," East had said. "Merr may be an ineffectual buffoon, but he's a *dangerous* ineffectual buffoon when he feels threatened. Ask Narses."

Deacon ground his cigarette out and got ready for work. There was no way to get Tara to safety as long as the Kid — as Deacon found himself referring to his shadow — was out there. So he would have to be made to go away.

Simple.

This time, he didn't worry about the gun. From what East had said, the Kid had to be in his natural state to be taken. And when he was like that, bullets — even the enchanted variety — wouldn't do much more than tickle.

So the first step is to get him to shift, Deacon thought as he took the stairs to the street. *No worse than sticking your head in a* svog's *mouth when it's teething.*

The early morning rush of workers hadn't started yet. The avenue was largely deserted, except for a few rag pickers going through the trash cans. They were in their own little worlds, and probably having a much better time than those who had to live in the real world.

The Kid still had his nose buried in his newspaper. At least he'd picked the sports section, but Deacon wondered if the little guy could even read. Shadows only needed to be able to tell one street from another to do their jobs.

Deacon crossed the street, heading for the garbage-strewn alley by which his target stood. He passed the Kid right by, not even acknowledging him, then stopped short. "You're reading that rag upside down," the detective said over his shoulder.

The Kid's lean, sharp-featured face twisted into a sneer. But he glanced at the parchment to make sure it was right side up, just the same. "Move along, Mister," he said in the best tone of implied menace he could muster on the spur of the moment.

Deacon leaned against a building and looked the Kid over. Short — in the neighborhood of the detective's shoulder; dressed okay; didn't look old enough to shave; lots of attitude. Sure, East said he was more than he seemed, but this type were all the same, Human or not. Just a jab here and there in the right places …

"Now that's not too friendly," Deacon said, mildly. "Tell me, Junior, does your mother know you're out?"

The Kid went so far as to lower his newspaper and glare at Deacon. "Keep asking for it and you're going to get it. I said to move along."

"Tough guy, huh?" Deacon asked, a mocking tone in his voice.

"I used to run into tough guys like you all the time when I was a sentinel. Yeah, they just about owned the world and no cell was going to hold them. None ever did, either; most of 'em ended up in the river. The ones we were able to find, anyway."

Now the Kid dropped his parchment to the ground and balled his hands into fists. His skin color was darkening, now almost a slate grey. "I've had all I'm going to take from you, buddy."

Here it comes, Deacon thought, while he said, "Run along home, son. A growing boy needs his breakfast."

The Kid's eyes blazed and a strangled cry of rage came out of his throat. Then he started to grow, and his clothes with him — *neat trick,* Deacon thought. All the while, his skin was getting darker and its whole texture was changing. A few seconds later, the runt towered over Deacon and his skin was hard as rock, for good reason. It was rock.

The Kid swung a wrecking ball with fingers at Deacon's head, but the detective ducked and he had to be satisfied with taking out the corner of a building. The impact hadn't even scratched — or chipped — the Kid's knuckles.

Deacon feinted to his left and went to his right, scooping up a loose brick and smashing it across the Kid's granite face. Result: one powdered brick and a sweet smile from the walking mountainside.

The Kid cracked Deacon with a backhanded left and sent him tumbling into the alley. Then he lumbered in after him, his shoulders scraping against the walls as he came. Deacon ordered the stars out of his head in time to avoid a kick and grabbed a piece of pipe.

Time to test 'Dr. East's prescription,' he said to himself as he smashed the pipe against the bridge of the Kid's nose. The pipe bent, but didn't break.

The Kid swung again and missed and Deacon landed two body blows with the pipe. Neither seemed to do much good and the back of the alley — a dead end in more ways than one, maybe — was getting closer all the time.

It's amazing how quickly the Human mind can move when it's

faced with being shut off forever. Deacon ran over his conversation with East five or six times in the space of a few seconds. The Kid was a 'shifter, he'd said, and his natural state was rock. And just like your average boulder, there was one point on his body that, if struck just right, would split him wide open. Unfortunately, East didn't know just where that spot was — or wasn't telling, more likely.

The Kid was having fun now, tearing handfuls of brick out of the walls and tossing them in Deacon's general direction. A sewer cover pried out of the ground turned out to make a great discus and ended up embedded in the far wall.

Deacon took a deep breath. He'd tried the obvious places and nothing. Time to do some thinking, before all his thoughts, memories and dreams ended up smeared across the alley floor. He took a swing for the Kid's left side, then his right. The first blow, the Kid took — but he blocked the second one.

He's protecting that side! Deacon realized. *Now let's find out why.*

The detective bored in, striking and then jumping back to stay out of the Kid's grip. As strong as he was, the Kid wasn't agile enough to block all the blows. Most of them rapped harmlessly off his stone hide, but the last one right below his armpit produced a very satisfying crunch.

Deacon almost tripped backing off to see if his gamble had paid off. The Kid just stood there looking shocked for a moment, then he started shambling forward again. This time, though, he was leaving pieces of himself behind as he moved. When his right arm hit the ground, he stopped to look at it like it was just any piece of rubble until the truth sank in.

If he'd been flesh and blood, he might have screamed. Spittle might have started leaking out of the corners of his mouth and his eyes might have bulged. They might even have produced a few tears.

But he wasn't flesh and blood. He was rapidly crumbling stone. If he had stopped moving and stood stock still, he might have been all right — eventually, the fracture would have fused together and he'd have been well, if not whole. Instead, his rage fixed on Deacon, he kept going, backing the detective up against the wall. He brought his left arm back for a killing blow and then stopped, choosing horror for the last expression he'd ever favor the world with.

First the arm split into three sections and dropped to the ground at his feet. Then his chest began to splinter, the cracks finally emerging from his collar and running up his neck. With a final, pitiful whimper — the only sound he'd made since his shifting — the Kid collapsed into a pile of debris before Deacon.

The detective had expected blood and gore, but there was none. The Kid had been rock through and through — the gods only knew what magics had allowed him to move in the first place. Deacon reached out and idly picked up a chunk of stone. The Kid's left eye stared up at him, accusingly.

He threw the rock away and walked out of the alleyway.

Tara was waiting for him when he got back to the apartment. He thought about saying something about her not waiting for his call, but then decided not to. She'd been watching out the window and, if she was glad to see him back, she did a good job of hiding it.

"What happened to the punk?" she asked, as casually as someone might ask about the weather runes.

"I told him you were leaving," Deacon replied. "He went all to pieces."

She gave him a sullen, angry look. "Who says I'm leaving?"

Deacon went over to her. She pulled away. "It's not safe right now."

She laughed. "'Right now?' That's rich! You've had your head on a block since I met you, Deacon, and you just won't be happy till somebody's lopped it off. And when it's all over, you'll come crawling back and want me to sew it back on for you. In the meantime, you figure you can start giving orders about whether I go or stay! Not in this life, pal!"

"We've been over this," Deacon replied, more anger than he'd intended in his voice. "I thought you understood."

"You mean *you've* been over this!" Tara said bitterly. "I went along, playing the good lover/nurse/best friend because I figured you'd have the sense to get out of this thing. Then maybe we could have a life together.

"Instead, I've got old perverts showing up at my door in the middle of the night, people watching my place, and gods know what else! When does it stop?"

"It stops when it's finished, Tara, like anything else," Deacon said. "That's why you have to leave — next time, they might not be content with just watching."

"No, Jack. No. It stops if you walk away from it right now. *We* can leave this behind. You can find other cases and I can go back to work. And if you don't want me to whore, I've got talents that don't require me to be on my back — or on someone else's. We could make it."

Deacon turned away. "I can't do that."

Tara grabbed him and spun him around to face her, tears welling up in her eyes. "Just tell me why, Jack. And don't tell me it's the nature of your business. Don't treat me like I'm just a stupid whore. Tell me the truth. That's all I ask."

As much as he wanted to, Deacon didn't reach out to her. "All right. I'll say this once and try to make you understand, then I'll give it up. They used me to set Larissa up and I can't forget that. No matter how far I run, I can't leave that behind. It's a wound that won't scar until I make somebody pay for her death.

"And if that isn't enough, listen to this: somebody once wrote that, when you believe in something — I mean, *really* believe in it — it owns you. Your life doesn't belong to you anymore, not totally.

"Now I don't believe in this crazy war, Tara. But Larissa did, enough to die for it — and gods help me, I believed in her. Maybe it'll turn out she died for nothing, but I'll be damned if I won't avenge her."

There was comprehension on Tara's face, and something

much deeper than that. She looked at Deacon as if she were seeing him for the first time. "You really loved her."

It was the first time Deacon had ever thought to put that word to it. Now, as he thought of holding the dying vampire in his arms in that tenement, he wondered if Tara was right. Despite what she was, there had been something in her to which he'd responded. Maybe it was nothing more than that she truly believed in something, a feat he'd never managed.

"Maybe I did," he said quietly. "She's gone."

"You still do," Tara said, less an accusation than a statement of fact. She reached out and took his right hand, cupping it over her breast. "I'm a living, breathing woman, Jack, and I love you. When do I become more important in your life than a dead vampire?"

Deacon kissed her with as much feeling as he could muster. She didn't respond at first, then yielded to his lips and the sensation of his hands exploring her body. When they broke apart, he brushed the hair from her eyes and said, "Please understand, Tara. I have to end this. Maybe then —"

She stepped away from him. "'Maybe' isn't good enough, Jack. If you think it's too dangerous to stay here, I'll go someplace else. Go off and do what you have to do." Her voice turned hard, the voice of a woman who'd spent her life on the street and had just remembered a vow never to be hurt again. "But I won't promise to be there when you come back."

Without another word, she walked to her bed, pulled a bag from beneath it, and began to pack her life away.

Chapter
Twenty-Six

Once Deacon had seen Tara safely installed at a new place —
the apartment of one of her former "colleagues," a strikingly tall
brunette named Kat — he caught some sleep. His inner alarm
woke him in the late afternoon, time enough to do what had to be
done.

East had traced Whisper down to the Staltonn flesh mill deep
in the heart of "Frenzy." He was supposed to be lying low there,
but a few 'shifters who talked too much said they had seen him
out by night. Maybe the stink of skin getting tanned was too much
for his delicate nostrils, nobody knew for sure. Anymore than
they knew how he had persuaded mill manager Darman Krog to
risk sentinel attention by harboring a now wanted man.

Deacon left the apartment and hopped a railrunner traveling
west. As far as he could tell, there was no one tailing him, but
laying a false trail would only cost him time. Better that than have
some of Whisper's friends show up at an inconvenient moment.

He changed cars three or four times, then took a cab back east.
He paid the fare and got out eight blocks from his destination,
then took a detour through a particularly desolate neighborhood.
Here, anyone following him would stand out, if only because any
noise in these burnt-out blocks was noticeable. Convinced that a
ghost wearing slippers and walking on tiptoe couldn't have tailed
him there without his hearing, he headed for the mill.

Whisper had chosen his refuge well. Staltonn was in financial trouble and had laid off their entire graveyard shift — an apt term, considering the line of work — and many of their day workers as well. All Whisper had to do was play it smart and he could easily stay out of sight for as long as need be.

The building itself was two stories tall, and almost as wide as a city block. The walls were of wood, though they were probably treated with spells to make them resistant to heat and flame. Fire was always a problem at flesh mills, and it didn't do to barbecue the inventory, even if the neighbors were usually well past complaining to the city about the smells coming from the place.

Deacon stopped into a bar and managed to find one of Staltonn's ex-employees. The guy had been out of work for close to six months, and still reeked of boiled skin. They said you never got rid of that smell, no matter how much you scrubbed. Once you'd worked in a flesh mill, you carried an invisible brand for life.

It only took a few drinks to loosen the man's tongue. Once you sorted through all the complaints about the working conditions and lack of a pension, a few helpful details began to emerge. Staltonn had fallen so far that it had laid off its mages. That severely cut into its manufacturing capability. The mill was now churning out ornamental "hands of glory," severed hands that had been pickled and turned into grotesque candelabra. Without the proper spells focused into them, they were no more than conversation pieces and worth very little on the open market. The ex-tanner said that management was so short-sighted that they weren't even selling what was left of the bodies to other mills — just burning them in the incinerators.

Deacon wasn't surprised. "Hands of glory" were fairly cheap to make, since for the spells to work, the hands had to be those of executed murderers. Plenty of those around, and selling them to mills saved the city the expense of burying the corpses. But if Staltonn wasn't able to scrape up the gold Galitia wanted, they would have had to look elsewhere for bodies, to the Cardiff Blacks of the world, and they'd done so. Selling bodies that didn't have the city's stamp on them somewhere was tantamount to admitting complicity in grave-robbing. At the least, Krog's neck would have been in a noose, and Staltonn would have been fined out of existence. No, much better to get rid of the bodies once the hands were removed.

All of which went a long way toward explaining what Whisper was doing there. If someone had tipped him to Krog's dealings with resurrectionists, the sorcerer could easily have secured himself a billet with a little old-fashioned blackmail.

Deacon bought the man a goodbye drink and left on a scouting expedition. He wandered the neighborhood for a while, memorizing the layout of the streets and alleys. Then he turned his attention to the mill itself.

The building had three entrances: double-doors on the west side with the firm's name and logo — a few disappointed and malnourished grave worms intertwined — with a short staircase leading up to them; a dull iron door on the north side that served as the employee's entrance; and a loading bay that could only be opened from the inside. He guessed that the former would bring visitors into the upper offices, which would be magically protected against the stench, as best as they could be.

There were windows only on the second floor, and then only on one side of the building, the north side. The Nivashi talisman works had been designed the same way, to allow the fat cats to watch their workers milling about in the "recreation yard." It was intended as a means of spotting trouble before it started. Instead, it had only allowed Gus Nivashi to see the rock thrown that would dash his brains out.

Put it all together and it meant access might be a problem. The preferred door was the one the executives used, if only for the sake of avoiding the mill floor. So Deacon decided to go in through the other entrance.

Nothing succeeds like surprise.

Deacon found himself a doorway from which to watch. He

waited an hour in the cold, trying hard not to think about Tara, their argument, what she might be doing now ... and with whom. He couldn't blame her for feeling as she did, but what he had said to her about belief had been the truth. This case owned him now in a way he couldn't quite understand — and as long as it did, he'd see it through to the end.

He was saved from such maudlin thoughts by the muted sound of a whistle and the emergence from the mill of the day shift. To a being, they were bone-tired, soaked in sweat, and stunk worse than the open grave Deacon had taken a header into in Starkwood. For a moment, he caught himself wondering how he would take Whisper down if he was busy gagging.

The workers rounded the corner of the building and went right past Deacon without noticing him. Most likely, you could have dug a pit and filled it with sharp stakes and these exhausted men and women would have marched right into it, too beat even to yell when they were impaled. It was surprising that the Staltonn people hadn't thought to try that.

Shortly after the workers left, the executives emerged from the west entrance. The contrast was striking: clean, pressed suits, soft, round faces that only sweated over the bills once a month, the latest dirty joke about Hugors making the rounds on their lips. A cab pulled up and whisked them far away from the hellhole they managed.

Finally, the security guard — probably an ex-sentinel — stuck his head out the back door and checked to make sure no one had hung around. Deacon ducked back into the doorway to avoid being seen. Once he was certain the area was clear — no one dead from overwork, no rabble-rousers holding impromptu guild meetings — the guard stepped outside, locked the door, and left for the night.

Deacon smiled. Another budget cutback: no night guard. Either that, or this old man *was* the night security officer and simply didn't care anymore. He would keep a sharp eye on the building from the bar down the block.

The sun had set now. A few minutes after that, the screaming started. The nocturnal cries of demented mages (and their subjects/victims) were what had given "Frenzy" its name. Periodic calls for the Elders to clean up the neighborhood and toss its residents in asylums, where most of them belonged, had long gone unheeded. Most ascribed this to bureaucratic indifference to the problems of the poor. The truth was that a squad of sentinels had been sent in, years ago, to roust some of "Frenzy's" harder cases. The conditions of the few who returned were enough to persuade the Elders that "Frenzy" was best left alone.

Deacon gave it another quarter of an hour and then crossed the street to the mill. He kept himself flat against the north side of the building, just in case someone was peering out the windows. Fortunately, there didn't seem to be any "watcher" wards in place around the door — employee theft wasn't a big problem at flesh mills.

The lock was only a few years old, but easy to pick. The door opened with a hiss like an angry snake and Deacon slipped inside.

The first thing that hit him was the smell. All-pervasive, overwhelming, a stink of the grave and of worse than the grave. The unmistakable stench of treated skin mixed with that of corpses, old and new, and the peculiar mix of chemicals that would preserve the hands to decorate someone's mantelpiece. Even though he had been breathing the foul air since he had entered "Frenzy," Deacon still wasn't prepared for the inside of the mill. He stepped outside again and retched as silently as possible.

When his stomach had settled, he went back inside to confront the second major feature of the mill by night. It was damn dark. He had thought about bringing a glowstone but rejected the idea for obvious reasons. He stood stock still for a few moments, giving his eyes a chance to adjust as best they could, then began to explore the immediate area.

❦

To his left, mounted on the wall, was the clock. Employees laid their left hands on top of it at the start of the day and the clock recorded what time they had come in and whether or not they had been drinking. Some people said it did a lot more than that, reading minds and keeping track of who hated the company and who wanted to start a guild. None of that had ever been proven and management wasn't saying, either way.

Deacon found the east wall and started to work his way along it. This was evidently where the gear no longer in use was shoved: bookbinding machinery, sewing stations, can upon can of indelible body paint, recycling tanks for the liquid preservatives. It all amounted to a mini-obstacle course for the detective, but at least nothing he stumbled over here had been alive recently.

It felt like an hour before he got close to the rear of the building. The smell was worse back here and it grew hot rapidly. Apparently, the incinerator wasn't shut off at night and the light of the flames spilled through the cracks in the iron hatch. Deacon could make out pallets stacked high with bodies. A few of the corpses even still had hands, meaning the extremities were either damaged or marked somehow, either with brands of tattoos. There were some people who liked their "hands of glory" marred for the color of it all, but they were rare. Naturally, bodies bought illegally to start with were non-returnable, so into the fire they went.

Now that he could see a little bit better, Deacon noted that the entire mill floor was dotted with pallets. Some held bodies waiting for carving; others boxes of hands to be dipped into the chemical vats; and there were other vats, too, with heatstones on low beneath them. Deacon made for those, almost tripping over an empty paint can on the way.

He was still several feet from the vats when his nose told him what they held. Flesh kept on simmer, something that didn't need to be done for "hands of glory." But a staple of paint production, another sin in the eyes of the sentinels. What kinds of items could incorporate human byproducts was strictly regulated by the city for health reasons, and paint hadn't been one of them the last Deacon had heard.

Gods and devils, Mr. Krog, you do have yourself in deep, don't you? Deacon thought.

And then someone turned on the lights.

❦

Deacon winced at the sudden glare and took cover behind a vat. Of course, there was no way to know where the newcomer was, but instinct told him the west side of the building. A catwalk ran along there so the executives could wander out of their offices and address the workers without having to go out on the floor.

He stayed still and silent and waited. When sounds finally came, it was from up above. Somebody was on the catwalk — in fact, it sounded like two people. And judging from the whimpers of pain coming from one of them, he would have preferred to be someplace else.

"Since you persist in being stubborn, we will begin again. Answer my questions truthfully and no more harm need come to you. Continue to lie and the pit that yawns for you will seem a mercy."

Whisper. Getting ready to play question-and-answer, it seemed. But who was the lucky contestant?

"I told you what I know, you … I don't know anymore!"

The voice was a little weaker, but there was no mistaking it. Gresh. When East said the boneyard had disappeared, Deacon figured he was in trouble for counting out a detective before he was cold and forcing Banff's exposure. He'd gone into hiding or Merr was disciplining him, those seemed the most likely explanations. And they might both be right: Merr casts him out, Gresh looks for a bed and a bottle, not necessarily in that order, and walks right into Whisper.

"Your attitude is … disappointing, Mr. Gresh," Whisper said. "I see I will have to attempt another adjustment."

There was a sudden explosion of light and a screeching sound that made Deacon want to unbutton his scalp and hide it under a pillow. Then Gresh began to scream.

Deacon risked a glance around the side of the vat. Gresh was suspended in the air, looking as if he'd been crucified, a green nimbus of crackling energy surrounding him. Whisper, his back to the mill floor, was watching the show. Even from a distance, Deacon could see that Gresh was the worse for wear. His mass of tissue was bloodied and torn in a few places and the bones of one arm were broken.

"If I wish, I can cause the aura around you to contract until it crushes you," Whisper said, emotionlessly. "Or I can draw the bloody mess that holds your persona out through an eye socket and introduce it into one of those vats down there. I have nothing but time."

"Told you ... everything ..." was all Gresh managed to get out before a seizure ran through him and his tissue started to spasm.

"So you've said. You have talked a great deal about Larissa, Deacon, and a multitude of others. But you have not told me what I want to know: where is Merr now? How much does he know about myself and my allies? What are his plans?"

Gresh's words came out in a ragged yell. "I ... don't ... know!"

Whisper reached out to grasp one of Gresh's ribs. With a shrug, he snapped the bone free and threw it over his shoulder. The clatter it made when it hit the mill floor was lost in his victim's screams.

"Is he bringing in another gem-bearer? Is he conceding Galitia to the Chaotics? Will he sue for peace?" Whisper asked, driving each question like a nail into Gresh's coffin.

"He never talked about it! I was only there a little while!" Gresh babbled. "He seemed to think Deacon had the jewel or could get it back!"

"Deacon is irrelevant," Whisper spat. "He doesn't have the jewel. He never had it. But if Merr is pinning his hopes on him, I will see to it that he is eliminated."

"Why ...?" Gresh managed, his voice fading out at the end.

Whisper chuckled. "For their own reasons, my employers wish to see Order broken in Galitia. They have retained my services to see that this occurs. Our philosophies are ... similar, it seems, and so I am more than willing to take their gold.

"Back to the subject at hand. You are a pathetic liar, Gresh, and my patience is not infinite. For some reason, my employers are getting nervous. Perhaps Merr has not crumbled as quickly as they expected. If I can deliver that old fool to them, their fears will be allayed and my purse will be the richer for it. Where is he, Gresh?"

This time, Whisper didn't even wait for an answer. He reached into the magical field of energy, a blade appearing in his hand from nowhere. With a practiced stroke, he slashed open Gresh's tissue and watched the blood flow.

Deacon pulled his head back and considered. Gresh obviously didn't know any more than he'd told. He didn't have the guts to stand up to this kind of torture and probably gave out with everything he knew in the first five minutes. The fact that Whisper was pushing the matter said that maybe somebody other than his "employers" was getting nervous. With an elderswrath out for him and gods knew how many sentinels working for Merr, his life wasn't worth an alchemist's promise. But if he could put Merr out of the way and Order fell apart in Galitia, he could live high for as long as the Chaotics were willing to have him around.

Eventually, of course, he'd get tired of playing with Gresh and Deacon was the next logical candidate for the full treatment. This made acing Whisper seem that much more appealing, though he'd prefer him alive for at least a little while to beat the identity of Larissa's killer out of him.

Deacon even had an idea of how to take him down, though it was a big question mark. Whisper had made a big show of the fact that guns couldn't hurt him, but Deacon was willing to bet that the bullet he'd shot himself with was plain old lead. He wasn't something out of the Wilderness — he was a sorcerer and if hit with the right spell, he'd drop like a headsman's trophy. And with some of his energy going toward keeping Gresh occupied, there might not be a better opportunity.

The detective glanced around the vat and saw that the assassin was still looking elsewhere. Deacon spun the chamber to the slug he wanted, took aim, and fired.

Chapter
Twenty-Seven

The bullet was a particular favorite of Deacon's and damned expensive. It was designed for use with sorcerers, although usually as a last-ditch measure. Essentially, it increased the power of whatever spell the sorcerer was maintaining at the moment. In this case, it meant Gresh would take quite a jolt from the field he was in, but Whisper would suffer the backlash.

The slug passed through Whisper's shoulder and took effect before he could react to it. The energy holding Gresh suspended flared briefly and the boneyard let out another yell as a few of his leg bones got crushed by the sudden pressure. Whisper grabbed his head and reeled backwards with what Deacon hoped was the grandfather of all headaches.

. Unfortunately, the spellcaster was down, but not out. He dropped to his knees in blinding pain, but somehow guessed the source of it and abruptly cancelled the spell that imprisoned Gresh. The battered skeleton hit the catwalk and came close to rolling off it, catching himself at the last moment.

With the spell gone, the agony eased for Whisper. He lifted his head and looked out over the mill floor with baleful eyes, mouthing one word: "Deacon."

Deacon fired another shot, this time at the catwalk itself. It hit the lower railing and electrified the whole apparatus. Gresh was too far gone to notice; Whisper levitated himself away and smiled.

"You save me the trouble of looking for you," he announced to his now-hidden foe. "Come out, Deacon, and we will settle this quickly."

Thanks, no, Deacon thought, smiling grimly as he examined the rune on the back of the bullet in the chamber. *I think I'll knock you out of the air, instead.*

He whirled, fired, and ducked back behind the vat. Whisper had certainly seen him that time, but with luck, it wouldn't matter. This bullet was Belrand's best work and it had Whisper's name on it.

Belrand had tried to explain how it worked once, but Deacon hadn't caught all of it. Basically, every sorcerer left behind a unique trail of energy when he cast a spell. Some rare individuals were able to trace someone by that energy — that's what Larissa meant when she talked about someone being "tagged." This slug, once it had a chance to get attuned to a sorcerer, would follow him until it found its target or expended its own magic in the attempt.

Whisper saw it coming and decided he'd rather not get hit. He started taking evasive maneuvers, diving and soaring in increasing desperation like a bat trapped in an attic. At one point, he plunged toward the mill floor, pulling up at the last moment beside a vat of chemicals. The slug, undaunted, bored through the vat and kept after him.

Eventually, Whisper ran out of steam, and well before the bullet. It nailed him in the calf and sent him into a spin. He had been close to the west wall and was able to twist his body around and land hard on the catwalk, where he lay unmoving.

Deacon watched him for a few moments, then shouted, "Gresh! Still with us?"

The boneyard didn't answer. But Whisper did.

"Worry about yourself," the sorcerer snapped. The heatstones beneath the vat behind which Deacon hid suddenly blazed to life. An instant later, the vat itself began to tip, boiling liquid flesh pouring over the lip.

Deacon ducked away, but not before some of the molten skin

hit him on the back, burning its way through his jacket and delivering searing pain. He screamed and rolled, trying to rub off the liquid fire.

The vat returned to its upright position. The heatstones cooled. Whisper laughed softly.

"You have an impressive array of tricks, Deacon. But you barely know how to use them, much less understand them. You can't hope to defeat someone with the knowledge at my command. You can't win."

Deacon found cover behind the hand-cutters and answered, "Sorry, pal. You can't expect me to stand still and wait for it like Gadsden did."

"No, I suppose not," Whisper said, bringing himself to a standing position with some difficulty. His trouser leg and shoe were stained with blood. "You are not *quite* the idiot he was."

"Thanks loads. How'd you get in to see him, anyway? Or was he expecting a fence post in the mail?"

"Gadsden cared for nothing but his own, sensual pleasures. My employers had been providing him with young victims — both boys and girls — for some time, in exchange for information. I simply caused him to see my weapon as what he wanted it to be: another less than willing candidate for his appetites. He was almost ridiculously eager to let me into his home.

"From there, it was easy. He never expected it, probably didn't even know that some of his colleagues had already been disposed of. I think, in the end, he was surprised that anyone thought he was *worth* killing.

"You would think that death by sudden impalement would be swift. But he suffered quite magnificently before the end."

Weapon reloaded, Deacon cast a look at the catwalk. Whisper was gone, but his icy words were still coming from there. Gresh had regained consciousness and begun to crawl toward an imagined exit. Deacon moved, trying to spot his missing quarry before he himself was spotted.

"Of course, Gadsden, despite his position and status, was insignificant," Whisper's voice was saying. Deacon made his way around the pallets of bodies, looking for any sign of his enemy. "But with his precious list of *tral* names gone, it meant Larissa would be slowed in her work. I was made to understand that she was the true target. With her destroyed, Merr's position in Galitia would become untenable and Order would collapse in this city like a wall of sand before the tide."

Deacon heard a faint hiss and, on instinct, dove. Twin hand-cutter blades, somehow freed from their boards, flew above him and lodged in one of the bodies waiting for dissection. A pile of boxes, each loaded with severed hands, toppled over.

"In the end, it was quite simple," Whisper continued. "I was to attract your attention in a spectacular enough fashion that you would feel compelled to share the experience with the vampiress. When she hunted me down, one of my employers would be waiting to finish her. You proved to be very helpful to their cause, Deacon — it's a shame you persist in making such a nuisance of yourself. Oh, and if you're seeking me, I'm up here."

Deacon turned. Whisper was back on the catwalk, leg apparently healed. The sorcerer bowed his head, acknowledging non-existent applause. "An old trick, detective. I establish for you the one place in which I am *not*; then I can safely return there with the knowledge that you will never think to look a second time."

Gresh had made it to his knees and was using the catwalk railing to pull himself up. Deacon didn't know where Gresh thought he was going to go or what he was going to do in his condition — he doubted if the boneyard did, either.

Whisper caught the movement out of the corner of his eye. Gresh was on his feet now, albeit unsteadily, but the charge he tried to make on the sorcerer ended up being more of a lurch. Whisper stopped him simply by laying a hand on his skull.

"Foolish. Very, very foolish," Whisper snarled. A fiery glow surrounded his outstretched hand, then spread the length and breadth of Gresh's skeleton. The bones turned orange, then red, then coal black. Finally, Whisper pulled his hand away and the skeleton crumbled into ash, the tissue they had protected hitting the catwalk with a soft, wet sound.

Whisper gave the tangle of muscle, nerves and veins a contemptuous look and kicked it off the walkway. All that was left of Gresh hit the mill floor and exploded into mist.

All of this had happened in the space of a second. Deacon aimed his gun, then turned at the sound of a crowd moving forward. The scene he saw was out of a nightmare — the bodies slated for incineration had crawled off the pallet and were shambling forward, the newly dead leading those who had been in the ground for weeks. And all of them were walking right toward him.

"I see no reason to soil my hands with your blood," Whisper said quietly. "Better to have you killed by your own kind: those too stupid to know when to stay dead."

Deacon fired a shot into the lead corpse that didn't do much more than slow him down. The detective backed off, but the dead were a gruesome army with eyes fixed on their objective and moved forward relentlessly, smashing whatever lay in their path. Deacon upset a pile of crates in front of them, trying to buy time to escape.

It was that last word — "escape" — running through his mind that made him stop. Something didn't *feel* right here. If Whisper had the power to raise the dead, why hire himself out to do other people's dirty work to start with? He could have made a mint in any city you could name — except maybe Guildsport, where they were so backward they were probably still leaving the dead out for the "rot fairy" to take in exchange for a gold coin under the casket.

The ambulatory corpses battered their way through Deacon's barricade. The detective gave it some more thought. If Whisper *couldn't* raise the dead, then …

Deacon smiled, then let out the best yell of pure terror he could manage. He broke into a seemingly panicked run, the dead obligingly trailing along behind him. He dodged around pallets and chemical vats, seemingly moving at random, all the while aiming for one spot: the ladder that led to the catwalk.

It all came down to how good of an act he put on. The corpses were certainly doing their part — Whisper was seeing to that. And Deacon had seen enough men broken — especially ones just in from the Wilderness — that he was able to do a decent imitation.

Decent enough, anyway. He reached the ladder and with a look over his shoulder and another scream, climbed it two rungs at a time. When he reached the top, he scurried along the catwalk and dropped to his knees in front of Whisper, sobbing.

The sorcerer suppressed a laugh and said mockingly, "There, there. Whisper will save you."

Deacon shot off his knees like a spring uncoiling and smashed Whisper in the jaw, sending him sprawling. "Thanks anyway. I do a pretty good job of taking care of myself."

Behind him, the illusory dead began to fade away. Below him, the items they'd destroyed were miraculously whole again.

Whisper tried to get up. He looked upset. Deacon soothed him a couple of times with the butt of his gun till the sorcerer lay quietly. The detective went through his pockets, but found nothing except a few bills and some Nivashi talismans. He took the lot and then noticed one thing more. Caught in the lining of Whisper's jacket was the tip of a thorn, sharp and thick enough that, whole, it must have been pretty mean. The look of it rang a chime in Deacon's head, but he couldn't place it. He took a handkerchief out of his pocket and placed the thorn inside, then stuffed it back in his coat.

Now there was nothing to do but wait.

❦

When Whisper came to, it was to see Deacon leaning on the catwalk railing, gun in hand. The sorcerer felt like his head was about to split open, and knew the detective would be happy to help it along. Of course, a spell in the right place would send the imbecile toppling to the ground. If only he could gather his wits and concentrate —

"Don't even think about it," Deacon said. "You so much as furrow your brow and I'll blow a hole in it. You and I are going to have a little talk."

 260

Whisper shrugged arrogantly. "I have nothing to tell you. Go ahead and kill me … if you can."

"Spare me the dramatics, Whisper. I'm through playing games with you clowns. You killed Gadsden; you betrayed Merr; you helped set up Larissa, maybe even killed her yourself. That's a lot in a couple weeks. You ever see what the sentinels do to sorcerers who step out of line?"

"No cell can hold me," Whisper answered with confidence.

"When they're done with you, they won't need a cell. A box will do," Deacon said, then added, "A *small* box."

"Is that supposed to frighten me?"

Deacon smiled. "Nope. That's supposed to fill you with hope for a better tomorrow." He bent down and grabbed Whisper by the collar, shoving the barrel of the gun under his chin. "*This* is supposed to frighten you."

When he saw a little of the attitude flee Whisper's eyes, he released him. "Okay, first question: did you kill Larissa?"

Whisper shook his head. "I would never have been able to get near her. She could sense when I was about. I was to act as bait for her."

"Why? Why were they so sure she'd come after you alone?"

"She knew me as Order. When she learned I was acting against you, she would assume I had defected to the other side. Her sense of duty and her damnable arrogance made her feel she must be the one to confront me. I do not know whether she intended to reclaim me for her army or destroy me. But all she achieved was one final death."

Deacon wasn't sure what she had intended, either. But one thing was certain, her killer had played her like a harp. "Who killed her, Whisper? Who are you working for?"

A sadistic look crept on to the sorcerer's face. "That would be telling."

Deacon grabbed him again and smashed the gun across his face. "Wrong answer. Try again."

Whisper wiped the blood off his mouth and smiled. "You might as well kill me. Even if I told you, you'll never find him in time."

"Try me."

Whisper's laugh was a little hysterical now. "You made the greatest mistake a detective can make when dealing with the netherworld, Deacon: you ruled out the dead as suspects. A corpse can kill with impunity, that's the beauty of it all."

Deacon rose and stood over the sorcerer, who was now beside himself with mirth. "He tried to slay both of you once, and failed. His second try was more successful with her. I trust it will be with you as well, detective. Tell me, do you think you will be able to murder me in your first try?"

"I wouldn't mind trying," Deacon answered, East's money suddenly feeling like a lead weight in his pocket. "In fact, somebody paid me just tonight to put you down. But I'm nobody's hired gun, Whisper — the day I am, I'm no better than you."

"Then call your precious sentinels, Deacon. And when all is done, I will escape them and find you again. Then this will be settled."

"No, it's going to be settled now," Deacon said, an angry fire in his eyes. "I'm not going to kill you, Whisper — but you're not walking away either."

Whisper saw the look on the detective's face and suddenly didn't look quite so confident in his mastery of the situation.

"Tell me something, Whisper. You're a big-shot sorcerer. Now, me, I don't know enough magic to change the glowstone in my apartment. How do you do it? How do you cast a spell? With your hands, maybe?"

Deacon fired twice. The bullets hit Whisper's wrists and exploded on contact, blowing his hands to pieces. The sorcerer's shock was too great to manifest in a scream.

"Or maybe you do it on your knees, huh, Whisper?" Deacon said coldly, firing twice more. The slugs mangled the sorcerer's knees beyond repair. This time the screams came, loud enough to wake all those dead men on their pallets.

"Hell, maybe it's all in what you say," Deacon continued,

shoving the barrel of the gun into Whisper's mouth, breaking teeth in the process. "You want to really impress me? Do one of your little tricks and keep from bleeding to death before the sentinels get here. I'd hate for them to miss their chance with you. You're taking the hard fall, pal."

Deacon pulled the gun out and wiped the barrel on Whisper's jacket. The sorcerer's face was twisted with pain but he still had the strength to spit out the words, "You haven't won anything. He has your woman by now. He'll kill her just like he did Larissa. And he'll enjoy her first … just like he did Larissa."

The detective grabbed the lapels of Whisper's jacket and yanked him off the ground, blood flying everywhere. "Tara? Who has her, damn you? Where is he?"

Whisper giggled. "Maybe here. Maybe there. You never can tell with a dead man. Think like a corpse, Deacon — you were one once, after all."

With that, the sorcerer's head dropped to one side. Unconscious. Deacon tossed him aside and made for the ladder to the mill floor. He had to get back to Tara and make sure she was safe. Then he would call the sentinels and tell them where to find Whisper.

And after that, I have a date with a dead man.

Chapter Twenty-Eight

On the long ride back to Kat's apartment and (hopefully) Tara, Deacon tried to keep his mind off the possibilities and focus on what Whisper had said. If the real killer was someone he'd thought was dead, did that mean he was back at square one? It didn't seem possible that any of the deaths in this case could have been faked — Gadsden staked; Gresh's substance scattered across the mill floor; Narses blown away; Black torn in half.

Which left two choices: Whisper was lying, or somebody who had died had the power to return to life.

And isn't that a pleasant thought? Deacon said to himself.

A few things had become clear. Larissa's death was part of an organized effort to undermine Merr and his agents in Galitia and leave the city open for the Chaotics or the war's "deserters" to take things over. Strangely enough, it seemed that Whisper and his bosses really didn't care who won, as long as Order didn't. But Whisper *was* a creature of Order, and there was no reason to think his employers weren't. Why would they want their side to lose, but not give a damn who won?

Unless …

Unless they wanted out of the army. With Order defeated here, there would be no generals to order them around. They'd collaborate with the winners — no matter who it was — and live out comfortable existences without their necks on the line. And the

 264

only way to ensure that happening was to sabotage Order's efforts to mobilize and hold on to this city. Most importantly, Larissa had to be killed to prevent any more recruiting.

It made sense in a twisted sort of way. If East had guessed that, it was no wonder he had turned to Deacon. When Order fell, its allies and pawns wouldn't last long under the sway of its enemies. Larissa had warned East that he would be sought out if the war went badly; he must have taken it to what little heart he had.

Or the whole thing could have been a blind. Maybe Whisper had become a hindrance and East wanted him out of the way. By sending Deacon, he gave himself time to grab Tara and use her as a hostage against the detective's future good behavior.

Deacon frowned. If East was legitimate, that scenario still rang too true for comfort. The information on Whisper's hideout had been too easy to learn — maybe his bosses were getting tired of him, or maybe they just didn't want to pay. They see to it East is tipped, knowing he's too much of a physical coward to do anything himself. When Deacon goes chasing off after the sorcerer, they put the snatch on Tara.

He put his theories aside as the cab slid to a stop in front of Kat's building. It was older and seedier than Tara's, if that was possible. At this hour of the evening, most of the tenants were working the street out front, their pimps keeping careful watch. Deacon scanned the line, but didn't see Kat or Tara. That feeling of dread that had been building started to feel like a bullet lodged in his heart.

He pushed his way past the whores and their would-be clients and went inside. Kat's apartment was on the third floor and the stairs were wooden and falling apart. He climbed them too fast for that to matter.

Kat's door was closed and locked. Deacon knocked, then pounded, calling for Kat or Tara. Neither answered. Finally, he put his shoulder into it and shoved, breaking the lock and letting the door swing open.

The place looked like a blackpowder bomb had hit it. Furniture was overturned, clothing was torn, and there was a smell of smoke and ozone still hanging in the air. Deacon pushed debris aside with his feet, all the while calling for the women.

It didn't take him long to find one of them. A trail of blood led from the bedroom to a closet. This time the door wasn't locked, but the woman behind it was hanging on to the knob for dear life.

"Let go of the door," Deacon said, as calmly as he could under the circumstances. "It's Jack. Let go of the handle."

There seemed to be a moment's hesitation on the other side, and then he was able to open the door. Kat was inside, bloody, clutching a torn robe around her body. Tears had streaked her make-up across her face. Even in the semi-dark, Deacon could see the bruises on her once-beautiful face. Her right wrist looked broken. As he reached for her, she pulled away.

"It's all right. It's all right," he repeated over and over as he led the stricken woman out of the closet and to a couch. It was a long while before she was able to say anything intelligible.

"Where's Tara?" Deacon asked, already knowing what the answer would be.

"He … he took her. She tried to fight, but —"

"Who? Who took her, Kat? Who did this to you?"

Her eyes went wide with fear. "No! No, I can't tell!" she shouted, bolting off the couch and heading for the kitchen area. Deacon caught her before she was halfway there.

"He said he'd kill me if I tell! Don't make me tell!" she pleaded.

"Take it easy. Nobody's going to kill you," Deacon assured her. "All right, let's put who aside for a minute. Tell me as much as you can about what happened."

Kat wiped the tears from beneath her silver eyes and did her best to compose herself. But it was obvious that the new calm in her voice was forced. She was half out of her mind with fear, and from what Tara had said, this was a woman who wasn't scared of much. While she talked, Deacon slapped together a makeshift splint for her wrist.

"Tara and I had something to eat. I … I said I'd have to go out soon, I had a call. She said that was okay. She didn't think she was in any danger. She said you just wanted to get rid of her."

Kat shut her eyes as if she didn't want to see the next part of her story replayed in her mind. "There was a knock at the door. I thought it was my client, but it ... it was him."

"Had you ever seen this man before?" Deacon asked. Kat didn't answer with words, but the frightened look on her face said it was a "yes."

"He pushed his way in. Said he was looking for you. Tara got angry and told him to get out. He hit her. I grabbed a cleaver and went after him, but he ... did this," she said, gesturing to her bandaged wrist.

"He knew who Tara was. He said if he couldn't have you, he'd take her instead. She tried to fight, but he just kept hitting her. When he was done, he turned to me and he ..."

The tears started falling again and her whole frame shook as she tried to suppress the sobs. "He ... did things! Gods, it was like being touched by a dead man!"

She drew her knees up to her chest and started to moan. She was retreating into herself, something Deacon couldn't afford. He grabbed her shoulders and shook her.

"Kat, listen to me! Tell me who he is and I promise he won't hurt anyone, ever again!"

It was no use. Her eyes had gone dead. She was off in her own little world where there was no violence or pain. Deacon wouldn't learn anymore from her.

Or would he? As he stood up, she reached out a hand to stop him. A small measure of sanity had returned to her and she was pointing toward a table by the bed. "He left something for you. 'A parting gift,' he said."

Deacon walked over to the bed, trying hard to ignore all the blood on the sheets. Resting on the nighttable was a single black rose, flecks of crimson on its stem.

He might as well have signed his name, Deacon thought, his gut filled with a hatred beyond anything he'd ever known before. And now there was a lot more than Larissa to avenge ...

Deacon found a phone. He got lucky — it was one of the kind

that read who you wanted to talk to out of your mind and dialed the number itself. Banff picked up after three rings.

"Sentinels, Banff speaking." No one who didn't know him would have been able to tell that Thom had been drinking.

"It's Deacon. I know the who, but not the where. There's one more lead to try. Have you got a temporal mage on staff anymore?"

"Budget cuts, Jack. Had to let him go. I've got one of his crystals yet. Might still have some power left. But these things are damn rare — have you got any idea how much trouble I'd get in if I gave it to you?"

"Not as much as we might all be in if you don't. Meet me at the alley where Larissa's body was found in fifteen minutes. And send somebody over to Tara's building — I've got an assault and rape over here. She needs a healer."

Deacon gave Banff the address of Kat's apartment and was about to hang up. Then something struck him and he added, "Thom? Don't tell Merr about this. This one's mine."

There was a long pause before Banff said, "All right, Jack. I'll give you as much time as I can."

❦

Although Deacon had known since his arrest where Larissa was found, this was his first visit to the site. Maybe it was because, by the time he'd escaped jail, the sentinels had lifted the wards and he figured the curious public would have tramped all over any clues that might have been left. Maybe he figured he was too close to the case to spot anything new, even if it was there.

Maybe it was just because it would hurt too much.

It looked like any other alleyway now, tenement on one side and warehouse on the other. Trash had blown in from off the street and covered its floor and rain had washed away the last traces of Larissa's ichor. Somehow, it seemed that the alley should have been different for what happened there, but the city didn't work that way.

Banff was already waiting when Deacon arrived. He pulled the timecrystal out of his pocket and said, "Got something to show me?"

Deacon pulled a parchment package out from under his coat, unwrapped it, and handed Banff the black rose. "It's not as good as a murder weapon, but it'll do the job."

Banff nodded, then turned to face the alley's mouth. He held the rose in one hand and the crystal in the other. After a few moments, the crystal flared and Deacon saw someone enter the alley.

It was Larissa. Even though he had known that the crystal, if it worked, would reenact the crime before them, Deacon hadn't been fully prepared for the sight of her. It felt like someone had stuck a knife in him and he started toward her, as if she were real.

"Stay still, Jack," Banff said. "Remember, these are only bloodshadows. The images left on this place by the violence that was done here. They're not real."

Deacon forced himself to watch the drama unfolding before him. Larissa was looking for something or somebody — Whisper, it had to be. Suddenly, her eyes looked over Deacon's shoulder, and the detective turned in time to see Whisper's shade climbing the fire escape. The bait was leaving; the trap had been sprung.

Now there was another figure in the alley, a tall, thin man with a walking stick in hand. He was on Larissa in two long strides, bringing the cane down savagely on her head and driving her further in. Reeling, Larissa tried to ward off the blows, but she was still too weak from her recent ordeal to fight him off. A few more blows and she went down, her coat opening to reveal her cold, white body.

Her attacker dropped his cane and reached into a pocket for a long knife. He knelt to the ground and exposed her throat, prepared to slice it open. But then his eyes and his hands wandered elsewhere. He would enjoy himself for a while before taking what he had come for.

Then, as if in mourning for its owner, Larissa's gem flared to life one last time. The light illuminated the features of her murderer: Cardiff Black.

❦

"That's enough," Deacon said, turning away from the vision. When Banff didn't immediately shut it down, Deacon shouted, "I said that's enough!" and struck the sentinel. The crystal flew across the alley and shattered against the wall. The bloodshadows mercifully faded away.

"Gods and devils, Deacon, you know how much that thing cost the department?" Banff said angrily.

"Put it on my tab. Black killed Larissa and now he's got Tara. He's been the one behind Whisper all along."

"But I thought you said he died in Starkwood."

"He did. I saw it. *After* he killed Larissa. But somehow he came back," Deacon said. "He and Whisper have been picking off Merr's people one by one, trying to drive him down. And Black figures once Order's gone here, he's safe."

Deacon took the rose from Banff, threw it to the ground and crushed it under his heel. "He's wrong."

"You want me to call out some men?" Banff asked. "He might be too much to take on alone."

Deacon looked at his friend, a strange light playing in his eyes. "I'm not alone, Thom. Larissa's with me. I'm going to finish this for her."

"Sure, Jack," Banff said, looking toward the street then back to the detective. "Where are you going to start looking for him?"

"I'm not sure, but I have a few ideas."

"If you need any help checking them out, we can —"

Banff's sentence was interrupted by a gunshot. The old sentinel grunted and fell to the ground, a bullet in his chest. Deacon looked up and saw the silhouette of someone peering over the edge of the tenement rooftop, gun still in hand. Then he was gone.

Deacon bent down to the sentinel, but Banff pushed him away. "Don't worry about me! Get that son of a bitch!"

Drawing his gun, Deacon climbed the fire escape ladder to the roof. As he stuck his head up over the brick ledge, two more shots rang out, the bullets whizzing past his temple. Deacon fired back and then vaulted the ledge in time to see his prey starting down the ladder on the opposite side.

Later, the memories of the chase would be a blur for Deacon. He reached the top of the fire escape before the gunman had made it to the alley floor. Knowing the shooter was gone if he made it to the street, Deacon slid down the metal ladders and hit the pavement only a few seconds after his man.

There was no time to dance, not with Banff bleeding a block away. Deacon caught the guy's gun arm and twisted it till something snapped, the weapon clattering to the pavement. Then he shoved his own gun into the man's back and marched him back to the other alley.

Banff was on his back, his breathing shallow. He had his pocket crystal set in his hand. When he saw Deacon, he said, "I called it in. The healers are on their way. Not sure why I bothered though — I know how bad off I am."

The sentinel coughed and a thin stream of blood started to flow from the corner of his mouth. "It's my own damn fault, too. I called Merr after I talked to you tonight. Told him where we were going to meet. Black must have had a way of intercepting the message."

"That's not hard," Deacon agreed, turning to the soon-to-be murderer. Beneath his trenchcoat, he wore the crimson robe of a blood cultist — the same robe worn by the group that had tried to sacrifice Larissa in the theatre.

"Where's Black?" Deacon demanded.

The cultist smiled. "I don't know what you're talking about. I follow no one's orders. I just like shooting sentinels."

Deacon forced the gunman back against the wall and then his eye caught movement on the pavement. It was a rat, a big one, coming out of its pile of trash to see what all the noise was about. Deacon reached down and scooped up the screeching thing, thrusting it close to his captive's face. The cultist flinched but the wall kept him from backing away.

"See this baby?" Deacon said as the creature fought to escape his grasp. "This rat's got plague. One bite, and so have you. Ever see a guy die of plague?"

The cultist had gone pale. Sweat was pouring off him. The rat was getting damn angry, but Deacon had it in such a way that its jaws couldn't reach him. That left the gunman the only target for its hostility.

"You —- you wouldn't!" the cultist sputtered. "You can't!"

Deacon's voice was a razor-edged whip. "Can't I? I'm no sentinel! I'm a soldier in a war and you're the enemy! You'll talk or by gods —"

"All right! All right! Just get that thing away from me!" the cultist shouted, sinking to his knees. "I don't know any Black! The high priest said I should come here and shoot whoever I found. But after I shot the old man I got scared and ran. That's all I know, I swear it!"

"Who's your high priest?"

"I don't know! None of us have ever seen his face!"

"Is this the same guy who tried to sacrifice the woman a while ago? The one who got his arm shot off?"

The cultist nodded, his face suddenly suffused with religious zeal. "That's right! But then his arm was returned to him, praise Erom!"

"Where can I find this high priest?" Deacon pressed. "Is he back at the theatre?"

"No. He's left us. He said he needed time alone to meditate."

And to wait for the dust to settle after Merr goes down, Deacon thought.

The cultist had started praying to Erom for deliverance. Deacon answered his prayers with the butt of his gun. That would keep him quiet until the sentinels arrived to pick him up.

"You black-hearted bastard," Banff chuckled weakly. "There hasn't been plague in Galitia in ten years."

"Guess he didn't know his history," Deacon replied.

"Got this all figured out yet?"

"Most of it. I'd be willing to bet Black's the high priest. He must have set up the cult as his power base before Larissa restored his memory, though I'm not sure how or why. He tried to sacrifice her in his capacity as cult leader — that was what Whisper meant when he referred to his 'first attempt' on her failing — but I showed up and took off his arm. He recovered from that, so I guess he could walk away from being torn in half."

"I still don't understand what this has all been about," Banff muttered. "All this death ..."

"It may be hard to believe, Thom, but I think it's about people who don't want to fight anymore."

Banff started to speak, then went into a coughing fit. When it subsided, he said, "Where are you going to start looking?"

"He's holed up in a cemetery, Thom. It has to be. Black's a ghoul and used to work as a graverobber. They're like second homes to him. And Whisper clinched it when he said I ought to think like a dead man."

"City's full of cemeteries, Deacon. And if he's got Tara —"

"There's one thing more," Deacon said, pulling the balled up handkerchief out of his pocket. He opened it to show Banff the thorn he'd taken from Whisper's jacket. "I finally remembered where I've seen this before."

The smile on Banff's face said he remembered it, too. "You've got him."

"And this one, he's not walking away from," Deacon vowed.

He turned at the distinctive wail of sentinel automobiles approaching. They weren't more than a few blocks away, from the sound of it.

"I'd better go, Thom. Some people still labor under the illusion that I'm wanted for murder."

Banff nodded. "I'm ... sorry I wasn't more help to you. I should have been stronger."

Some part of Deacon wanted to tell his old friend that everything was all right, he had only done what he thought he had to. But the memory of Narses shot to pieces kept intruding, so he said nothing. Instead, he stripped off the cultist's coat and slipped it under Banff's head, then turned and left the alley.

It was time to close this case.

Chapter
Twenty-Nine

The cab came to a stop abruptly. Deacon climbed out and paid his fare. The driver sped off without waiting for a tip. He'd given Deacon more than a few strange looks on the way, wondering why he wanted to be taken to a cemetery at this ungodly hour.

"Kinda late to be mourning, isn't it?" the driver had asked, trying to be funny.

"I'm going to a funeral."

"Who died?"

"Nobody. Yet."

Alone now, Deacon turned to look at Asiah Cedar's dream come true.

Cedar had been one of the "big rich," back when that meant running the city directly instead of through front men. He'd made his dough in import/export, a pleasant euphemism for smuggling. As a child, he'd had a love for puzzles and an obsession with his inevitable death.

That was what had led him, sixty years ago, to construct Cedar Park Cemetery in the exclusive southwestern section of Galitia. It was billed as the ultimate in security against resurrectionists and their like, a place where visitors could reach only the specific grave they requested of the gatekeeper and none other.

His method proved to be simple and effective. Sorcerers on his staff created a type of hedge, one whose shape could be manipulated with the right spells. Two meters thick, with intertwining branches and wickedly sharp thorns, the hedge was virtually impenetrable. Cedar had it planted on this site and carved into a maze, within which the bodies of those who could come up with the gold would be buried.

The whole thing provoked outright laughter on the part of graverobbers. No walls? No padlocks? Not even guard wolves? Cedar had to be kidding. But he knew things they didn't, like the fact that the maze could be manipulated if one knew the right spells. Tell the gatekeeper where you wanted to go and he would shift the pattern around and let you travel there — but nowhere else. Step out of line and the maze would close in, turn you around, and its punishments were the stuff of legend. The lucky ones who tried to knock over Cedar Park in the early years wound up fleeing the place in terror; the unlucky ones were lost inside for months and ended up candidates for burial themselves.

Ironically, Cedar's fortune was lost when a few of his trade caravans disappeared in the Wilderness. He ended his life just one more poor bastard in a city full of them and was planted in Starkwood.

The thorn caught in Whisper's jacket had led Deacon here. No sentinel who had ever done "grave and grin" — late night drive-bys of cemeteries to make sure the guards were awake and the dead where they belonged — could take that little item for anything but part of the Cedar hedge.

This particular graveyard only needed one guard, the guy who ran the maze. His station was a booth off to the side of the entrance with adequate wards but nothing special. His life insurance policy was that everyone knew if anything happened to him, the maze would slip out of control.

As Deacon approached the booth, it became obvious that someone didn't care about the potential threat the hedges posed. The red stuff on the windows wasn't tomato soup. The gatekeeper was slumped on the floor, head beaten in and lower right arm gone missing. *Black must have wanted a snack,* Deacon thought.

The detective started toward the entrance of the maze and then stopped. There was one other reason, besides indifference, why Black might have felt secure in killing the guard. If he had mastered the spell that controlled the maze, he would have nothing to fear from it. And he would have a living fortress around him that an army of sentinels couldn't penetrate on a bet. Suddenly, this job had gone from dangerous to suicidal.

"But I don't really have much choice, do I?" Deacon muttered to himself.

The answer came from within the maze, from every direction. Black's voice. "Of course you do, my boy. You can turn right around and leave me to my night's amusement. There's no need for war between us."

Deacon didn't bother to answer. Instead, he plunged into the maze, gun in hand, the image of Larissa dead at Black's hands burning in his brain.

"Surely you're not so enamored of this girl that you would risk your life for her?" Black continued, his voice carried by every branch. "A common flower of the street? Galitia is filled with them. And you don't have it in your heart to begrudge an old man his pleasures, do you?"

Deacon had a choice: right or left. He chose left. At the first turning, he broke a branch off the hedge to mark his passage. It grew back before his eyes. Undaunted, he took the handkerchief out of his pocket and tore off a strip, draping it over one of the thorns. This time, the hedge did nothing.

"You have always been too concerned with the welfare of others, Deacon," Black said, with exaggerated politeness. "Why, it wasn't so very long ago that you were offering me money to leave Galitia. Remember the outcome of that, my boy? It will be no different now, save that you may see more familiar faces in the beyond."

Deacon spotted the first set of gravestones. All the same family, and not wealthy enough to afford the heart of the cemetery. He sidestepped them and made another right, coming up to another intersection. This one was protected by a marble statue of Atad, the legbreaker for some god or other. Today, Atad wasn't content to just stand and menace: he was moving and talking, although it was Black's voice coming from his cold lips.

"You had your measure of blood from Whisper. Your friend Banff — if he lives — will clear you of Larissa's murder. The whole matter will be settled and you'll have been well-paid for your efforts."

Atad raised his mace over his head. He meant business. "Don't make me kill you, Deacon," Black was saying. "It'd be a hurt to me to be without you. You have been run through a maze since all this began, and it has been a pleasure to watch. I'd hate for you to end bloody and broken."

"That makes two of us," Deacon said, firing twice into the statue. Atad exploded into dust and rubble. His arm and mace fell intact and split a tombstone down the middle. "We don't have to do this the hard way, Black. All I want is your head and I can go home happy."

Atad's mouth was still moving, though lying a good meter from the rest of him. "You'll never take me, Deacon. I've planned too long, risked too much."

"You're breaking my heart," Deacon replied acidly. He had wanted to make another right, guessing it led further into the heart of the maze, but the hedge shifted to block his passage. So left it would have to be. "How much planning could you have done? You didn't even know what you were until a few weeks ago!"

The hedges got a good laugh out of that. "You mean you never guessed, Deacon? I must confess I'm surprised. I was aware of Larissa, Merr and all the rest from the very beginning. My 'panicked graverobber' act was just that, an act for your benefit … and theirs."

"If Larissa didn't bring you back, who did?" Deacon asked, slipping through a gap in the hedge. It led to a small tomb — and a dead end. He turned around and retraced his steps.

"No one, detective! No one had to, that's the grand jest of it! Nine hundred years ago, Deacon, I was a soldier in a great war. I marched into the field along with thousands of others, fighting for something, I knew not what. I was wounded in battle and someone decided to erase my personality until the day I would be needed again. But I was not so weak as they supposed — I resisted, and retained my consciousness.

"Oh, I played at believing myself a mere Human, and in the chaos of what they called 'the Godwar,' no one took any notice of me. I was but one more warrior being buried for some long-distant tomorrow, and if my eyes seemed brighter and my step livelier than my fellows, it was a small matter. I fooled them all then, just as I fooled Larissa into believing she had restored my memory."

Deacon made two quick lefts and the hedge closed behind him. Trapped. He bent down and started to pry the branches apart and create an opening, but the thorns grew to twice their size in an instant and one stabbed him in the hand. He cursed and pulled away.

"There'll be none of that," Black warned as the hedge shifted again. "You must play by my rules now. Now where was I? Ah, yes, the peace. I spent nine centuries living a lie, dreading the day the war would return here and I would be called upon again to fight. Oh, I never minded the killing much — it was the idea of dying that disturbed me.

"Shortly after I came to Galitia, I hit upon an idea, a wonderful idea! I was a creature of Order, you see. But if there were no Order, there would be no need for my services, no army in which I would have to serve. As the time drew near and I saw events occur which must surely draw the warring parties back here, I set my plans in motion."

The path down which Deacon walked had narrowed suddenly, forcing him to squeeze his way through, thorns tearing at his clothes. The thought that all Black had to do was squeeze him between the hedges and play pincushion did nothing to comfort him.

"So you set up your own cult," Deacon said. "Ready-made spies, right?"

"Very good," Black replied, sounding like an approving schoolmaster. "It appealed to my sense of humor to pose as a

Chaotic high priest and draw in some of the more respectable members of Galitian society for my plans. They could see and hear things I could not — at least, not without betraying that I was not the humble repairman I pretended to be. I even crafted a god for them to worship. Knowing that all cultists really want is more — more power, more sex, more pleasures of every kind — I simply reversed the word and 'Erom' was born."

"Then what? You passed the collection plate and held bingo games?"

Black didn't laugh. At least, the hedges didn't seem amused. "Cults are like the leaves of a tree, Mr. Deacon. The slightest shift in the breeze can be felt by them, long before the roots are aware. Give them their share of excitement — arcane rituals, a few killings — and they're perfectly content. Through them, I found Merr, Gadsden, Chase, and even Larissa. She was the one who had to die for my plan to succeed, for she was the key to Order's efforts in this city. But first she had to be isolated, drawn out.

"That was where Whisper came in. He killed Gadsden; Chase, a lieutenant of Merr's and barely a player in this game, fled to East, seeking counsel. East obligingly sent him back out into the streets, where Whisper beheaded him. Larissa was now alone and abandoned, except for you."

Deacon turned a corner and found himself confronted by one of his own markers. He had been shunted back to the outer edge. Black could run him in circles until he dropped without even trying hard. Deacon found a tombstone and sat down to think.

Black hadn't shut up. "I confess, you were a problem at the beginning and I was forced to set Whisper on your trail. The Chaotics made an effort to eliminate Larissa and you interfered. They made a second attempt — with a bit of help from information from my cultists — when you found Gresh, and again you and she escaped. When you came to me with your ridiculous offer, your noble effort to 'save' me from a life of horror, I thought Fate had delivered the means to ending your annoyance."

"And you killed me," Deacon said absently, not wanting Black to think he wasn't paying attention. The beginnings of a plan were taking shape in his mind, but it would depend on surprise.

"Yes, I felt it would save a good deal of time if I slew you then and there. Unfortunately, Larissa and Gresh chose that moment to appear and I was forced to concoct a fable to allay any suspicions they might have. Worse, you responded to the dear girl's pleas and returned to life. Most inconvenient."

"Sorry," Deacon answered, eyeing a patch of hedge. It had struck him that, when he'd broken the branch off and later pushed some aside, the hedge — and Black — had reacted. But his cloth markers had stayed put, meaning Black might not know they were there. In other words, he was only aware of what went on if the hedge was disturbed or harmed in some way.

Deacon smiled. The spell that controlled the hedge had to give the caster a mental link to the plants to enable him to control the maze's defenses. But links work both ways …

"Fortunately, you chose to turn on Larissa and go your own way. This was my opportunity to see her dead and take her gem out of play. Alas, things did not go quite as I'd planned."

Deacon rose and checked the load in his gun. It would have to be the right mix for what he had in mind. "Putting it in small words you might understand, you screwed up. Larissa was starting to get suspicious and sent out the fake Narses as a test. You fell for it and she thought somebody on her own side was feeding info to the enemy. She still hadn't guessed that that somebody *was* the enemy. Worse, his death brought me back in. You had to take care of Larissa before I was all the way back.

"You tipped your cultists off about where she was and they put the snatch on. Then you sent Whisper to me to try and scare me off, and as insurance in case this latest murder attempt didn't pan out. A sick little bird let me know where she was and I showed up in time to save her and blow your arm off. How'd you grow that back, anyway?"

This got a chuckle out of Black. "Yes, and your avian friend will pay dearly for his interference when all this is over. As for the arm, it's one of my minor talents. I am of the stuff of graves, Deacon. I can draw upon the earth and its dead to make myself whole. Thus, my death in Starkwood, though unplanned, was no more than a minor inconvenience. I can't be destroyed, therefore —"

Deacon fired three times, blowing a big hole in the hedge. Black stopped talking long enough to let out a yell. Deacon dove through the gap he'd created before the hedge could react, rolling and coming up on his feet on the soft turf on the other side. The path turned right up ahead and Deacon broke into a run, trying to take advantage of Black's distraction.

It was working. The thorns were making a good try, but they were about two steps behind their target. There was still no way to be certain which way was the right way, but Deacon guessed Black would be right in the center. And if he'd hurt Tara, all the graves in Galitia wouldn't be able to put him together again.

He was getting closer and Black was getting his wits back. The statuary was making a bid to block him, but a few well-placed shots turned them into so much powder. Deacon reloaded on the run, narrowly avoiding a barricade of thorns that erupted out of the ground.

Deacon reached another crossroads. His choice was left, but the way was narrow and long. He tore off his trenchcoat and tossed it on to a hedge to the right, letting the thorns tear into it and rip it to shreds. While Black was occupied with that, he went left and made it through unscathed.

Now he could hear something, but it wasn't a continuation of Black's life story. It was Tara and she was crying. He let the sound guide him through the maze's heart until he reached a last turn. Through a rapidly closing gap, he spotted her in a clearing.

Deacon vaulted a tombstone and burst through the tiny opening, thorns tearing at his arms as he went. His momentum carried him toward her and it was only then that he saw the look of fear on her face.

He turned, ready to fire, but Black was waiting with a pistol of his own. Instead of Deacon, it was aimed at Tara. The ghoul didn't look happy.

"I can't match your prowess with this toy, Mr. Deacon, but I can assure you that if you fire, she dies."

Deacon glanced at Tara. She was pinned to the hedge by thorns that had pierced her hands, blood running freely down her arms. Her clothes had been torn and there were bruises on her face and neck.

"Tara?"

"I'm … I'm all right," she answered, not very convincingly. "Gods, Jack, he's a —"

"I know what he is," Deacon said, turning to look at Black with hellfire in his eyes. "Let her go. She was just your bait. It's not her you want."

Black stood there, gun in one hand, cane in the other. His black suit was dusty and worn and he looked paler than usual. But his eyes blazed with madness — or maybe just the sense that he was finally going to win his private war.

"Don't be foolish, Mr. Deacon. The villain only lets the damsel escape in poor fictions. I am a poor man, a humble man, and I have had to do many things in my life that I did not want to do. There is no nobility left in me, only a desire to survive."

Deacon shook his head. "East said the same thing when I first met him. 'Anything beyond survival was meaningless,' he said. But he never explained how a life that consists of nothing beyond making it to the next day is worth living."

"I wouldn't expect you to understand," Black said, smiling. "You're limited to just one lifetime and know from birth that it has to end. It's very … different the day that you realize it *doesn't* have to end. Why should I risk death in a war, the winning of which would not benefit me?" he asked, as if it were a challenge.

"I don't know," Deacon answered. "But I know Larissa didn't view the war as something to die for. Instead, it gave her something to live for. And you betrayed that, Black, betrayed her."

"She was a foolish woman!" Black raged in response. "She could have looked around her and given up her notions of marshalling an army. She could have conceded the futility of it all and she would have been alive today."

"No. She would have been as dead as you are. As dead as

you've been for nine hundred years."

"You know, I expected her to cry out for mercy, Deacon. She regained consciousness before I was done, you see. But all she did was call for you, the one who had made it possible for me to lure her to her doom."

Deacon said nothing.

"I pocketed the gem, of course, and Whisper masked it from Merr's probings. All the while you were hunted by those who desired it, it rested with me. I went through the motions of searching your friend's shop, and bargaining with you, for Gresh's benefit — and yours. Had things gone badly, I would have bought my safe passage from Galitia with the jewel. Now I shall simply destroy it, worthless bauble that it is."

The gem. Suddenly, Deacon could see so clearly the dream he had experienced in jail. Larissa, killed for it, but then emerging from its depths again when her enemies were destroyed. Had she been trying to tell him something through that vision?

Deacon searched his memory. Larissa had come to him, whole, and … there were tears in her eyes. Regret that they had been lost to each other.

In a way he couldn't explain, he understood. Some small part of Larissa was bound to that gem. It was waiting for something to set it free — and he was the key. Though he had grieved for Larissa, he had never shed a tear. Tara had forced him into recognizing that he had loved her, but he had never allowed himself to *feel* that love. He had risked all to find her killer, telling himself it was the right thing to do, never once admitting how much his heart had driven him.

It was easy to explain away. There were a thousand reasons why it had been better to lock the real feelings away, bury them in anger over her death and how he had been used to bring it about. But there was no sorcerous spell or supernatural power that could unlock her spirit from that jewel.

Only something uniquely Human.

"You've been an excellent opponent," Black was saying. "I will miss our little game, Deacon, but it's time to end it the only way you could end. You never belonged in the netherworld and it is time to usher you out. Put down your gun."

Deacon only half-heard him. His thoughts were fixed on the memory of a woman, one struggling to be Human as much as any living being. When he saw her clearly, for all she was and was not, he saw the truth as well and knew it could be his weapon.

In the end, there was no great, transcendent moment. Just simple words spoken in his mind and in his heart.

He didn't see the gem start to glow, though later he would imagine he did. But there was no mistaking the ghostly figure who suddenly stood beside Black, her eyes on Deacon, her arms outstretched.

"I'm so very sorry," Larissa said softly. "I would have liked …"

Black wheeled and fired at the image, screaming, "No! You're dead! I won't let you live again!"

The spectre vanished. Deacon fired, the bullet tearing through Black's gun arm, shearing it off. A second bullet caught him in the gut, sawing him in half, gore spilling out on to the ground. Deacon fired a third time and caught the ghoul's throat, the slug tearing head from shoulders. The expression on Black's face wasn't one of anger or some unspoken vow of revenge — it was no more than fear of what awaited him in the darkness.

If he reached there. Already, Deacon could see his severed limb moving to rejoin his torso. He was about to shoot again when the left arm, still bearing the cane, lifted the deadly instrument.

Deacon hit the ground as the lightning bolt from the cane's head tore through the air, striking the hedge and setting it aflame. Tara screamed. Deacon dove for Black's sundered corpse and wrested the cane free, then pulled Tara loose from the thorns that held her.

The flames were spreading rapidly across the maze, acrid smoke rising to obscure the moon. Deacon plunged the cane into the fire and returned with the torch to set Black's body ablaze. The assorted parts began to writhe and blacken, and Deacon felt a weight lift off his soul as the ghoul turned to ash.

"Jack, we've got to get out of here!" Tara shouted as the maze

284

twisted in its death throes. "This whole place is going to go up!"

Deacon started to move toward her, then his eyes caught something among Black's remains. Its facets reflected the flames all around, but the heat hadn't touched it. The detective scooped up the jewel and slipped it into his pocket.

Then he and Tara left Hell to its feast.

Epilogue

Deacon sat behind the desk in his office, his feet up, a glass of ale in his hand. The healers had put salve on his burns and bandaged him in places he hadn't known he'd had, but a cold one was still the best medicine.

Tara had joined Banff and Belrand in the hospital. The pawnbroker would be back in his shop in a week or so, and Tara would be physically whole not long after, though it would take a while to get her over her trauma. Banff's bullet wounds would heal, eventually; his account of the events in the alley — and what had led up to them — meant Deacon was in the clear on Larissa's murder. The possessed Mallory's death was being written off as an accident. Strings had been pulled and Banff was looking at a promotion rather than early retirement.

Deacon was looking at two of the uglier faces he'd seen since Cedar Park burned.

Merr sat on one side of the room. Redge, stark naked and transforming more than ever due to sheer tension, lay on the other. Both had come about the gem. One — maybe both — were going to be disappointed.

"This is as much your fault as anyone's," Deacon said to Order's top man in Galitia. "Black should never have gotten as far as he did. He, Whisper and a few cultists almost cost you the whole damn city."

Merr looked more uncomfortable than angry. There had been no way to keep the scribes away from the cemetery fire, but so far Deacon had kept his mouth shut. If that changed ...

Redge snorted. His wild boar aspect was appropriate, if not becoming.

"Think that's funny? What if somebody on your side gets the same idea?" Deacon asked. "Maybe some of your recruits aren't so thrilled about giving up what they thought were their lives to fight a war that's been elsewhere for close to a thousand years."

"Ridiculous," Redge said, spikes emerging from his flesh. "Impossible."

"Suit yourself," Deacon said, glancing at the one empty chair. He had tried to find the "deserter" who'd talked with him near Starkwood, but no luck. Still, the chair itself was enough to make the other two nervous.

"Let's get down to business. How much do you want for the jewel?" Merr demanded.

Redge slithered up to the desk. "You promised it to me, remember? I do."

"I remember. I also remember that both of you tried to have me killed at various times during the past few weeks. Things like that tend to hurt my feelings. I'm a sensitive guy. Ask Whisper — if he ever gets out of the prison hospital."

"We had a bargain!" Redge insisted.

Deacon eyed him coldly. "I lied. I do that. We all do. Get used to it."

That shut the Chaotic up, for the moment. Deacon continued, "The jewel isn't for sale, gentlemen. But I don't want to keep it, either. What the hell am I going to do with it?"

"Then why won't you sell it?" Redge said testily, struggling to sprout wings.

"'Cause it isn't mine to sell. And if you start flying around, so help me, I'll plug you. This baby belonged to Larissa Martel, my client, and was stolen from her when she died. I recovered it in the course of solving the case and that gives me sole discretion as to its disposal."

...con flipped the jewel to Merr, who came close to dropping
it. ..o, here. Whether or not it's the smartest thing to do, it's what
Larissa would have wanted done."

"Unfair!" Redge hissed. "It was promised to me! Be assured,
Deacon, I will not forget this!"

Deacon slipped his gun out of his jacket and pointed it between
Redge's now hooded eyes. "Don't push me, Scales. It's been a
long couple of weeks and I'm cranky."

Merr didn't say anything. Deacon didn't care.

"Now get out, the two of you. I have a business to run," Deacon
said, gesturing toward the door with the gun. Merr left in a hurry;
Redge took longer and grumbled a hell of a lot.

Deacon had all of a minute's peace before a cane rapped on his
door. East shuffled in, looking every day of his gods knew how
many centuries. He also looked amused.

"Good evening, Deacon," he croaked. "You're looking well.
Have you started counting the days you have left yet?"

Deacon took a long drink and stared at East. "Nope. I never
learned to count that high. What do you want, East?"

"You think it's over, don't you?"

"No. I know it's not," Deacon answered, soberly. "Whisper
kept talking about 'employers.' Black wasn't in this alone, he was
just the prime mover. Might be all the rest will go back to being
good little soldiers after what happened. If they don't, well, that's
not my problem."

East laughed. "You're a very poor liar, Deacon. You've been
touched by the netherworld and survived. You've seen things few
of your kind ever have before — although, if this war proceeds as
I expect it will, more and more Humans will have to learn to come
to terms with what exists beside them. And you are not so much
of a fool that you think you can go back to your dirty little world
of divorces and blackmail as if nothing had happened."

"Watch me," Deacon replied.

"No, Deacon. You watch yourself," East said, suddenly very
serious. "I like you. I don't know why, for you're nothing like me,
and I am the only one I have ever had any real use for. But you

have made some powerful enemies in Galitia and the shadows may not be so friendly to you as they have been in the past."

"Is that what you came to tell me?"

East shook his head, with some effort. "Not entirely. I also came to get my money back. You didn't kill Whisper, as I hired you to do."

Deacon aimed the gun at East, almost casually. "I haven't killed you, either. I'm considering the dough a downpayment for that."

East shrugged. "Very well. I wish you good fortune, Deacon. And if you must lay down your life sometime soon, I pray it will be for a worthy cause — say, my continued existence. Be seeing you."

When the old man was halfway out the door, Deacon called out, "East!"

"Yes? What is it?"

"You knew all along, didn't you? About Black, the cult, all of it."

East smiled. "Perhaps. I may have had my suspicions, but lacked the will to see them proven, one way or the other. If I did, well, that is my secret. And there have been far too many secrets shared already, my boy."

With that, he was gone. Deacon turned and looked out at the night and the city. He had seen parts of it he had only dreamed existed and parts he hoped he would never have to see again. And maybe he had learned, when it was all over, something of why Larissa had chosen him for this dark ride.

He poured himself another glass and raised it to her memory, before letting the cool, amber liquid wash away his pain.

ck Deacon

✠ **AGILITY 9**
Dodge 13, maneuver 11,
melee combat 12, stealth
12, unarmed combat
14, unarmed parry 13
DEXTERITY 10
Fire combat (pistols 15),
lock picking 12
ENDURANCE 10
STRENGTH 9
TOUGHNESS 10
INTELLECT 11
Deduction 15, first aid 12, perception
15, tracking 13, trick 14
MIND 8
CONFIDENCE 10
Con 13, interrogation 14, intimidation 15, streetwise 12 (Galitia
14), survival: urban 14, willpower 15
CHARISMA 9
Charm 11, persuasion 12, taunt 14
Life Points: 7

Equipment: .38 revolver, damage value 14, ammo 6, range 3-10 (0/+1)/25 (+1/0)/50 (0/0); trenchcoat; 250 *vens* in bills; trenchcoat; fedora; dagger, damage value STR+4/18, *incinerate* spell focused in, effect value 30, three charges remaining

Background: Jack Deacon was born 35 years ago in Eldred, in northern Galitia. He was apprenticed at a young age to a wood-worker, but his inability to master even the most basic spells led to his being dismissed. He became a sentinel in Galitia, a job he quit six years ago, disillusioned. He set up shop as a private detective and has ground out a modest living doing divorce cases, debt collection and a little strikebreaking. He maintains some contacts among the sentinels and has a few regular snitches scattered around Galitia. His latest case brought him in contact with the top echelons of Chaos and Order in Galitia, acquaintances he'd just as soon forget, but probably won't be allowed to.

Larissa Martel

AGILITY 15
Dodge 18, maneuver 17, stealth 19, unarmed combat 17
DEXTERITY 10
ENDURANCE 14
Resist fatigue 16
STRENGTH 15
Lifting 17
TOUGHNESS 14
INTELLECT 9
Deduction 10, divination: wizardry 11, divination: vitomancy 12, first aid 13, perception 12, trick 12
MIND 9
CONFIDENCE 11
Faith (Akar) 13, intimidation 15, shapeshift: mist 15, streetwise 13, survival: urban 14, willpower 15
CHARISMA 11
Charm 16 (seduction 18), persuasion 14, taunt 14
Life Points: 8
Alignment: Order 5
Arcane Knowledges: Living forces 2, entity 2

Spells: *Intuition, sense demon, sense the living*

Background: Larissa is a vampire, roughly 105 years old. She was killed 85 years ago by her then lover, whom she later condemned to a death by blood starvation in revenge. She has lived in Galitia all her life, serving as the bearer of the gem of restoration, and her most recent career was as a merchant.

Larissa has the ability to shapeshift into mist and enhanced Agility, Strength and Endurance. She is virtually immortal, but must consume Human blood at least once every three days or perish from blood starvation. She is resistant to non-enchanted metal weapons, but has a vulnerability to wood and a limited vulnerability to sunlight.

u Gresh

AGILITY 8
Dodge 9, melee combat 11, unarmed combat 13, unarmed parry 12

DEXTERITY 8

ENDURANCE 15
Resist fatigue 17, resist shock 17

STRENGTH 15
Lifting 18

TOUGHNESS 7/18*

INTELLECT 6
Apportation: technomancy 8, science: metalsmith 9, trick 7

MIND 6
Conjuration: vitomancy 8

CONFIDENCE 9
Alteration: technomancy 12, intimidation 16

CHARISMA 7

Life Points: 4

Alignment: Order 1

Arcane Knowledges: Living forces 1, metal 3

Spells: *Facade*, various metalwarping spells

Equipment: Bone spikes, damage value STR+4/19

Background: Gresh is a veteran of the first Godwar, whose true nature was hidden under a facade of normal Humanity when that conflict shifted to another plane. He has lived several illusory lifetimes in Galitia, working as a metalsmith.

His true form is that of a *drask*, a massive creature whose bone exoskeleton serves as protection for the soft tissue that houses his intelligence. Gresh is able to cause bone spikes to grow from or withdraw into his skeleton.

*Toughness stat before the slash refers to inner tissue; Toughness stat after the slash refers to his bone exoskeleton.

THE POSSIBILITY WARS

Storm Knights   *by Bill Slavicsek and C. J. Tramontana*

What were the first few weeks of the invasion of Earth like? Who were the
heroes who stepped forward to stop the Gaunt Man and his Possibility Raiders?
Find out in Book One of the Possibility Wars, as Earth is held hostage by invading
realities. $4.95

The Dark Realm   *by Douglas Kaufman*

Book Two of the Possibility Wars Trilogy, as a brave team of Storm Knights
travels to Orrorsh to confront the unspeakably evil High Lord known as The Gaunt
Man. $4.95

The Nightmare Dream   *by Jonatha Ariadne Caspian*

The conclusion of the Possibility Wars Trilogy! The Storm Knights are Earth's
only hope in a race to prevent its annihilation! $4.95

Out of Nippon   *by Nigel Findley*

This full-length novel takes you from the intrigue and manipulation of the
realm of Nippon Tech, to the horror-haunted jungles of Orrorsh. There, corporate
greed and scientific experimentation clash with the occult and the ancient terrors
of the land. $4.95

Strange Tales from the Nile Empire
                          edited by Greg Farshtey, Greg Gorden and Ed Stark

A short story anthology of evil villains, pulp heroes and daring adventure in
the Empire of the Nile — a realm of two-fisted, guns-blazing, non-stop action!
$4.95

Dragons Over England   *edited by Douglas Kaufman and Ed Stark*

A new queen shares the throne of the British Empire. Elves, dwarves, and
fairies roam the Scottish countryside. Join the quest to rid the fantasy realm of
Aysle of evil and darkness in this short-story anthology. $4.95

Mysterious Cairo   *edited by Ed Stark*

Last of the "free cities" of the Nile Empire, Cairo is the heart of the pulp-
fiction realm. Weird scientists outfit pulp heroes with strange weapons,
hardbitten detectives track gangsters through the underworld, and new Storm
Knights are created in the war against evil. Short stories in the pulp magazine
tradition. $4.95

WEST END GAMES®

RR 3 Box 2345 • Honesdale, PA 18431

Please send me the items I have checked.

SHATTERZONE™

❏	21101	**The River of God**	$4.95
❏	21102	**Sole Survivor**	$4.95
❏	21103	**Beyond the 'Zone**	$4.95
❏	21104	**Shattered and Other Stories**	$6.95

TORG™

❏	20601	**Storm Knights**	$4.95
❏	20602	**The Dark Realm**	$4.95
❏	20603	**The Nightmare Dream**	$4.95
❏	20607	**Out of Nippon**	$4.95
❏	20604	**Strange Tales From the Nile Empire**	$4.95
❏	20608	**Mysterious Cairo**	$4.95
❏	20605	**Dragons Over England**	$4.95
❏	20609	**Interview With Evil**	$6.95

PARANOIA®

❏	12303	**Title Deleted for Security Reasons**	$4.95
❏	12304	**Stormshooters & Troubleknights**	$6.95

I am enclosing $_____ (please add $3.00* to cover postage and handling for the first item and $1.25 for each additional item).

Send check or money order — no cash or C.O.D.s, please.

❏ Please send me your catalog of games and books.

Name: _____

Address: _____

City: _____

State: _____ Zip: _____ Tel: (____) _____

*For deliveries to Canada, add US $5.00 for the first item ordered and US $2.50 for each additional item.

Allow 4-6 weeks for delivery.